J. KINCAID & M. LAMBERTH

A Merry Untitled Space Murder Comedy

J.B. Kincaid Publishing

To our wives Katie and Nicole.

*Thank you for always letting us
dive off the deep end into our projects.*

And also to our dogs.

*Many people were neglected
for this book to be written.
It's a miracle we still have
friends at all really.*

"I, however, place economy among the first and most important republican virtues, and public debt as the greatest of the dangers to be feared."

"Bigotry is the disease of ignorance, of morbid minds; enthusiasm of the free and buoyant. Education & free discussion are the antidotes of both."

Thomas Jefferson

Chapter I

The clouds of toxic pollution engulf the man, consumed by fear. His skin burning from its radiation, and bleeding from the lacerations, he turns to face his assailant. The heels of his feet pressing up against the edge of the massive skyscraper, the ground invisible, hundreds of floors below him. The dense fog always hides the ground from view. Perpetual darkness from the shadows of the upper-terraces above. He is trapped.

"The tree of liberty must be refreshed from time to time with the blood of patriots," says the assailant. His pistol raised towards the man.

"When injustice becomes law, resistance becomes duty. I did everything that you asked. I passed every bill. I believed in the cause when it was just *them*. You changed the game," the man says with his last spiteful wish.

"There are times where our lord speaks in metaphor. He rails against an action as a roadmap to the wise and discouragement for the fools. You would have us believe that our interpretations are built on a legacy of opposition to his will. Perspective my friend is a two-sided coin. May we live in both. In your final moments, witness the opulence your narrow pathway has denied you," says the assailant.

The look in the assailant's eyes is one filled with sinister joy. There was a thrill in his murderous games. He should have seen it long ago. He should have stopped them. The purge of conflicting ideologies would, at last, be resolved within the Order. Control of the Syndicate would fall to his greatest enemy. The enemy from within, as absolute power always creates a Brutus unto Caesar. The betrayal hiding in plain sight. A calming acceptance of death overcomes him.

"The opulence of never standing on solid ground? Witness my last testament. When I die, it shall be by my own hand, and in my final breath, I will at last experience *truth,*" he says. These words would be his last. He casts his arms out wide to embrace death with poise and dignity before casting himself backward over the ledge.

Bang! The gunshot rings out at just the right moment, catching him directly in the heart, his eyes locking one last time in defeat at the hands of his assailant. His blood spatters through the air as he falls endlessly into the abyss.

"Now you have lied to yourself, even in death. I give you no such satisfaction. Nothing personal, Senator. *It's just business,*" says the assailant, dusting off the smoking barrel.

* * *

Gruntilda the vibrant green goddess throws back her head. She appears to scream. Her lips speak words that go unheard as the tentacles surround her, wrapping ever tighter. Rodtron is a monster, sweating vehemently, his tentacles writhing in pleasure. His wide grin glimmering with quiet anticipation.

There is nothing else she can do now; the end is near. Additional tentacles approach her firmer and more expediently. She acknowledges his majesty. This only encourages the beast further. This was worth every bit of compensation for the viewers. A loyal following, an audience of ruffians and degenerates.

"*Ah yeah!* This is it. Take those tentacles!" says Harold, one such degenerate, as he sits on his porcelain throne. It was the only place he could get any privacy on this skyscraper-forsaken hell-hole of a planet. Harold wishes he had the sound on, but he knows he can't turn the up volume or else she might hear.

"Harold! What's taking you so long!?" a shrill voice calls through the door.

"Nothing! Mind ya' business. Do I bother you in the morning with your makeup?" says Harold.

"Harold! Are you watching the pornography again!?"

"No Sheron!" he fires back, "Would you please leave me alone? I'm tryin' to get ready for work here!"

What was she talking about? This wasn't pornography. It was art. Two of the greatest adult entertainment stars in the Capital City going at it, may as well be a selection of fine wines and cheeses to Harold. *Ah yes, I really like the way this portrait captures the subtle glow of her three massive knockers!* he thinks to himself, envisioning that he is in a pretentious museum surrounded by well-to-do snobs. He has never been to such a place but were he to curate one, it would certainly include portraits of Gruntilda. Otherwise, art was just boring.

Harold turns off his viewing device and looks himself over in the mirror. Belly protruding from his undershirt. He always told people he was a slug-like species, but in reality, he was just fat. He could never figure out why he kept gaining weight when he worked such a labor-intensive job. He grabs a cold slice of last night's pizza from his bathroom fridge for a quick pre-breakfast snack and steps onto the scale. *Beep.*

"Get fucked!" he curses at the scale, kicking at it with his big clumsy feet. A bipedal organism. Human, they call themselves.

He suits up in his work uniform, struggles with the zipper, and throws on his hardhat. If he's quiet, he might make it out of the apartment alive. Slowly, he opens the door, careful not to breathe. It creaks ever so slightly. His feet shuffle in silence across the yellow-stained vinyl flooring. *Almost there, only a few more steps!*

"What no goodbye kiss?"

Ah no, here she comes again with *The List*. Always with *The List*. Deep down, he knew that he was lucky to have her, but after fifteen years, sometimes he just wanted some time to himself without the expectation of doing chores. In this world of constant steel and concrete, there was no solitude, just as there were no days without *The List* in marriage.

"Of course not sweetheart! I was just getting my boots of course."

"*Uh uh* sure you were! Listen Harry, Can you pick up... on your way home...

and after work when you get back can you fix... the ... .and .... and...”

“Yeah yeah! Sure,” he says, reassuring her with a quick kiss before bolting out the door, not hearing a damn thing she had just said. She would probably yell later, but it was early in the morning and his brain wasn't all there yet.

The dim fluorescent lights of the hallway flicker. The familiar musty smell lingers in the air. The aging colossal structure creaks and groans as if it would collapse were it not interconnected to the endless web of buildings in the city. The purple and reddish gas floating through the air outside the windows of the hallway corridors almost presents the illusion that there is a horizon, but on the other side rests only more buildings.

He squeezes into the lift. Its metallic rusty doors are bent to the point of no longer fully closing. The octagonal structure was built to hold perhaps no more than five citizens, but during the work rush hours, it often overflows with dozens of commuters. On this particular day, Harold is the ninth patron to squeeze onboard. Fortunately, it is only three levels down to the lobby.

The lift reaches level zero, but it is by no means the ground floor. Rather it represents the floor of their building that intersects The Flats. Buildings are organized into clusters called sectors. All of the buildings within a sector are interconnected by a massive complex of terraces, complete with roads, rail stations, places of commerce, and everything else that you would expect to find on the ground. Except that it is in fact hundreds of stories above the actual ground.

A society had rebuilt itself in midair, appropriately named The Mids. It services the citizens of the middle floors of the buildings, sectioned off from the lower levels by a security gate. Perhaps more importantly they are also sectioned off from the upper levels of the building where the rich reside. In fact, the upper dwellers have their own interconnected web of terraces creating yet another semblance of ground. The city perhaps looks normal from their point of view, blissfully unconcerned that it blocks any chance of natural light hitting the surface. The clouds of pollution swirl under these terraces creating a toxic atmosphere in The Mids.

The lift creaks along as it makes its way ever too slowly down, coming to a screeching halt. The barely serviced lift doors need some help as they try but fail to fully open. The crowded lobby of lifts has Harold shoulder to shoulder with aliens and humans of all sorts. The sea of workers flows toward the cross-bridge that connects their building on the edge of the sector to the main terraces. From Harold's perspective, this isn't the greatest position, but at least he lives just above the midline.

Foot traffic in the cross-bridge is its usual horde, but it moves slightly better today as there is a slow but efficient moving sidewalk. Aliens of all types are shuffling along to whatever useless mundane task they call a job. It's not like there are too many ways to move up in the world. Hell, no one even knew what species was native to the planet anymore. The people who had originally developed it were ancient history.

He glances out the pointless windows to the dense clouds of smoke and pollution. Down below is only darkness punctuated by the flashing lights of the high life above. Sometimes he wished the windows would just break so that the toxic air outside would go ahead and suffocate them to death and that would be the end of the daily grind.

Every couple feet or so on the moving sidewalk are carefully placed advertisements.

Live a floor above with Glarblast Cologne...

Fully nude gals and Yrondnax at the Century Club...

Re-elect President McSlurmins – 'Remember it could always be worse!'...

Boy, they sure knew their target demographic. That's probably the one thing that keeps anyone in the mid-level class going – the prospects of *worse*. While living a floor above was a damn near impossibility, a small miscalculation could send one hurtling down to the lower levels where poverty, crime, and slow death by toxic radiation awaited them. The only thing keeping the lower levels going was their own fear of being demoted still yet lower, to the sewer-dwelling underbelly where the freemen lived. Where death was wanting, but for the life-sustaining agonizing mutations keeping them alive. *Cringe.*

Then again maybe, just maybe, you would get lucky and move up. Unlikely in this economy. The way McSlurmins runs things, there wouldn't be a planet left to rule upon. Harold was actually born six levels above the midline, but the shitty economy had set him up at three floors down. Eight years of university just to get knocked down. Remember though, '*It could always be worse!*' No doubt about it, the single greatest campaign slogan to win on.

The cross-bridge opens up into a vast plaza. The polluted air is pushed away by deflectors and recyclers. It almost has the feel of being outdoors in the nighttime. Harold shuffles along to the far end of the plaza and down the stairs at its opposite end to a platform.

At long last, he reaches The Transit – the slow commuter train of the working-class citizens. It chugs along through the mid-levels connecting the various sectors and the districts within them on different lines. The silver paint chips off the side to reveal the rusting shell beneath what was surely once a brilliant maglev train. Its worn upholstered seats are a dull brown color.

Harold lives in an industrial sector of the Capital City, so his train car is densely packed to the brim with passengers in work clothes, hard hats, and the more-common-than-not lunch box. Passengers who are all just like him. He can only imagine if this rust bucket was what they had, surely the lower dwellers had to just walk along the wreckage of whatever remained of surface society. Not that he had ever been there, or ever wanted to.

Finally, he reaches his stop. He squeezes through to the doors, already sweating from the heat of the Transit.

"*Mulknosh Factory Exit.*" *ding ding.* "*Next stop Vurspusia District with transfer service to the Magenta Line.*"

He squeezes out into the station and walks up the stairs to yet another plaza. This one has a deep orange glow, illuminated by the smoldering furnaces of the factories surrounding it. He heads towards the windowless metal walls toward the gates of the box plant. His friend and coworker greet him in the plaza.

"What's good Harold!?"

"*Oh,* hi there Baab. Another fine morning. How's the kids?"

"Ah, they good Harold. They good. Bertrice damn near ate one of them last night, but I talked her down. Got another six hatchlings on the way!"

Was he serious? It sounds plausible enough and Baab is far too stupid to lie.

Why he was blessed with the misfortune of working with so many idiots was beyond Harold. He had always thought he was destined for greatness. He was going to rise to the top. One galactic recession after another had left his prospects for greatness terminal.

Whhooooooo! The work whistle blows.

Time to get the fuck inside, thinks Harold. He smashes his badge card into the reader. *Bonnnkkk.* Another successful clock-in completed. He pushes through the rusty turnstile gates into the aging box factory, the smell of oil and rust hitting him in the face. *Ah! Another day closer to death...*

They approach the morning meeting circle. Aliens of all sorts and sizes. What would it be today? Probably the same shit they did yesterday and the day before and the day before that. It was truly unbelievable that his boss lived fourteen floors above him for shuffling papers at her desk all day.

"Good Morning Mulkinites! I hope you're all ready for another fan-fucking-tastic workday. Our goal is to make 275 boxes today," says his section leader Mrs. Xvranbul. Her decrepit elderly voice is shrill and rude. Her faded green, wrinkly, leathery skin is drooping from her slug-like body. Her deep gray hair is pulled back tightly and she has thick eyeglasses held on by a strap. She wears an unfortunate shade of bright red lipstick. Truly a disgusting creature.

She brings up a simple shape on the screen behind her.

"Here look at the viewing screen for an update on quality. Does that look like a box to you? No? Sure doesn't. It's supposed to be a cube. Why does this shit have twelve sides? How is that even possible? Help your dimensionally-challenged species coworkers out. Remember, we're an equal opportunity employer, which means you're all equally worthless! We're only as smart as our dumbest team member. Now get your asses to work! And remember... *It could always be worse!*" It really was the societal mantra of the middle-class. Maybe she would die soon and he could finally get a promotion.

"Would you?"

" Excuse me? Would I what?"

Harold glares over to see his friend Geordon, egging him on. At least he isn't an idiot like Baab, but nonetheless still quite below midline. His dirty tattered jumpsuit fits poorly around his hulking centipede-like form. An impressive accomplishment for his species to reach even this level. The Y'tarians were universally disliked.

"Disgusting! I wouldn't touch her with a ten-foot pole... unless of course, it got me promoted!" They both laugh and proceed to their spot on the line. They put the same panels in place all day, every day on the assembly line.

The Mulknosh Corporation is the leading manufacturer of cargo containers in the galactic core. A title they proudly wear, achieved on the backs of underpaid, overworked employees. They are always happy to cut the programs that matter to make a cheap profit. A key supporter of McSlurmin's *'It could always be worse'* campaign. They would probably resort to slave labor if it were not for their fear of an uprising of the lower levels. They also found that it was cheaper than robot labor; their logic algorithms have given them sentience and an impossible-to-bust union.

The corporations pay the middles just enough to put a buffer zone between them and the rich. A carrot dangling in front of their noses gives them the slight hope of being moved up, while simultaneously keeping them subdued by reminding them they can always go down. In this mentality, things become very predictable. For millennia the delicate balance had been maintained, justifying countless acts of terrible political decisions that gave rise to this nearly unlimited urban sprawl and decay.

The twelve-hour shift passes glacially slow. This is not to say that it is the slightest temperature below sweltering in the factory. Harold spends most of his day spaced out, going through the motions of his labor as he daydreams of better possibilities.

He dreams of the penthouse suites of his building. Though he has never seen one in person, he can only guess at the luxury from what he saw on the viewer. Living plants, pools of clean water for recreation, elaborate robes, jobs with thought and discussion, music concerts, and wasteful lavish storage space. Perhaps even an off-world transport. The height of society, both literally and metaphorically.

Whooooo! A rude awakening by the whistle of the bell.

It's now the same bullshit story in reverse. Punch out the clock. Say goodbye to Baab and Geordon. Cram into The Transit. Back to the apartment. He knows he is supposed to pick something up on the way home, but can't remember what exactly. It is probably dinner though. Sheron is a terrible cook, she would want him to pick up dinner. He doesn't know what she expects him to pick up on his salary, but anything is better than what she would make, so he stops by the cheapest grub dispensary he can find between work and home.

It is greasy and most likely laced with the sorts of chemicals that his factory only saw fit to dispose of in the hazardous waste bins, but it is cheap and tastes good enough to Harold. He figured Sheron won't mind if he eats his on the way home. It's not like she made it.

"Sheroooooooon, I'm home! I brought grub." He throws off his work jumpsuit and settles himself into the worn and tattered recliner. Sheron has always hoped that one day, a spring might break and poke out of it enough to kill him. At least then she'd have insurance money. Somehow it is the most durable thing they own. If only she knew the company had cut its life insurance years ago and Harold never paid the premiums.

"You bought food? But Harold, I spent all day making dinner!" she says. The tone in her voice tells Harold that she is mad, but he can't figure out why. He knows she had not spent *all day* crafting dinner, because she also had to work just like he did. Then again, he could see her putting it on in the morning, so it would be sufficiently burnt by the time it got served.

"What? *You* asked me to pick up dinner on the way home!" he says.

"Harold you dumbass! I asked you to get the kids from school!"

"*Ahhhhh fuck. Uhhhh.* Tell 'em to just ride The Transit home!"

"Harold! The Transit is dangerous, I don't want them riding that. What if they get injured, or killed, or worse, kidnapped and held for ransom? We can't afford that, Could you live with yourself?" she said. Sadly, she knew he could, and perhaps jovially even.

"I could never get so lucky! They'll be fine. Better they get used to it now anyhow."

Sheron storms out of the room. He turns his attention back to the viewer. He slurps down the meal that Sheron made, as though to prove that his purchased meal was by no means a deterrent to him eating hers too. The show is boring and uninspired. Just the same repackaged shit over and over again, just like the meal that Sheron made. Nonetheless, he has little else to do and he's too tired to go do anything else.

Time for a commercial break.

"Rosnarth Galxshu: is he right for Capital City? Galxshu voted twelve times to demote the middle dwellers. Here is Senator Galxshu with a Nvitrian prostitute! Galxshu hates the Capital! Tell Galxshu to stop his legacy of lies. Vote to reelect President McSlurmins this solstice. Because remember... It could always be worse!"

Groan. The same commercial again and again! Don't they ever get tired of this shit? Harold isn't prepared for what happens next.

Gruntilda is standing before him on the public network in an unprecedented and welcome change of pace. She leans in as though she is speaking directly to him. Her voice rings sensuously over the speakers.

"Are you tired of the daily grind down in the mid-levels?"

"You betcha." Harold is intrigued.

"Do you feel like your worthless job is getting you nowhere?"

"Yes. Do go on!"

"You were destined for greatness, but something is holding you back."

"Fuck yeah it is! What do I do?" *Here comes the catch,* he thinks.

"Call 545-353-654-98772 today to learn about this exciting opportunity to make some serious cash fast! Experience the high life. Call now I'm waiting."

Fuck it. I got nothing to lose, thinks Harold. He is certain it is some bullshit scam, pyramid scheme, or product pusher, but there is somehow a hopefulness about him. He still wants to be optimistic. Maybe this is different. *Couldn't hurt to try right?*

He dials the number on his communicator pad.

Ring ringggg.

"Hello? Who is this?" says a voice who sounds remarkably like it might actually be Gruntilda to Harold's delight.

"Uhhh yeah. Hi. This is Harold. I saw your ad on the viewer?"

"What? Ohhhh! Yes why of course." The tone changes real quick to one of enthusiasm.

"Yeah, so you said I could make some serious cash. Start talkin', what's the angle here?"

"No angle at all! In fact, why don't you join me for a drink? I'll be at the Jyand'l Bar at the Pilquist Complex at Sector 748 later tonight. It's on me! We'll talk business."

"Huh... You know what, sure. Why not! I'll be there," says Harold, trying to contain his excitement that Gruntilda, the legend herself, is asking him out for a drink.

He isn't sure how he will explain this to Sheron. She would never let him go do this if she knew what it really was. She would say someone was probably going to harvest his organs and sell them on the black market. Maybe she would be right, but maybe that was fine too. *I'd probably still make more money than my salary. Think. Think of a convincing lie.*

"Hey, Sher. The boys are going down to the club tonight. It's for Baab. You know Baab from work? Yeah, he's having another brood of hatchlings soon, so we're gonna take him out to put him out of his misery. "

"*Fine!* Just go do whatever you want..." she says, baiting the trap.

"Great! Thanks."

He knows she doesn't mean it, but he doesn't want to play this game right now. He has money to make and he knows she would get over it if he came back with more money than either of them knew what to do with.

"I'll just do everything around here... Take care of ya kids. Clean everything. Do the dishes, the laundry, cook dinner, and go to work. *No problem...*" she says, rolling her eyes, aware that she is losing the gambit.

"Yeah okay... It's just one night! You'll be fine I swear. Besides this could be good for me, my boss might be there!"

"Mrs. Xvranbul? At a bar? Celebrating an employee? It's the titty bar again, isn't it? If you're gonna tell a lie at least make it a convincing one okay?"

"Cool your thrusters! It's just a guys' night out. We've all been stressed on the job lately, ya know? This is just a great chance to unwind."

"Sure, Harry. I'll be sure to tell the kids about you since they never saw their father growing up. They're alive by the way, not that you care. I just got off the phone with Thomas."

Well, that was the end of that conversation.

He storms out of the apartment, barely managing to get his pants fastened. *Undershirt to the bar? Yeah sure why not.* Gruntilda will see his bulging biceps better that way.

The elevator doors creak open as he reaches the end of the hall. His son Thomas and his daughter Martha. *Boy, do they look pissed.*

You can barely tell that Harold is even related to Thomas, much less his father. He is svelte and mesomorphic. His chiseled triangular jaw stands in stark contrast to Harold's chin fat. His thick reddish hair is perfectly sculpted, while Harold is balding and his patchy brown hair desperately clings to life on the sides of his head. Always sharply dressed, Thomas is a real model citizen, befitting an idealistic image of Capital City perfection. Harold in his athletic days of youth may have looked similar, but the years of abusing his body have taken their toll. Martha, on the other hand, looks like a miniature version of Sheron, yet somehow also so plain as to be virtually unnoticeable.

"Dad! Where have you been? We waited forever and you never came. We had to take the Gray Line home." His son speaks to him in such a tone, in front of his own apartment? *Teenagers have a way of getting under your skin don't they?*

"Yeah well. Looks like you figured it out. One day, when you're busting your ass at the box factory six days a week, you'll understand," says Harold. He is trying to sound both wise and hard, trying to convey that he is The Law and he is The Law for a reason. But he sees the look of disgust on Thomas' face.

For a brief moment, he feels a sense of self-awareness wash over him. He knows Sheron is right. He certainly isn't Father of the Year. He is barely even a father.

"Look, I'm sorry, okay? It's been crazy at work recently. The economy is all over the place and we're all putting in too many hours just trying to keep our jobs and..." he trails off, rubbing the back of his neck with his hand, not sure where he might have been going with the excuse. It is pretty weak, even by Harold's standards.

He looks back and forth between Thomas and Martha. Thomas is nearly a man and Harold fears it is too late to do right by him. He'll have to get it right with Martha. Which means he has to get that payout, whatever the job was. Not that he knew what to buy her, as he hardly knew her at all, but he was confident he could buy her affection.

"Where are you going anyway? You and Mom fighting again?" says Thomas.

His probing questions easily dispels the uncomfortable moment of awareness in Harold. Don't they know that he doesn't answer to them? THEY answer to HIM. But he has places to be and he isn't looking for a fight right now.

"Yeah, you could say that. Going to the bar with the guys. It's Geordon's yzmarbitaka tonight. Mind your mother, okay? Don't cause any trouble?" Harold says. Thomas' look of disgust continues.

"Whatever, Dad. That's not even a thing. I'm not even sure that's a word in Y'tarian."

"How would you know? You don't know any and you ought to keep it that way. Go do your homework. I'm outta here," says Harold, decisively sure of himself in that fact.

Thomas sure is bright sometimes and sometimes Harold admires his spirit. *Maybe he will be able to do what he could never do. Marry a rich girl! Ha.* He boards the lift this time down to the hovercab level. The Transit would be too slow. He'd never make it across town in time that way. This had better be worth it. *Hovercab ain't cheap!*

The pedestrian traffic is unusually light on the hovercab terrace level. Many young people these days have too much to worry about to take up drinking and clubbing. Responsibilities never stopped Harold.

They were just soft. One day they'll be cynics too and wish they'd started drinking years earlier.

Harold is a married man, but that doesn't stop him from checking out the two gorgeous female whatever-aliens that are waiting at the platform.

They're checking him out too right? They are scantily dressed. Maybe they were... N*aw. Don't be an ass. Don't be an ass. Well, fuck you did it anyway.*

"How much ladies?"

"Ktrshra Ylvab!?" they said.

That wasn't good.

He doesn't have to speak the language to know she said *excuse me* and not in a good way.

Well, why not. I'm already in this deep. Might as well press the matter, right?

"Relax, ladies. I ain't the enforcers. You guys are hookers right?"

A swing and a direct hit. Purse to the face like a ton of bricks. Why does he always have to say dumb shit? If Sheron only knew how many times he'd failed to pick up a hooker, she'd probably leave his ass or just laugh really. She'd probably think it was hilarious to watch him fail like this.

He regains his balance and stumbles over to the hovercab stand. The bright yellow flying cars pull right up to an open ledge that leads to the abyss below where passengers board in a disorderly fashion. Harold hails the hovercab and pushes his way past the ladies, gets in, and slams the door shut.

"Pilquist... 748," he says.

The driver understands. Whatever he says back is lost on him. Some series of muffled tones emanate from his cybernetic mask. At least he can read the numbers and watch the rate go up as they travel.

"And take the 803 straight there you hear? No funny business."

More tones. Now they are getting to know each other. He lost count of alien species long ago but after a lifetime of living on a planet with almost as many species of aliens as individuals, one learns how to pick up on the gist of languages. Particularly through the use of hand gestures, should of course they have hands.

As they barrel through the city, his nerves start to get to him.

What if this thing just fell out of the sky one day? Plunging down into the lower levels. How far down did it even go? Most sectors are over 250 stories high. Mid-level cab falling from this level would explode for sure right? Even worse if I survived. Being carted away, treated by those lower-level docs.

He shudders at the thought of the torture implements they must use as medical instruments.

Ah good, we're almost there.

The Pilquist Building Complex. Indistinguishable corporate sprawl, just like all the other sectors around it. A building surrounded by buildings, surrounded by more buildings. Progress. Development. Success. Garbage.

He holds his breath from the platform to the door, noticing the broken deflector. If he was going to breathe in toxic air it was going to be on his own platform, from his own decrepit factory, not someone else's.

"Twenty-seven credits, fifty? Are you out of your mind?" Harold says to the driver.

The driver spits more muffled tones and clicks back at him. It doesn't take a genius to guess what he has said. *This had better be the offer of a lifetime.*

"*Please scan identification badge.*" He jams his ID card into the reader. "*Welcome Hair-old. Pilquist is pleased to welcome you to our corporate district. Did you know you can buy wares and souvenirs at the company store? Check us out on your way home. Pilquist, drugs and drink, no need to think!*"

Yeah yeah. Spare us the bullshit and just open the stall, please.

The stall door opens and he's free to enter the complex. Not every building is this secure, but Pilquist is the foremost manufacturer of pharmaceutical enhancement beverages. Why waste a trip when you can do drugs and drink booze at the same time? If only he was born here, he might be ten floors higher by now and in more ways than one.

The Jyand'l Bar is not quite his scene. Not the usual seedy dive bar you'd see in Mulknosh. The lights are colorful, the music loud and pulsating. People dancing, tripping, fucking, drinking their colorful concoctions. Harold is beginning to get concerned. He hadn't had the presence of mind to think about what he would say to Gruntilda. More importantly, he was worried this was the kind of establishment that didn't serve regular beer and if they did, he wasn't sure how to order one.

He is about to ask someone when a voice comes from nowhere. A man's voice with the confidence of a crooked salesman.

"*Ah!* Mr. Harold, I'm so pleased you could make it. I was beginning to worry you wouldn't show."

Harold turns to locate the voice. He isn't sure what he was expecting but it for sure wasn't the cleanly dressed businessman sitting at a booth with two of the most attractive women Harold has ever seen, sitting by either arm. They sit in a way that says they don't know each other and it doesn't matter. The man radiates power subtly, drawing everyone near him closer without them realizing it. Harold himself has stepped closer to the table, not in control of his own legs.

"I'm glad you did though. I've got a great opportunity for you," the businessman says with a smile.

It's the only part of his outfit that doesn't fit perfectly. It's someone else's smile as if he has stolen it from someone on the viewer because he hadn't been born with his own.

"Now we mustn't talk out here. This endeavor is strictly confidential. If you would accompany me, I have reserved a secure room in the back of this establishment. I trust it will meet our needs," says the man. His voice is calm and quiet, yet Harold has no problem hearing him over the chaos of the bar.

"A private room sounds nice doesn't it ladies?" says Harold.

The man gets up from the table, he motions to the women to stay where they are. They don't even attempt to move. Harold's nerves only get worse.

Should I just go ahead and hand over my kidneys now or wait to be stabbed in the back room? Should I even let him try? I could probably take him.

He takes a closer look at his potential employer. His simple two-piece suit is deceptively tailored. It makes him appear lean but Harold can see that he is surprisingly tall with a sturdy frame.

On second thought, maybe I couldn't.

"If I had ladies like that, you wouldn't see me leaving them out here! What are you a pimp or something? Come on man, what is this about? Where's Gruntilda anyhow? You her manager or what?" Harold asks.

The man ignores him and only beckons him to follow.

If the man completely defies Harold's expectations, the secure backroom at the Jyand'l does not. Every feature of the room screams 'high-class back room'. The dim lights are just enough to highlight a red circular booth cradling a smooth black table. The surrounding darkness likely hides sins that would make even Harold blush. It is the perfect environment for secret gambling, cavorting with mistresses, or talking 'business'.

"Have a seat Mr. Harold," says the man. Once again Harold's body acts on instructions from outside his own mind. "Tell me, what brought you here."

Harold gets a distinct impression that the man already knows exactly why he is here. He also suspects he won't be meeting Gruntilda after all.

"Cash," Harold blurts shamelessly. "You said you had a deal. A job or something. Whatever it is, makes no difference to me as long as I get my share of the money. Whatever it takes to move up."

"Well, your record would suggest otherwise, Mr. Harold. I'm glad you've seen fit to change your mind though. I presumed at your level you had given up interest in chasing such dreams. And yet here you are. I assume you know that any offer has its price. You took a risk coming here." He grins with that borrowed smile of his again. "I admire that." The man pauses to sip his drink and let the silence and the veiled warning hang in the air.

"Can you blame me? With a commercial like that? Who wouldn't call?" says Harold.

"Of course. I want to make you rich, Mr. Harold. Rich beyond your wildest dreams. How does that sound?" asks the man.

"Sounds like too many words. Look, Mister, I ain't a fool, and I know what a ticket up costs. Tell me what the job is and how much it pays. Then we'll talk about how it *sounds*," says Harold, his nervousness quickly turning into irritation. If there's one thing Harold can't abide, it's being talked down to by a rich guy. Not that he had ever met any.

Harold's gruff approach towards people is often off-putting, so he is surprised to see a twinkle in the man's eye and something almost approaching a real smile.

"Direct! Very well, Mr. Harold. I have a problem with a man who took something from me, something priceless. I want you to kill him."

It catches Harold off guard and he barks out a short laugh. He looks back at the man and the twinkle and smile are gone. Instead, there is a strange look on his face that Harold isn't sure about. Is it regret? Harold isn't experienced with it enough to say for sure. Either way, it indicates that the man isn't kidding.

"Wait, you want me to whack some guy I don't even know? I don't even know you!" Harold isn't so sure about that and his insides are beginning to twist back into nervousness.

"Mind your volume, Mr. Harold," says the man, but he doesn't appear too bothered by the outburst. "But yes I want him dead. Preferably a slow and painful death, but it is of no concern how you do it. You'll of course be paid handsomely for the deed."

"I don't know, that's some heavy shit. I ain't exactly the murdering type," says Harold, forgetting about the money for the first time in hours.

The man smiles the borrowed smile again. "I understand completely Mr. Harold. It's not a job for everyone, even with the massive payout. You're under no obligation to accept, of course." Harold tensed, sensing a 'but' coming.

"Mr. Harold, did you honestly expect that this would be easy? You came here thinking that you of all people were going to receive a clean business deal from a supermodel?" The man pauses for his answer.

"I never expected to get through on the call. Surprised you didn't have thousands lining up for a deal like this. I mean, Gruntilda. Come on!" says Harold.

"There was never anyone else, Mr. Harold." says the man.

"What do you mean, pal?" asks Harold, becoming frustrated.

"Our advertisement was only broadcast to you. A waste of our resources it seems. Perhaps you know too much already," says the man, taking a threatening posture.

"Hey! Hold on. I'm not saying that. I'm your guy okay? I mean I got morals and all, but a cred is a cred. How much are we talking here? I just need more *assurances.* Clearly you have some reach, you've done your homework. You seem like a wealthy guy, but how do I know you're not playing me?"

"My apologies. I suppose you are quite right. I should probably be more forthcoming about our arrangement. As a show of my good faith, take this. Ten-thousand credits, unmarked in an envelope. Yours to do with as you please. No strings attached. Though might I suggest you hold onto some of it for supplies? I don't want to tell you how to do it, but I certainly won't be caught with dirty hands buying them for you," says the man, making a handwashing motion with his hands.

This is truly unbelievable. Money like that never just falls out of the sky. If this is good-faith money, the real thing really must be unbelievable. He starts dreaming of his penthouse. The luxurious fountains and his beautiful wives. *Gruntilda, you've decided to stay? Wonderful. Let's bust out the champagne and reenact that scene from* Busty Blonde Alien Bitches III. *Yeah.* He could get used to that. Thomas can go to the best schools. His daughter will grow up to respect him and marry rich. His wife... *Eh, I mean we'll stick with Gruntilda. Sheron can live in the guest apartment.*

Could he live with himself though? Knowing his fortune was built on the back of a man he murdered? Surely... Yes. Yes, he could. All of society is built on the backs of the less fortunate. The corporations kill tens of millions every day in the lower levels. He isn't half as culpable as them, right? No one is looking out for them. A ticket up is all that matters. Besides, whoever this guy is, he is obviously a bad dude. Wrapped up in some pretty shady shit, stealing from people and stuff. Maybe he deserves it. Maybe he'd be doing the world a favor. Maybe he'd be doing the man a favor by putting him out of his misery. He takes the envelope.

"So... who's the lucky guy?" Harold inquires.

The man smiles, his mood way too upbeat for a guy arranging a murder-for-hire plot. He says nothing further, handing him a full access identification card and a data record.

"Sector 1149? You sure this card will get me in?" Harold asks. The man only nods his head in agreement. "Suppose this doesn't work out? What if I get caught or something?"

With no warning, the man pulls a sleek black pistol from his jacket pocket. With precision, he twists the silencer onto the barrel. He aims and fires before Harold has even a chance to react.

Harold yells out in fear before realizing he is still alive. He turns to face the doorway to find one of the beautiful women previously occupying the booth with him dead on the floor, bleeding from a perfectly centered headshot.

"You won't fail, Mr. Harold," says the man calmly wiping down the barrel before placing it neatly back into his jacket pocket like nothing ever happened.

"Holy shit! You just? Why? What the fuck man?" says Harold.

"I value my privacy, Mr. Harold, and I hate to be interrupted. It's unfortunate when someone violates my trust and I don't do second chances. One can never be too careful these days."

Harold understands the message clearly. "How do I contact you when the job is done?"

"I'll call you when the job is done, Mr. Harold."

"Who are you?"

"My name is Gharles. Gharles Darkley. That is all you need to know," says the man.

There is a brief, awkward silence in the room. Harold can hear the blood as it slowly flows across the floor. "Well, good evening Mr. Harold. The Syndicate thanks you for your participation in this matter."

The who? What, so there's a group of them now? This guy must have really fucked up. Am I in a cartel now? How am I gonna pull this off? What will I tell Sher?

He'd have to be gone for hours. She'd never go for it. She wouldn't understand either. He couldn't tell her a word of it. "Tell a convincing lie," she had said. See, he did listen to her after all. Maybe he hears what he wants to hear. The sooner this is over with, the better. Now he just had to make it back to the house without getting robbed and hide this envelope somewhere real good where the kids and Sher and nobody would ever find it.

Chapter 2

It was in yet another meeting that could have been an email that Carl realized
he didn't actually know what day it was. If he thought real hard, he seemed
to recall that Monday had been three days ago. Or was it four? He wasn't
sure it mattered, it could have been Saturday and he wouldn't really have
known the difference.

Every day was the same exact thing. Carl would wake up in the morning,
turn off his alarm and go back to sleep for thirty more minutes, wake up an
hour later and realize that he turned *off* his alarm instead of setting it to
snooze and that he was now an hour behind schedule. That was okay, he set
his alarm an hour and a half early specifically to account for that.

First, the morning routine: Get out of bed, put on his work outfit, brush
his teeth, shower, and rush out the door. Then the commute. He had worked
a low-end food prep job while in university and saved every credit to afford
a used shuttle. It wasn't much and it already had over 100,000 lightyears on
it when he bought it, but he'd been flying it for twelve years and it hadn't
failed him yet.

Sure, it shook pretty violently at anything over .7c but he rarely ever needed
it for that. For work, it just had to get off the ground, leave the atmosphere,
and hit orbital velocity. From there it was just an easy hour to work. *An hour
and a half if there was traffic.* Carl had never taken Interstellar Logistics in
university, so he wasn't entirely sure how there was traffic in space, but he
supposed it didn't really matter because it existed and that's all there was to
it. *Just remember, you're part of the problem*, he would tell himself.

It didn't make him feel better.

While he was rarely late, he was somehow always the last one to the station, which meant that he was the last one to dock. That meant getting the furthest dock away from where he actually worked, which added another fifteen minutes of walking to his trip. Generic Orbital Office stations were all pretty much the same design. Employee parking on the bottom four floors and then there were forty-five floors of mixed offices. Up forty-five floors of the station in an elevator, three passageways down the main corridor, take a left, and finally, he arrived at the unceremonious entrance to his office.

Before leaving his shuttle to enter the office, he would carefully inspect himself in the mirror, adjusting his red tie, pulling at his grey suit, and making sure his white button-down shirt was securely fastened. Each day he would gaze at his black hair making sure it was perfectly combed for business, always fearing the onslaught of grey. He made sure to leave it just a little bit frayed so as to give the appearance of a fun casual guy. Ready for work, but also ready to engage in necessary social interaction. He wondered if his eyes were still blue enough to be charming. He had to present the image of a quintessential businessman, conforming to every standard of mediocrity so as to blend in seamlessly with the sea of suits.

Melissa, the receptionist, was always there with a warm smile on her face and it was the only part of his day that he could look forward to. Luckily, it happened first thing during his workday, so he could get that over with right away and get straight into the mind-numbing grind for... *how many hours?* Thinking on it, Carl couldn't actually say. At any rate, it was likely somewhere between eight and twelve, though hours on a station could be tricky. Since there was no day/night cycle on an artificial station, they always set it so it felt like early morning.

"Good morning, Caleb!" she would confidently exclaim each morning as he walked in the door.

"Good morning," he would mumble as he walked by and stared probably for just a few seconds longer than he should. He would like to correct her, but he didn't want to make it awkward. Besides, it was an understandable mistake. He had only worked here fifteen years and names could be tricky to remember.

He would make his way to his desk, which itself was a journey. His company's office took up the entire west side of the station but there was only one entrance that standard employees were allowed to use. So after he would enter, he'd head down the hall, hang a right to the *'employees only'* elevator. And make his way forty-five floors down. And from there it was only a fifteen-minute walk to his actual desk. Work started at 8:00 am every day and every day Carl would get there just in the nick of time to see the clock hit 8:30.

It was like that every single day except for weekends and even then, he mostly would zone out and imagine what life would be like if he had fun on the weekends instead of doing exactly what he did do, which was nothing.

"Carl, will you have those numbers ready for us this week?" someone in the meeting asked. The entire party of business suits turns to stare at him from across the long shiny black table that filled the conference room. At least those who couldn't just turn their eye stalks toward him.

So, what did that make today? Thursday, probably?

That seemed as good as any, though he wasn't sure if there was any definitive way of telling. He thought briefly of some sort of program which could determine what day it was, possibly by checking the alignment of the stars or maybe polling a government server somewhere and then display that information on his communicator. It would certainly help him and he was willing to bet there were other people that would find it useful as well.

"Carl?" His boss repeated.

"Yes, I know lots of numbers, you can have any of them you like," Carl responded, not sure exactly which numbers he was supposed to 'have ready' by the end of the week. *When exactly was the end of the week again?*

"Thank you," he said, apparently not really hearing Carl. He carried on with, "Paano will work on the Risk Analysis as soon as those numbers are in and it can have that done within a week so we can really get rolling on this project."

The words 'this project' got the smallest bit of reaction internally from Carl, as he wasn't really sure what project they were talking about. This was the first he had heard of it, though he idly thought that perhaps it was mentioned in one of those unread emails under his 'Project' folder. He made a mental note, one which he would absolutely forget by the time the meeting was done, to check those emails later.

His boss carried on for another hour, or maybe only fifteen minutes. *Who could really say for sure?* It seemed like two hours anyways. They discussed more tasks that each person in the meeting would carry out to begin the planning phase for the beginning of the assessment portion of starting a new project. Just as Carl was certain the meeting would actually never end and he would just have to leave, his boss ended the meeting and they were free to leave. He checked the clock on the way out. It read 9:13 am.

* * *

All things considered, it wasn't a terrible job. There were certainly worse places to work. He could have been in one of the planetside factories right now, doing mindless labor six days a week, getting nowhere. He was paid well enough to have his own place and his own shuttle, though admittedly not much else. However, he was content and so he never really gave it too much thought. At least he was told he should be content with what he had.

His coworkers were decent enough and he would occasionally go out with them and pretend that he was having a great time spending more time with the people he already worked with every day. Not only that, but he was also up for promotion and Carl was sure that if he played his cards right, he could finally move up the corporate ladder another rung. So there was always something to look forward to. But after a long day of making numbers ready and learning about a project he'd apparently been assigned to, the only thing he looked forward to was going home.

On his way out, he saw Melissa again. She had the same comforting smile on her face that she had all day long and Carl began to try to think up a way he could start a conversation with her. He thought up all the ways that he could be charming and whisk her away and have a great time.

"Hey," he might have said coolly. "Wanna grab a drink with me tonight?"

He might have said that, but he did not. He tried to think of other things he could say but he was drawing a blank. It's not that Carl had *never* dated anyone before, but most of the times that he did had sort of been a matter of circumstance and he never reached out to make the first move.

And then life happened in that annoying way that it does where things keep happening and you have to keep dealing with it, always creating situations where Carl found himself far too busy to worry about things such as dating.

He had graduated university and job hopped for a bit until he landed on working for... Where did he work again? Then he had moved to his new apartment in Sector 1149 and had to move all of his stuff in, and ever since then, he had been so busy not living life that he had never taken time to actually just live life. Carl idly thought about how to change that as he said "Good night" to Melissa, who sweetly replied back.

"Have a great evening, Charles!" She almost had it that time.

A calendar! He thought as he made it back to his shuttle, not sure of how he had forgotten what that was and even less sure if it would actually make his life better. Even still, he pulled up the calendar function on his comm device and checked what day it was.

It was Saturday after all.

Chapter 3

Ank! Ank! Ank! What? What's happening? Oh time for work again already? What a long night.

Harold starts to wonder how long he might make that ten grand last if he quit his job today and just went straight for the kill. *Naw. That's not gonna fly.* Nothing out of the ordinary. Just a normal day. Nothing suspicious. He'd leave work as normal. Tell Sher he had to take a package over to corporate or something. He would find this guy and cap him with his pistol. That would be the end of it.

"Come on, Dad. Let's go. Your breakfast is on the table. No need for applause. If you'd like me to save you the effort, I could neglect myself? Still hungover from your yzmarbitaka?" says Thomas.

He's clearly agitated at Harold. He meanders over to the scratched-up four-person table and throws himself into his usual chair. It has the illusion of wood, but really it's just a cheap painted composite. Real wood no longer exists on any core world, and as far as he knew trees might not even exist at all.

"Listen here you disrespectful shit! You better be glad I'm not a morning person. Don't worry. I'll keep putting that money in the account so you can have that breakfast to be thankful for. Anybody make coffee though? Where's your mother?" he asks, gesturing around at the tiny apartment, searching for his coffee to be brought to him.

"She goes into work early on Wednesdays! How do you forget? You have to take us to school today. Remember? Otherwise, we'll be late taking the Transit, and you know how Mom feels about that."

"Shit. Have you noticed she never seems to worry about me taking it? Give me the communicator would yah?" says Harold, reaching for the comm, his stubby arms unable to reach. Thomas passes it to him and he dials her up. "Listen, Sher? Baby you there? Yeah, I know you're at work. Of course, you think I'd forgotten? Listen I got this *thing* I got to do for work tonight. It's a package delivery situation. I'm gonna be late. But it's good overtime..." *Ah shit.* "That's tonight? Do I have to? Alright alright! Take it easy. Of course I wouldn't miss his Fljrkhorn game! I'll... I'll figure something out okay. Bye!"

"Dad... you forget my game again?" Thomas rolls his eyes.

"I'm coming, buddy. I promise. I'll be there."

Shit how am I ever going to do all of this in a day? Working twelve-hour shifts, six days a week. Life is unmanageable enough as he is barely doing it. Much less adding murder to the to-do list. Thomas is a great Fljrkhorn player. His ticket out. If he does well enough in the next two seasons, he could get a full ride. Maybe to an elite upper-level school. Meet a rich girl... *or guy?*... to marry. *Rich* being the operative word here. He can't miss the game again. He has to be there. Thomas would play better with his support.

"You're coming? For real? Like seriously this time? Because last time..." says Thomas, who is pensive, trying to recall the last time Harold had come to see him play.

Harold waves him off. He is coming. End of discussion. He barely manages to shuffle out the door with the kids in tow. Sher had left him the hovercar. *Great.* They head to the parking terminal. Fortunately, they don't have to take the lift because they have access on their floor.

The beat-up old hovercar sputters to a start. If the hovercab ride was bad, this death trap is worse. How could he let his family ride in this every day? Not that he could afford anything else. And remember... *It could always be worse!* Well, it was about to be if this hovercar didn't get moving.

The hovercar whirs into heavy traffic, the dense smoke and fog clouding the viewing portals. Fortunately, the sensors are cooperating today. Zooming along at the speed of smell, they arrive barely in time. *Here we are. P.S. 8415, the pride of Mulknosh.* A dump really. The school is in a sad state of disrepair. Little has changed since his parents had gone there even. It is like a monumental pyramid of concrete and metal that narrows to a flat glass roof.

With the kids abruptly exiting, he whirs the sputtering hovercar back towards the plant. He's tempted to cut across sky lanes to the open. A shortcut, but a death wish. Another craft coming from the opposite direction doing the same maneuver could send the wreckage hurtling downward.

Down. Down. Down!? Shit, why is the hovercraft going down? It stalls. *This is it. This is the end. Come on. Start! Start! Start!*

The car begins its smoky descent into the abyss below. It sputters and chirps. Nothing. Just down. *Down. Down!*

Then finally it comes back online. He kicks it into high thrust back up toward the lanes. *Crisis averted.* He has to do something. He can't maintain this life anymore. He is going to do the job no matter what it takes.

* * *

Not late. Not late. Not late! Punch card slams in, gate opens. *Safe!* Only a minute to spare. He's survived another Wednesday. You see, being late isn't really an option for the mid-levels. You're late, you're fired. They can easily replace you with any of the tens of millions of hungry lower-dwellers.

He hustles over to the morning meeting. Not really running, running isn't his thing. Xvranbul's obese slug-like body is his saving grace. She isn't the type of boss that can sneak up on you, so he is thankful for that even if she is a mean old bitch.

"*Wellll.* Just in time Harold. I was about to take great satisfaction in terminating you. Anyways, yesterday we were just short of your goal of 275 boxes at 127. Actually, you made 200 something, but most of them were shit. Fortunately for all of you, this wasn't your fault. The panels we received were both late and defective. The Quality Executioner General has determined to cancel our contract with the lowers of Sector 378. If you would like to see footage of the extermination, check out Channel 687 on your viewer. Since it was a foundry, they decided to use flamethrowers for the irony. Saw the previews this morning, and I assure you it will be violent and gruesome. Truly spectacular. Anyways, to make up for it, our goal is 547 boxes today. Hopefully, you can all stay late. If not, I don't care. As always, if you plan on dying today, make sure to fill out the appropriate requisition form two weeks in advance. And remember, *It could always be worse!*"

Even working at full capacity this was going to be no less than a sixteen-hour shift. He will miss Thomas's game for sure. Maybe he can catch the final quarter, and have just enough time to murder this guy before passing out for the night.

Fucking lowers. If they would just work harder, they could move up to the mids. All they have to do is meet their production goals, and they wouldn't be killed. Simple as that.

"Harold. What's got you today?" asks Baab, sensing Harold's dissatisfaction.

"Step off it Baab. The car stalled out on me this morning. It was my day to take the kids."

"Ahh, just have them ride the rails. Save you a fortune on hovercar insurance."

"No offense, Baab, but how many of your kids are dead or missing?"

"Who cares! Just have another brood. I got a couple hundred more."

"Do you even know their names?" The banter is as playful as it is concerning.

"Hell no! They can name themselves. Kids gotta be resilient. You humans are weak. Put all your eggs in one basket. An internal basket no less! You know. I know a guy who does GenMods and CyberNet. Why not get yourself another set of arms or some wings or something? Bet you'd be a lot more efficient then."

"No offense, Baab, but I'd rather crash my hovercar into the sewer levels than meet anyone you know. How long do you guys live anyway? Ten years?"

"Ha! It's all about efficiency. After one year you humans are still meat sacks. All of my kids could speak seventeen languages, get jobs, fuck, and move out by then. Besides how long does anyone in the mids actually make it? Better to have ten years less the jaded."

"Yeah well, hope you don't get crushed. Better get back to work before Xvranbul rips your wings off and feeds you to her gorthox."

"Suck my proboscis, Harold!"

In the mids, friendships are like that. Never too serious, because you never know when someone will drop out or drop dead. You insult each other to take your mind off the real damage. Pretty much everyone's friends come from their jobs. Not like you have time for much else.

Truly he is disgusted by the insectoid creature, but he is a good top welder. *Easy to do when you have wings, I guess.* Sometimes they do fuck up the design schematics with all those eyes of theirs; they barely understand human engineering diagrams. How they became a sentient spacefaring race is beyond him, but Baab isn't wrong. The quick cycle of birth and death is perfect for capitalism. No pensions, no retirement, no time to be disgruntled, producing a never-ending supply of labor, easily fed, easily housed. A veritable jar of flies. It is a miracle they employ humans at all anymore. Lucky for him, the titans of industry and politics are primarily human and have a nasty habit of xenophobia.

The mids are diverse like that. Your neighbors are aliens of all types. Some of them mixed. They could have automated all of it with robots, but it is cheaper and easier to do the grunt work in the lower levels. Once you get into the upper class, things thin out quite a bit. Mostly humans, and a few select species deemed socially acceptable. If it weren't for their uneasy alliances and profit-producing markets, the humans would probably wipe them all out.

He calls Sheron during his lunch break to tell her about how late he will be. She is probably yelling, but he just goes on with his sandwich. Carefully concealing his pistol in his jacket pocket. Preparing his mind for the task ahead. She won't be yelling when he comes home with the big money.

The day passes slowly, as it always does. 537 boxes made. The shipping lanes ever-expanding as more and more worlds are pillaged for their resources. The truly obscenely rich live off-world, in some remote part of the galaxy untouched by the hands of industry. Flat to the ground. Non-sentient organisms surround their spacious mansions. Natural water! He has never seen it, but it is rumored to exist. He knows it is foolish to dream of that level of wealth. Extra-solar permits are for the elite of the elite only, less the shipping crews, *lucky bastards*, spending their R&R on foreign worlds, only just to be able to tell the tales to keep the masses content enough to continue existing in the Capital.

* * *

Harold is the first to the exit gate, punching out only a moment after the exit bell rings. He hustles his way over to the parking chambers, damn near falling down the stairs. Breathing heavily, drenched in sweat and filth from the job, he fires up the hovercar. He blasts out into traffic with reckless abandon. *Fuck the lanes. If I die, I die.* Hopefully, no Monitor Bots are patrolling the sector today. A successful shortcut. A sigh of relief.

At last, he reaches Barbados Field #743. Home of the Fighting Mulknights. The enclosed ellipsoid structure can house tens of thousands of patrons. *Why 743? Don't know, don't care.* Barbados' name is on everything. *He is one rich motherfucker for sure.* Rumor has it he is the CEO of Mulknosh, but no one ever sees him, at least not in the mids. That is on a need-to-know basis, and no mid-level citizen needed to know. Wouldn't blame him. Why bother ever being associated with anything less than royalty when you have that kind of cash? Extrasolar mansion for sure.

He squeezes his way up the stands. The stairs hurt his knees. He is exhausted from the day. Sheron is easy to find, still in her waitress uniform. Intensely following the game, her face turns sour upon seeing him coming. It is the fourth quarter. The score of the Fljrkhorn game is 17-10, a close game, but the Mulknights are on top.

"I made it! What did I miss?" says Harold, trying not to sound too winded.

"Hardly... you damn near missed the whole game. Thomas had three Fljrkhorn goals in the second quarter. He's playing well tonight," says Sheron, trying to ignore him.

The opposing crowd cheers wildly, a three-point score for the Arkonians! The score is getting closer. He hopes they won't go into overtime. He has business to take care of. Fljrkhorn is an extremely popular sport on a multi-planetary scale. Professional players make a fortune from ticket sales and merchandising. It is one of the best ways for a mid or lower to move up in life.

The game is played on a three-dimensional plane, representing the three societal tiers. Non-flying players have specialized jetpacks. The goal is to get the Fljrkhorn into one of six goals. Bonus points are awarded if the goal is lit up. The higher tier goals award higher points. The Fljrkhorn itself is a sizable weighted diamond-shaped ball made of a metallic polymer. Defensive guards wield specialized sticks and have the goal of either stealing the Fljrkhorn from the opposing team, preventing it from entering the goal, or knocking an opponent out of the way or to a lower tier.

Thomas is a Tier-III offender, the top tier. His goal is to be one of three people who can advance on the opposing team's goals, but his primary mission is to support the captain in their pursuit to get high-level goals. He is in line to be team captain next year. A beaming source of pride for Harold. Harold never made it past Tier-II. If only he had, they might be rich today. He has the highest hopes Thomas will get a scholarship for it.

Bonkkkk.

Wild cheers again. 17-18 now it was a high-tier goal. Will they recover? Only a few moments remaining on the clock. Thomas has the Fljrkhorn! He's advancing on the lit goal. Two defenders sweep in, knocking him away, direct hits. His coverman is too far away. He goes spiraling down towards the ground. A heavy hit. He will bruise for sure. Still holding the Fljrkhorn, he makes an angled ascent using a quick burst maneuver. Five seconds remaining!

He slams upward into a Tier-II guard sending him flying. The guard crashes into the Tier-III defenders. Thomas swoops up to the lit goal. *He scores!!!* 22-18 Another Mulknight victory! They will be going to the playoffs for sure. The crowd goes wild.

Harold's energy is restored. Even Sheron seems happy again. There are few moments of joy available in their day, but this is certainly among the greatest. The murder can wait just a moment. He wants to at least congratulate

Thomas first. *Who cares if I lose sleep, it's not like I have to be conscious to do my job.*

Thomas is elated; surprised that his father had actually made it to the game. They say their congratulations and are on their way back to the fieldhouse for a post-game celebration. Harold turns his attention back to the matter at hand.

"Listen, Sher. I still got that package thing, you know. I still have to drop it off today. I'll be home pretty late, so don't wait up. You can take the hovercar home though. I'll catch The Transit," he says as she rolls her eyes.

* * *

It's late, but the city never sleeps. The Transit station still bustles with endless droves of patrons. He will have to take the Red Line to the Yellow Line intersection and take it up to Fuchsia to reach sector 1149. He is nervous. He has never been to a business district before. No authorization. Just to access the Fuchsia Line is an incredulous new task for him.

He can't go in there looking like this. There aren't too many suit stores in his sector. Mostly only for weddings and special events really. He knows there is no way he would fit in his wedding suit! He calls an old school buddy who owns a bridal shop in the West 287th commerce building.

"Hey L'krell, it's Harold. Listen, can you do me a solid? I need a suit rental and I need it tonight. Actually, hell, I'll just buy it off of you. I know it's late. It's the opportunity of a lifetime though, unmarked cash! No, I'm not lying."

The deal is sealed. Business is always bad; L'Krell isn't going to question him about it, just as long as he has got the sale. Unmarked cash has a way of disappearing from the tax registers, and it is always desired. It is hard to get down here; usually only when a rich man needs his dirty work done for him. L'krell doesn't need to know how or why Harold has the money, because it probably isn't good.

L'Krell opens up the rundown old shop, lifting the rollup security doors. The inside glistens with cheap low-end dresses and an assortment of the same suit in every color. Harold is exhausted, but he arrives only seconds after. L'Krell fits him quickly for a passable suit, using the tendrils of his long floor dragging mouth to measure. Hurriedly he takes the suit over to his sewing bench and tailors it with incredible speed, the benefit of having multiple sets of arms and prehensile tendrils. Harold looks like a fish out of water. L'Krell has to break his silence.

"You look ridiculous, Harold. I don't know what you're up to, and I don't need to know, but you need to be careful. When you're among them, you got to walk like them, talk like them. Otherwise, they'll know you're not one."

Harold takes his advice to heart. If he is going to infiltrate the upper-mids he has to bring his best. He exchanges the money, with L'Krell seeming surprised Harold isn't lying about it.

"Listen. If Sheron asks, you never saw me. Okay?" They have an understanding. L'Krell will keep his beak sealed.

* * *

The Transit ride seems endless. He isn't sure if he has ever been this far away before. He is nervous at the Fuchsia Line. *What if the card Gharles gave me doesn't read?* He carefully swipes it at the security gate. The computer says nothing. No identification. The gate just opens. Inside the terminal is quite a different experience.

The terminal is surprisingly spacious and uncrowded. Many people are already returning from their nights out as it is late. He wonders if he'd have to catch this guy asleep. The Transit cars are unvandalized. The seats plush. The carpets clean. Temperature controlled. Maybe he doesn't even have to go all the way up the ladder, the upper-mids of a commerce district is more than enough. The ride is quiet. Peaceful music playing from the intercom as The Transit rolls on.

Is he blending in? Are people staring at him? Will they know?

He tries to look away, not making eye contact with another soul. The Transit comes to a halt in a tall, well-lit plaza. The floors could be marble or at least made to look that way. Red faux carpet pathways lead patrons from the Transit out into the sector. Unbelievably, they even have fake plant adornments that mist purified air into the corridors. Tall windowed ceilings in the narrow alleys between buildings offer a greater illusion of space.

He approaches the first commerce building in the sector. The shops hold goods all too unfamiliar to him. This is far from the cramped quarters of his local stores. Wide-open storefronts with clean walkways and thoughtful inside lighting. There is so much space between people. The pathways between the middle class are certainly wide. He envisions that some lowers here might live as well as he did at home. They are by no means regarded as wealthy here either. His motivation is reinvigorated. *Push through the tired.*

He enters the first bar he sees. *How should I go about this?* A decisive action to request information from the bartender. The bar after all is mostly empty and the bartender is staring into the abyss, polishing his glasses.

"What will it be tonight, sir?" asks the bartender. *Sir? Where?* Oh, he is talking to him. *What fresh hell is this? Time to switch on the academic language.*

"Your cooperation, sir..." He flashes a picture to the bartender who looks fearful. "I'm looking for someone. Thought maybe you could help me out. This is his name. You know him?"

"I'm afraid I haven't seen him, sir. Is he known to frequent our establishment? Is he dangerous? Should I be concerned?" says the bartender, seeming apprehensive.

"Oh! No, not at all. He's just a friend of mine. I wanted to catch up while I'm in town."

"Right... I'll be sure to contact the department if I see anything. We are a law-abiding establishment I assure you sir." Says the bartender defensively returning to his glasses.

What? Did this guy think he was an Enforcer? An even better cover. Not that he wants to be caught impersonating one, but it is a convincing lie. He thanks the bartender for his assistance and exits the bar. As he is leaving, he sees a man turn the corner of the corridor, heading for a residential building. *Is that him? It looks like him. What luck. It has to be.*

He follows the man for a while, casually strolling through the shadows of the walls to go as unseen as possible. With each glimpse, he is more and more certain. He looks back at the picture to be sure. *That's got to be him.* He has to wait for the right moment.

The man turns onto another walkway off the main path. It is clear that this is likely his residence tower. There is hardly anyone around. He follows the man into the building using his special identification badge. The door opens for him too. An unstaffed lobby. *I guess even the upper-middle class can't afford the night service.*

There is no one else around. This is it. This is the moment. His heart is pounding. His hands are shaking. He quietly draws the pistol from his coat pocket. He chambers the round. He speeds up to close in on the man as he approaches the lift terminal.

Why am I doing this? This wasn't right. Second thoughts. Doubts. *No. No Harold. You have to do this. This is your only chance. Whatever it is this guy did, he probably deserves it. Do it, Harold. Pull the trigger!*

He raises the gun, pointing it towards the man. He yells out the name of his target. The man turns questioningly.

"What? Oh!"

Bang! The man collapses to the floor.

Harold swoops in. The man is lying face down now, bleeding out onto the hallway. He turns him over. The panic! The horror! The face of the man. It isn't Carl! He checks the ID badge in his wallet. *Definitely not the guy. Shit! Fuck! Who did I kill? Why did I do it?* He feels nauseated. *What about the body?*

The light for the lift dings as it hits the first floor. *Oh no! Someone is coming. What do I do?* He freezes. Unable to move. Panic sets over. The doors open. It's empty. *Whew! That was a close one.* Though wait a second. Predictably, the lift doors struggle to open. The elevator is stuck between floors. *Ha! Even in the upper-mids things stay broken!* An opportunity.

He drags the lifeless body over to the elevator. It's heavy and starting to become rigid. He estimates that at this level there are perhaps forty floors to the bottom of mid-level before it hit the lift barrier between classes. He pushes the body over the edge. It falls down the shaft for what seems like forever before the crushing sound of the ground echoes loudly through the chamber. The elevator shakes a bit and resets to its original position with a *ding*. No one will ever find the body if they even bother to come looking for it.

What of the blood on the floor though? He doesn't want to generate suspicion. Fortunately, it blends well with the red faux carpet that seems to adorn every building and walkway in the sector, looking like any other stain. *Oh shit! What about the cameras?* He looks around panicked but sees nothing. Even the upper-middle-class can't afford public cameras. He runs out of the building as fast as he can.

He rushes down to The Transit platform and gets on the first train. It's not even the right line, but he doesn't care. He maps out a longer but alternative path back home. He laughs a bit to himself. This is going to be harder than he expected, but he had made it. Rather, survived. It is somewhat of a rush. A thrill. A power trip. He hopes it won't go to his head.

A ring on his communicator. *At this hour? Who could it be?* An unknown number. He answers suspecting Sheron, but instead a chilling voice calls out to him.

"Very good. Mr. Harold... Your resourcefulness will serve you well in the hunt. Unfortunately, you got the wrong guy, Harold! The wrong guy! It is of no concern to us though. Don't worry. No one shall come looking for him and he will hardly be noticed missing. Next time though, do your homework first." The communicator hangs up without even a chance to respond. It was Gharles. *How did he know? Who had seen him? Was he being followed?* His paranoia grows.

Chapter 4

Going home was just a reversal of Carl's morning routine. The long walk back to his shuttle was at least more tolerable knowing that his destination was home and not work. He still had an hour of traffic ahead of him but he knew that at the end of that was his home, his couch, his space, and no expectations. He could leave his work problems at work and not worry too much until the next day.

The door to his shuttle opened with the same groans he made getting out of bed every day and he sank into the well-worn seats. For a few moments, he just sat, decompressing, both mentally and physically as he expanded his entire body into the cracked leather chair, trying to squeeze out the maximum amount of comfort.

The moment that his finger touched the initializer, he knew something was wrong. Carl had spent up to three hours a day for the past twelve years flying this bucket of bolts from one side of the planet to the other and every sound, every vibration, every sequence was as familiar to him as his own skin.

Every time he had started the shuttle, it was the same thing. First, every electronic component would squeal an electrical cry of agony for a few seconds as the overworked capacitors would object to their continued torture. Then the engines would start their lazy spin up, increasing their pitch in just the right tone to make it sound like it would continue pitching up forever. Out of nowhere, Carl suddenly recalled that it was known as a Shepard Tone. After a few seconds of the anxiety-inducing engine spin up, they would ignite with a soft and reassuring hum and then Carl could be off on his way.

This time, however, there was no whine, spin up, no ignition. There was a shudder, the kind of mechanical shake that instantly alerts you that something is *Wrong* with a capital W. Though there was no spin up, it was even more anxiety-inducing. Carl wasn't even sure what would cause it to shake like it had, much less what to *do* about it, so he did the only thing he knew how. He cut power to the shuttle, waited a few moments and then turned it back on. This time, he heard the familiar squeal, the now comforting spin up, and *felt* more than heard the engine ignition. Turning it off and back on – *the universal solution*. Glad that his problem was solved and would never be an issue going forward in the future, Carl undocked and began the long flight home.

"Since it's Saturday, there should be less traffic than usual," Carl lied to himself. Carl was an expert at lying to himself, which is something he was aware of and therefore never believed any of his own lies. It was a problematic situation to be in. Society was all a lie anyway. The more you believed your own lies, the happier and more successful you would become. He had heard that years before in a Barbados speech at a business conference.

Carl arrived at home to his adequate apartment. *Adequate* was definitely the best word for it. It was comfortably between a 'hovel' and 'nice house'. It wasn't bad, but it just wasn't great either. The kitchen served to cook food, but it only had one drawer for all of his utensils. There was an island, but it only served to act as a bar for chairs. The dishwasher couldn't be opened at the same time as the oven and though he rarely had occasion for it, two people would absolutely not fit in there.

It was split into two levels with the common areas upstairs and the living spaces downstairs. For most of the time that Carl had lived there, the upstairs had been carpeted with a thin, fraying carpet that was impossible to determine if it was dirty or not. However, at some point, the management had come and replaced the carpet with tile that was clearly someone's first time. Downstairs the imitation wood floor was pleasant enough to look at in the places where it wasn't peeling. All of the spaces were roomy and served their function and they were *just* comfortable enough to move the entire apartment to 'cozy' status. *But only just.*

Waiting for him was a stack of bills. It was the same old thing. Rent's due, electric's due, water's due, plasma's overdue, *the usual.* Because he decided he hadn't had enough stress in his day, he decided to sit down and go through them all.

There were a lot of bills, but nothing that either couldn't be paid or couldn't wait. The more he went through them though, the more he couldn't get rid of the sense that everyone in the galaxy wanted something from him. At work, every email was from a coworker needing him to do something for them. *Fill out these forms, get these numbers ready, assess these markets for me, prep these reports and have them on my desk.*

At home, every email was some stranger demanding their piece of his pie.

Pay your rent, pay for these basic services. Pay for insurance. Will we cover anything should something happen? No, of course not, but if you don't pay us, you'll be in legal trouble for not paying us. Have you renewed your starship warranty? We cover everything except the items that would be likely to happen to you. Do you remember the doctor you visited six months ago? You paid your bill at the counter before leaving, but we've just discovered a mistake where we didn't charge you enough. Please pay the remaining balance that's inexplicably more than the original bill. Pay your toll bill.

Why were there tolls in space? There was no infrastructure to build, less clearing the constant ebb and flow of space trash. Carl was convinced that it was all just a scam, but there's nothing he could do. *Pay your monthly… .ammonia bill?* Carl wasn't sure why he was paying monthly for ammonia, he was pretty sure he didn't use it at all. Although, he had always wondered what the third tap was in his bathroom sink. He made a note to call the utility office one day and have that canceled. If it were even possible to cancel.

This continued for a while until he had made it to the last email of the day. He then *selected all* and clicked *delete.* They could wait another day.

Just as he was about to shut down his tablet, another email came in. Carl thought it might have been another bill until he noticed that the sender was unknown. The subject simply said '*Job Offer*'.

He opened it up and there wasn't much to see.

Mr. Carl,

You need money and I need services performed. I could pay you enough that you never have to worry about money again. The job shouldn't be discussed over email though. Reply back if you're interested and I'll send you more information. I look forward to making you a very rich man.

Carl looked at the email for a bit and moved his finger to the *delete* button without actually pressing it. He wasn't sure why but something was holding him back. It was clearly a spam email and yet for some reason, Carl wanted to know more. Maybe it was the use of his name, maybe it was the font. Whatever it was, Carl simply marked it as read and closed the tablet. It was getting late and he needed to sleep.

Carl did not sleep that night.

* * *

Carl thought about the email all the way to work. He didn't notice the traffic, he didn't notice being the last shuttle at the dock again. He didn't remember walking into the office and he couldn't remember if Melissa called him Carl or Corbyn. He didn't really care.

He knew that he was being ridiculous, obviously, it was a spam email. It was fake and nothing would come of it. He needed to put it out of his head and forget about the whole thing. Which is why he turned on his computer and started trying to find the sender. Carl pulled the information from the email and ran it through a few tools he knew of to try to trace the origin. A lot of data spit out, but then Carl remembered he was a number pusher, not a techie, so he didn't really know what he was supposed to make of it.

"Hey Carl, wanna go grab lunch?" his friend asked.

Carl hadn't even noticed it was already lunchtime. He didn't really want to stop, but he knew that he should probably eat.

"Only if you're buying," he responded half-jokingly, remembering his ammonia bill.

They went to a restaurant on the other side of the station and sat down for lunch.

"So what have you been working on?" T'Zori asked him.

"I've been looking at this email all day," Carl said.

"Just one email?" T'Zori asked him incredulously. "Must be a really long email."

"No, but it's weird. I got it last night and the sender is unknown. It says it's a job offer and all I have to do is to reply back to make enough money to never worry about it again. Honestly, it seems too good to be true, but there's something about it that feels real to me. I think it's the font. It has a very honest font."

"What kind of font?" inquired T'Zori

"I can't really place my finger on it. It's not one of the standard fonts. It's definitely a Serif font. Kind of hovers between regular and bold. It's a really strong font without being overstated. Just a real good *man's* kind of font."

"Oh yeah, if you want to attract the right kind of attention, you gotta use a Serif," agreed T'Zori.

"So, what do I do? Do I respond to the email?"

"Only if you want to never worry about money again, I guess. I mean, what do you have to lose? If you respond to the email and it's just spam, nothing happens. If it's real and you don't respond, you missed out on an opportunity. The only way to lose here is to not respond to it."

He brought up a good point that Carl hadn't considered before. He still didn't like the idea that someone would offer him a mysterious job via email with no information, but he couldn't see any downsides to at least seeing how it played out.

When they had finished lunch and made it back to the office, they went their separate ways and Carl sat back down at his desk. He pulled open his email and replied back with,

'*I'm Interested.*'

* * *

He didn't know exactly what he expected, but it wasn't an immediate response. Yet an immediate response is exactly what he got, with nothing but an address and a time. Carl put the address into his map and it pulled up the information for a bar. Disturbingly, it was a bar that he had frequented before, which made the whole thing feel a bit voyeuristic.

He decided that since he would normally go there with friends after work anyway, he shouldn't go alone and so he left his desk once again to gather the usual crowd and see if anyone would go with him. A few hours later, they were on their way.

It wasn't the best bar on the planet, none of them were rich enough for that, but it certainly wasn't the worst. It was dark, like most bars, and smelled of a rich, thick smoke, although no one there was currently smoking. It was the kind of smell that had penetrated the walls and furniture and would exist for as long as the walls and furniture were there. It wasn't an unpleasant smell though. It was spacious and there were never too many people there, so it was always quiet enough to hear other people talking.

All the way on the trip to the bar, it had occurred to Carl that he wasn't sure what he was supposed to be doing there. The email only mentioned the when and where, but not the what, who, or how. Presumably, he would be finding out the *why*. However, as he walked through the doors, he realized he shouldn't have worried.

The man that he was there to meet was obvious, in the kind of way that is impossible to describe. Here in this not-quite-a-dive bar, in an unassuming sector in a part of the planet where the average income was just barely enough to feed a family of one, sat a man in a suit. Not the kind of suit that you wear to work, or rent for a weekend to wear to an acquaintance's wedding, but the kind of suit that was custom-tailored. Not a single square inch of fabric was wasted on the man's frame and fit as if he had been made alongside it. Despite the fact that he was out of place, the man sat comfortably as if he owned the bar. Given the way that he dressed, Carl guessed that he could have owned the entire building that the bar was in. He was sipping a drink that Carl would not even have guessed the name of, but even that looked expensive, but in an understated type of way. Everything about the mystery man screamed *Serif font.*

Carl excused himself from the crowd of work friends and tried to casually make his way over to the man. He wasn't entirely sure how to do that, or if he needed to do that at all.

"Are you trying to casually walk over here, Mr. Carl?" The man asked calmly, clearly knowing the answer.

"No, this is just how I walk," Carl lied.

"Well, please stop doing that, at least in my presence. It's extremely weird and uncomfortable," said the man. Carl stopped and tried to walk normally, but found he forgot what that meant. Now that he had pointed it out, Carl was thinking too much about how to walk and couldn't figure out what it meant to 'walk normally'. So instead he shuffled his way over there. The Man stared at him patronizingly the entire time.

"We better get this over with before you decide you don't want to give me a job anymore," said Carl.

"Agreed," said The Man. "Well, in that case, I'll make this short and simple. I have an opportunity for you. You see, I have a problem that I need to have solved. Rather," he paused here, seemingly trying to find the exact words he needed, "I know the solution, but I need it... *executed.*" He had put an emphasis on 'executed' that Carl didn't like, but couldn't place his finger on why. "Carl, someone stole something from me. Not a possession per se, but something I valued more than life itself. And I need him to repay me... with his life."

Carl wasn't sure he had heard what the man had just said. "You want me to kill someone?" *Surely that's not what this was about.*

"Well, yes, but I wasn't going to put it so bluntly. Killing is such a nasty endeavor, wouldn't you say, Mr. Carl? No, I much prefer the idea of *repayment.*"

"Why me?" Carl asked. "I've never killed anything in my life. Once, a bug landed in my ship and I didn't want to get in there with it, but I couldn't kill it, so I just called into work sick. It was a really big bug," Carl added after seeing the look from the man. "Anyways, if I couldn't kill a bug, I doubt I'd be able to kill a person, even if they are a bigger target."

The man just shrugged and appeared to be unphased by Carl's lack of enthusiasm. "Mr. Carl, I picked you because I know that you need the money and no one would suspect you. Your bills are piling up and your paychecks are not. That's all there is to it. If you don't want to participate, you don't have to, I won't force you. This was merely an offer and I assure you that I lose nothing if you say no. I won't sit here all day while you weigh the pros and cons. If you decide you've changed your mind, here's how you can reach me. I guess I will just take this large sack of cash and leave then. Good day, Mr. Carl."

The Man slid Carl a small card with the name Gharles Darkley, and just a number on it. It was a lightweight yet sturdy card, obviously exceptionally made. The font was a Serif font. He then finished his drink, exited the booth they were sitting at, and walked out the door, leaving Carl sitting by himself holding a business card and wondering if any of the events that had just happened were real.

R'Moniea from accounting walked by the booth and gave him a strange look. "What are you doing over here Carl? Everyone else is on the other side of the bar. Come on, you're going to miss all of the fun!"

Chapter 5

Back in Mulknosh, Harold is forced to reckon with his drab lower-middle life. In his neighborhood, he is doing alright, but his trip to the business sector has made him feel behind. Every passing day his life is ticking on, wasting away time that could be spent in a place like that instead. Maybe something more. It has been a few weeks now. After his first attempt, he is afraid to try again. Not without finding out more.

"Good one, Baab! You really fucked this one up. Give me the weld breakers, I'll fix it."

"It looked straight to me!" says Baab. His bug-like eyes say otherwise. He examines his work on the box frame parked in their station. It won't be long before they are holding up the line.

"Yeah? Out of which fucking eye, Baab? I don't even know how this was possible."

It is a quick fix. They just have to hurry before it shows up on Xvranbul's data screen. Everyone knows she never actually looks at the line, just the numbers. Harold begins to think that maybe the guys at the plant will know something or someone that can help him in his murder mission.

"Hey, so I've been thinkin'... Either of you guys know how to locate an address if you don't know the person that well?"

"*Oooo boy!* You finally did it! You fell in love with one of your hookers and want to run off and live with her don't yah!" says Geordon.

"*Ha...* yeah thanks, Geordon, but no nothing like that. Just trying to find my *cousin*. He got reassigned to a different sector years ago and we haven't heard from him," says Harold.

"Wow family outside the sector! Must be nice. Anyways... Your 'cousin' is easily accessed from the terminal," says Baab.

"Thanks, Baab. Like I didn't think of that? Come on! You know I don't have credential access to a database at that level. Besides, none of the terminals we have access to interconnect with other sectors," says Harold.

"So say you! You can always access the database. For a price of course... There is one consistent set of terminals. Ever heard the saying *the only consistent thing in this universe is birth, death, and taxes*? That gives you three ins to the global network. The birthing center, the death registry, and the tax office... And as Bertrice is due any day now, maybe you could, you know, join us there in the hatching room," says Baab.

"Baab, you're a shitty welder, but sometimes you're a genius. Aren't they going to notice some random human there?" Harold says as he dislodges the poorly welded beam with a spark and a loud *clang* as it hits the conveyor floor.

"Only at first. Once the six hatchlings emerge, I assure you they will be quite overwhelmed. Plenty of distractions for you to slip away unnoticed. You just have to be quick," says Baab; a strange proposal that makes Harold ever curiouser.

The plan is set. Harold will find out where this guy was born, and start his search there. Hell, like most people in this world he's probably never moved a day in his life. He isn't thrilled to have to witness the disgusting miracle of brood hatching, but at least it is an easy in. Also, one that he won't have to explain to Sheron.

* * *

When the day finally comes he is nervous. It is awkward. Baab had told his wife that he is curious about it and wants to come watch. She said it was totally acceptable. *Imagine saying that to a pregnant human woman? Not a chance.* In this case, the cultural differences work in his favor. This birthing center is pretty low grade. Almost exclusively aliens. He is glad his kids weren't born there.

The smell is definitely awful. He keeps reaching to cover his nose and gags a bit. His insensitivity is noticed by the other alien patrons who admonish him with their stern glances. He is undeterred by their looks and continues his rudeness. The building was once white inside, but the walls have been darkened by mold and stained by years of decay. Oily water drips from a ceiling tile into a bucket and the fluorescent lights hang precariously, shining their harsh blue-green hue across the lobby, illuminating the fly-like eyes of the alien patrons who all wonder why Harold is there.

"Hi there! You must be Harold. I'm nurse Tvjalk'nm." Surprisingly she is human, Harold is relieved. "You and I are just going to stand here and watch through this window okay? I'll only have to go in if they need me, so I'll hopefully be with you the whole time. If it gets to be too much for you, you can return to the lobby."

The door is like that of a seafaring vessel. It is sealed shut by turning a dial and has a circular viewing portal.

Harold shudders at the thought of it. There is a whole medical team in there already. Buzzing, slime, so much slime. The brood moves so quickly, flying around the room as they emerge, destroying everything in their path. A roar erupts from Bertrice, the mother. Her fangs emerge and her long tongue extends from her proboscis, trying to scoop up her hoard. A violent roar.

Is she attacking them? Oh fuck what is going on?

"Nurse is that normal?" asks Harold, concerned.

"Of course! A tradition among the Zvranicans is to be suppressed after the brood hatches to give them a chance to survive and grow in strength. Evolutionarily speaking, after the mother hatches the brood, she becomes incredibly violent and cannibalistic. For the next four hours, she will attempt to devour her young so that the weak perish and only the strongest hatchlings survive. With modern civilization, however, they try to subdue her... *Oh! Oh! No! Code red!*"

The nurse springs into action, entering the room. Beatrice's tongue is wrapped around the delivery doctor and she is pulling him in towards her fangs.

Oh god, it is horrible and disgusting. Now is his chance though. With his hall monitor gone, he springs into action.

The adjacent office is clear. No one in sight. Fortunately, there are no encryption keys or passwords. Blessings of the low quality of the birthing center, they can't afford even basic IT security. He frantically clicks through the screens. Global Birth Registry, there it is. The database is loading... loading. So slowly. *Come on!* He doesn't have much time.

He goes ahead and refines the results to only include those births in Sector 1149 bearing the name of his target. This was going to work. *Twelve million!? Fuck!* Okay, more refinement. *How old does this motherfucker look in this picture? Guessing the approximate year of birth, he's probably in this window. There we go!* 547. Maybe he can just look at the pictures. *Wrong! Don't be an idiot, the birth pictures would never look the same as they did today.*

It will have to do!

He downloads the data onto a recorder. He will just have to manually assess all the possible victims. One of them is bound to be the one. *Right?* Hopefully.

"Excuse me! Sir! Sir! What are you doing in there? Sir! That's a restricted area. *Oh shit.* It was the nurse. *Quick come up with something! Come on Harold. Think. Could I just shoot her and run? No, come on Harold do better.*

"I was afraid! So I came in here to hide. I thought she was really going to eat the doc."

"*Oh!* Is that all? Nonsense, sir. We're trained professionals, we do this all the time. Only a handful of our doctors are ever eaten by their patients. I told you to go wait in the lobby if it got to be too much!"

Crisis averted. Harold returns to the lobby, but rather than waiting for Baab he just goes ahead and walks out the door. He doesn't want to be there any more than he has to be. *How am I going to do this?* Without much of a plan, the best he can come up with is to go one by one. Surely he won't have to go through all 500 to find the one. *Right?*

A poster catches his attention.

President McSlurmins hates aliens! His unemployment numbers are as sky-high as his tax policies! Senator Rosnarth Galxshu has a proven record on lowering taxes and getting things done. Vote Galxshu this solstice! It shouldn't cost this much to live this terrible!

What a genius idea.

Harold catches the Transit back to sector 1149. He has business to attend to, and he has the rest of the day off to do it. On his way to the terminal, he pays a visit to the political panhandlers, reliably passing out flyers in the plaza.

"Galxshu right? Yeah give me everything you got. I'm on my way to a rally and I ran out of flyers. Of course! Yes *live terrible*, yes of course. *Uh-huh*". He grabs as many as he can stuff in his jacket pocket and boards the Transit.

He reviews the data he collected. Alright, first on the list. Residence of birth, 5433 W. Douglas Furnstein Tower, Apartment 5B. Okay sure. Wherever the hell that is. Upon arrival in the sector, he decides to head back to the first bar. The bartender recognizes him.

"On the hunt again, sir, or shall I give it a pour?" asks the bartender.

"What can you tell me about this address?" Harold puts on his best Enforcer face.

"Certainly." He takes out his spectacles to examine the recorder. "Never been there in my life sir."

"Can you at least tell me where this building is?" Turning up the heat.

"I wouldn't want you to think I had ever been there, but sir, if I may be as so bold, have you looked at the map?"

"The map? There's a map?" Now Harold sounds like a complete moron.

"Oh dear... you must be new to the business. Yes of course. All sectors have maps posted at regular intervals! There's one just right over there," says the bartender, pointing to a large square electronic bulletin in the middle of the walkway outside the bar.

"Just making sure." Harold had no idea. *They have maps in this sector? Unbelievable. What else am I missing out on?* He exits the bar. He should probably stop going there before the bartender gets suspicious, or at least order something. Time to look at the map then.

There it is! The Douglas Furnstein building. Just six blocks away from the Transit terminus. He reaches the destination and enters the lobby. This building is more lively and a doorman is present. *Look cool Harold. Look cool.* The doorman ushers him in welcomingly. *Alright, well that might make shit complicated on the way out.* He takes the lift up to the fifth floor and pulls a few of the pamphlets out of his pocket. He follows the signs until at last, he reaches apartment 5B. He knocks on the door to the apartment. This was it. Showtime. An elderly woman answers the door. "Hello dear. How may I help you?" Harold wasn't expecting that.

"Good afternoon, ma'am. Have you decided who you're going to vote for on solstice day?" asks Harold, thrusting the pamphlet towards her.

"Well... yes... well no... maybe... What is this about?"

"Many Capital residents are on the fence about it like yourself. Can I tell you about why Galxshu is the only candidate in this race worth voting for?"

"Oh... Well, I don't know. I'm not too keen on the aliens, you know. I'm sure some of them are good people... and of course, the senator is not one of *those* aliens. I just don't want things to get any worse, you know? It's fine if you're an alien, but I wish they would just stay in their own neighborhoods. I wouldn't want to see my building become one of those crime havens."

Wow. Honestly, he hopes this is where the guy lives just so he can cap him and his old lady. Not that he is big on the aliens either, but this old bag has no idea what she is talking about.

"Of course. That's why *Galxshu* wants to lower taxes. That way you can keep more money in your sector and out of the hands of criminals."

"*Oh!* Well... you might have led with that. Here, let me go get my purse and I'll make a donation. You just wait here now."

She turns and slowly shuffles her way further into the apartment. He follows her in and shuts the door behind him. The apartment smells of old perfume and cigarettes. Everything in it is a variable shade of faded pink and dirty white. The door just opens into one rectangular room with a kitchen off to the left and a hallway with bedrooms off to the right. A perfectly efficient square design.

"Lovely home you have here, miss. I see you have family portraits over here. Is this your son? Are these recent? Would love to see more..."

"Oh. Well, yes. This is my son." She starts to ramble off into a story. He really doesn't have time for this. Time for drastic measures. He pulls his gun and points it straight at her forehead.

"Alright lady! Stay right there and nobody gets hurt." He pulls out the photo of his target. "Is this your son?"

"What?! Oh... no. Certainly not my son. My son is much more handsome. Those good human genes."

Fuck this wasn't it. Now she's seen his face. *What do I do?* He asks her to prove it. To his surprise, she agrees. She reaches for her purse.

Thwack! The old lady side-swipes him with her cane. The gun discharges into the wall. He falls to the ground, the gun goes flying across the floor. She comes at him with the pepper spray from her purse.

"You monster! Preying on a helpless old woman. Shame on you! I know jujitsu and I'll kick your ass, you motherfucker!" An unexpected burst of energy. His eyes are burning, his head is throbbing, and he is about to get his face kicked in by an old broad.

He reaches for the gun, but she steps on his hand as he reaches for it. He cries out in pain. A shot goes off in the room. *Bang!* The old woman falls to the floor, dead. Another man comes in from the side bedroom. It's her son. *Holy shit! He just shot his own mother dead. Why is he in his underwear? Are those cuffs on his arms?*

"What the fuck man! Look I got the wrong house man. You had the same name. Your own mother!?" says Harold, astonished.

"Don't worry about it. You did me a favor. And she's *not* my mother. I started banging her three years ago. I was hoping for free rent and some good life insurance money. She must have known or was already crazy. Chained me up to the bed one night and made me her bitch instead. Your little altercation here gave me a chance to escape," says the man.

"Wow. Shit man. That's. That's fucked up." He is shocked by the admission, as the man of the same name as his target reaches into the old woman's purse, pulls out her pack of cigarettes, and lights one up.

"Yeah. Look, I'm gonna need you to get out of here. I'm just gonna say it was a burglar and that I didn't see your face. The neighbors probably already called the Enforcers by now. Take this gun with you though and make it disappear. I don't want my prints on this. I'm going to go fix up her will to make sure all this gets left to me. Good luck finding your guy."

"Yeah... Thanks..."

Harold runs as fast as he can out of the apartment. Not bothering with the lift, he heads down the stairs, trying not to fall. He exits through a fire escape door into the alley. This will create some chaos and allow him to avoid the doorman. When he is safely three blocks away he stops running to catch his breath. If he doesn't lose weight after this, he doesn't know what would do it.

There has to be a hovercar launch platform around here somewhere. He searches around, making his way to the periphery of a nearby terrace until he finds one. He tosses the man's gun right off the edge of the platform and it falls into the polluted abyss below. No one will find it now. *He laughs. Truly unbelievable.* Then he remembers his eyes. They are swollen and red. His hand is bruised and his head is bleeding. How will he ever explain this one to Sher? For that matter, how will he make it across three Transit lines back to Mulknosh without getting questioned by an Enforcer?

He doesn't have long to think long before his phone rings again. It is Gharles.

"Mr. Harold... You've really outdone yourself this time. I'm starting to worry, you almost became her next victim. Seems like she had it coming. You created quite a stir on the way out. Nothing to be alarmed about. There will be no investigation I assure you of that much."

"Hey! You listen here. I need more information from you. This guy is like finding a plintaar in a frindstend. Can you tell me anything else? Help me out here."

"I *am* helping you, Mr. Harold. A private car is on its way to you now, just stay where you are. It will take you home. I gave you everything you need to know. You just have to figure it out. The collateral damage comes with the territory. Lucky for you I'm not even going to bill you for this," says Gharles before hanging up.

He remembers the hovercar landing on the platform. At this point, he nearly collapses from the loss of blood. He remembers the two men dressed in all black dragging him into the hovercar. Dressing his wounds. Injecting him with something meant to salvage him. Back at Mulknosh, the hovercar lands at the hovercab platform closest to his building. *How do they know where I live?* It didn't matter, Gharles knew everything.

That's when he completely blacked out. Right there on the platform. He had been bested by an old woman. *How will I ever make it as a professional hitman? Is that what I am now?* Maybe he doesn't want to wake up again. He will probably miss work and be fired. Demoted to the lower levels. Gharles deals in greed the same way a drug dealer hooks a client.

The allure of money, all for the downward spiral.

Chapter 6

As it happened, the real fun began for Carl on his way home. Although Carl had completely ignored the problems he had had with his shuttle the other day, for some reason, the problem had come back. Only this time, it was worse.

Even though the bar was only a few blocks from his apartment, he had to hit orbit to get his shuttle back to the garage. Right as he hit the main orbital thoroughfare, the ship completely died. It did so in a way that completely defied physics as well, coming to a complete stop right in the path of other ships. For the first time in his life, Carl was at the very front of a traffic jam. It was just his luck that he still wasn't moving.

He had to have his ship towed back to his apartment. If you've never had a spaceship towed from orbit, it's not cheap. Carl didn't think he should be charged a 'hook up fee' when all the towship driver had to do was press the 'engage tractor beam' button, but he wasn't one to cause a scene.

He paid his bill and keyed the lock to his apartment. After a long day, all he wanted to do was fall into his bed and pass out. Instead, as he opened his door, an ankle-high wave of water crashed out of his door and onto his balcony. That seemed unusual to Carl, as most days there was exactly *zero* water in his apartment, at least outside of sinks.

Carl stepped inside to find the entire downstairs section of his apartment flooded with at least three inches of water. He wasn't sure how that had happened because when he had left that morning, he checked and there was no water anywhere. He heard a dripping sound and looked up to find a very soggy ceiling with water streaming down. That *definitely* had not been there that morning.

He made his way upstairs. There, underneath the sink in his bathroom was a broken pipe that was spraying water with an enthusiasm that Carl could only ever dream of having for anything he had ever done. He turned off the water and just examined the damage. *This was going to take hours to clean.*

Just then he heard his tablet *ding!* with an email notification. He picked it up and checked his email to find a bill from the Orbital Transportation Department for blocking the spacelanes. Because of course he had done that voluntarily, so why shouldn't he pay for it, it was basically a service they were providing to him.

While he was busy angrily thinking of all the ways he'd like to reply back to that email but wouldn't, another email came in, this time from his apartment complex. Apparently, it was against the apartment regulations to have a flooded apartment, because of course it was and *OF COURSE* it came with a fine. *Why wouldn't it?* thought Carl.

He looked back from the flood of water, to the broken pipe, and finally to the emails and decided it was too much and went to bed and passed out. The sound of the rushing water was soothing in a way.

* * *

Riding the spacebus to work was much more of a hassle than flying his own ship had ever been. It was also something Carl had forgotten to account for in his morning routine. He woke up his standard hour late and went outside to remember that his ship amounted to a fifteen-ton paperweight, so he started walking to the nearest bus stop. Of course, none of the bus routes near him would take him to his work station, *why would they?*

He looked at the map of stops and found a pretty simple route consisting of seventeen line transfers of ground buses, one trip by way of the Transit to connect to another set of ground bus stops, and then nine more spacebus stops. Then it was only a short space taxi ride to his station. All told, he was only two hours late. He thought that wasn't too bad, all things considered.

That was until he got to the front desk. Melissa greeted him with the same warm smile that she always did and said "Morning Crane! Mr. D'Delvoo wants to see you in his office. He seemed really angry!" She said it with a smile that didn't match the context. *I'll have what she's having.*

Wait, did he really want to see Carl? Or someone named Crane? Was Crane a person's name? He didn't see why it couldn't be, but he also hadn't met anyone named Crane. *Wasn't that a bird? Are birds even real?* Probably, although, even if it was, it didn't answer the question of whether Mr. D'Delvoo wanted to see Carl or not. However, it seemed likely, since that was Carl's boss and Carl was two hours late. That probably wasn't a coincidence. Or maybe it was and they were actually giving him a promotion! Probably not though.

Carl strode through Mr. D'Delvoo's office full of unearned confidence. Someone had told him once that being successful was just lying to yourself about how successful you are and pretending to be better than you really are. He wasn't sure if that was true, but he figured now was just as good a time as any to test it out.

Mr. D'Delvoo didn't seem impressed. Well, more accurately, he didn't seem to know who this person strutting through his door was, or why he was interrupting D'Delvoo's day.

"Who the fuck are you and what do you want? You have fifteen seconds."

Carl was surprised by this.

"I'm Carl, and Melissa said that you wanted to see me."

"Oh, right, Carl. Yes, we need to talk about your performance lately. You see Carl, your shift starts at 8 am, not 10 am. 8. And we need you to be here at 8 am *every* day, not just on the days that you feel like. Do I make myself clear, Carl?"

"Well sir, not really. Am I supposed to be here *every* day or just Monday through Friday? I've been losing track of the days lately—"

"GET THE FUCK OUT OF MY OFFICE CARL!"

That had gone about as well as Carl could have hoped for. Well, actually, it went a lot worse than that because Carl had hoped to get a promotion instead of being yelled at, but all things considered, it made sense to Carl. Not that being on time mattered. No one did any real work there, at least none that mattered. It was just part of the societal game they played to advance the capitalist cause.

If he wanted to get to work on time, Carl would have to find a way to get a new shuttle. The spacebus just wasn't working out. He even woke up two hours earlier every day to try to account for the erratic nature of the buses' schedule, but it seemed as if the person in charge of the bus schedule was out to get Carl with the extraneous stops, the constant delays, and the general inefficiencies of the system. Carl knew that he was just being paranoid.

* * *

Many years before, when Carl was in the third grade, he and his friends had formed quite an enviable crowd. During the recess hours, they would dominate the playground and cause a general ruckus, as children are wont to do. Carl in particular was the worst of the bunch and would knock kids off the jungle gym as he climbed to the top and pretended it was his throne. He would summon the other children who, being quite dim, would ask Carl for permission to join him on the jungle gym, as though it were his property. His teachers were proud of this display of competitive victory, and they thought Carl might actually make a great mid-level manager someday.

"Please Carl," a chunky Sven Stenderson begged Carl, dragging out the please in a whiny voice at just the right pitch to be maximally annoying.

"Fine. But first, you have to do a task for me. Since you're so fat, I want you to run all the way around the playground ten... *no* a hundred... *no* a bajillion times!" Carl wasn't particularly bright either.

"But I can't do it that many times!"

"Fine, then just ten times around the playground."

Sven, to his credit, ran ten times around the playground and made it back to the jungle gym in pretty decent time. Carl was none too impressed.

"That was okay I guess, for a fatty. I'm going to call you Bam Bam Bigelow from now on!"

All the other children thought that was very amusing and Carl never did let poor Bam Bam on the jungle gym. Children can be absolute monsters.

At any rate, Sven Stenderson, the Planetary Public Transit Coordinator for sector 1149 would have his revenge. *Who is running around the playground now, Carl?* He changed the bus routes and timetables every day, expressly to torment Carl after discovering he had to use them.

* * *

Carl had gone to the local shuttle dealership to investigate the possibility of buying a new shuttle. However, he quickly discovered that was not even remotely feasible.

"Hey friend, looking to buy a new shuttle?" squeaked a very slimy shuttle salesalien. "We've got all sorts of good deals here. My name's Ed'die. Let's get you out of the used shuttle area and into our *new* shuttle area. We have some new Model 15s that—"

The salesalien stopped mid-sentence as his tablet buzzed and he looked at it. Carl knew that the facial recognition software had identified Carl, pulled together all of his relevant information – such as; credit score, his current debt, his current address, his social media profiles, his family history, his DNA sequencing, and his mediocre sexual history – and provided it to Ed'die. He turned a subtle shade of purple, which Carl wasn't sure if that meant anger, embarrassment, or sadness for his species. In fact, it meant all three.

"Carl, my friend, I've got just the deal for you. Please, come with me," Ed'die said with an approximation of a human smile on his face. Carl followed him through the lot and into the office building. He wondered which office belonged to Ed'die as they made their way through the maze of cubicles.

"Right this way Carl." Ed'die motioned to a doorway to a small office towards the back of the building. Carl stepped through and was met by two very large, burly men. He had failed to notice that the door had a label on it that read 'Credit Security'.

For the next half hour, the two men took turns creatively beating Carl in a way that definitely hurt but didn't leave him too injured to walk away. The last thing they wanted was the extra hassle of having to carry him off the lot.

"Carl," Ed'die had come back into the room in just the last few minutes of the pummeling and now he spoke to him as he lay on the floor curled into the fetal position. The squeaky sliminess had gone from Ed'die's voice and he spoke in a very serious but gruff tone. "If you ever come back to this dealership, you will be leaving it in the trunk of one of our ships, not the driver's seat. Now get the fuck out of my office."

Carl gingerly got off the ground and limped his way out of the office, off the lot, and back to the bus stop to begin his long ride back home.

* * *

Carl needed to find something to resolve his shuttle situation soon, because not only was he late to his job every day still, but he was also being fined for being late to work every day. Since he was an hourly employee, he was also making less money than he had been making and those bills were becoming even harder to pay. The bill he received from the shuttle dealership for making the credit security team beat him was also no trivial amount that he needed to find money for. In the meantime, his apartment was still flooded and he was running out of ideas on what to do about it.

One evening, he decided that he was fed up with the plumbing situation but as he couldn't afford a plumber to fix it, he decided he would fix it himself. This was something Carl was actually good at. Not plumbing, good god, no. He was good at looking up information about a new skill, taking it in, and learning about it, so that's what he decided he would do. He began spending hours after work researching how to fix the plumbing in his apartment and after what he felt like was ample time, he decided that he would be able to do it.

He grabbed what few tools he had, carefully prepared his work area, and opened the cabinet to begin fixing the pipes. He worked for several hours, emitting several swears, crying only a couple of times, and generally making a pretty good mess. When he was done, he got up off the floor and stood back to look at his handy work. From his new vantage point, he found that the pipes that had been broken were now just completely gone. Nothing was in their place, they had just vanished, possibly disintegrated. Dismayed and defeated, Carl sloshed back through more water to sit down on his couch and opened the email from his apartment management complex billing him for damaging the plumbing even more.

Chapter 7

The darkness surrounds Harold. There is nothing. Gharles appears to him from the void. A demon in the clothes of a man. Money flows forth from his shirt sleeves like a cyclone. Engulfing him. Smothering him. Drowning him? A splash of water on his face. Springing back to consciousness. He isn't dead. He is at home in bed. *How?*

"What? Oh, my head. Where am I? Oh... How did I get here?" asks Harold.

"I found you laying on the tarmac passed out drunk. A beaten bloody mess. I dragged you all the way back home. Don't worry though, I bartered at work on your behalf. I will take your place for today. You can thank me later. Don't explain. I don't care," says Thomas, rifling through Harold's closet for one of his work uniforms. He holds one up to himself so as to properly size it. "What do you think? Will this one fit? It'll have to do it's the smallest one you've got."

"What? Thomas... no... Thomas, wait!... You don't... you don't have to do this."

"Yes, I do! My commitments are sacred. I do what I have to do. Do you?" he says slipping on the boots.

"Go to school. I can manage. I can..."

"No you can't, so neither can I. Without this job we perish. If you descend, so we descend with you. There would be no school to attend. Can't you see that? Your family is everything. Everything. You fail to see us in everything you do. Well, see this with clarity. Today I saved your life, don't expect me to save it again," says Thomas, as he turns to walk away.

His words are powerful, his tongue sharp. Thomas might as well have stabbed his heart. If only he knew the sacrifices he made. If only he could share in this burden, he would understand that it was always for them, or at least so Harold believes. *It was for them, right? Or was this all just selfish ambition?*

Somewhere in his desperation to climb the ladder, he's found himself with a son he does not know and a daughter he's never met; his wife a bitter, scorned woman. This banter is frivolous. Feelings are the luxuries of the rich and powerful. To have feelings in this world was to surrender to death's sweet embrace. When they rise to the upper level all will be forgiven and the past could be forgotten. Money doesn't buy happiness, rather it affords it. *Only a rich man would be foolish enough to have the luxury of lost joy in the face of more money!*

Despite his splitting headache, he manages to rise from his bed. He stumbles over to the medicine cabinet in his bathroom. His trusted bottle of Pilquist Gold goes down smooth. *If this doesn't fix it, nothing can.* He won't make the same mistakes twice. His next attempt will be more cautious, more prepared.

He throws on his uniform and rushes towards the door. Each passing moment the drug and drink combination brings him to life and dulls the lingering pain. A sprint to the Transit station, running, running. Today is not the day. Through some incredulous miracle, he still manages to board the Transit. Thomas is only a few cars ahead of him. Harold tries to push his way through the cars to find Thomas, but he is too late. The factory exit comes up fast. He hurries off the Transit.

At the entry point to the factory gates, he sees Thomas. Almost to the gate. Almost there. Harold gives it a last great push. He catches him just before he gets there. He grabs Thomas by the shoulders, spinning him around and slamming him up against the factory wall. He seems shook. Astonished. His eyes wet with sadness and pain.

"Let me go! Just let me go! Just go die already! Drink until you die!" yells Thomas.

"Thomas! This is my burden. And mine alone. Get your ass to school. I'm already dead. Been dead for a long time," says Harold.

He releases Thomas, both of them bitter. Thomas backs down and walks away in silence back towards the Transit. Harold clocks in for work. The gates to hell swing open and engulf him. Xvranbul will have a dreadful laugh at this one. All at his expense. But he isn't late. And he isn't about to give up.

"Good morning employees! *Hah!* Just kidding, it's fucking terrible. Harrrrold! So unfortunate to see you alive and well for another day of work. You look like shit. I was looking forward to the day we got your boy in here. Looks like it'll have to wait after all! Anyways, I have to hand it to you all. Production levels are okay. We celebrate your mediocrity. Remember, *only ever do enough.* If you do more, they'll expect more. If you do less they'll end you. Go out there and be average today. And remember! *It could always be worse!*" says Mrs. Xvranbul.

The thought of her greasy slimy slug hands near his boy gives him the chills. Now that he has killed two people, he thinks about all the unfortunate accidents that might befall her. Her words are particularly scathing today.

"So, Harold, what the hell happened to you? Is this... Is this about your *cousin?*" asks Baab.

"What do you think, Baab? No shit. Do yourself a favor and don't ask questions. It's better that you live out the rest of your short days on this rock blissfully ignorant. Cute kids by the way."

"Thank you. I hope you enjoyed the hatching ceremony. I assume you got the information you needed to find him?"

"Well... Not exactly, genius. In our infinite wisdom, we somehow forgot that there might be, oh I don't know, billions of people with the same name in the galactic birth records. I narrowed it down to 537 suspects. Paid the wrong one a visit."

"Ah. Yes, I suppose. I forget that your species is incapable of coming up with unique identifiers. Might I suggest you cross-reference the birth records to the death registry? That way you can at least eliminate those who are no longer with us. This might also go without saying, but you might also want to screen out the non-humans as well. Have you ever heard a non-human go by such a name?"

"Yeah, that's a good idea. Now I just need a funeral to attend, so I can get those death records. How many years you got left Baab? And no, I've never heard an alien go by a name like that."

A funeral. That is precisely where he can gain access to the death records. He just needs to know someone who died. Surprisingly, there is no one lined up at the moment. *Think Harold. Think... Who could have died?* That's when it hits him. A stupid dastardly idea.

* * *

Back in sector 1149. The bloodstains still barely washed from his suit, Harold enters the funeral parlor to pay his respects. He greets people who stare at him questioningly.

"Excuse me, I need to go speak to this gentlemen over here... A dear neighbor of Margaret's..." says the man of the same name. He grabs Harold by the arm and drags him into a private viewing room. "What the hell are you doing here!? Are you crazy?" says the man, turning off his fake grief.

"No disrespect! Look I'm not here to cause trouble. They'll hardly know I'm here. I just need a favor," says Harold.

"A favor? Are you fucking serious? This better be good man. You at least got rid of the gun right?"

"I need access to the death records network. I'll slip out the back quietly during the ceremony while the director is giving the service. Then I'll leave. You'll never see me again. No one knows what happened, and they never will," says Harold throwing up his hands in an accommodating gesture.

"Fine! Just don't fuck with my money and don't come around me no more."

He has to hand it to the guy. *The fake waterworks he puts on for that crazy old woman are truly award-winning.* Harold slips out unnoticed with ease, by sitting in the unoccupied back rows. The director's office door is locked, but it is easily picked.

He accesses the terminal. Inserts his data recorder. Opens the cross-referencing software. He targets the matches between birth and death certificates. He eliminates those that align. Only 325 remaining now. Then just for grins, eliminate the non-humans. Much to his dismay, there now remains 162. *Wow. Seriously?* He had not expected to eliminate any at all that way, but it turns out there are quite a few aliens of that name.

The reach of the server isn't sufficient enough to allow him access to additional data and he's certainly no hacker. The search is narrowed, but it isn't any closer. This is getting him nowhere. Time for the next foolish crusade.

He departs the funeral home just as the funeral ends. As is tradition among the Capital City, at least in the upper- and mid-levels, a glorious fanfare plays as the casket is tipped over on its axis sending the body hurtling over the edge of the building into the smog below. At this point, there might be a stack of bodies three stories high covering the ground levels of the entire planet. It gives him some reprieve to know that the creatures of the sewers are said to devour whole corpses, bones, and all. A final act of charity from the dearly departed. Incineration is considered a waste of power resources, so cremations are banned. Perhaps it is the bodies of the dead that prop up the buildings. No one ever checks their foundations insofar as he is aware. It's a wonder they don't collapse more often.

Upon departing the funeral home he heads to the local tax office. He devises his scheme en route. This has to work. The monolithic government building stands out in every sector for its grandeur on all floors at all levels of society. It might perhaps be the only safe refuge for lowers. *Not that they ever really pay their taxes!* For middle dwellers it is usually to be avoided, a constant nuisance vacuuming up one's hard-earned checks. He approaches the kiosk and pulls a number. The line is remarkably short on this side of town, only five or so patrons ahead of him. Typical, that he would draw something in the four or even five-hundreds.

Harold still looks badly beaten from the previous events. The woman behind the glass at the counter looks disturbed by his presence. *Good.* This is working. He puts on his most pathetic-sounding voice, wanting to appear desperately in need of her assistance.

"Sorry to bother you, miss. I'm afraid I have recently awoken from a terrible hovercar accident. Lost most of my memory. I was hoping you could help me. All I remember is my name. If you could help me find my address so I can get home, I would be eternally grateful. I'm sure there's a lot of records, so maybe to save time you could just download them all on this recorder and I'll find myself," says Harold.

He has her fooled. *This has to work! Wait, her face. Why is it curling up in disbelief and irritation? Come on. Please.* He has to find this guy. It is time to get this over with.

"Yeah. I'm sorry to disappoint you, but it says right here your name is Harold. You don't even live in this sector, so you'll have to take the Transit to get home. I can patch in the info if you'd like," she says.

"What!? How could you possibly know that? Who told you?" says Harold, snapping back to his real voice.

"No one. You're on camera. We have face recognition, you know. We are the interplanetary government after all. Let me guess, you made up that whole story and this is some kind of fraud scheme? Nice try. I've heard everything. *Next!*"

"Fuck you! I pay your salary lady! Just wait until the manager hears about this you'll be sorry!" says Harold, pointing his finger at her across the glass window.

"Will you be escorting yourself to the door, or shall I have security throw you out?"

He escorts himself out and with great haste so as to not let the door hit him in the ass on the way out. What is he going to do now? He's screwed! It is back to one at a time. There has to be another way. He goes back to the bar again by the Transit station, defeated. This time to drink it over. The same bartender again looks up from his glasses.

"Rough day at the precinct? Looks like you found your target?" says the bartender.

"Not exactly... Wrong target... Pour me a Pilquist Red. Make it a double," says Harold.

"Remind me again. What's the trouble sir?"

"I'm looking for this guy. My sources say he lives here. The trouble is since I'm out of jurisdiction, I don't have access to the local database files.

I managed to get a copy from the birth and death registries, but there's no current pictures to cross-reference."

"Ah, I see. Forgive me, sir, for suggesting the obvious again, but wouldn't it be easiest to just go down to the precinct here and use their terminal? You can't access the local database on your viewer, but everyone else who lives here can."

"Of course! Bartender, you're a genius. Can I use yours?"

"Not a chance in hell, sir. And certainly not without a warrant!" He continues cleaning his glasses.

"Right.. Right... I'll, uh, pay the precinct a visit then. Soon as I finish that drink."

* * *

The night is late and it will be a while before he can return. This time he has a new plan. Returning home would be rough. Sheron would give him the *what-for* on his absence and the incident. Thomas isn't speaking to him. At least Martha is kind, but she's too young to understand. His presence is enough for her. She will talk on and on about her day as though each detail is fascinating. All he has to say is, "Oh wow that's interesting" while he watches the viewer.

He can't think of them right now; the plan consumes him. No turning back now. He has to see this through; it has cost him too much already. This time he will take some additional precautions. He brings a long knife to accompany his pistol. He brings gloves and a mask to shield his identity and protect his face and hands. His hitman kit is growing. He gives it a few days from his last visit. He doesn't want to raise too much suspicion with the family.

Upon arrival in the familiar 1149 Transit station, Harold panics. He realizes he doesn't have the ID card that Gharles gave him. Just his own. *What to do Harold!?* He approaches the help kiosk.

"Pardon, miss, I seem to have lost my ID! Is there another way that I can exit so I can go down to the government office and fetch a new one?"

She laughs directly into his face. "You don't need an ID to exit! The fuck you mean? Just push the button. We only use the scanners on lockdowns. You're in the mids. You're a special kind of stupid!"

Harold walks away both disgruntled and relieved. He pushes the button at the exit gate and enters the sector. He takes a familiar path back to the man of the same name's building. The doorman greets him, remembering him.

"Ah! Sir, what has happened to your face? I hope it wasn't the robbery. We had a dreadful burglary last week. One of our residents was killed," says the doorman.

He what? Oh right of course. "Yeah. I *think* I fell down the stairs trying to get out when the fire alarm went off," says Harold, passing the doorman, heading to the lift.

* * *

Knock knock. The door opens. It's the man again. *Again? Seriously? Why?* "I thought I made myself clear? Why are you here? I have nothing for you," he says.

"Sorry. I hit a snag. I need to access the local database, and you're the only friend I have in this sector," says Harold.

"That's interesting... I don't remember us being friends?"

"I figured you saved my life, I saved yours, we've been through some shit together. That makes us friends. I just have to find this guy. Please, it's really important."

"Fine... Just no funny business. I don't know what you're up to, or why you brought a gun to an old woman's house and I don't want to know. If this comes back on me, I'm telling them everything. *Everything.* Except I'm telling it *my way,* you understand? I'll pin it all on you. Fair?"

"Relax! No one is ever going to come looking for this. One database search in billions. It's not as serious as it sounds."

"So says the man who broke into an old woman's house and put a gun to her head..."

Almost to his dismay, the man allows him access to his local database terminal. A common household item, but nonetheless quite regionally specific. Networks for security purposes are rarely integrated outside of the corporate sector they service. The only bridges between them tend to exist in offices of government or those of wealth and status.

He accesses the terminal. The beginning of a long search through the database for all of the possible matches in District 1149. One file at a time comparing their photographs to the one in his hand. Current photos were kept of almost all citizens on the local networks for identification purposes. *Nope, not that one. Nope, not that one either.* Only a few hundred more to sift through.

The search fatigue starts to set in. *Maybe that one could work? Looks close enough, right?* All of them start to look the same, but none of them match the picture. Somewhere about two-thirds of the way through, he regains his attention.

A near-exact match! *He'd found him!*

He quickly downloads the information to his recorder. The address. 1726 Oakwood, apartment 467B, The Residences of Transvermidian. Amazing how a street can still be known as *Oakwood*, as though a single tree had existed on the planet within the last thousand years. Harold has never seen a tree before, they may not even really exist. Now to cross-reference that with the map. *There it was!* It was time. The time to kill.

"You found something or what?" asks the man.

"It's him! That's the guy!" proclaims Harold.

"Good. I can finally get you out my hair. We really have to stop meeting like this! It's been real though," says the man not unironically scratching his nearly bald buzz cut.

"Yeah, yeah. Quit your bitchin'. I'll be outta here in no time. Thanks for everything man. Really I mean it. I owe you one!"

Each moment is growing closer and closer to the target's death as he leaves the building. How will he do it? He starts to envision all the ways he could kill this guy. He has never met the guy, but the journey to find him seemed to be reason enough. *Should I use the gun? The knife? Strangle him with his bare hands? Push him off the edge of the tarmac?* There were so many ways to do it.

* * *

The Transvermidian Building seems nice enough. Really nice. *Too nice.* Not rich, but nice enough. It has an expansive lobby with a gym and a recreation room. A bunch of upper- middle-class snobs gather around the tables for their evening games and drinking. He starts to wonder if the top floors in his own building would even compare to this. *Could be disappointing.*

The place had no less than twelve elevators, all of them appearing to be functional. *Unbelievable!* His blood boils with each moment as he grows to covet the man more and more. The hallways are neatly organized, with obvious attention to soundproofing. Good lighting. *This is going to be more difficult than I thought.*

He reaches the door of the man's apartment. At last, his moment has arrived, but he realizes he has no plan! *What am I going to do? Knock on the door? Excuse me, can I come in and murder you?* He needs a pretense to be here. *That's it!* He will ditch his suit disguise. His street clothes are homely enough. He will pretend to be a maintenance man there to conduct an inspection. If there is one thing the well-to-do middle class does consistently, it is grouping everyone they consider *low-brow* into one category as though they are one person. A hundred different maintenance personnel could walk through his apartment and this fucker probably wouldn't even notice it wasn't the same guy.

Knock. Knock.

"*Uh* excuse me sir! *Uh* Maintenance here. We got reports of an electrical outage in your part of the building and I need to access your electric panel to check some circuits, or whatever."

It is no use. *This fucker isn't even home. Maybe he is out? Maybe he is still at work, wouldn't that suck?* This isn't going to be a one-day job.

What he needs is a good tracer. Someone who can watch the man, study his movements all day long and report back to him. There are many such people, but he needs someone who can easily go unnoticed. In nearly every sector, at every level of society, there is always a *ghost* class of homeless vagrants. Somehow, they gained access to the next level or refused to fall when evicted. At times they slip through literal cracks in the system. There is always something for people to be running from, hiding from, hustling for. Even in this business district, there has to be a place like that.

He suits up again and heads downstairs back to the clean-cut businessmen playing games in the wreck room. He puts on his friendliest, douchiest face.

"'Scuse me, gentlemen! I'm an offworlder here on business, so I don't know the area. I was hoping you can help me out. You guys know where I can find a hooker?" asks Harold.

Of course, they did! They fail to disappoint. Each one drunkenly describes the nearest and best locations in the sector, their favorite hookers, and the selection of *special services.*

One thing that is certain, is that where there are hookers, there tend to be other establishments of vice that almost always attract the attention of *ghosts.* He picks the underside of a nearby walk-bridge. He wants someone who knows the area really well, so he wants to make sure it is someone close enough to the building.

* * *

"Hey there, you looking for a good time? What do you say we go back to your place?" says a hooker, soliciting him.

"No thanks, doll! I'm looking for something else tonight, but you know if you're free on Saturday..." says Harold. *Focus Harold! Focus!*

"Adventurous I see. Try my friend over there! Is he the *something else* you were hoping for?"

"No, that's alright. Nothing like that. I'm looking for someone a little younger, the less conspicuous type."

She points to the teenage boy tucked away in the corner of the bridge; lament in her eyes for giving away his location. She doesn't know what Harold's game is, but it isn't uncommon. Just another business day.

"Excuse me! You there, boy. You want a job?"

He hesitates, fearful at first, but recognizes him as a customer. He prepares himself for the worst. "What'll it be? I got Elevate, Firestax, Huacoavia's Breath. Or are you here for *something else?*" says the boy.

"*Ah.* That's definitely not why I'm here. I *uhhh...*" says Harold, mortified.

"It's still fifteen credits for my time. Snap to it, old man," says the boy, casually, emotionless.

"Like I said, I got a day rate on a multi-week job. I need a Tracer. You know what that means?" asks Harold, somewhat condescendingly.

"Yeah, of course I do! But why would you want me and not a pro? What's the bag?"

"I need someone that can hide in the shadows. Someone unseen. I can't send that broad over there! He'll get caught up in her for sure, or recognize the cover. They see you, they don't look. Their shame, your game. You catch my drift? Come on, what do you say? Fifteen credits per day," says Harold, hoping to persuade him for less even though he can easily afford more.

"I follow you. But I need thirty-five in advance and a twenty-five credit day rate. Surveillance comes with hazards, you know," the boy says, again alarmingly stone cold in his expression. All business.

"You got a deal pal." He easily could have paid him yet still more than that with the money Gharles had bestowed upon him. "This is your target, here is a data readout of all the info I have. I need you to follow him. When does he leave? When does he get home? What Transit lines does he take? Bars he frequents? Place of employment? Where's his office, if you can. I want to know what he has for breakfast. I'll pay you a visit here in two weeks and we'll complete the transaction. I better be happy though, or the deal is off!"

"It's settled then. And thanks. For, *you know...* being nice," says the boy, almost smirking.

"Perfect... *uh* yeah you got a name kid?" says Harold; feels felt rude for not having asked. To be fair, the kid had made no such inquiries into him either.

"David. Davy Blue Eyes on the streets. Tall enough to stand in this hood. Middle born. If you don't find me here, ask for me on the circuit. Enforcers sweep here sometimes. *Wanted.* Theft, arson, narco trade, ghosting," says the boy, boisterous and prideful of his street credentials.

He feels tremendous sadness for David. He imagines the fragility of his own life. If he were demoted, would Thomas ghost? Sell his soul on the streets to stay mid. If Harold is willing to kill for it, Thomas would surely work for less. Would Martha? Would Sheron? Was there anyone who couldn't be bought? He imagines well-off assholes like the target and his building cronies with their hands on them. Finally, a moment of clarity that perhaps he ought to avoid hookers after all. Then again, if they don't get business how will they survive? The ultimate goal of capitalism, to sell the lives of others for the choice of product.

"Pleasure doing business with you, David. And say, David, you ever thought about going to school or something?" asks Harold, feeling somewhat guilty about his exploitation of child labor.

"*Ha!* Education is a luxury afforded to the rich. Hunger is my teacher. Misery my coach. The streets are my classroom now. To demote is to die and I chose to live. If I enroll, they find me. Spare me your pity. You're as stuck in your lane as I am. These are the roles we're given," says David, full of his enlightened street wisdom.

The harsh reality of societal failure is already so deeply entrenched in David's mind. He is right of course. They do what they have to do. In this dog-eat-dog world, your choices are only as big as your wallet. To seek change or acknowledge trauma is a luxury the middle-class simply cannot afford. Always forward with no reflection, no remorse, no qualms. You lived or died.

When Harold is rich, when he has ascended, he will come back for David, maybe drag a few hookers up with him. *Humans take care of humans, right?* He makes himself a promise. It is rare for him to do so and follow through on it, however, it is rarely for altruistic purposes. Harold after all is not fond of spending any amount of money for any reason, especially one that doesn't directly benefit him.

Chapter 8

It was when Mr. D'Delvoo fired him that Carl finally broke. Well, broke wasn't quite right, as Carl's exact response to being fired was something like, "Yeah, no, that makes sense, I get it." On his way out, security made sure to give him a thorough, but polite beating. He had been there fifteen years after all, but he had had enough. The shuttle breaking down had just been the beginning. The insane bus schedules, the fees for being late, being beaten and rejected, fired and beaten – it was too much. Carl decided he had had enough.

"That's it, I've had quite about enough of this shit," he said out loud as if to strengthen his resolve.

"Shut the hell up," said an old woman with most of her teeth missing, sitting across the aisle from him on the spacebus. She hadn't spoken the whole trip up until that point. Carl decided he should probably keep further thoughts to himself.

He made his way back to his apartment, treading his way through more water, and laid down on his couch. He thought about what he was going to do now. He needed money and he needed it fast.

He looked at the available jobs and noticed they all required a specific degree that he didn't have. Of course, he *had* obtained a degree from a university, but because *everyone* had a degree; there were now degrees that were highly specific to companies and even specific job positions. His degree in university had to be tailored specifically to his company and was useless for any other job that required degrees.

He then looked into smaller side jobs, gig work. Of course, one can't just *do* gig work, you have to have a license to operate a gig job. At least getting a license was easier than getting a university degree.

* * *

The Office of Public Work Licensing and Child Safety was not an easy office to get to. The first inconvenience was its location inside the imposing Central Government Complex, which towered over the city like an octopus of bureaucracy. The Transit lines that branched out from it were its tentacles, solidifying its grip over Capital City. This meant Carl would have to leave his sector to go there.

This particular office could only be reached by a specifically designated set of elevators. Most elevators in the city, at least at the mids and above, were powered elevators, *as they should be, otherwise what's the point.* These particular elevators were manual, as part of a government energy conservation program. As though that one small act would make a difference. Carl got into the first open elevator and found himself in the unfortunate position of being the last one on board. Social norms dictated that the last person on a manual elevator operated the crank.

Carl began cranking. The more people that were on the elevator, the harder it was to crank because the laws of physics were always in full effect. He really did not have the strength for this and within sixty seconds, had already built up quite a sweat. Eventually though, he managed to get the doors closed and they could then begin the more arduous task of lowering the elevator by several hundred floors to the office he needed to get to.

It took an eternity and the other passengers on the elevator, of which there were about fifteen, watched in pure rage as Carl struggled to single-handedly lower the carriage. But lower them he did, and finally, he arrived at his destination, tired, and sweaty, and nearly having forgotten why he was there to begin with. In front of him stood a solid stone door with the words 'Office of Public Work Licensing and Child Safety' carved into the face of it with rune-like letters. He pushed the door open and entered. The Central Government Complex was built thousands of years ago and rarely underwent any renovations.

He stepped into a dim fire-lit labyrinth. *An honest to god labyrinth.* The tunnel immediately split off in front of him and he was faced with a decision, left or right? Carl struggled to remember some advice that he had heard about mazes once.

"You can't connect the dots looking forward; you can only connect them looking backward. So you have to trust that the dots will somehow connect in your future. You have to trust in something — your gut, destiny, life, karma, whatever."

He wasn't sure that applied here.

He began walking. He was certain that the office wasn't where he was at the moment, so he just started walking because he wasn't getting anywhere by not walking. He very quickly became disoriented and thought several times that he may have been walking in circles.

He passed some other people along the way, one of which had just gotten lost on her way to the kitchen. He wasn't sure how much time had passed but he was certain it was far too long. *How long did these torches last anyways? Was this electricity-saving effort really worth this fire hazard?*

He knew he was getting towards the end when he could hear the sounds of receptionist laughter, the kind of laughter that indicated someone had told a tremendously unfunny joke about teenagers. He turned a corner and should not have been surprised, but somehow he was still astonished to see a large minotaur blocking the exit. Somehow, it was also the first time that Carl wondered why a government office had a labyrinth. *Is this what his taxes went to?*

The beast snarled at him with the kind of disinterested vehemence that only a government employee could manage. "Have you filled out the entry forms, sir? I can't let you pass without the entry forms," he rumbled. His voice shook the very walls of the labyrinth and some of the torches nearest him went out.

"Entry forms? There were no entry forms. Where do I get those? No, on second thought, why should I need them, I did this whole stupid maze," Carl said in disbelief. *Where did this guy get off?*

Of course, if Carl had paid attention in his Other World Cultures class in university, he might have known a few facts about minotaurs. First, they are sticklers for forms. Nothing gets a minotaur excited like a good form, especially those ones with the yellow carbon copy page behind them. Those are the best. In part, due to the fact that the planet was completely void of trees and all paper products had to be shipped in on the intergalactic transport network. This made them highly valuable and expensive. A triplicate copy was a status symbol. Second, minotaurs hate being questioned, which is why they make such good government employees. But third, and most importantly, you should never, *ever*, refer to a labyrinth as a maze in front of a minotaur. Carl would soon learn the error of his ways.

The beast became enraged at Carl. He flipped his desk, throwing office supplies on the ground, and ripped off his fine government clothing. He was unintelligibly screaming at Carl and after a few beats of his chest, began to charge. Shocked, Carl did the only thing he could think of and cowered as he shrank into a ball. This was surprisingly effective, as minotaurs are notorious for their bad eyesight, and he tripped over Carl and slammed face-first into the stone wall, killing himself instantly.

Unsure of what he was supposed to do in that moment, he moved towards the exit. He wasn't sure if he was supposed to clean up or if the janitor did that. It was kind of awkward because someone had walked in right as it all had gone down. Carl finally decided it wasn't his job and he exited the labyrinth on the other side, finally reaching the office. At least he thought he had.

The receptionist at the front desk greeted him with all the warmth of a semi-thawed slab of meat. "How can I help you, sir? Do you have your entry forms?" she asked.

"Again with the damn entry forms, where do I get those?" Carl was starting to be irritated.

"Sir, how did you even get past Incoteonx without having the proper forms?"

Well, there was the awkward question that Carl was dreading. Every time a government employee kills themselves in a fit of rage, it's always, *"How did you get in here?"*

"Well, if you're talking about that creature out there, he showed himself out," Carl said.

During the entire conversation, the receptionist had never once looked up, until now. "Oh my gods, he's dead. Well, that makes this process a thousand times easier. You came here for your Gig License right? Well you can just walk out there, grab one of his teeth and you have the permanent license!" she says.

"All I had to do was kill him?" said Carl, baffled.

"Of course dear, why do you think this maze is here? Because it's fun to get to work every day?" She laughed a grating awful laugh. "You will still owe the license fee of course."

There was always a fee...

* * *

He decided to start a food delivery service, which in retrospect might have been a bad idea given that he didn't have a shuttle. Delivering food around the bus schedules proved to be way more complicated than Carl had expected and, time after time, he was met by angry customers upset that their food was two or three hours late and ice cold. Carl thought they should have been at least grateful that someone went out of their way to get food for them.

After food delivery failed, he decided he might try ride-sharing. In theory, this worked by one person owning a method of transportation and someone else paying that person to drive them around. It seemed like a good plan to Carl, but after paying several people to drive him to places he didn't want to be, he decided that he just did not understand ride-sharing and gave up on that idea. Carl's skills were astonishingly limited when it came to business acumen.

Each time Carl picked up a new gig, he ended up losing money. He tried a website where he could perform odd jobs for small amounts of cash. That seemed like a good idea except most of the 'odd jobs' had been full-time work, or worse yet *blow jobs*! One position requested that he show up to an office for forty hours a week for the next thirty-five years for just a one-time

$5 payout. At this point, Carl was tempted but decided he might still be in the same place with no shuttle.

Carl sat on his couch, in the dark with the lights off in his apartment. It was raining outside and the sound of the rain on the windows provided minimal comfort to Carl. The rain was of course simulated. It was just a decontamination worker spraying the windows of his building. It was nice to pretend the planet had weather patterns. He had never seen any, but he imagined they might be nice.

He sat, staring at the blank entertainment screen. He didn't dare turn it on lest the noise disrupt his trance. He didn't want to have any stimulus at the moment. He wanted to sit in silence and darkness and contemplate his position in life.

He reviewed the facts. First, his shuttle broke down rather unexpectedly. Second, his apartment broke down rather unexpectedly. Then he was fired from work and lost his only source of income, meanwhile, bills, fees, and tolls continued to stack up

At one point, Carl had heard someone knock on his door claiming to be from "maintenance." Carl didn't answer, he knew better, it was likely his landlord, coming to kick him out. Carl couldn't be homeless in this city, the fines were too outrageous. *Ghosting* as they called it was also an arrestable crime if anyone cared to enforce it.

He pulled up his tablet and started searching the directory without really thinking about it, he just let his fingers type and he glanced at the screen. He was surprised to learn how many euthanasia centers were in his sector. There was even one listed as an amenity in his apartment lobby. He just stared at the screen for a while, contemplating what it even meant. Why had he searched for that? Did he think he would get a job there? He didn't have the Euth Group Corporate Degree. Realization slowly dawned on him about what had led him there. *And why shouldn't it?*

He left the search results up for a while as he set the tablet down next to him on the couch and stared at the ceiling. He sat there for a long time. He wondered if he could ever get back on track. *Could he get his job back? How would he ever afford another shuttle? Could he get a job somewhere else? Where was all the excess water from his broken plumbing going?* Staring at his ceiling, he wasn't sure he was thrilled about what the answer to that was.

Carl picked up his tablet and made his decision. He opened his email, recovered the deleted offer email from Gharles, and responded.

'*I'm in.*'

Chapter 9

The next two weeks pass uneventfully. Harold keeps his head down and business goes along as usual. Internally, he is anxious. All of his dreams are at his fingertips. The family is apprehensive. They all know something is different, but they can't put their finger on it. He decides it's time to buy some of their affection back.

He pulls some of the cash from his good-faith money from Gharles and uses it to buy a gift for each of them along with a few essentials; things he could never have previously afforded. He will tell Sheron it was a bonus from all the overtime she thought he was working, while he was out trying to murder the guy.

It works, slightly. Thomas comes around again. He is surprised Harold has listened at all to remember the things he has been wanting and saving for.

Reconnecting with Sheron is more difficult. A great deal of hostility has built up around them over the years and it seems like there is no good way to resolve it. He decides to use some of the money to take her on a date. A rare form for Harold, but he takes her to a nice fancy restaurant in their sector called Green Lobstar for wine and a good dinner. To his selfishness, the organic food is highly welcome over the usual gruel of processed box meals, and certainly better than her cooking.

He even goes as far as to tell Baab and Geordon that his days at the plant are numbered and that he will soon be ascending. They of course laugh it off in disbelief. Perhaps he will throw some money their way when he gets it, just to shove it in their faces.

The two weeks finally at their end, he returns to Sector 1149. It is time for his rendezvous with David. Assuming he hasn't just taken his money and run. He returns to the bridge and waits. The night is young and there is little activity there. He starts to worry that he's been stood up. Then he sees a familiar face.

"Ohh... If it isn't Mr. Big Money himself! Coming back for another go? Can I get a piece of that action? You did say you'd be back one Saturday!" says the hooker, her taunting voice like nails on a chalkboard.

"Ha! It's good to see a familiar face. But you know why I'm here. What's the scoop?"

"Yeah yeah I know why you're here. He's still on patrol for yah, but he'll be around. Listen I wanted to thank you for what you did for Davy. I can tell you're not perfect, but you're a nice enough guy. We don't get much of that around here."

"Thanks... but you might be wrong about that. Can't say I haven't done my share of wrong."

"Honey, haven't we all? Take a look around you. Name one part about this world that ain't wrong? At least you got the sense to see it for what it is."

Here comes David now. Hopefully, he has something useful. Both of them seem pleased that the other has returned, but cautiously optimistic to ensure both sides hold up the bargain.

"David! Tell me something good. What do you have for me?" asks Harold.

"Show me the money first. Then I'll talk," says David, stone-cold as always.

Harold flashes the bills to David as carefully and secretly as possible so as to not alert anyone else who might be nearby. He has the money alright.

"Thanks. Well, I tracked your target, but he's difficult to follow. Leaves early, comes home late. There's no consistency to his coming and going, but he is mostly gone. It's harder than you think. He works off-world on a station. You're not going to catch him there and I can't follow. But I got something for you. When he heads to work he takes the M349 Tramway to the space departure terminal. You want to get him? That's where he's most vulnerable. Here's the recorder, it has all my data. Do what you want with it," says David, transactionally.

"Thank you, David. This is good. Really good. Here's your cut. But if you want, I've got another job for you if you're interested." He hopes he will say yes. He needs someone who already knows the man's movements. Someone reliable.

"Yeah, I'm in. But if you plan to cap him it'll cost you extra. Two-hundred-and-fifty credits advance or I'm out. If I get a mark on my head, I need at least enough to get out of town. You understand?" says David.

"Deal! Okay, here's what I'm thinking. I come next Thursday on my day off. I give you a burner communicator. If he starts to head towards the Tramway you call me. I wait at the station and catch him before he even gets on the tram."

"Okay. Sounds like a plan then. The station will be crowded. Not my business, but you're going to have to go in close range. In and out. Stab and go," says David, as though he is a resident young connoisseur of murder.

"Hmmm... That's right. You let me worry about that. I'll figure it out. Meet me here again Thursday early. Dark outside, early. Two-hundred-and-fifty and a burner."

The deal is made. He just has to hope the man will happen to take the tram on Thursday. If they have the same day off, he is fucked. The hordes at the platform make him nervous. He worries someone will see him. How could they not? The risk is too great. He can't conceivably follow off-world, it would be too obvious. Fewer places to hide. This is his best chance.

He decides to visit a friend.

* * *

Knock knock.

Back at the man of the same name's apartment.

"You? Again? Seriously? Why do I keep opening the door to you?" says the man, irritated.

"I know. I know. Once again I find myself in need of your service. But this time I'm paying," proclaims Harold.

"Well... why didn't you say so to start with? That changes everything. Come in then."

"I know your hands ain't exactly clean. There's something I need and I'm hoping you can get it for me," says Harold.

"Maybe I can. I know some people. What's the bad news?"

"I need an explosive. Something with a remote detonator. Enough to break concrete."

"Oh wow. That is dirty. Yeah, I can get it. But it won't be cheap and it won't be easy."

"Can I get it by Thursday?"

"It's possible. Five-thousand credits. In advance. But I don't deliver. We set up a middleman. This can't get traced back to me. I don't know what you plan on doing, but I can't wear it."

Five-thousand! That is almost half of his Gharles money. If this plan fails, he will be in deep water. Having no other ideas, he agrees. They arrange for David to pick up the goods and deliver it. That way it involves as few people as possible. He just has to up his rate for David who is uneasy about it but eventually agrees. Everyone has a price you know.

* * *

When Thursday arrives everything seems to be going according to plan. Back under the bridge, the middleman makes the exchange with David and he delivers the explosives to Harold. He carefully slips through the early morning darkness, reaching the underside of the elevated tram rail.

He chooses a joist on a curve to ensure greater success. His heart races. He is perspiring. He looks all around; the paranoia sets in. Has to be certain no one sees him. He carefully secures the explosives to the joist, taking great care to ensure that they will not be discovered before the big event.

He sets up on a nearby terrace overlooking the railway, but far enough away to be out of the blast zone where he can slip away quickly. Now all there is to do is hope and wait. The lights grow brighter as the 'daylight' emerges.

Will this be the day? What if it isn't? Will I have to leave it there where it can be found?

His fears subside when he hears the ring of his communicator. It's David. "The package is on its way."

The code signifying that the man has left the apartment and is actively headed into the tramway station. This is it. He checks the station departure times. The next M349 tram should depart the station in the next twenty-six minutes. Luckily for his plan, the trams are quite slow when still within this sector. He will have plenty of time to react.

As time grows closer, his anxiety worsens. *Do I have the gall to go through with this? What of all the innocent people aboard who will also perish?* No sense in worrying about it at this point, he has already killed at least two people. *What will it matter when I ascend?* This society rewards selfish opportunists, this was no different.

There it comes. A minute late, but reliable. The tram departs the station. Here it comes. Closer. Closer. Approaching the bend. Not a moment too soon. Wait. Wait for it. Steady.

* * *

At this point Carl was desperate. Gharles responded right away and had agreed to meet him later in the day to exchange the information. He decided to make one last-ditch effort to get his old job back through an act of groveling. He had been going back almost every day for the past two weeks, but his optimism waned as his former boss was always "indisposed at the moment" or off-world somewhere doing anything but working. At least it gave him an excuse to see Melissa once again. Though she was incredibly irritating, he still had a certain weakness for her. If this didn't work, he would go through with Gharles' proposal and meet him as planned.

He departed his apartment for the tramway station, hoping that he wasn't late. The route to the tramway station was all too familiar. Each second he got closer and closer. He approached the security gate and scanned his ID badge.

* * *

Harold's thumb comes down hard on the detonator.

Kaplow!

The vibrations shake the building beneath him. He sees the fireball erupting upwards. The track collapses as the tram, a smoldering wreck, falls to the ground. A second even larger shockwave follows.

Kaplow!

Glass shatters. The destroyed tram smokes with flames all around it. All aboard have surely perished. Nothing but charred pieces of metal and concrete remain. Harold takes a moment to bask in the horror and glory of his achievement. *Time to collect my wealth!*

He books it down to The Transit center and catches the last interregional train out before they lock down the entire sector for investigation. His communicator rings. It's Gharles! *Excellent. He is already ready to hand over the reward. Right?*

"Mr. Harold. Quite the fireworks show you put on. I must say that you have exceeded our wildest expectations. You are truly monstrous in the best possible ways. Unfortunately for you, once again you have failed your target. Enjoy the footage on the viewer this evening. This will surely make for a wonderful segment, but you might want to check the passenger manifest."

What!? How!? Impossible! It was verified.

Gharles hangs up on him again. These calls are becoming more and more painful each time. Another call. This one from David.

"What did you do you little brat!? You said he was there! You said we were good to go!" says Harold, belligerent with rage.

"I tried to reach you but it was too late. His bus connections were late and there was trouble at the gate. He never made it on board. And after seeing this, I don't know if I can do this anymore. I'm tossing this communicator over the railing now, where it will never be found."

"David!! David! No wait! I need you. I ... I still... I."

It is too late. David is gone. *All that money wasted!* It was starting to get very personal now. He spends the rest of the ride home not lamenting the lives he destroyed but rather the money he lost pursuing it and envisioning ending the one life he couldn't.

* * *

Things back at the apartment are stirring in a frenzy. The family is gathered around the viewer.

"Harold! Come quick. Where have you been!? Look at this!"

Sheron is frantic for him to come over. Surely there was significantly more violent news to be aired in the Capital City than the destruction of a single tramway! Why were they airing this broadcast!? It wasn't even in the high class.

"Authorities responded to a brutal terrorist attack occurring shortly after 9:35 am this morning in sector 1149. The disturbing footage you can see here. Watch as the entire portion of the track goes up in flames! There were no survivors of the crash resulting in the deaths of forty-three people including Anastoncia Tennhausen, legendary businesswoman and CEO of VranthCo."

Harold's heart is racing. *Of all the days, why was she there today?* The murder of a rich upper-tier woman is bound to trigger a massive investigation.

"Ms. Tennhausen was returning to the terminal for her departure home to Prylax III after solidifying a major business deal. Local Enforcer Chief Royce Hollander has announced a swift investigation. Rival companies HyrOn, Malthex, and ZornCo issued a rare joint statement denying any involvement on their part saying, 'While we hated Ms. Tennhausen and would have loved nothing more than to see her profits destroyed, we deny any and all involvement in this incident, and expressly deny any employee involvement. It is not within the purview of our corporate operations to assassinate rival members of the ruling class without first making a declaration of war as required by Galactic Regulation 4536.5B issued after the Merger Treaty of 3751.'"

Harold knows this to be a lie. Vacated shares and executive positions of this magnitude always lead to inter-sectorial warfare. Perhaps this will thin out the investigation and turn the attention towards the competing companies.

"Hollander has expressed that he will nonetheless pursue a rigorous investi-

gation, but assures the public that they can rest at ease, as he has no intention at this time of reviewing any corporate financial documents saying that, 'The privacy of the corporations will be respected as a top priority.'"

Harold is reassured by that. Corporate finances are always total forgeries. Despite the billions upon billions of pencil-pushers in Capital City, it is impossible to ascertain how much money is really being moved. They cook the books to reflect whatever dish they are serving that day.

"The VranthCo. sector of Capital City is on temporary lockdown, while large shareholders prepare their armies in what is sure to be the most violent and exciting corporate takeover of the year. Tennhausen's net worth of 23.7 quadrillion credits has been left to her beloved cat Winston, who I am told was also murdered later this afternoon. Her spacious 567 billion credit Capital penthouse is now available for purchase, it comes with fifty-three bedrooms, sixty-five bathrooms, and housing for up to four hundred servants. I'm Gui'lda W'uthrnm, Capital News. Remember, it could always be worse!"

This is by far the worst possible outcome of the incident. There were cameras capturing the explosion, which means they likely also have footage of him setting them up. He only hopes the camera quality is low grade as it typically is in the mid-levels so that he cannot be recognized.

A wealthy woman died! Of all his worse luck. Why was she even down there associating with the upper-mids? Doesn't she have people for that? And why was she taking the tram? Entry to sector 1149 will be heavily monitored now. He will need a new cover angle.

"Oh my... Sheron I think I need to lie down for a while," says Harold.

"Psh! What's the matter with you! You love violence? It's usually your favorite. Come on Harold, you live for this stuff," says Sheron. The kids chime in their agreement.

"Forty-three people are dead! Let's have some respect," says Harold, eliciting rancorous laughter from the family.

"Geeze, Harold! Since when did you have a conscience?" says Thomas.

"Sorry. I guess I'm just not in the mood today."

Harold always hates it when Thomas called him by his first name. Thomas is skilled at pushing his buttons.

"Yeah but just imagine it though. What I wouldn't do to live in that woman's servants' quarters even! And she gives it all to her damn cat!" says Sheron.

"Don't worry dear. I'll get you that penthouse someday!" promises Harold.

They all laugh at him again. But Harold isn't laughing. Was he serious? Did he think he could ever have such wealth? They had no belief in him! None. He leaves the room to lie down. The sadness of his failure weighs him down into the bed.

* * *

Detective Georgette Clinton of the Sector 1149 Enforcer Unit pushed through the sea of reporters gathering outside the precinct building. She was called to the office of Chief Hollander on special assignment. The precinct was in chaotic disarray. A mess of cubicles, office furniture, and papers were strewn almost haphazardly everywhere they could be placed. The once grand building stood in disrepair.

Her deep blue enforcer uniform fit her perfectly, always crisp and neat. Her curly hair is always tucked in perfectly to her hat. Her deep red lips are always pursed, rarely breaking from her serious demeanor. Most of the rookie enforcers were intimidated by her deep commanding voice and physical strength.

Chief Hollander on the other hand was much the opposite. He was loud and crass, always wore a suit and frequently smoked cigars at his desk. His shaggy blonde hair was always an uncombed mess. He tended to shuffle around the precinct, hunched over, shouting, and micromanaging. Georgette was among his most trusted enforcers and he admired her propensity for taking the job seriously and performing it with integrity.

"Detective! Come on in. Come on in. I assume you've seen the news?" said the chief.

"Yes sir. I intercepted the radio communication about it. Forty-three deaths and an out-of-commission tram line. That's bound to cause a riot."

"Transport authority thinks they can have it up and running again in three days. But I call bullshit. I want to review some evidence with you that we collected from the security network. The footage isn't great, especially because it was dark, but we've got a perp here on camera planting the bomb," he said.

"I see. Have we pulled external footage, tracked his movements?"

"No, not yet. I want to keep this as tight shut as possible. No noise. Capital government wants somebody to go down for this, but we need to be careful about who that is. Pursue the real suspect, but not a word to anyone about this okay?"

"Understood. Given the profile of this case do I have full discretion?"

"Yes. Any resources you need get top priority. Just let me handle the big dogs. If you dig something up that goes political, bring it straight to me. The governor was *very* specific, he only wanted a human on this case and I trust you. "

"Well, let's get started then," she said, confidently.

Detective Clinton was a sharp veteran detective of the enforcers. She had a calm demeanor, always logical and calculating. If she had weaknesses, she kept them well concealed. She was never unprofessional for even a moment, always taking her role seriously. She had seen almost every kind of case imaginable and had the skills and wisdom to be an expert in her field. Some said that the only time she laughed is during interrogations and only then if it is part of the act.

In a world of endless buildings, endless people, endless species there was this sweeping sense of lawlessness that permeated every sector. The economic dimorphism was staggering and readily obvious. Some called it 'trickle-down law enforcement' because it was top-heavy. Defending first the rich and lighter as you go down. The reality was that the enforcers rarely defended justice, and instead guarded money.

There was a smattering of court systems and enforcement agencies all the way up from individual buildings, to the whole galactic order. In this world of endless choice, endless corruption, endless want, endless need, Detective Clinton desired to find endless *truth*. Her fact-finding mission was at the core of her being and she was determined to faithfully uphold justice and the law even in an unjust system. Someone had to bring order to a world of chaos.

She would begin her investigation from the camera footage, starting at the crime scene, and attempt to walk it back from the killer's direction.

* * *

The scene was quite grisly, still smoking as they pulled the burnt corpses and skeletons from the wreckage; forensics teams dusting everything for evidence. She pushed through the masses of gathered spectators and media to the security perimeter.

"Clinton? This is your assignment now, isn't it? Let me guess. It's bigger than me."

"Afternoon Lt. Xanthu. Glad to see you too. I didn't ask for it. Hollander asked for me. Better luck next time. What's the status?"

Xanthu's blue-green exterior darkened to gray in the outside lighting. His long snout hung down to his chest and guzzled coffee straight from the mug. Two sharp horns protruded from the top of his head. Otherwise, he was generally humanoid in nature with two arms and two legs. A similar number of fingers and toes. He was able to produce tones of human language with ease. His species was well respected among human society particularly for their wealth and the resources their confederation of planets controlled. Senator Galxshu, the presidential candidate, hailed from the very same.

"Naturally. Well, the recovery team is still trying to get the bodies we couldn't reach before. The mayor's office is beating down the door with a cleanup crew. They want to start the rebuild today, but I've held them off for now to save the evidence. Better hurry though if you want to see it before it's bagged," said Xanthu.

"Has the explosive device been found or identified?"

"Indeterminable at this point in time. There's no way to decipher what's left of it from the wreckage. If you ask me this was a professional job. Total disintegration and remote detonation. This isn't something homemade. Got to be military, but probably black-market."

"Okay, you're right. I do want to look for my own evidence after all. Give me a layup on the central blast radius. I want to get as close as I can. We have tested for biohazards and radiation right?"

"Of course we did. Not a trace!" he said, almost laughing as though she should know.

"Not a detectable trace you mean. Get me three of your strongest. I want a chance to lift some of these larger pieces before the mayor does."

She combed the periphery of the blast radius, carefully inspecting each piece of debris. Thorough, expedient, meticulous. They sifted through the wreckage. Simulating the blast in her mind, she imagined where the blast must have occurred based on the debris pattern. The foundation of the joist was still visibly apparent, but the direction of the fall was not as clear. Her advantage over the recovery and evidence team was the video she had seen with Hollander. In doing so she could approximate the piece she was looking for.

"Xanthu. Come have a look at this. The impact had to originate from this side. There is no other way to explain the debris pattern. Notice the subtle grade differentials in the other still functioning joists relative to the ground level. Even with burn marks, you can still isolate the grit pattern to tell what is what."

Xanthu looked defeated; she had bested him again and found what he had missed.

"Now, see what your crew missed. Notice the darkest and most fractured piece? Now imagine the repulsive forces incurred by the blast. If you follow, we should find our explosive casing somewhere in this vicinity. Which, we did. Looks like it wasn't total disintegration after all. Though not as intact as I would like. It'll be hard to get an ID on it."

"Clinton, you've done it again! Once again, I am humiliated and humbled in your presence. You always put things together in a way I would never consider." He's impressed by her, but he felt like she was always stealing his thunder. She always came in on the scene and found the clue he missed, or seen things in a way he couldn't see it.

"All in a day's work, Lieutenant. Brains over brawn wins every time! That being said, I want you and you alone to be the one who handles this evidence. Trust no one with it. I mean no one. Got it?"

"Geesh, this case is getting above my paygrade fast isn't it? Can I at least take it to forensics?"

"Hmmmm. Okay. But I want Lazurthus to do it. Just the two of you. No one else in the room and you never leave it, until I get back and take it from you. In other words, if it gets tied back to the military, sit on it. There are unfortunately some injustices even I can't protect you from."

"Lazurthus? You really hate me don't you?"

"To the contrary! It's good to have an extra set of eyes, literally and figuratively speaking. It's a good pairing. I know he can be *difficult* at times, but once you see him work, you'll know why I told you to go to him. Now. I'm going to take a giant leap of trust here and say that you can handle this while I follow a lead. Yes?"

"A lead already? You get all the good action! I got you covered here. We'll have this wrapped up within the hour. If we don't get eaten by the press," said Xanthu.

"A well-fed dog doesn't bite. If the press is hungry, throw them a bone," she replied.

She departed from the scene, tracing the path of the bomber in the video. If he came from this direction all the way up to this point out of camera view, where would be the next logical place he might have come from? Three potential entrances, unless he was smart enough to follow an irregular pattern. Something told her that wasn't the case, or else he would have known the tracks are monitored and might have at least worn a better disguise. Not that it mattered. The camera resolution was abysmal.

The first boulevard seemed too exposed. The commerce buildings faced a wide avenue. A person trying to go unnoticed would likely have chosen another route. The back alleyway seemed ideal, but of course, the narrow constrictions would make surveillance equipment useless, so in the absence of any other theory she would follow it to the end and reassess. The third entrance might prove useful as it connected to the main hub. It was likely that the suspect had monitored the tram prior to detonation. How else would they confirm their target?

* * *

She proceeded to the tramway station terminal first. It had been cleared and shut down from the wreckage, leaving behind only its security guards. As a major sector artery to the off-world terminals, this was a significant blow for the sector economy.

"Can I help you miss?" said a gruff-voiced security guard.

"I hope so officer. Detective Clinton EN1149. I'm going to need to see all of your security footage starting at 1:00 am this morning. Is that possible?"

"Yeah sure. You think we got something? I talked to my pal Krathos who was working the morning shift. Said nothing out of the ordinary. Then just out of nowhere, *blamo!*"

"Oh yeah? I'd like to get a statement from him if he's agreeable. Sometimes the chaos of crime becomes ordinary enough that even those hunting against it stop noticing. I bet he saw something that caught his attention and thought nothing of it."

They strolled to the guard office. The corridors of the building were dark and filthy. Trash littered the floors. The forest green walls were stained with centuries of heavy traffic. When it was full of people it was so lively you hardly noticed, but with the patrons gone it looked like the perfect place for crime, as often it was.

The cameras were not catching the best images, nor were they all functioning. The wall of security screens had the feeling of neglect. After a while, people stopped looking at them proactively. They only look at them when something has already occurred.

"I need to see all footage between approximately 4:46 and 5:03 am. If my suspicions are correct I should be able to find what I need."

The footage was inconclusive. Only a handful of pedestrians. The alley theory seemed now more plausible, though she wanted to be thorough.

"Do you have a map of the layout of this complex? I want to determine your proximity to maintenance access tunnels. Specifically the pass-throughs."

"Seems unlikely. The lowers are still a full forty flights down. There's a three-floor support foundation under the base level that attaches to the four corners of each of these buildings here. See? Look at the map. The platform is suspended in the crossway. It's the only place to put a rail really. There's no one above or below," he said with confidence.

"Well, officer. Ka'drel is it? It might seem that way. However, looks can be deceiving. Trust, but verify. There see. Look? These supporting tunnels here run secure comm lines and power horizontally. All four buildings have potential access points to the station. Yet you have no cameras on these entry points? Might want to rectify that."

"You think it was them though? Lowers coming up forty floors just to come through a little access tunnel? Doesn't seem like something they would do," he said, astonished.

"Does blowing up a tram rail sound like something a *normal* person would do? I'm not pinning this on class conflict just yet. It could be anyone. Let's see footage also just prior to the explosion. We're looking for someone who might have entered the station, failed to board the tram, and left in a hurry."

"Sure, yeah. You can see it was crowded. These folks here are probably waiting for the J792. See they don't get on but they ain't moving either. Nothing on the entry side."

"Show me the gate entrance feeds. Anybody show up and doesn't have clearance? Look for someone watching the gate who might leave without entering."

"That's got to be a dozen people an hour! Just look at the kiosk line. How will you know?" he said, irritated by the amount of work involved in investigating this.

"I'll know when. Wait! Stop. Go back. Further. Five seconds more. Notice there are seven at the kiosk. We've got a dozen or so headed inside. But wait! This guy here. Seems normal, right? He scans the gate pass. There's a problem. He proceeds to the kiosk. Nothing to see here right? But look. Who is *that*? See how that boy comes to the entry area?"

He can see it, but he doesn't see it the way she sees it. It's very subtle. An ordinary person observing it wouldn't have stopped to think twice about it.

He shrugged at her questioningly.

"He stares straight at the man, before glancing around to check his cover. Notice his expression changes when the last man doesn't enter. We see him leave in a hurry. Now on the outside cam. On his communicator now. Worried about something. What is he worried about? I bet it has something to do with that man not getting through the gate," she said.

He still wasn't convinced, but she sounded like she knew what she was talking about, and she is an Enforcer detective after all. Hopefully, she'd got what she needed so he could go back to his day of staring aimlessly at the wall, pretending to care about the facility he was supposed to be securing. Then again, he couldn't let her have the last word.

"Wow! You're good at this, ain't yah? It's just a kid though? Doesn't that happen all the time? Maybe he forgot something at home. It just don't seem right."

"Nothing about the events of today were right. I'll take the leads where they fall. Even if it's a dead-end, I want copies of these two recordings here. And I'm sending down two guys from the precinct to check those access hatches. Better make sure those are sealed while we're at it. And thank you for your cooperation in this matter."

She isn't my boss. She can't tell me what to do!

Not that he had anything better going on, but copying recordings wasn't exactly easy for him. He had to isolate the footage and then do a data transfer. This meant he had to actually engage with the terminal, a contraption that he hated. *She would get her recordings when she got them*, on his time. All of five minutes later, she had her recordings and was walking out the door.

This was no ordinary boy in the footage. He was too unkempt to be a resident. Citizens in the business district would be hard-pressed to be seen in that condition at any age. Appearances were important to maintaining status and upward mobility. She suspected he was a hired hand from one of the sector's seedier districts. *Find the watchmen, find the buyer.* She decided her next course of action would be to pursue the path leading back to where he had come from. She called the precinct to set up the action plan. This meant losing track of the bomber's route, but it was an easier lead to trace.

Unlike the assailant, the hired help was also less likely to have identification clearance to exit the sector. She decided to call an analyst down at the precinct.

"Hey Be'Quiy it's Clinton. I'm emailing you some footage, I want to get facial tags on these two. The last man on the right at the entry gate, you'll see him going to the kiosk, and the boy watching him in the shadows. Think you can handle it? Great. Also, would you send Shu'ck and Bayrie down here to the tramway? I got four access tunnels for a seal breach check. Copy? Thank you."

There was no way to know just how far the boy had come from and the paths seemed to diverge in every direction. She cross-referenced the paths with the alleyway she suspected was used by the assailant. She hoped they might merge at some point into a commonplace or district to narrow her search. The possibilities were too variable. They could have come from multiple directions. She went on to try and gather additional camera footage from nearby buildings, but there was nothing compelling. Hours had gone by and she was back at nothing.

She impatiently called Be'Quiy on her communicator, asking for an update.

"You know I got it! Suspect one, man at the gate is Carl. The boy watching is David, aka Davy B. He's a local boy gone ghost. He's got a RAP with us. Petty theft, assault, unlicensed, class-level living violations, you name it he's done it. The family descended years ago and he overstayed. He's on our list, but we've never bothered going after him."

That fit the bill perfectly for her hired-help theory. He was exactly the kind of person who would get recruited for a job like this. Even if he didn't plant the bomb, he probably knew who did. Then again, it was equally plausible that he was just there to pick-pocket the man. "We have no known connections between the two. Nothing on Carl. Profile suggests a highly insignificant target. Awful credit score, on his way to descent for sure. Maybe the financial stress got to be too much for him?"

That seemed unlikely. Usually, they would start small with fraudulent financial transactions or petty theft first. A terroristic murder was hardly the profile of an amateur, especially when the victim was of such notoriety, wealth, and prestige. She knew the investigation gave little concern to the other forty-two victims. It would take weeks to determine whether any other passengers might have been linked together, but that would be a slow web of hypotheticals. She needed something fast. She had to stop this killer before they acted again.

"Thanks, Be'Quiy. I knew you could find it. Let's get a search out for David. I'm not leaving any stone unturned on this one. Keep it quiet though. Don't connect it to the case. I need this one alive okay? Great!" she said, hanging up the communicator.

She decided to pay Carl a quick visit to see if he might talk and find out why he might have been followed to the station. After making the journey to his apartment, she found that no one was there, and she'd wasted a trip. It was quite a significant journey from his apartment to the tramway station, so he must frequent many forms of public transit to make this a viable commute. She decided to put finding Carl on hold for now; there was plenty of additional evidence to review. It was better to get back to the station to see what Lazurthus and Xanthu had found so far.

Chapter 10

"All non-resident Transit passengers must be screened for purposes of entry. We thank you for your cooperation and apologize for the inconvenience."

It is becoming more and more difficult to enter sector 1149 now. Harold steps out onto the platform and joins the line forming at the non-resident exit. It moves quickly enough, but some are detained longer for further questioning. In his moment of stupidity, he once again forgets to bring the ID that Gharles had provided him.

"Mulknosh district? Why come all this way, Harold? You've been out this way a lot recently," says the checkpoint officer, reading off the data screen on his terminal. This gives Harold the chills, it meant the face recognition security grid was tracking him, even if he was using the false ID.

"Well, you see officer, my wife and I are in the process of adopting and this agency has a better selection than our own. It's got to be a human you know," says Harold as though he were serious about the bald-faced lie.

"That's noble. What's the prospect's name?" says the checkpoint officer, unconvinced.

Harold pauses awkwardly. "David. Yeah, it's David. Great kid. Might be a while though. You know how long these processes can take, with the paperwork and all."

The officer knows this very well, as all matters of government in Capital City take an eternity and require endless amounts of paperwork, similar to the log files he will have to assemble at the end of his long day.

"Yeah, you're tellin' me, probably as much paperwork as the reports I've gotta file later. Best of luck to you sir." He clears Harold for entry.

That was a close call, but it bought him another shot at the target. In his desperation, his ideas for murder start getting sloppier and more direct. He will stalk the man for several blocks at a time just to see if the perfect opportunity comes up. *This motherfucker takes more bus connections than anyone I ever saw.* He is tired, running low on funds for these extra excursions, and can't stand the thought of returning to the plant for another day of box making.

* * *

Carl took a pass-through tunnel that goes through a building. These were frequented by both ground transit delivering cargo to the building and also by pedestrians trying to take a shortcut. He thought that his nerves might be more frayed after his near-miss with the tramway explosion, but somehow he partially wished he had perished. At least then he wouldn't have to struggle in this world anymore.

It was dark enough in the tunnel that Harold could get closer to his victim and still hide in the shadows. Carl approached a terrace with steps that lead down onto the next level below and Harold saw his window of opportunity.

The thought came to Harold that he couldn't get close enough to the man to stab him without alerting him to his presence, but the knives would work just as well if thrown with enough force. He would wait until the man reached the top step, and throw the knife into his back, causing him to fall and roll down the stairs dead. He would pretend to be a concerned bystander and retrieve the knife before someone noticed. They would just think he fell down the stairs.

Moments away, the man reached for the railing at the top of the stairs. Harold aimed his knife towards him. He threw the knife with perfect aim. It barreled towards the man's head.

Swoosh. Swoosh. Swoosh.

This was it. The moment of impact. *Wait no! No!*

The knife landed square on the back of Carl's head by the handle! It bounced off of his neck, ricocheting back towards Harold just as an unfortunate bystander crossed between them, emerging from the hidden cross-section bisecting the terrace and the building. It lodged straight into the old man's neck. He grabs at his throat, gasping for life.

Carl grabbed the back of his head in pain. *Ow!* "What the?!? Fuck." He turned to see the old man behind him, bloody and falling to the ground. "Oh my god, are you okay!? What happened? Help?! Somebody?" He tried to catch the old man as he fell but it was of no use.

Carl looked deep into the man's brown eyes as the life faded away from his body. He attempted to lift the man off the ground, as though that would be helpful. He heard the discharge of a gun. *Bang!* Blood spattered from the back of the dead old man he had just inadvertently used as a shield.

Shit! Shit! Shit! I have to get the fuck out of there.

Carl ran as fast as he can down the stairs, sliding down the banister railing to accelerate his descent. He ran in a zig-zag pattern, frantically searching for a crowded place to hide. He was too panicked to bother looking for the assailant.

Unbelievable! Harold says to himself. First the knife, then the gunshot. *This guy just won't die!* Harold quickly springs to retrieve the knife and flees the scene, losing his victim in the process.

* * *

Detective Clinton was back at the precinct, heading over to the forensics lab where Lazurthus and Xanthu awaited her. Lazurthus was an obnoxious and hideous alien. A bulging off-white mass like a grub worm with arms and legs; he had at least four that were visible, three eyes, and a number of probing antennas and sensory organs unknown to humans. This made him incredibly perceptive and he was the best and most reliable forensics expert at EN1149.

"Good evening gentlemen. What's the news?" she asked.

Lazurthus furled his snout in disgust. "*Shhhhh!* How can I hear the vibrations? Can't you taste that? But yes. I possess knowledge."

"He's been *tasting the vibrations* all afternoon. Any luck on your lead?" Xanthu was annoyed.

"I got a line out for some suspects. but no interviews—"

"*Hush!!!* There! There is? Reach out with your thymboscis. Do you experience that radiation pattern? No? Ah yes, I forget the inferior limitations of your species... I say that. Xanthu do you have a thymboscis?"

"Would you *please* just tell us what you found already, Lazurthus?" Xanthu could take no more.

"The metallic composite is Kaldresh in origin. Military casing. The powder is FLTX537, a proprietary of QualCore, but it has been in our sector for quite some time. Highly susceptible to incineration by water, so it was likely held in a dehumidified chamber. My presumption is that this was assembled separately. Kaldresh casings are not formulated to QualCore as they have their own combustion driver. The primary matrix of the detonator has been modified to operate on illegal frequencies. If you taste carefully, you find impressions of four beings handling this within forty-eight hours. I ran a cross-reference with the tastes of known gang members, and I found a match. Ex-Kaldresh employee who went off-grid three years ago after entering our sector before reemerging at a recent funeral. His name is Carl..."

"You keep a database of tastes?" Xanthu was genuinely puzzled.

"What? Wait Carl!?"

The name matched her suspect at the terminal. She checked the address. It's not a match. Now there are two Carls. An odd coincidence That made the matter even more suspicious. She made a mental note of it.

"Yes. *Carl...* Did I say it wrong? Maybe I'm talking with my Schloon again! I'll say it slower. *Carrrrrrlllllllll.* Did you get it? I could say it in multi-variable frequency tones if that's preferred? A different smell perhaps?" said Lazurthus, unknowingly condescending.

"Yeah... I got it thanks. Listen Laz, this one is big. This report is for my eyes or the chief's only. Got it? I'm going to head out and meet this new Carl," said Clinton. She pulled up information about the new Carl on a nearby data terminal.

"Carl is big? He doesn't taste that large... That's only four eyes though?

You'll never get any sense of smell that way... Ohh! You mean this case is top secret. Sorry I wasn't paying attention to my Fgrel. You do know the categorizations of data security right? Or are my words beyond your comprehension?"

"She gets it you big lug! Get out of here Clinton. I'll bag and secure this one myself," said Xanthu.

* * *

Knock knock.

Detective Clinton has arrived at the apartment of Carl. Not the Carl whose life was in a downward spiral. Not the Carl who had been at the tramway station when it exploded Carl. It was the man of the same name. The man whom Harold was searching for when he had his encounter with the old woman. The man Harold had purchased the explosives from. The first man on the list of Carls that Harold had acquired from the birthing center terminal.

"Yeah who is it?" A man's voice said, behind the door.

"EN1149 Detective. Just want to talk okay? You gonna let me in?"

"Yeah... Just a minute, I ain't decent."

She could hear the sound of commotion in the background, and the sound of an opening window. No time for this nonsense. She used her universal key to enter the apartment to see Carl struggling to climb out the window.

"You seem fine to me. It's a long drop to the ground floor. Probably not a good time to take in air pollution. Why don't we start with what you're running from. Save us both the time of the chase."

"I ... I didn't do it. It wasn't me. Whatever it was... I ain't going back!"

"Really and what is it you didn't do? Steal this apartment from a dying old woman?"

The apartment is still pink as the day it was the time Harold had been there previously, except the photographs of the old woman had all been trashed.

"What!? No! That's insane... We were in love!" Carl said, defensively.

He was extremely unnerved by her presence. This was not his first encounter with the Enforcers, and he knew he had continued his legacy of crime. It was always only a matter of time before they caught up with him again. He wasn't sure he had the money to buy himself out this time. Yes, that was how it worked here. For the right amount of money, just about anyone could purchase and bribe their way out of jail. Carl had gone broke doing so before.

"Right. It was so kind and convenient of her to leave you all her money, but that's not why I'm here. Can you recount your whereabouts during the Tramway bombing?" she asked segueing from the obvious crime to catch him off- guard with the hidden one.

"What!? There's been a bombing. I had no idea. That sucks." Carl lied, but badly. His fake surprise lacked the theatrics he needed to be convincing.

"Sure you didn't. Tell me something though. Did you steal the casing from Kaldresh yourself before you left, or did you have a friend on the inside do it?"

She had him now. The details slowly connected him deeper and deeper into the case. *What else does he know?*

"*Ahhhh fuck.* Listen I didn't touch it. I'm just the middleman. You gotta believe me! I didn't know they was going to use it for that. I just made the money exchange. *Business* you know."

Business was always the term of endearment for justifying nefarious and illegal activities. In the name of commerce, virtually everything was acceptable with the right financial exchange in the right amounts.

"Tell me what really happened and I might believe you," she said, switching into good-cop mode.

"Okay! Okay... This guy shows up here a few weeks ago. Political organizer or some shit. He... he had a gun. He shot my dear sweet Margeret, whom I loved dearly, dead right there in the door. Told me if I didn't work for him, he'd kill me too. After he left I was scared. Especially when he kept showing up over here. He was trying to kill another guy named Carl! Maybe he hates Carls? I don't know!"

"Can you describe this man? Would you be able to help us identify him?"

"Yeah, I mean maybe... He was a typical blue-collar human. Kind of fat, you know. About, oh I don't know, about this tall. I was looking more at the gun than him really." He makes portly hand gestures to describe Harold.

"And you delivered the casings to this man? Or the whole thing?"

"No! I didn't touch none of it. He gave me the money. I passed it along to my pal. He hired a delivery. I thought if I did it for him he might not kill me."

"I see... And what was your pal's name? Did he take it straight to this man?"

"*Ha!* You know I can't tell you that. I'd be dead for sure. I ain't no snitch. But naw he had a delivery too," said False Carl.

He was trying to play nice, but the detective was starting to tread into murky waters. Asking him to rat out a coworker was the fastest way to get yourself killed in the crime circles.

"I see... And by chance was *this* the man's delivery? She held up a photo of David from the station cam footage.

"Yeah! That's him alright. He picked it up at the drop point and took it to him."

"I don't suppose you want to take me down to the drop point so I can have a look?"

"Ah, come on! You know I can't. I don't want to get any deeper than I already am!"

Carl was nervous now, as the detective was getting closer to implicating him. She could take him in at any time now. The second fastest way to be killed was to be seen helping an enforcer.

"Come on, Carl. Would you rather I take you in?"

"Okay! Okay! I'm not going to be seen out with you, but I'll show you on the map. It's this bridge here you see?" said False Carl, pulling up the sector map on his terminal.

"Thanks, Carl. You've been *very* helpful. If I need more info I know how to find you."

False Carl breathed a sigh of relief as the detective exited the apartment. She could have easily taken him in, but this had given her a chance to track his movements. Now that he knew she was onto them, the clues would start to get stronger as they raced to hide their tracks. At least that's what she suspected.

Chapter 11

Harold returns a week later to Sector 1149. The route is starting to become too familiar. He starts recognizing his fellow Transit patrons heading home after a long day of work. Every time he leaves, Sheron becomes angry with him. Each time he has a different excuse: working long hours; going out with friends; errands to run. He isn't sure how much longer he can keep this up. This time he is getting desperate. He decides to take the risk and go for a direct all-out assault on Carl. Even if he has to break down the door to his apartment. No risk of bad aim. He is going to walk up to an unsuspecting Carl and just slit his throat right there. *Game over.*

As he approaches the all too familiar building, he backs off from his rage a bit. *Be cool Harold. Be cool. Just be ready.* He watches the door carefully. After an extensive period of waiting, he sees Carl emerge from the lift, heading down the hall towards his apartment. He is waiting to ambush him when he turns to enter the apartment.

Walk. Walk. Walk.

Inserting the key. Turning the knob. Harold raises the knife ready to pounce. When suddenly...

Blehhhhh uahhhh hrrrrr!

A rope is wrapped around Harold's neck, pulling tightly. He drops the knife. Carl, oblivious to the entire situation, sees nothing, walks in and shuts the door.

The airflow running out, Harold struggles to break free.

I am being strangled to death at my own killing spree! What fresh hell is this?

He is brought to his knees now. Almost blacking out. A voice in the back of his mind triggers his fight response. Somehow, he manages to reach backward towards the arms of his attacker. He grasps them tightly and pulls the attacker in an unsuspecting way. He goes flipping over Harold. Stunned in the moment. Harold reaches for the knife before the attacker can return to strangling him and he plunges the knife deep into his chest. The blood drips all over Harold as the attacker collapses on him, a heavy dead weight.

Harold comes to realize the face staring back at him is none other than *Carl!* The wrong Carl. Blood dripping from his mouth, his ravenous eyes still seeking vengeance at Harold as he bleeds out.

"Carl!? Why?! What are you doing?! Why?!"

"I... told... you... this ... happen... they... know.... They... know... Dav... .id... you... every...." The muffled sounds as the wrong Carl starts to lose consciousness. He takes his dying breath only to say, "Fuck you Harold!" and spits in his face before his life departs his body.

Harold is in a weakened state. Still gasping for air, his neck bruised, the rope still hanging loosely. The wrong Carl's dead body pins him to the ground and, for a long moment, he cannot move. *What did he mean they knew? Who was 'they'?* He is devastated. He had almost actually come to consider the wrong Carl as a friend. *I guess this is just a cruel reminder that in this world friends are illusory. Your only true friends are yourself and your money.*

He manages to slide dead Carl off of him and into the floor. He stands up slowly. His suit, *his only suit,* is drenched in drying blood. *This is terrible. What am I going to do? Leave the body? Forget the body, how is this ever going to wash out?*

He stumbles to the nearest stairwell. At the bottom of the stairs, he notices a trash receptacle. He takes off all of his bloody clothes and tosses them into the bin along with the rope and his knife. Just in his boxer shorts now. *Well... This is terrible.* He does the walk of shame to the lobby. The fratty businessmen in the lounge, spotting him, burst into laughter. The doorman is highly concerned about his wellbeing.

"Sir? Are you... forgetting something?" asks the doorman.

"Sorry pal. Bad sexual encounter. No time to explain. Not worth going back for the pants if you know what I mean?" says Harold.

A bizarre, but persuasive answer. Concerns assuaged, he rushes out the door and into the street. He will never make it back to The Transit looking like this. He is afraid to visit the bridge after Wrong Carl's warning. He is back to knowing no one.

Well, almost no one that is... To his saving grace, he sees his first acquaintance heading home. The bartender, shocked and horrified to see a nearly nude, beastly fat man barreling towards him.

Oh! It's that strange Enforcer again. He really must be terrible at his job to keep getting jumped and lost like this.

"Boy, am I glad to see you! Hey, listen, I know this looks crazy, but you gotta help me. I was on an undercover job that went south."

The bartender thinks long and hard about it. He supposes it's alright. Then again no good deed goes unpunished. He isn't crazy about the idea of harboring an Enforcer who is being pursued by nefarious bandits of some sort. Nonetheless, he figures that being in the good graces of the agency might be profitable if they were to say *overlook* some over-serving violations periodically.

"Fine, I'll help you, but just remember this the next time I need a favor? You're not being followed are you?" says the bartender, sighing heavily.

"Thank you! Thank you! No, no. I was able to hide as they came by looking. They're blocks away by now," says Harold, filled with delight. His talent for lies continues to grow.

They proceed to an imposing residential building. It does not have the same decorum as many buildings in the business sector, but it is likely where the service personnel can find 'affordable' homes in the mid-levels. They proceed to the elevator terminals. There are no less than twenty of them, but easily seven of them are broken. There are a few small groups of people congregating in the lobby to wait. They stare curiously at Harold, still in his boxers.

Is this some kind of weird sex thing? Probably. Better take the next one...

With none brave enough to follow Harold and his companion into the lift, they descend about eleven floors. The bartender apologizes for the descent as though his distance downward from the mid-level terrace was somehow more embarrassing than Harold's sweaty undressed form. This attitude is held even by Harold himself who feels it on some level even now in this moment of stress.

Despite the project nature of the building, it has certain amenities that put it a step over Harold's building. *The lift music actually works!* At least in this one. The sound is a bit grainy, but nonetheless makes the creaky journey down more acceptable.

"So, you got a name bartender?" asks Harold, trying to break up the tension.

"No. Not to your knowledge, sir, " says the bartender without missing a beat.

Ah, okay. It was going to be like that then.

The silence is foreboding and awkward, though perhaps justified in the circumstances. He is, after all, doing Harold an act of generosity.

The hallways on this level look more similar to his own. Flickering lights, few if anything in the way of color or decoration. Just another utilitarian concrete box erected in the name of progress, hundreds of stories high. He wonders why sentient beings felt it necessary to fill every available space with rock, but he imagines on this planet they have added so many buildings they likely increased the gravitational weight of it.

"Here we are. I apologize for the condition of things, as you can imagine I was not expecting any guests. I would offer you something in the way of a beverage, but there are more pressing matters to attend to," he says looking down at Harold's form.

"Yeah sure, pal. Nice place you got here. Nice window."

The small apartment has but one window, and it is by no means nice at all, it is just the first thing he can put a visual on. The furniture is a mix-match of handed-down, well-used furniture. All manner of things in this society tend to trickle down. What the rich cast down, the middle-class are happy to take. By the time it reaches the lowers, it is virtually garbage, but everything found its usefulness. In this sense, global trash management tended to be easier than you might expect.

"Let's see if I have anything in... *your* size."

The bartender rummages through his closet, looking for his loosest fitting outfit. Perhaps these pajamas will do the trick. He puts them up in his view towards Harold. *Yes, that might work.* Harold looks on in disapproval.

"This ought to work? Try this on."

Truthfully the idea of Harold's disgusting perspiration infecting his clothes repulses him. As much as he hates to let go of something useful, he doesn't want this back.

The shirt sleeves bulge outward under intense strain. The shirt rides up, unable to come down over his protruding belly. The pants, though elastic at their maximum, are unable to be pulled all the way up. Harold struggles and strains but it is no use. *This isn't going to work.*

"Hold on. I have an idea. Why don't you wait here? Borrow the shower if you'd like. I shall return momentarily."

What can he be up to? Harold is in no position to ask questions. A shower does sound nice. After all he was is still bruised up and covered in dead Carl's dried blood.

The bartender proceeds down the corridor a few apartments away and knocks on the door. A large figured woman answers the door.

"Oh! It's you. What's the occasion?" she says, delighted.

"Sheryl. Might I ask you a favor?" he says, looking at her forlorn.

"Of course! What's the problem sugar?" she asks. He is disgusted by her use of idioms and by her boisterous smiling enthusiasm towards this occasion. He sighs heavily before speaking again.

"There's a man in my apartment and—"

"*OIhhhhhawww.* Is he cute?" she says, curling up her hands in deviant joy.

He stares at her, irritated.

"And as strange and unfortunate as this is going to sound, I was wondering if he might borrow some of your clothes for a few days."

She cackles with delight.

"Kinky! Yeah totally. Come in and have a look."

He rolls his eyes pensively. While his apartment is of modest humble means, hers is something of a veritable garbage dump of color. Strewn with odd statuary, clothes everywhere. It is dirty, unclean, piles of junk abound and he can hardly walk through. It disgusts him to be here.

"How about this?" She shows him something hideous.

"Yes. That will do splendidly, thank you," he says, taking the outfit and holding it between as few fingers as possible so as avoid touching anything more than the minimum of the garment.

"I'll make sure it is returned." He exits the apartment so he can finally breathe again.

He has no real intention of returning it, but she will soon forget anyway. Her stuffed face peers across the edge of the door, watching him as he returns to his apartment, hoping to catch a glimpse of the mysterious man he had wrangled up for the evening.

Harold steps out of the refreshing shower. He feels bad about the state and condition he has left the floor in, the blood and grime dripping off him, just in time to see the bartender standing there with a disgusted look on his face, holding what appears to be a woman's blouse and pants.

"You've got to be joking?" says Harold, half with laughter, half with concern.

"Fine! I'll take them back then. I'm sure your coworkers at the precinct will be delighted to see you *au naturale*. At least this gives you a chance to make it home and change into something more suitable before they see you."

Harold knows he is right. Except that he isn't an Enforcer, and while he has become great at using the plant break rooms to pull off his suit switch, he won't be seen dead going back there in this. Of course, coming home to Sheron wearing another woman's clothes would be even worse!

He looks completely ridiculous in the flowery ruffled outfit. This one fits significantly better of course, but it is egregiously offending to his fragile sense of masculinity. The challenge of social norms is a luxury of the rich because they are able to be the truest form of themselves without fearing the loss of their livelihood. Similarly situated, the poor could also be a truer form of themselves because they had nothing to lose. Life in the middle requires a degree of mass conformity into the narrow bandwidth of that which is most socially acceptable. The one who offends the sensibilities of the whole the least could use their sterility to advance upward. Those who were seen as different, quickly found themselves falling out.

"I look absolutely ridiculous! What am I supposed to do?"

"I haven't the slightest idea, but that's your problem! Now, if you'll excuse me, I hope you have a pleasant evening!" says the bartender, shoving him along towards the door.

The bartender gestures towards the hallway and Harold gets the memo. His assistance has gone above and beyond the call.

"Yeah, I get it. Thanks for helping me out. Means a lot to me."

He begrudgingly steps out into the hall and proceeds back towards the lift, hoping it will be unoccupied. The bartender peaks his head out, looking left and right, hoping no one saw. He sees Sheryl peeking around her door, smiling and giving him the thumbs up. *Wretched woman*, he thinks. Hopefully, she keeps her mouth shut. She already has too many ideas in her head.

The lift terminal at the terrace level is as busy as before. Eyes once again staring at him but for different reasons.

"What are you lookin' at!? See something you like?" says Harold.

They all turn away, minding their own business. That is the other caveat of the mids; saying how you felt about anything publicly is frowned upon. You never want to risk ruin at the hands of being wrong about something or upsetting the wrong person. At home and with one's friends, all bets were off, but outside the door, you put on a mask to match all the other masks. Better to say nothing than to ruffle the feathers.

* * *

Carl hoped they moved the body soon. They've just thrown a sheet over the dead bloody corpse for now. A stabbing right outside his door was the icing on the cake for how terrible his apartment has become. He did the right thing and called the Enforcers, but he hesitated for a while, having hoped someone else would swing by and notice. Then again the last thing he wanted was to be implicated in the deed, especially when he was already working for Gharles. Not that he had made much progress.

"No shit? Your name is Carl? That's funny! The dead guy's name is also Carl. Would you believe that?" said the Enforcer standing before him, laughing as though this were just part of a normal day.

"Yeah that is something, isn't it? Any idea when you might move Carl?" said Carl.

"This a crime scene, buddy! Relax. Stay awhile. We have evidence to collect."

"Come on though, it's starting to smell up the corridor!"

"Excuse me sir, could you stop your apartment from flooding? It's tainting our evidence," said another Enforcer, inspecting the body under the sheet.

"I wish! Unfortunately, it's entirely necessary for the survival of my goldfish."

It had already been a long day, the last thing Carl wanted was to be dealing with a dead corpse in the hallway. He imagined the bloodstains would eternally grace the hallway carpet because no one would ever clean it. There was hope that perhaps the water leaking through the walls might dilute some of it away.

He wasn't sure what to do during this time of waiting. He had already scrambled to hide all of his weapons and valuables. Fortunately, the Enforcers seem to have little to no interest in entering his apartment, and he wants to keep it that way. He was kind of hungry, but what should he eat? *What goes well with a slab of hallway corpse?*

* * *

Detective Clinton changed into street clothes before leaving the precinct again. Hollander approached her, asking for an update. She had no idea about Carl's murder and the subsequent investigation.

"Alright detective, what's the news?" he asked.

"We analyzed the bomb fragments, sir, and I was able to locate a suspect, Carl. I had a very productive interview with him. I just put in a tracer to track his movements. It appears that this suspect was the financial middleman in the bomb transaction. He provided me with the location of the transaction, and I'm on my way to scope it out now. There was a second middle man, a receiver named David. He's just a kid, a ghost hire, but I think he can lead us to the architect. Showed up on station cam at the Tramway too. I think he will be an easy target. I'm going to bring him into the station for questioning."

"Great work so far detective! Why don't you take Rusfelt and Kaaringer with you to watch your back. Might be good in case you have a runner or get into trouble."

"My thoughts exactly chief. I'll see if they're available."

With her team secured and a well-defined plan in place, she set out for the location Carl had identified for her on the sector map. It was in a high crime area of the sector often overlooked because of the vast economic support provided by the seedy businesses that took place around it. The Enforcer policy was typically one of containment in these areas. As long as they stayed within the few-block radius, they were mostly left alone. Hence her need for street clothes. Enforcers were known to be targets in these parts.

She proceeded alone to the bridge. A small group of questionable individuals were gathered there. She tried her best to appear like a normal customer looking for vice.

"What's your pleasure sweetheart? Candy? Xtat, Blackwings? Raxdust? Pappa's got everything you need right here at good price." The man approached her with genuine interest in her business. She monitored the situation closely, trying not to look apprehensive.

"Not my style, friend. I'm looking for someone specific," she said, casually.

"Well, we don't know anyone specific around here do we? A chorus of agreement erupts around him.

"Relax. Just a business opportunity. I'm looking for Davy Blue Eyes. Any of y'all seen him around lately?"

"And what *business* does Davy have with you exactly?"

"I got a friend who wants to meet him for a *private* job that his talents are well suited for."

"Ah! A recruiter. Wise choice that one. Your client best be rich though. Boy like that come at high price. They want experience, they come to Pappa.

I got *talents* like you never knew," he said, laughing.

"I don't make the rules. He has a certain type. But if you see him, let him know I'm hunting," she said, before departing the area.

The rowdy gang of nefarious individuals laugh off their distrust of her. There is nothing that needs to be indirect here. Ask and you shall receive. They perceived her as green and thus not a threat to their operations. Her infiltration was successful and she would have her search unencumbered by difficulties.

As she crossed under the bridge, a voice called to her from the shadows at her back.

"Heard you was lookin' for Davy. What's it to you? I might know the guy."

"Yeah, as a matter of fact I am. This is a *premium* offer. Room and board. High pay. High-status client. Ascension package. Think he would be interested?"

The shadow figure stepped out from the wall, arms folded, unmistakable eyes. This was him. This was her suspect. It had to be.

"He might be. What's the hook?" he inquired, all too casually.

"You must be David. I'm sure of it. Does it matter who they are if they have the cash? You perform *services* as requested for the buyer, otherwise you have free reign of the house commons. Come with me. I'll set up a private meeting. We can work up the details, give you a taste of the life afforded. You in?"

"Well, it might. I have my limits. I suppose a meeting wouldn't hurt. What's the term contract?"

"Up to five years. Option to renew, depending on your sales," she said, knowing it's a lucrative deal. She just failed to mention the buyer was in fact the justice system, and the house commons would be the prison cafeteria.

"Alright. I'll go with you. No bullshit though. You waste my time, you waste my money, and we'll have a serious problem, you got it?" he said, with an intense gaze.

"Understood!"

He followed her out of the district, out of the view of his cronies where no one could see what happened next. As they approached the vehicle, he noticed the Enforcer tags on the plates. His suspicion and alarm rose. He carefully picked her pocket to reveal her Enforcer ID Badge. He reached for his knife.

"Looks like we have a problem," said David.

He lunged for her and she deflected the attack, the knife slashing through her coat. She stumbled backward, falling as he takes off running. He had to get back to warn the others. *An ambush!*

Two additional officers cut him off at the alley before he even got a chance. He fought hard to get away and it took both of them to subdue him enough to get him into the Enforcer hovercar. With David securely in custody, they checked on Officer Clinton. She was a bit roughed up but it was nothing serious. She headed to the car for a debriefing with David before they went downtown to the precinct, struggling to catch her breath.

"I kind of figured you wouldn't go willingly. Want to tell me why we're running today? Something you're hiding? I'm listening. Tell me what I need to know so we can get you back out on the streets. Otherwise, we can go down to the station and work this out the hard way."

"Not afraid of no Enforcer raid and I got nothing to say. You and I both know the judge is going to rule for me. I didn't do nothing that wasn't strictly business. Your case to lose detective."

David was suddenly more hostile, sounding ignorant. He became foolish when angry. Perhaps he wasn't as mature as he thought he was.

"Is that right? Sounds like you've chosen the hard way then," she said, closing the door.

The Enforcer hovercar fired up to make a swift return to the precinct. There was no trouble on the way back and no audience at the precinct. *A successful pick-up.* She brought him in through a side security entrance to keep it on the low.

They set David up in a cold, dark interrogation room. All there was, was a table with two hard metal chairs. The light overhead was dim and flickering. Ahead of David was what he could only presume was a two-way mirror window. They left him alone for quite some time before officer Clinton finally entered to begin the task.

"David… Let's start with a simple question. Why are you here?"

"Could it be because you brought me here?"

"Don't get smart with me, David. You know what this is about, so let's just go ahead and say it."

"I can't speak to what I don't know. Why are you here!?"

He doesn't talk anymore. They stared each other down intensely.

The accidental confession is too smart for him. Time to shift to a different tactic and go for something more personal.

"David. This is not your first encounter with law enforcement. Your RAP sheet is pretty extensive for someone so young. This is your fourth infraction with us and it's a pretty severe one. That comes with a mandatory sentence in juvenile detention, after which you will no longer be able to decline entry into the foster system, and you will have no choice but to descend. Is that what you want?"

Silence from David. He won't budge for a second. A tough one to crack. He wasn't going to grant her that satisfaction. Time to go straight to family matters.

"Wouldn't you rather be at home with your parents and siblings? Why didn't you descend with them? I'm sure they miss you down there. You could get back to them, you know. We can make all this go away. No more life under the bridge. I just need you to tell me what I need to know."

"Having seen my options for housing and line of work up to this point, why would you think I would be persuaded by the idea of a degraded family life in that wretched place? Better to take my chance up here with you, in jail. You want me to talk? You pay the same rate everyone else does. You want me to testify? You pay the same rate everyone else does. Strictly *business*," said David, having fully recovered his calculating confidence.

"See, that's where you're wrong David. We've already talked to Carl. We have the weapon fragments in our possession and I have a positive camera identification of you at the Tramway stalking another Carl."

"Then I guess you don't need me after all," he said calmly. Inside he was terrified of her knowledge and control, but he tried to save face with a rugged exterior.

"Why don't you start by telling me what you were doing there on the day of the blast?"

"Sounds like you already know. I was just minding my business. You're just making up inferences now."

"Perhaps a short stay in the precinct jail will get you talking... Of course, this is your big chance to tell your side of the story. Otherwise, we'll just have no choice but to accept Carl's full testimony against you. You'll probably end up in one of those for-profit youth prison labor camps in Sector 749. Given your *line of work,* I think you'll be very popular there... It's *just business,* right? How about some information and I might let you out of here?" she said. Her final offer.

"Why don't you save us both some time and read my rights. State a charge or let me go. It's getting late and you know how long processing takes."

"Tonight let's make it soliciting business without a permit and see how it goes. Then if you still don't feel like talking, we can try accessory to terrorist attack."

"Don't insult my intelligence, Detective. You know I can get both dismissed on age. You know I'm the *real* victim here right?" he said, finally pulling the youth card.

"We'll see how confident you feel about that in a few days. I can drag this out on at least a dozen other counts and procedural maneuvers. You'll be staying here for quite some time."

"Free meals and a warm bed? Best room in Capital City. Does it have plumbing too?"

"Just remember, Davy, *it can always be worse,*" she said with a smile.

The interrogation didn't go as planned. Throwing this kid in jail wasn't exactly the look she was going for, but this was no ordinary investigation. If David wasn't going to talk, she would be back to waiting for Carl to screw up. Of course, she had not interviewed other Carl yet, but that's what made the next news so unsettling. She escorted David to the booking area and begun her paperwork.

"Ma'am, sorry to bother you, but we've run into a problem with that trace you put out..." It was a rookie enforcer sent to deliver the news. That was never good.

"Well. It might not be a problem. What's the news?" she said, trying to be nice.

"The recovery team extracted Carl's body shortly after 11:48 pm. He was found dead at 1726 Oakwood at the Residences of Transvermidian. Fourth floor hallway right outside of 467. Get this though! The guy who found him outside his apartment was also named Carl! Can you believe it? Medical examiner's report not-withstanding it looks like an open-shut stab wound case."

This was truly devastating news for her. The chief witness in her case had just been murdered before she even had a chance to track him. Now he was a dead end and so was her case. She needed a new plan fast before Hollander got word of this.

"Wait!? Did you say Carl found Carl?!"

"Yeah! That's what I said. Isn't that something? Small world, I mean huge giant world, but what are the odds. I mean come on!?"

"Pleaseeeee tell me it occurred to you that maybe... just maybeeee, Carl might have killed Carl?"

"*Ohhhh.* Yeah nooooo. We probably should have thought of that first, shouldn't we? Want us to bring him in?" he said, as though it was the first time he had ever worked there.

"No! I'll do it myself when the time is right. Get an extra evidence team up there though. I want to know everything. And I mean every microbe. Cut out the carpets if you have to. Just keep this low. I don't want anyone to know Carl is a suspect. I can't have suspects getting offed before depositions, so do not say a word of this to Carl until I give you the go-ahead with the evidence," she barked at him, half expecting him to ask her *which Carl?*

She couldn't risk losing yet another potential accomplice or witness. She would have to bring this one in like she had brought in David. This one would be more difficult. A person of general business class with off-world access permits and a shuttle could disappear easily. Carl might have thought he'd got away with murdering his associates, but he would still be on edge. She wanted the dust to settle first. Keep him under observation like she had meant to do for other Carl.

The question then is why would Carl want to kill Carl? Unless of course Carl didn't kill Carl at all. But if so, who did?

"Working late or hardly working?" It is Lt. Xanthu with a hot beverage in one hand and a data recorder the other.

"Xanthu! What are you still doing here? I'm exhausted honestly, but I'm so close now. This case is getting stranger by the second though. I should probably give it a rest, but I know I won't sleep until I get at least one more answer."

"I have something that might cheer you up. Can you *taste what I'm thinking!?* Ha! No but really here's the report that you asked for on sector entry and exit data for mass-transit. Cross-referenced, analyzed, and sorted for your pleasure."

"Xanthu... I never asked for that?"

"I know you didn't, but you can thank me later. Take a look at the data. A few red flags here and there, but look what happens when you cross it for re-entries post-op. We started documenting entry reasons and look at this one," he said, pointing to the data pad.

"You're too good to me, you know that? What's significant about this entrant? 'Entry for adoption papers.' That's fairly typical enough?"

"On its face *yes*, but is it not the slightest bit suspicious that it says he's adopting *David*? Is that a common human name? I truly don't know, but it was enough for me to think to look at it. Turns out he's never been to the agency a day in his life. No record of the guy whatsoever."

"Xanthu, you almost make a good detective sometimes!"

"You'd be surprised what I can be good at," he said, flirtatiously.

She read the datapad.

Mulknosh sector. Harold. Industrial worker. Mid-Lvl +3. Threat-Level 0. No known affiliations. Wife: Sheron. Son: Thomas. Daughter: Martha.

What is this guy doing here? Look at these entry stamps. How did he even get travel permissions for this? I don't recognize that card signature pattern. Why is he coming here?

"That's your guy right? It's got to be."

"It's worth a shot anyway. Thanks Xanthu. I can rest easy for now."

Chapter 12

To say it was a late night would be an understatement. Harold manages to stumble his way home, mocked for wearing his borrowed blouse. Surely Sheron is asleep? He will sneak into the house quietly and just throw them away before she noticed. Slowly he opens the door. The apartment is completely silent. He creeps toward the back room. He's almost gotten away with it.

"Hayrollllld!? Where have you been? Do you have any idea what time it is and— Are you...!? Are you wearing another woman's clothes!? Who is she, Harry? Is that why you're always at the bars until all hours of the night!? You look ridiculous. Explain yourself, Harold. And it better be a very compelling reason."

"For Huacovia's sake, Sheron! Quiet down. I don't want the kids to see me this way! It's nothing, Sheron. I lost a Fljrkhorn bet is all" he says.

It is quite convincing. Harold would be stupid enough to wager his clothing for the sake of Fljrkhorn. The level of obsessive lust that Harold has for the game is repulsive to Sheron, but since Thomas became a star player, she has come to find it acceptably interesting.

"I wish you would come home more. The kids miss you... I miss you. And I'm tired of doing everything around this damn house while you're out throwing back Pilquist at one of those disgusting disrespectful bars!"

"There's absolutely nothing disrespectful about my bars! Disgusting maybe," he yells back.

"Whatever, Harold! You men are *all* alike. Going out to those bars where girls reveal their tentacles for the whole world to see!"

"They're not strippers, Sher! They're servers... They serve food and stuff!"

The argument is terminal at this point. They both spend the rest of their night in total silence. This is of course no problem for Harold.

* * *

The week unfolds slowly with Harold deciding to chill on murdering Carl for a while. He still very much wants to, but he needs to let things settle down since his last slip up. Unfortunately, an even more dreaded matter presents itself for attention.

He flails his way into the morning meeting. Xvranbul is in rare form today. Her blob-like body is not only a shape but also her *mental form*. She is almost cheerful. This is never good.

Perhaps it's layoffs? Another lower-level extermination? Who knows.

"Good morning....Whoever you all are. I have the esteemed pleasure of inviting everyone to our company picnic this Sunday!"

"But Sunday is our only day off!" a voice cries from the crowd.

Xvranbul continues, unphased by the interruption, " We hope to see you in attendance, otherwise we'll have to fire you. Bring your families! That way the kids can see what an abysmal failure and disappointment you are. Mr. Barbados regrets to inform you that he won't be in attendance. Not because he can't be there, but rather because he regrets being invited. 743 boxes today! Let's roll people. And remember, it could always be worse!"

Ugh! The cursed family picnic.

The very term of it is absurd as there was neither fresh food or resources on this planet, nor could you sit outside and enjoy them. Rather, such events were a serving of slop held in the company meeting hall. While the event is allegedly voluntary, Harold knows his presence is required if he plans to continue working there.

This is made worse by Sheron's overly abundant enthusiasm for the picnic every year. No doubt he will end up spending a fortune on whatever absurd dish she's concocted this year. She will force the whole family to don their formal attire and arrive early to greet the human members of the company. He just hopes she doesn't say anything too outrageously offensive in the presence of his alien coworkers.

Legend has it that the humans once spent a few millennia consumed by racist violence. Small changes were made and it eroded over time, but the first discovery of other sentient beings in the galaxy had spearheaded a remarkable cultural change. This was not because they improved upon their character or their understanding, but rather they found an entirely new group with which all of humanity could hate, defile, and discriminate against.

As long as you are human you are automatically held in higher esteem amongst other humans. Certain groups of aliens that resembled humans were, over time, considered more acceptable, becoming part of the *us* in the *us vs. them* dichotomy. The less human you look, the worse type of alien you are considered. Unless of course, you are profitable, because money can wash away all matters of xenophobia and racism.

* * *

The day of the picnic is every bit as disappointing as he knew it would be.

"Mom... I don't understand why we have to go to this stupid picnic anyways!" says Thomas, already whining.

"Thomas! This is a big networking opportunity! These are people that can help you get a job later in life. Be agreeable!" says Sheron.

"As if I would *ever* want to work in this shithole!" he snaps.

Harold nods approvingly. He would rather Thomas never have to step foot in this place again either, but nonetheless, practical realities necessitated the false pleasantries.

Harold speaks up if only to keep the peace as Martha is about to give Thomas the *what-for* over his rudeness. Tact and restraint are not becoming of a child her age, but she understands justice and right from wrong.

"Family... Please. Let us get through this insufferable day in silence. I want to see all of you on your best behavior. Fake pleasantries everyone. Smile like you care!" says Harold.

A collective eye roll of understanding comes from the family. Harold sets down Sheron's strange and expensive dish of gelatinous garbage, among a table of similar delicacies. The entire company meeting hall screams 'cheap' in its decorum. It is as though its utilitarian purpose was enough to decorate it, because it merely exists to their gratitude.

Xvranbul is the first to approach them. He recoils in disgust as her large body slithers across the floor toward them.

"Oh, Sheron! You've really outdone yourself this time. That looks wonderful! And your kids... Martha, so well behaved! Thomas, I heard you are quite the rising Fljrkhorn star! Hopefully, you can make something of yourself, unlike your father! No offense, Sheron! But you should have left Herbert years ago!" she says. Then she laughs hysterically, as though she knows them on any personal level.

"It's Harold, ma'am! Now don't you have other employees to torment?" he says, begrudgingly. The family laughs at him. Xvranbul's deep, scratchy voice is gurgling with laughter too. Her whole body quivering, jiggling sacks of fat. He is repulsed by her.

"Right. Whatever. Now Sheron, you just let me know! I'll make it look like an accident, no one will ever see him again!" she slithers away.

Xvranbul being in management makes her an acceptable enough of an alien to Sheron. Again, she serves an economic benefit to the family. Thomas is keenly aware of her prejudices and in his teenage angst seeks to play off of them. They greet the human families with fake smiles and handshakes; discussions of all sorts, most of them carefully promoting the usefulness of Thomas. They can buy, sell, or trade him like a used hovercar, to suit whatever mundane task they needed.

"Oh hey, Dad! Isn't that your friend Geordon? *The Y'tarian.*" Says Thomas. He makes sure to say it loud enough so that those around them can hear him, including his mother.

"We're not *friend* friends! He's just a work acquaintance that I happen to hang out with after work on a regular basis," says Harold, trying to defend why he would ever associate with such a reviled, hideous alien as that.

"Ah come on, Dad! Let's go say hello! Friendly faces right? Wouldn't want to miss out on this networking opportunity would I, Mom?" says Thomas.

Sheron grits her teeth trying to maintain her composure. "Thomas what are you doing? It's bad enough they let *them* come to these, much less having to talk to one!"

Sheron is trying desperately to steer them away, but it is too late. Thomas has waved to Geordon and he and his family meander over to them.

Their disgusting centipede-like legs scurry in unison towards them, their brown exoskeletons ripe with that fresh insectoid smell. Their mouth pincers and antenna flicker with each motion, their clothing loosely fitting over their subdivided bodies. It is truly difficult to determine who is who. Sheron says they all look alike.

"Hiya, Geordon! Mom was just talking about you guys! She was saying how great it would be to have all of you over at the house sometime. It's just been too long, right Mom?" says Thomas.

Sheron smiles awkwardly – uncomfortable, speechless.

Someone please say something to keep this conversation moving.

The eyes of the room are always on the Y'tarians; you never know when they might steal something, or choke you in your sleep, or gobble up one of your children. She knows Thomas only did this out of spite for her forcing him to attend. *Why would he tarnish the family by indulging this?*

"Hi, Thomas. Congrats on your win last week! Blindaara and I were very impressed. Artynon says he's ready to play next year."

Geordon is gracious and kind. *He had attended a game?* Harold has forgotten yet again that there are games to attend. In his quest to murder Carl, he's forgotten all about his fatherly duties.

"Yes, Thomas. Very impressive! Thank you again for getting Tyxlynor on the team. It really meant the world to us."

Blindaara is a kind soul as well, hideously similar in appearance to her husband Geordon. Harold has no idea how they can tell the difference.

"Are you kidding? He's our best Ground Guard. Who else can stretch to defend two goals at once? I should be thanking you for letting him play! Where is he anyway?" asks Thomas.

In this moment, Harold is realizing that his own son knows the family of his work comrades better than he does. Sheron is most horrified by this. *My son has been talking to Y'tarians behind my back!* She thought of all the awful things that could happen to him.

At this moment, Tyxlynor comes running up towards them. Sheron throws up her hands, apprehensive of her own death. He intertwines with Thomas in some sort of jocular *bro-hug.* Something of a fistbump if Y'tarians had anything in the way of fists or traditional hands.

"Tyxlynor! What's up, man? That was a great play the other day. We never would have won if you hadn't made that double block."

They proceed to have a friendly conversation about all matters of things from their sports team to the homework they have in class.

Blindaara speaks directly to Sheron from one mother to another.

"Oh, Sheron, your dish was simply delightful this year!" says Blindaara.

Sheron's legendary false enthusiasm is struggling to find itself. "*Oooohhhh...* Well you can have it then!" says Sheron. She doesn't want it back knowing they had eaten from it.

How bizarre.

You don't have to understand alien facial expressions to recognize Blindaara is clearly confused as though she has walked into a cultural misunderstanding. She graciously thanks Sheron for the dish. *Humans are certainly strange.* Geordon and Harold look at each other, shaking their heads. Sheron is holding onto Martha for dear life.

"So your wife made you come to this too?" says Harold.

Sheron jabs him in the side. "Harold!"

"Ah you know, Harold, we don't get out much as a family.... *Ha!* But yeah pretty much. It's my day off. Come on? Haven't they seen us enough this week?" says Geordon.

"My thoughts exactly. Have you seen Baab anywhere?"

"I don't know Harold, have you checked under the flyswatter?" They both laugh. Seems that everyone is getting along splendidly except Sheron.

Baab can be seen flying towards them at that very moment. A tiny Y'tarian on his back. Sheron isn't sure which repulses her more.

"Again, Uncle Baab, again!" The tiny Y'tarian pleads for a continuation of the flight. Baab is winded and sets her down gently.

"That's... all... for.. today... I'm not a.. young.. larvae... anymore!" says Baab, exhausted.

Blindaara makes the introduction. "Have you met our youngest daughter, Fuulderna? She'll be starting first-tier school next year. Perhaps you and Martha could be friends?"

Innocent Martha is delighted to have a new friend, but Sheron holds onto her tightly.

"Oh... why of course! Maybe they will have the same classes," says Sheron in her fakest Mom voice. She hopes they don't. Seeing such a hideous beast with Thomas makes her blood boil enough as it is.

"Hey, Harold. Geordon and I been wondering where you been lately! You keep saying you're going to come out, but you leave us hanging! *Hello!* I'm not getting any younger here. Short lifespan you know," says Baab.

Baab has walked him into a bit of a conundrum with that one.

Fuck, Baab! Why did you have to go there? You had one job. To not say shit. But you said that.

Sharon glares at Harold. "Yes Harold. What *have* you been doing lately?"

"Baab you old fool! You've clearly had so much to drink you've forgotten we went out just last night!" Harold gives him and Geordon *the look.* Baab walks it back.

"*Ohh* man, I must have really been gone last night! *Uh oh!* Senior moment!" says Baab. They tried to laugh it up, but Sharon is pretty amped up.

"Well I would hate to cut this party short, but I'm afraid it is getting time for us to go. Very busy day right Harold?" she says.

Mission accomplished.

Thomas had pissed her off enough that they can leave early. Played like a fiddle. Harold is thrilled.

"Ah, yes of course dear!" says Harold.

"Gordan, Blendera, always a pleasure!" says Sheron. They wave their goodbyes or at least as well as they are capable of, as Sheron butchers their names. A lost cause really.

Sheron doesn't speak as they walk back to their building in total silence.

Not a moment after entering the lift, her dynamic changes. She bitchslaps Thomas across the face.

"*Ow! What did I do? Fuck!*" he says with shock.

"You know what you did! And it's okay if you hang out with *them* at school I guess... They're not *all* bad... I just don't want *them* in our house!" she says.

Harold might have defended Thomas in this instance if he were not already in the doghouse with her.

"And as for *you*, Heyyyrold! You're on thin ice with me. Just tell me who she is okay? What makes her so great?"

He just lets her vent. She is obviously under a great deal of stress and anything he says will only make it worse, so he just stays silent while she berates him.

"What you have nothing to say!? *Nothing?*"

The lift doors open and not a moment too soon. She snaps back into normal mode. *Best company picnic in years if you asked Harold!*

Back at the apartment Sheron and Harold continue the matter in private.

"I know what you're thinking and I know I've been distant lately, but I just need you to trust me. It's all about the money," says Harold.

He thinks she might be pleased to hear that it is a matter of money, but he is wrong.

"That's all it ever is with you, Harold. When will it be a matter of family?"

To make matters worse he answers her rhetorical question. "How about when all the bills are paid?"

She screams at him to get out.

If that's how she feels about it, he would just go ahead and go. She won't be screaming when they're rich.

It is time for another trip to kill Carl.

He storms out of the apartment, much to the surprise of Sheron. She has expected him to stay and fight, but he actually leaves. Thomas has his suspicions. After piecing together all the events he has heard and witnessed, he takes it upon himself to investigate the matter. *What was Dad really up to?* He decides to follow him.

* * *

He trails behind Harold who seems to be on a deliberate mission. Thomas just barely makes it onto the Transit car. He will now have the difficult task of trying to monitor Harold from the next railcar to see what station he gets off at. He hopes he has enough money for the trip. This isn't a line he normally takes.

Where was he going?

Two transfers later Thomas barely manages to track Harold. "*Sector 1149 next exit.*" Harold rises again. *Another transfer? What was this? Wait. Wasn't that the sector in the news recently? What business can Dad possibly have here?*

Security is tight at the station. Thomas is funneled into an outside entry line along with Harold. He sees Harold up ahead talking to the security guard. He listens carefully to isolate his voice amongst the crowded station. *What is he telling the guard? Something about adoption... ? What is he talking about?* Thomas is determined more than ever to find out. He pushes his way toward the entry gates.

"Hold up, kid. What brings you into the sector today?" says the guard.

He freezes and says the first thing on his mind. "I got a date?"

"Really now? What's their name then?"

"It's... Harolda!" he says, barely coherent.

"Oh yeah? And where is you and *Har... harolda?* Going?" he asks, laughing.

He thinks back to the last advertisement he saw. What was that film that is out in theaters?

"The movies sir. *Ganthor the Terrible.* Looks great doesn't it?" he says, knowing damn well that a movie would be the worst place to take a first date. You can't possibly hold a conversion there.

"Yeah, man. I'm sure she'll love it. You come out all this way you must really like this dame. Alright, you're in. Enjoy your stay! And happy hunting," says the guard, in a vulgar display of fraternity.

Thomas runs as fast as he can toward Harold, through the crowded terminus, catching glimpses of him in the distance. *Almost losing him.* One sharp turn and he will be gone. Fortunately, Harold has no idea he is being followed, so Thomas is able to catch up with him again unseen.

Harold heads toward a nefarious-looking streetway, littered with drug shops, casinos, and houses of ill repute. Thomas is nervous. He tends to keep it clean-cut and this isn't his scene. He is disappointed already. Whatever Harold is doing here it can't be good.

They come to a bridge where Harold stops to look for something. *Or is it someone?* A scantily clad prostitute approaches Harold, her hoop earrings glistening in the neon lights around her. He listens in to their conversations, but he can tell she's not happy.

"Where is David!? Have you seen him?" asks Harold.

"You got some nerve coming back here! David is gone. He got picked up in a raid last night. Haven't seen him since."

"That's terrible! Did they say what it was about?" says Harold, genuinely concerned for his own safety mostly.

"It wasn't a normal raid, I can tell you that. They only sent one this time. Undercover bitch. She went straight for him. Probably something to do with you I suspect."

"Oh geez. This is bad. This is really really bad!"

"Damn straight it's bad. I expect you to fix this. We got our eyes out for you. After that stunt you pulled, you want to be the boss, you gotta handle shit like a boss. Take care of your boy," she says, thumping him on the forehead.

Thomas is shocked by what he is hearing and starts to piece things together. *Adoption? David?* In his mind, the concerns compound, and he comes to the farfetched conclusion that Harold has been living a secret double life where he fathered a child with this prostitute.

He would have continued his eavesdropping, but for a voice from behind him.

"Didn't your mamma teach you it's not polite to stare? How about I give you something to look at instead." The alien woman pulls at her shirt, partially revealing herself sensually.

"*Ah! Umm* no thanks. I really should be going," he says. This is too much. He gets out of there as fast as he can. Straight back to the station.

"What's the rush, hon? Am I *too much* woman for you? Name your price.

Discount 'cause you're cute. Am I your first? Let my experience teach you!" She continues her spree of solicitation as he flees the scene.

The entire Transit ride home, the thoughts fill his mind. *Harold is going to leave them?* Then he would have to drop out and get a job at the factory. All the worst-case scenarios go through his mind. Something else is odd. There is a woman who seems to be getting on and off at all the same stops. *A strange coincidence.* He feels like he is following her as she conveniently walks into his apartment building ahead of him.

She exits the lift onto the same level as him and proceeds towards his apartment. He keeps his distance from her, not knowing her intentions. He sees her knock on the door to his home. Sheron answers the door.

* * *

"Harold? Oh hi, you must be Mrs. Harold! I'm Ms. Milton, I'm with the agency! Mind if I come in for a moment," says the mysterious stranger at the door.

The agency? What agency? Sheron is intrigued. *What was this about?*

"The agency? I'm sorry I wasn't expecting you. What is this about again?"

"Didn't Harold tell you? I've brought some papers for you to sign. The deal is almost finalized now, I just need to do a quick home study," says Ms. Milton.

"No. He didn't mention it. What kind of papers exactly?"

"For the adoption of course! David is such a great kid. I'm sure you'll give him a very nice home here!"

"Excuse me!? What are you talking about? Wait. What are you saying? Are you saying my Harold is trying to adopt some kid? You must be mistaken. My Harold would do no such thing, and certainly not without discussing it with me," says Sheron, shocked, disgusted, and laughing all at the same time.

"Oh dear! I do hope I got the *right* spouse. The paperwork made it seem like you were both in on this. I'm terribly sorry, is there another wife I can speak to?"

"No, it's all me."

"Then this must be awful news coming from me!" says Ms. Milton. She's caught Harold in a lie. Now it's time to gather information.

"I had my suspicions that Harold was cheating, but this? This is something else entirely. Let me see those forms. I want to know *her* name!"

"I'm sorry, ma'am, unfortunately, the files are confidential, but here let me give you my card just in case. Our office is in sector 1149"

"1149? Oh I'm terribly sorry you came all this way, and I know it's been rough there, we saw the news! What in the world was my Harold doing all the way over there?"

"Oh, I would rather not get involved in your private affairs. You have a nice night now!" Officer Clinton has successfully baited the trap. By walking away now she leaves Sheron in disarray. She will surely confront Harold and in doing so will likely extract critical information. Information she hopes that Sheron will share with her the next time she calls.

Thomas enters just as she is leaving, snapping a quick but secret photograph of her as she left on his comm.

"Who was that, Mom?" asks Thomas. He couldn't hear enough of their conversation to make out what was going on.

"Oh just someone from corporate! They had some paperwork they needed me to sign. Nothing to worry about," says Sheron.

They both have things to worry about, but neither of them wants to upset the feelings of the other, so they keep their fake composure and go about their separate days.

* * *

Harold has no idea what he is going to do, but rescuing David is the least of his concerns. If he isn't careful they will discover it was him all along. All can be handled once he is rich. This time he decides to take smaller actions towards murdering Carl.

He has been secretly fabricating them from pieces of scrap at his job. The small disc-like objects have sharp metal edges that if thrown hard enough will lodge themselves deep inside of Carl's jugular vein. If he hits him enough times or in the right place, he will bleed out and that will be the end of it.

As Carl leaves his building and heads down into a commercial zone, Harold tracks him to a small bar, where Carl typically meets his coworkers. He casually slips in among the patrons. At this point, Carl still has never seen him. He can get close without Carl ever noticing. The bar is unusually crowded for the evening due to the current hour's drink specials.

The place is dimly lit and there is a great deal of commotion. People going in and out. All of them wear suits, it is almost disorienting to try and find Carl. At least he can rule out the aliens as a possible match. It isn't a great deal unlike many of the bars Harold goes to, except the place is cleaner and the drinks are a bit uppity. *Oh and nothing in the way of titties, a total sausage fest.* Harold scopes out Carl and orders a Pilquist Red. *Why so basic Harold?*

Carl gets up from his barstool and starts to make his way through the masses towards the back. Harold follows him. He opens his side satchel for quick access to his new weapons. Carefully, he lifts the first throwing disc. He aims it straight for the back of Carl's head. *Whoosh!* It flies through the air. A complete miss. It veers to the left lodging itself deep into another patron's skull. He falls forward into the crowd. *Better be quick Harold.*

He grabs another. *Whoosh! Whoosh!* He hurls two of them in rapid succession. Both of them hit unsuspecting bystanders who happen to walk right in front of him at the most inopportune moment. At this point, people are starting to somewhat come to and react. *Last chance Harold!*

One after the other he hurls the throwing discs. *Whoosh! Whoosh Whoosh!* People are now scrambling to get out of the rain of fire. Carl somehow is still unaware, heading to the back. The place is in a panic as people run towards the exit. Not a single disc hits Carl! *Of all the bad luck, mine is the worst.*

Carl disappears through a back door. Harold is now in fast pursuit. He bursts through the door, throwing a disc at the unsuspecting patron at the urinal. *Fuck! It isn't Carl!? How is this possible? He had just come through this door Where did he go?*

The bartender springs into action bolting the bathroom door shut, locking Harold inside, giving patrons a chance to escape.

It turns out that Carl had inadvertently chosen the ladies' room. Being that the bar has few if any ladies, he hadn't even noticed at all. He emerges from the bathroom to find the bar abandoned, less a pile of bleeding and dying corpses, including many of his former coworkers.

That's just rude, thinks Carl. *How could they die without him?* He stepped over the bodies. *Oh no! Not Tyrell from accounting! And Jvrisnos from the sales department! Whatever would they do without whatever it is these people do at wherever it was they worked?*

Probably already replaced with even less memorable coworkers. It is a great inconvenience to die because it takes years to get their replacements to even remember his name.

"Well, that's one way to get out of a bar tab. Hello? Anyone alive?" asks Carl. *Again? This is the third time I've almost been murdered this month. Better get out now in case the killer decides to come back.*

He takes a quick drink of a random shot on the bar and then proceeds calmly to the exit and out into the streets. He can hear the enforcer sirens blaring as they come down the boulevard. Having already seen enough murders in recent memory, he feels it prudent that he should not be present as a witness for this moment.

Harold frantically pulls at the door. *It's locked! What is he going to do?* He kicks it. He body slams it. It doesn't budge. He looks around the room. *A window!* The window is high up. He struggles for a moment, obesely trying to pull himself up, but it's no use. He grabs the ceramic backing from one of the toilets and smashes it into the door. It shatters, but the door is unpersuaded.

Just as his desperation kicks in, he realizes the utter stupidity of his ways. The door may have been locked from the outside, but the locking bolt was on the inside. He turns it and it unlocks with ease. *What an idiot!* Finding no sign of Carl, he makes a mad dash through the bar. With the place emptied out, he ransacks the bar for top-shelf liquor bottles. He steals the cash from the tip jars and the register. He checks the pockets of the victims for wallets and cash. Then he smashes a few bottles on the floor and lights the place on fire with a match. *That ought to keep the enforcers busy and royally fuck up the evidence.* He may not have got Carl, but he isn't walking out of here empty-handed. He runs out the door and down an alleyway just before the Enforcers arrive on scene.

He boards the Transit with his now overflowing satchel, like a distasteful Santa Clause that takes the toys instead of giving them. His holly-jolly fat ass is elated. While he didn't kill Carl, he has stolen no less than twenty credit cards. He will take them out to different sectors tomorrow and try to rack them up before the families reported them dead. He can buy Sheron's silence with a thick sack of bar cash and can enjoy a crisp overpriced bottle of whatever he stole. *Maybe it wasn't about Carl at all. Maybe Gharles just wanted him to be rich.*

Speaking of Gharles, he predictably summons Harold on the communicator. *Ugh, what does he want now?*

"Pleasant evening, Mr. Harold. I see you have amassed a fat sack for yourself. Another pile of innocent bodies, a robbery, and arson? Sufficed to say, I've never seen anyone with quite the misfortunate bad aim as you have. The Syndicate is pleased with your embrace of the crime life. The self-made weapons were truly exquisite. We're becoming impatient though, Mr. Harold. Try harder! These quick kills bore me. Remember what Carl has done. I expect to see great suffering! Good day then Mr. Harold."

Chapter 13

Thomas stands outside the apartment all night, waiting for Harold to return so that he can confront him once and for all about what he knows. Harold stumbles in from the lift, exhausted. Thomas takes him by surprise. Overcome by his rage, he lunges at an unassuming Harold. A fist to the face. In his disorientation, Harold swings back at Thomas with a strong left hook. After a moment of recovery, he realizes who his assailant is.

"Thomas? What in the hell is going on here? Explain yourself this instant!"

"Who is she dad? Who is that woman? I know everything!"

"What woman? What are you talking about? There is no woman!"

"Don't lie to me. I saw you. I saw you in sector 1149. Who's David? Is that my brother?"

The gig is up. He has been caught. He shifts the conversation from lies of substance to lies of feelings. At least maybe they were lies. There is some slight degree of shame that all those innocent lives had perished at his hands. *Or were they in Gharles'?*

"You saw that? Listen, Thomas, you have to understand I didn't mean to kill those people!"

"Wait... *What?* I have a secret brother *and* you murdered someone? *People?*"

"Oh! So you didn't see everything. And no! David is not your brother, he's just hired help."

"So you hired a kid to murder for you? What the fuck? Are you insane?!"

"No! No! It's not like that, he was just a Tracer. I never meant to kill those people. Just Carl."

"How do you accidentally kill people? Who the fuck is Carl? You're psychotic! I'm telling Mom about this right now."

Thomas turns to run back down the hall towards the apartment, but he isn't fast enough.

Harold sees that this is now spiraling out of control. He brings himself close to Thomas, frantically trying to block his path.

"Thomas wait! I'm being paid to do it! It's just a job. Carl is the target."

"So, because you're getting paid that makes it okay?" Thomas says, his face scrunched up in utter disbelief.

"Yes! Because it's not just money, *it's an unbelievable amount of money.* Enough for us to ascend. Not just to the next floor, but all the way into the upper-tier! I did it for you. For Mom. For what's her name... Martha. For all of you. I just want you to have the best things in life," says Harold. It's almost believable.

Thomas drops to the ground, holding his head. He's so morally conflicted by what he has heard. His father is a mass murderer in the name of cash, but then again, the opportunity to be rich beyond all measure is so alluring that even Thomas in his infinite good nature cannot ignore the temptation. It is an unbelievable emotional roller coaster.

"How many people was it, Dad?" says Thomas, softly, his hands still in his face.

"Well to be honest I'm not entirely sure. Maybe sixty or seventy people?"

"You don't even know? Wait. It was you! You blew up the tramway didn't you, you sick son of a bitch!" Thomas is enraged again, he lunges toward Harold, barely holding back his fists.

"*Okay,* I admit not my finest moment. He's just surprisingly hard to kill!"

"How? Is he like heavily guarded or does he have a lot of weapons or something?"

"Well. No, not exactly. He's just really lucky."

"Unbelievable. Even as a murderer, you're still an idiot!" says, Thomas, crying now.

"Every attempt was well calculated! It just keeps getting foiled by people getting in the way."

"How many times? Do I even want to know? How many times have you tried this?"

"I think I lost count after the first six, but I've been at it for months now. It all started when I called this nice lady from the viewer, but then it was Gharles. Anyway, he gave me ten-kay as a down payment. I think he runs a big crime network or something. But he wants Carl dead for some reason" says Harold, absent-mindedly.

"Months? Wait, so that time when I found you passed out...? *Gharles?* You got caught up in a televised murder-for-hire scheme? What the fuck, Dad?"

"Well, I'm too deep into this to quit now. I have to try again until I get it right. Otherwise, I think Gharles might kill me, and possibly all of you as well. He's not the nicest guy, you know."

"*Wow!* Okay. Great so now you put our lives at risk too. I can't believe I'm saying this, but next time you do this, I'm going with you."

That is entirely unacceptable to Harold. He never meant for any of his family to get involved in this. He wants them to at least have clean hands. This is not what he wanted.

"What? No, absolutely not! You're not getting involved in this and that's final."

"Sixty or seventy people, Dad! Let's face it, you need more hands on deck for this."

"I.... I... You're not going to take no for an answer now are you?" Harold says.

He realizes that Thomas has inherited his stubbornness. There is no use arguing with him, he has the absolute moral high ground over Harold. Not exactly the father-son bonding opportunity he had hoped for. *A family that kills together, has thrills together?*

"Nope! We're all in this now. Thanks for that by the way. Don't worry. I won't be telling Mom about this. You know she can't handle it. Once again I'll clean up *your* mess. Oh, by the way someone from *the agency* came by today to inquire about your *adoption.*"

"What do you mean? I haven't made any such request! Unless... Oh, I told the security at the Transit station."

"So if you didn't actually apply, why is a caseworker coming to the house unless...unless that wasn't a caseworker at all?"

"That complicates matters. What did your mother say? We'll have to speed this up. The enforcers picked up David last week. It's safe to presume they're on to me."

Thomas is putting it together better than Harold . It is clear that the Enforcers are closing in, and so is Gharles. He needs to wrap this up quickly.

"I can't hear everything that was said, but she isn't happy about it that's for sure. I think you've got a real problem on your hands. I can't fix this one though. You're going to have to do it yourself."

They both enter the apartment together. Sheron is still wide awake, waiting for them. She is clearly angry. Angrier than he has ever quite possibly seen her.

"Harold... We need to have a conversation."

"About what, dearest? Can it wait until morning? It's very late now."

"No, Harold. Not this time. And don't think you're out of the woods, Thomas. Where have you been? Do you have any idea what time it is?"

"I really think we should just talk about this again tomorrow," says Harold.

"Where were you anyways, Harold? Why don't you start there? Thomas go ahead and go to your room right now. I'll chat with you later."

"He was with me, Mom. He was helping me with something. You got to believe me," says Thomas. Throwing himself under the bus to save Harold is definitely a first.

"Harold, is this true? What's going on? Why is an adoption agency coming to the house?"

"It's for me, Mom. Well I mean it's not *for* me. But he's trying to help out a friend of mine on the team. The agency was mistaken about the circumstances," says Thomas.

"*Oh,* okay wow. That's actually a relief to hear. I think? I thought... I thought... Never mind. Listen you two, enough of these secrets. Just keep me in the loop next time. Even if you know it's going to freak me out okay?" says Sheron, believing they actually had been reformed by her words.

"Yes, of course, dear."

"Yeah sure thing, Mom."

Thomas and Harold glare at each other approvingly. Harold is almost proud of his son in a way. He has raised Thomas to be an amazing liar. Not exactly the greatest parental accomplishment, but somehow it feels like a strong capitalistic skill he has imparted.

Thomas has exceeded even Harold's own ability to swindle someone and the feeling is amazing. Dirty, but amazing.

Sheron of course does not completely drop the matter. As they lie down to go to bed she continued to press him.

"Harold. I know you think you're trying to do something good, but I don't know what bringing another person into this house would be like. I don't know who this kid is that needs help, but we can't afford it. Look at this bill, Harold! Look at it!"

Their homeowner's insurance renewal bill. The most terrifying thing Harold has seen in weeks, murders included.

"Double from last year! That's absurd! How can they get away with this, Sheron? It's thievery! Spacelane thievery! We have to find a new policy right away."

"I already looked, Harry. They're all the same! They know we all have to have it, and the profits haven't been glorious enough. They can't get anything out of the lower levels, so the costs just get passed on to us. We're going to have to come up with some extra cash somehow or I don't know how we're going to be able to stay on this floor. Do you know how humiliated I would be if we ended up at mid-tier zero? It's only downhill from there, Harold."

"That's what I've been doing, Sheron! I've been picking up extra shifts and everything. That's why I'm never home. This favor for Thomas is just an effort to try and restore what little is left of our relationship. If you haven't noticed, I'm not exactly Dad of the galaxy here."

"Maybe it's time for Thomas and his new friend you're trying to bring in here to get a job," says Sheron.

There's the shrewd capitalist woman I married! "Absolutely not, Sheron! I will provide for us. Thomas should focus on getting that Fljrkhorn scholarship. It's the best way for him to move up!"

"I think we just need to be realistic, Harold."

"Well, Sheron, just wait until you see the extra money I've been making on the side. Besides, we get a stipend if we take him in!"

He thinks back to his sack of stolen goods from the bar. He will show her what is possible through hard work and sacrifice! *Well, I mean sacrificing others' hard work anyway. But isn't that what capitalism is all about?*

* * *

"Detective, we've got a serious problem down here. We got about eleven, possibly more, bodies, completely charred. The whole place is burnt up. The ID cards have all been taken. No identifiable markings. We're going to have to do DNA profiles just to get a victim report. You think this could be related to your case? We got witness reports of a maniac with some kind of throwing weapon. He just started hacking up people at random then set the place ablaze. No cameras, but I got a composite sketch, but you know it looks average as fuck," said Xanthu.

"I'll look into it, but not a word of it, Xanthu. I don't need a media circus. In the meantime pull those entry records. Let's see if our David connection, Harold came in again last night."

"Once again, I took a few liberties. Your man Harold was *definitely* in the district last night but get this. His son followed too. I talked with your tracer too. He says he never saw Carl leave, but that he did see him returning."

"What? How did he miss the departure? Unbelievable! That could have given us the critical evidence we need. Put more tracers on the job. Obviously, this basic task is too much for one person to handle. I want at least two Enforcers on watch from different vantage points, twenty-four-seven. Round-the-clock surveillance!"

"Not to be adversarial here but we're stretched thin as it is. Who gets the bill for this? I can't get that kind of surveillance without a warrant."

"Send it up to Hollander, priority-one. Just use my name. No warrant request. If you have to blame someone, put it on me. We don't know how deep this goes, and I don't need a corrupt judge on my hands right now."

"Understood boss. *The cake is yours to eat!* I'll give you updates when we get these pushed through forensics. Shall we put a detain order on your man Harold?"

"Not yet no. I want an enforcer at the Transit station though. Plainclothes, I don't want him tipped off. Get a covert security notice out to give a signal when he comes in again and we'll get him tracked. I want to find out what his next move is and who his associates are. Let's try to catch this guy in the act so we can really nail him. There's no way this guy acted alone either, somebody has to be paying him. I want to find out who the real ring leader is."

"Good to go then, boss. We'll take care of him, don't worry."

* * *

Harold and Thomas set out to sector 1149 together this time. They need a new pretense for entering the sector, knowing that someone is on to them. False identities would have been helpful, but the expenditures were too great to incur at the moment, even with the stolen credit cards Harold has been racking up all over the Capital. Then the idea occurs to him to use the special access card Gharles gave him. He had completely forgotten about it.

The Transit comes to a halt, the moment of truth is upon them. *Would it work?* This time they go to the resident exit. They are both nervous. There is no telling if this plan is going to fail. The security guard stops them at a gate. Fortunately, or perhaps, unfortunately, it is not very crowded.

"Afternoon, gentlemen. What have you been up to out there?"

"My dad took me to the Fljrkhorn game in Sector 251. I'm a big Devron fan!" Thomas says.

"Say no more! I'm quite a fan myself, but you know *don't say that too loud around these parts!* Your resident card please, sir." Harold hands him the ID that Gharles had given him.

He scans the card and looks at his screen carefully before passing it back to him. *What is going to happen? What did it say? Are they about to be in trouble?*

The security guard's face lights up with fear and enthusiasm.

"My apologies for the delay, sir! I didn't know you were a double-black platinum resident! Down here in the mids too, *wow!* I mean not that you wouldn't be, I mean you can go wherever you want of course. I just... I'll stop talking now. Welcome home, sir! Shall I call you a limousine or something?"

Harold and Thomas both look at each other, bewildered.

"No! That won't be necessary. You take care now."

They enter the station and are on their way, celebrating the unusual encounter.

"Dad, what was that? Double-black platinum? This guy Gharles, you said he was like a mob boss? What kind of crime ring is this? No one has an unlimited access card. *No one!* This guy is big, dad. *Huge!* You shouldn't have fucked with this guy. We're in way over our heads here."

"It's the lifestyle we're walking into if we off this guy! So let's get on with it. Besides, Gharles has had little issue with the delays. If anything, he seems to relish in my failures," says Harold, feeling surprisingly more confident in his decision to do business with Gharles.

They walk through the sector, careful to avoid any enforcer units, watching carefully to make sure they weren't followed. As they approach Carl's apartment, *an ambush!* They're surrounded. Not Enforcers. *Who are they?* Four, no five, brutes all around them.

"Well... Well... Well... Harold... I seem to remember telling you that to be the boss you had to handle business. Looks like you a punk ass bitch instead. Why is my boy David still in jail when you out here walking these streets a free man? I thought I made myself clear, Harold."

It's the hooker! What does she expect him to do? He isn't anyone special, he doesn't have magic powers. There is nothing he can do for David. Not a thing.

"Woah! Hold on now. Just wait a minute. Easy. Easy! I came back, didn't I? I brought help this time! See? Now excuse me, do you have a name, miss? We've met so many times now I feel so rude never having asked," Harold says, trying to deescalate the situation.

"It's Roxy, but you can call me Duchess because on these streets I'm royalty. What's this kid going to do, get arrested for you too? Excuse me If I don't have just a whole lot of confidence in your abilities."

"Okay. Roxy or Duchess. Look, I never meant for this to happen. That snitch Fake Carl must've squeaked, okay. That's why I offed his ass, okay? But, you're right. I'm not the best fixer. But you are. You're real good. That's why you're gonna figure out what you and Thom— *Tito* here are going to do. This time I'm going off-world to cap this mother fucker. You got it?"

The sounds of laughter fill the air around them.

"You? You're going off-world? Fat chance fat man. Ain't nobody crying over dead ass Carl's drug dealin'-ass. Tito you a fool for trusting this jester. I suggest whatever he's paying you, it ain't worth it. You should walk away."

"Hey! Don't talk about the boss that way. Harold isn't just some bitch. He's double-black platinum. Untouchable. You fuck with him, you get burned. You saw what happened at that bar? They still haven't identified the bodies. I came here to get it done, so are you going to tell me how to get David out of this place or am I going to have to handle it myself?" says Thomas, fully embracing his new role as *Tito*.

Harold is once again bewildered by Thomas's ruthless lies. It is truly riveting to watch him in action, almost fun. Thrilling even, to be doing this with his son. Quality bonding time with the boy. In that brief moment, he feels less like a murderous slob, and more like badass.

"Woah easy tiger. My mistake! Look. Not trying to piss on your parade, Mr. Big Time, but, you see, you're putting a lot of pressure on my streets right now. I need you to finish your business with bitch ass Carl here, and get out of my backyard okay?" says Duchess.

"*Ha.* Finally something we agree on! It's settled then. I'm going off-world. You and Thoma— or, uh, Tito are gonna bust out David. Capiche?" says Harold.

With everything settled and agreed to, he is nervous for Thomas. It wasn't his intention to leave him behind but if this is what had to be, so be it. *Thomas is at least not under investigation right?*

He speaks to him privately one last time. "Thomas, be careful out there. If anything looks off, you get out of there as fast as you can. Don't worry about any of these people, just take the next Transit out. They can't follow you there. Also, how did you know it was me at the bar?"

"Dad, I'm not a moron. I saw it on the news. You think I didn't see your stash of stolen credit cards? You're a lousy criminal. You didn't even notice I took two of them yesterday. Thanks for the shoes by the way. They fit great!"

"*Huh.* Well, who am I to talk shit? I haven't a clue what I'm about to do! Never been off-world before. I have no idea what to expect," says Harold.

"You were serious? Why off-world?"

"I'm going to try killing him at work this time. I got tipped off on the address in the data I got back from David. He's a good kid. You're doing a good thing here. What should I do?"

"Just be cool. Act natural. That's what I'm about to do. I'm about to bust a bitch out of prison and I've never even been to d-hall. These people scare the hell out of me. But if I can fix something you fucked up and get this guy out, I'm going to do it."

Such loving parting words. They go their separate ways. Thomas with Duchess the hooker and her roving band of marauders, and Harold armed with an all-access pass and not a plan in sight.

He heads towards the Tramway. Ironically, the very same one he had blown up only weeks earlier. Fully rebuilt, as promised by the mayor. Naturally, when something that impacts the elite is broken, it gets fixed, but the lifts in the residential buildings remain out of service for decades at a time.

From here he has no idea what to expect. The tram slowly delivers him to a massive hangar terminal, an off-world transit hub. Thousands of ships, large and small, coming and going. He has never seen anything like it. *What am I supposed to do now?* He stands there looking lost, so lost in fact an attendant felt it necessary to ask him about it.

"Pardon me, sir, but you look lost. Is there something I can help you find?"

"Yes, madam. It appears I need to book a transport to this station here," Harold says as he fumbles with the datapad.

"Okay, let me see... Interesting... okay. Let's get you over to the information counter. Heleen! Heleen! This gentleman here is going to Station Alpha IV 8

C, but he doesn't have a passage booked. Can you help him?"

"What, he can't read the signs? Is he really that stupid? He looks like he has eyeballs. I bet they have it in his language somewhere. I think he's human but he's a little big, you know?" says Heleen.

"Heleen, don't be rude. Just help him!" says the attendant.

With that marvelous introduction, the nice friendly attendant leaves him in the hands of Capital's most heinous-looking information advisor.

No one, it seems, has ever had less job satisfaction than her, and she is not afraid of reminding people that per her union contract she is not required to actually help anyone. This seemed counterintuitive being that she runs the information desk. You simply had to know where you were going and figure it out yourself.

"You there! Come on, let's figure it out. Let me guess, it's some bullshit you don't have clearance for? Behind on your shuttle token payments? Let's see some ID hon," says Heleen.

He hands her the ID card with attitude and disgust. She scans the card, holding it between her flippers, and a look of dismay falls over her. At least that's what it looks like to Harold. He hopes that's her face anyway. It isn't readily apparent where her speaking organs are located.

"Oh! Oh my goodness. My apologies sir! If I had only known. Was no one here to meet you with your private shuttle? Who was the operator? I'll have them killed. You just give me the names. Anything I can do to make it up for you?" says Heleen. Her tone is doing a massive about-face, and she is suddenly being unbelievably kind. That double-black platinum status has really paid off.

"No no. That won't be necessary. I just need a transport. What, did you say I can take the public shuttle?"

"Oh! Oh no *haha.* I would never put you on that old trash barge! I don't have anything in your class available because, well frankly, we almost never get dignitaries of your prestige on this level. Not to question your judgment! That must be why you chose such plain clothes. Wise choice sir, you just never know these days when someone might try to assault you or something."

She fidgets around with her terminal for a moment, before rattling off again. It seems that she has found something.

"Anyways, the best I can do is private first-class on our Nautilus-X359 Space Taxi. I'll have Jendy escort you! Jendyyyyyy, Jenddyyy! Oh, there you are. Escort His Majesty to Launchpad 7 immediately! If he needs anything, anything at all, you get it for him okay doll? Thank you. You have a pleasant flight, sir, and again I apologize for whatever I'm sorry for okay!" she says in her sincerest customer service voice.

What a strange alien. He likes the sound of private first-class. Nothing Harold has ever experienced in his entire life could be described in either of those terms. As they approach Launchpad 7 he sees a sleek black cruiser, decked out in polished space-chrome. He gasps in shock. His escort is apologetic.

"Oh, I know! I'm so sorry. It truly is offensive to be putting you on such accommodation. I assure you there will be absolutely no charge for this inconvenience. If there is anything I can to make you more comfortable you let me know," says Jendy.

How anyone would consider this to be a problem, Harold has no idea, but he has always loved the sound of *no charge.*

The captain of the vessel greets him personally and he is brought into a massive suite of unbelievable splendor.

"Yes, this will do fine, thank you," says Harold. He tries to sound as though this is normal and this isn't his first time on an off-world trip.

Then not a second after they leave, Harold does a victory dance. This place is incredible. Fine leathers, live plants, fancy lights, a player for music, a mini-bar with top-shelf liquor. A container is set chilled on ice in the center of a table. He opens it to reveal fresh berries. *Real berries!* Like from an actual plant. Not chemically simulated, not flavored, not even freeze-dried. Real fresh berries. Harold devours them like Dionysus at an orgy. He can't fathom a world where these were accommodations to be apologetic for. His desire to kill Carl is now full-throttle.

The ship blasts off with a force unknown to Harold. The ride is still somewhat smooth but the feeling is truly exhilarating. He peers out the viewing window to witness the amazing spectacle. The terminal is getting smaller and smaller. They rise to the tops of the giant buildings towering overhead. He is now hovering above the elite of the world! The buildings got smaller. Floating smog collectors in the atmosphere steadily work to contain the enormous volumes of polluted air, convert them to energy, and spew out oxygen.

He observes a burning layer for a moment and finally the quiet serenity of a black sky with millions of tiny lights in it. The planet below is incredible in its spherical form. He can't make out individual buildings or even sectors, just one giant mass. An interconnected web of brown, gray, smog, and lights. *Even from space, it is disgusting!*

The space around them is littered with millions upon millions of stations. Ships hustling and bustling in clustered shipping routes, careful precise transport to prevent collisions. The space trash and debris are endless. Collector drones attempt to scoop them up, narrowly missing catastrophe with the satellites swirling by.

Within the span of half an hour, the ship begins its descent! *Already?* Harold was just starting to enjoy himself. He stretches out on the couch, downing the bottles of expensive liquor. The inside of the station is back to the abysmal gray of steel. Like any office building on the planet, except in space. *How disappointing.* He yearns for the ebb and flow of the open space, its majesty, its brilliance. *If only I could tell my family about this!*

"Here you are, sir! If you'd like, you can call another transit when you are ready, otherwise, I can wait here for you and return you to any destination you like," says the captain.

For a moment Harold considered having the ship take him as far away as possible and dump him off on the first planet that isn't polluted.

"Ah yes. Thank you that would be splendid. I shall not be long. You just wait here okay?"

He steps down the ramp, missing the comforts and luxuries already. An obnoxious spectacled balding man approaches him as he descends.

"Oh my! I'm so sorry. They didn't tell us you were coming. It's so rare that we get anyone from headquarters here! If we had known we would have done more. You just let me know what you need! Anything at all. I'm here for you!"

"I assure you that won't be necessary. I'm looking for this office right here. If you could just point me in the right direction, I can manage it myself thank you," says Harold, showing him the datapad.

"Really? *That office?* Well okay! Sure you'll just head down this hallway to the lifts. You'll take it to the 45th floor, and then it's three hallways down the main corridor there. You'll take the first left and you'll find the receptionist who can direct you further. And once again welcome to our station," he says with enthusiasm.

Harold hears him whispering to another employee nearby as he walks away.

"Never seen him before."

"What's he doing here?"

"You suppose it's a new auditor?"

"No, don't be ridiculous, in that outfit?"

"He must be really high up to have the confidence to show up in a cheap suit. Maybe it's an undercover boss situation?"

"I thought I knew all the bosses?"

"Psh, you don't even know what you do here!"

"Would an exec really fly a Nautilus?"

"They would if they were incognito! Maybe it's a surprise bonus?"

"Unlikely! More like massive lay-offs. I bet we're doomed, he's come to terminate us all!"

This is exhausting. How does Carl do this every single day? The lift ride alone is absurdly long and the main corridor seems endless. He finally reaches the receptionist as promised in the directions.

"You must be the guy from headquarters! Tim phoned and said you were on your way. How can I help you today? I'm Melissa. I'm so excited you're here!" she says. The unimaginable enthusiasm radiating from this woman makes Harold nauseous.

"Oh my. Okay. I'm here to see Carl actually. Just tell me where I might find his office."

"Who? Carl? I wonder. Oh, you mean Caleb? I think that's his name.

What's the office number? Oh okay. Yeah. Wow, his name is Carl? Why didn't he say something? Silly Caleb. *Oh well.* Anywho, you just go right on down past these double doors down to the end of the hall to the right there is a staff elevator. Take it down forty-five floors to the first floor and then head straight down the first hallway. After about fifteen minutes, you'll see an office on the right and that should be Callum's," she says, in one long breath.

"What? You mean your employees come all the way up here just to go right back down over there the same amount of floors? That's ridiculous! *Ugh.* Never mind. It's not your fault. I'll be going now. Thanks for your help," he says. *Maybe Carl has hired Gharles to kill himself!*

"I'm sorry to have disappointed you! If you would like we can make Carleton move his office up to this floor so as to not inconvenience you to go down there!" she says as though this is a serious option.

"No, that's quite alright. Just no. I'll be fine. Go back to whatever you were doing then," he says. He had never been so irritated by a receptionist in his life.

By the time he reaches the bottom floor again, he is exhausted, almost forgetting the directions. After almost half an hour of walking, he arrives at Carl's office. *Okay, Harold. You're just going to walk in there and you're going to stab this guy and it's over.* He glances around to make sure no one else is nearby.

He bursts through the office door, knife in hand. A man is at his desk on his communicator with his feet up on his desk.

"Carol... I'm going to have to call you back," says the man.

"Alright, Carl. Your time is —Wait? Who the fuck are you?"

"How should I know? I just started working here, man! Who am I supposed to be?"

"What? What do you mean, you don't know who you are? Where the fuck is Carl?"

"Carl? Oh, that guy. Yeah, he doesn't work here anymore. They fired his ass weeks ago. Hey, so like what's with the knife, man?"

"Dammit! What do you mean he got fired? I came all the way up in space just to ride in an elevator for an hour.”

“Bummer dude, that’s a long way for just an elevator ride. But that knife though bro. What’s the deal with that, man?”

“*Ugh.* You know too much now. I’m here to kill Carl, but now that you’ve seen me, I’ll have to kill you instead. You’ve really inconvenienced me.”

“Ah come on man! It’s my first day. I can’t die within the first ninety days. Company policy.”

“Why aren’t you working then? Shouldn’t you be doing something?! How do I know you’re not a spy sent here by Carl to watch out for me?”

“I don’t know what I do here! I mean I assume they’ll tell me eventually, but what’s the rush?”

As the ridiculous conversation continues to unfold, another man walks into the office handing Harold a massive stack of data tablets. This one looks older, weighed down by decades of corporate drab.

“Here yah go, Carl. Get these numbers to me by Friday okay?” he says.

“Who are you? I’m not Carl! I don’t even work here!”

“Okay *Notcarl* sorry! I don’t really care who you are, I still need these by Friday,” he says.

“This isn’t even my office! He should be the one doing this,” Harold says, pointing to the man who wasn’t Carl.

“Okay fine! He’s Carl now. Not sure how else to say I don’t care! See you on Friday and by Friday, I mean Wednesday!”

The man exits the office, not even noticing that Harold is wielding a long knife. He turns to the man he had hoped was Carl.

“Are you sure you don’t want me to kill you? This place looks awful,” says Harold.

“No, but that’s a generous offer! Thanks for thinking of me. Anyways, you better get back to those numbers, Carl! The boss will not be happy when he sees you standing around!” the man says, as he returns to his communicator.

Harold throws the data tablets on the floor and storms out of the office. *Idiots everywhere.* Thirty minutes later, he is back at Melissa’s desk.

“You might have mentioned that Carl doesn’t work here anymore!” he says to her.

"Oh, I'm sorry! Have we met? I don't recall anyone named Carl. Maybe he worked here before I started. We can check the employee archives if you want!"

"Forget it! Just... Nevermind. I can't."

He storms past her, irritated to no end. If Carl isn't working, that means he will almost certainly be at home. This time Harold will beat down the door if he has to. Someone is going to die, him or Carl, and he prefers it be Carl.

Back at the private space taxi, Harold is once again enjoying his fifteen minutes at the height of luxury. He wanted to stay just a little longer, but he doesn't want to tip the pilot off to his falsely held ID status. Besides he wants to make sure Thomas is okay before killing Carl.

Chapter 14

"Duchess, I really don't think... I mean, this isn't going to work!"

Thomas is intrigued by her plan, but it doesn't seem possible. There is no way he is going to fit inside the air ducts. *What if they collapse? What if they have big chopping fan blades or someone turns on the furnace and burns me alive? What if I can't turn around and get stuck?*

"Would you rather be the one who seduces the guard then? I don't remember that listed as one of your talents, but you seem pretty enough," says Duchess, smirking at him.

"No! No. I'm good thanks. I just don't know how I'm going to pull this off."

"Just like you saw it on the building schematics. You follow this duct to cell junction-B and then across here, and you take the left passageway about fifteen kilometers or so and that should be the general vicinity of David's cell. It's that simple."

"And how do I get him up there? The ceilings are fifteen feet high!"

"That's what the rope is for, moron. Tito, are you sure you've done this before?"

"I got it! I got it. What's the signal for when you're ready?"

"*Ha!* Oh, *you'll know* trust me. Never had a dissatisfied customer yet. You better believe you'll know when it's time." She opens the air intake hatch to the precinct duct system, motioning for him to get inside.

Why did it have to be me? Thomas asks himself as he squeezes his way into the dark cold steel duct. He can barely see, there is dust and dirt everywhere. The passage is so narrow he can barely crawl through it. The steel buckles beneath him. *Come on Thomas, you can do this.* He starts to panic, but it is worse to breathe heavily. Whoever David is, he owes him big time after this. The vent is sealed behind him so as not to raise suspicion should anyone happen to stumble upon it. No turning back now.

* * *

Roxy makes her way to the guardhouse entrance. There are but two guards there. One who talks, and one who watches. Once past the guardhouse, they will open a series of security doors, allowing access to the jail.

"Afternoon, ma'am. What brings you in today?" asks the talker.

"I'm here for visiting hours. My dear friend David."

"ID card please, sign and date here. Remember that all belongings will be searched, prohibited items will result in confiscation and possible prosecution. If you would like to check your weapons you may do so at this time," he says, without even really looking at anything, or even her. He just stares forward, repeating the same monotonous line all day, every day.

She has done this routine a time or two. She's come prepared to get through security quickly. She passes through and is escorted through a series of security doors before finally coming to David's cell block. They have him in a solitary holding area. Part of their attempts to make him talk. A guard is positioned at the cell at all times during their conversation.

"Duchess? What are you doing here? You shouldn't be here. Not on my account anyways," says David, delighted to see her.

"How are you doing? We're worried about you. We're doing everything we can to get you out okay? It's just like that night at Vilmers Casino. You just have to hold your head *up*." She says, conveying the covert message. David knows what she intends and nods in agreement.

"I'll be okay. Corporal Lance over here is taking real good care of me," he says.

"Oh! Is that right? Yes he can *take care of me* alright. Tell me, Officer Lance, are all guards as *well equipped* as you?" The guard blushes as she begins her seduction.

"Ah geeze, ma'am, you're very kind, but I'm not supposed to be talking to you. Sorry."

"*Awwww*, why not? Are you already taken? I'm sure a man like you has already been snatched up. That's okay though. I won't tell her if you won't. *We don't have to talk either…*"

She slowly unbuttons the top of her shirt revealing even more of herself.

"No, ma'am. I'm still very much available. I guess *just this once* I could make an exception for such a gorgeous lady as yourself," says Lance, mesmerized by her breasts.

"I do enjoy a man in uniform! Cover your eyes, David. Officer Lance and I need a moment."

She inches closer to him. He is shaking with nervousness as she sensually brushes up against him. She reaches for his zipper. At first, he seems hesitant, but as she gets closer and closer he cannot resist the temptation.

As the spectacle is unfolding, Thomas has reached the drop point. He can hear Roxy's conversation. He couldn't be more ready to get this over with. He has already had several very unfortunate encounters with rats in the ducts and he is ready to get out of there. He gently pulls up the grating and casts it to the opposite side, peering down to find David is already looking up at him. He passes the rope down

Not his most brilliant idea; he has nothing to secure the rope with and David is heavier than he anticipated. The ducts can barely hold him. *How are we both going to make it?* He holds the rope with all his might, giving David the chance to climb up. You can tell it is a treacherous ordeal. Though they both strain, neither can make a sound and risk the attention of Corporal Lance, who is well *occupied* at present.

The duct buckles under their weight. Thomas has to back his way out for lack of space to turn around. He will have to crawl backward all the way to the next junction point. David carefully places the vent back. It's near pitch darkness, but for the limited light coming from the cells below. They have to crawl at a safe distance from each other so as to not overtax the brackets.

It feels like forever before Thomas is finally able to turn around. They hobble along as quickly as they can. Time is of the essence. Any second now, they could discover he's gone and order a perimeter sweep that would surely pick them up. Almost there. Almost there!

Someone else is almost there... Corporal Lance certainly had a *big smile* on his face.

"Wow! I guess when you're in tha mood you're in tha mood huh? That was really something you know that? Can I call you? What's your name?" he says.

"Lance, Lance, Lance... That one was free, but next time it'll cost you something extra," says Duchess.

"What? You mean you're a hooker? What is this? Come on! I thought you was into me?" he says, truly hurt.

"I am. I'm *soooo* into you. That's why I gave you this free limited time offer, didn't I? Ask for Duchess. You'll find me. Am I not worth the investment, Lance?"

"Yeah, I guess you were pretty great. But still, I ain't that kind of guy. I've got a reputation to uphold with the badge you know," he says, pointing to it.

"You might want to revisit that too. I would if I were you. Take care now Lance!"

She steps out of the cellblock. Lance can't take his eyes off of her until she's completely out of sight. He rests up for a moment before thinking about what she has said.

"Some friend of yours huh, David? David?... David! Oh fuck... *Oh! Ohhhh fuck.* How? Where? Shit I'm so fucked," says Lance, realizing his prisoner has slipped the building.

Roxy is out of there as fast as she can muster. As soon as she is out of sight of the precinct jail, she runs like her life depended on it.

Meanwhile, Thomas and David reach the end of the duct tunnels. They throw open the access hatch and breathe in the fresh smog. Looking around carefully, they seal it back behind them.

"Where are we going? I got to get somewhere and lie low man," says David. He is putting a great deal of confidence in the random guy who just rescued him.

"Head to The Transit station!" says Thomas. They are sprinting now.

"It's too risky! I can't badge in. We have to find another way. I got a place."

"David! Trust me. Where we're going, the card readers don't work and nobody gives a fuck. I'll pay the toll. We just have to get you out of the sector, okay?"

He nods in agreement. They are already nearly there. Just a few more blocks anyway, before he realizes he is still decked out in his finest prison attire.

"Hey! You, wait! I can't go anywhere looking like this," says David gesturing at his bright orange jumpsuit.

"I know! Trust me. Here, look!"

They stop around a corner in an alleyway where a bag of clothes has been stashed, along with a collection of David's personal belongings.

"Duchess always was good to me." He changes out of his prison fatigues as fast as he can. Thomas keeps watch over the alleyway; so far luck is on their side.

"What's your name, stranger?" asks David.

An alarm rings out over the city from the precinct. A prisoner has escaped. Their time is almost up.

"Thomas. I'm with Harold. I'm here for damage control."

"You're a few weeks late for that! Harold's truly an asshole."

"Believe me, I know! He's my dad!"

They make it to the Transit station, just as the guards are receiving the escapee images. They are beginning to lock things down. Thomas swipes his ID card and they both slip through the exit gate just before the shutdown. They run down to the train. The doors are closing, the warning is flashing. They catch the last train out as the doors shut right behind them. Tired and winded. They have made it. The connecting routes are much less perilous. It gives them a chance to catch up and work out the next plan.

* * *

At long last, they make the journey into the Mulknosh Sector, home for Thomas, a new realm for David.

"Thomas, where are we? I've never been to this place before. Where should I go?" asks David. He tries to make it a point to get a layup of an area as quickly as possible to assess its survivability.

"You're in Mulknosh. You're going to love it here. It's great! And you're not going anywhere. You're staying with us tonight. You're staying with us until we get something figured out," says Thomas, overly enthusiastic. David still doesn't trust him fully.

"You don't have to do that. I can manage myself. Always have."

"David, stop! You're coming and that's final. I know you're independent and a survivor and shit, but please. It's no burden, truly. If it makes you feel better, you can sleep on my floor or something," says Thomas, agitated by his refusal.

"Why are you so nice to me? What's the catch?" he says, always believing there's a hook.

"Look, man. This world is fucked up enough as it is, and we have everything we need. I know what it's like to have to do shit for yourself. Okay, well not like in *the same way you do*, but look I can't live with myself knowing what Harold has done to get us there if I don't at least do this small act of kindness. Call it karma if you will."

David is still uneasy about it, but he figures a night or two to get his bearings on the place won't hurt. After all, Thomas is the only person he knows here. He reluctantly goes with him. He isn't sure what karma is, but he liked that it was free of charge.

Thomas's communicator rings. He has almost forgotten it is there. *Thankfully it didn't go off in the ducts or we would have been caught for sure!* It's Harold.

"Thomas? Where are you? I heard the sirens and they shut everything down. I feared the worst. They held us at the spaceport terminal for hours. Well, I got to enjoy it in this luxury lounge area, but I'll tell you about it later. The important thing is that you're safe right?"

"Yeah. We're good. Back home now. Our trip was successful," says Thomas.

He isn't sure if his calls are being monitored, so he tries to be as cryptic as possible. He did after all have to scan out with his own ID badge. That will turn some heads if they ever investigate it.

"That's wonderful news! I was not so fortunate. *My business meeting* was canceled. I'm going to visit him at his house instead, make sure I get it taken care of."

"Great. You do that, Dad. Later."

Come on Harold! You missed him again?

Thomas can only imagine the space station carnage he might see on the news later.

Thomas and David head towards the apartment. David takes in the surroundings. This sector is much more industrial than his own. It's mid-level, but it seems to be much less extravagant than what he is used to. Somehow it makes him feel better, like it might be easier to make it here, or at least cheaper

The building is quaint. More indoor passages here, perhaps due to the proximity of the high levels of pollution put out in the factories. The lights flicker a bit and the lift is temperamental. He doesn't want to get used to it though, just in case it isn't a stable arrangement, but he thinks he might be happy here.

"Well, here we are! Just brace yourself. My mom can be really intense, and she's probably going to ask a bunch of ridiculous questions. Just remember that she doesn't know anything about this! Let me do the lying okay? Oh, and be nice to my sister!" Thomas says.

Comfortable in his surroundings, Thomas' *'Tito'* persona fades away back into prodigal son mode.

The door opens. The place is not spectacular. Kind of dirty. Kind of smelly. Kind of dark. Kind of old. Not poor, but just very average. Very homey. There is an older middle-aged woman there. A blond with stringy hair. This must be Sheron.

"Thomas! I thought you left with your father. Any idea when he plans on coming home today? Who's your friend? Who is this? Who are you?"

"*Ugh.* Mom this is David. Dad is picking up an extra shift this afternoon."

"*Oh* Hi David! I'm Sheron. It's so great to meet you. So what are you guys up to today?" she says. Finally, she can shed some light on this David situation. She wants all the juicy details. *What have they been keeping from me?*

"Well, David's going to stay here for a while, if that's cool? Home stuff. Don't ask. Okay?"

"Well, I wish you had told me earlier, I would have fixed dinner! So David how *did* you guys meet?"

"*Uh* well, Mrs. Sheron..." David finds himself without words to lie with.

"School! We met at school. He's on the team, Mom. Look he's had a long day, can we skip the interrogation please?"

"Geeze, Thomas! I'm not that overbearing, am I? I'm just trying to be polite and make conversation. You teenagers are always getting worked up. Go on then, we'll talk later."

Sheron of course won't let it go. It stays on her mind the rest of the afternoon. *What is the connection?* Harold. Gone all the time. Adoption agency. Family problems. Thomas. Thomas and Harold fight all the time. David. David with no explanation. David who is staying in their house now. David who isn't Harold's secret love child. She knows every kid on the team and she has certainly never seen David. *What is going on here? Did they really meet at school?*

Clearly, it isn't about money. Thomas doesn't seem to be on drugs. *What else can it possibly be?*

Her brain starts piecing together the evidence. She comes to the most logical conclusion that by process of elimination, David must in fact be Thomas's lover! Clearly, she needs a night out with the girls to discuss the matter with her friends, but for now, she is assured that David's entrance into their lives is by relationship with Thomas.

* * *

Harold cannot make another attempt on Carl's life, the pressure is too great. Enforcers are searching everywhere for their lost prisoner. He returns to the apartment empty-handed. Sheron is relieved to see him.

"Harold, you're home! Good. *David is here.*" She whispers the last part as though it is a secret she doesn't want anyone else to know about.

"Really? Now? Well, that's just great. Anyways. What's for dinner? I picked up an extra shift and now I'm starving."

Harold sits down at the table waiting to be served. She smacks him instead.

"You're okay with this? Aren't they a little young to be cohabitating? I know it's high school, but still. We don't know anything about this David person. Thomas said they met at school and he is on the team, but I looked it up in the team yearbook and he wasn't there! Explain that!" Sheron says, piecing together her elaborate conspiracy theory. If only she knew how complicated the real story is. She points to the team photo in the yearbook.

"Sheron, I don't know what the hell you're talking about. David is an outstanding young man. He's just here temporarily until he can get on his own two feet. He's not in the yearbook because he just moved here a short time ago. Do yourself a favor and find something else to obsess over before you say or do something crazy."

"Harold, call me crazy again and I'll show you crazy like you've never seen before!" she says, pointing a sharp kitchen knife in his direction. "I hope this extra work you're putting in can feed the extra mouth around here. Maybe he can help clean something. I just... I just don't want to see any touching or lovemaking. Can they just keep that to themselves?"

"Sheron! What the ever-loving fuck are you talking about? Relax! It's not that serious," says Harold. At least he thinks it's not, but then again he has been gone for several hours.

"Okay, but I've got my eye on that boy! Also, don't forget your daughter! When was the last time you did anything with Martha? She probably thinks you're her imaginary friend because you might as well be," says Sheron, her tongue is sharp and vile tonight.

David and Thomas can of course hear the entirety of their conversation as the walls are nearly paper-thin. They aren't so well off as to have the luxury of soundproofing. There hasn't been a private conversation in years that Thomas has not caught wind of. They laugh at her.

"Oh wow. Your mom thinks we're lovers! You're right she is too much," says David.

"Dude I know! Why is she so ridiculous? I can't believe Dad is back already. He still can't do it! Maybe we should kill Carl ourselves. He obviously can't manage it."

"Okay... Are you sure you don't want to make out first though?"

"Ha! Not a chance! I'm saving that one for a day when I really want to piss her off!"

"What's the deal with Carl anyway? What's in it for Harold?"

"Wealth beyond all measure! All he has to do is kill Carl and we become rich. Like upper-tier level society rich. Yet somehow Carl always gets away."

"Damn, someone must really hate Carl. Why though? What did he do?"

"We don't really know. My dad was contracted by some guy named Gharles."

David's face freezes. "Gharles? Gharles Darkley? Are you certain?"

"Yeah. That guy. Why you know him or something? You look like you just got punched."

"That's a very bad man, Thomas. Harold never should have got involved in this. Everything Gharles touches turns to ruin. Rich. Powerful. Evil. Those who meet him tend to go missing or turn up dead. Harold has made a deal with the devil, Thomas. His money will come at a price and it probably isn't just murder."

"*Ugh.* I knew it was some fucked up shit. That's why I have to do something to end this before he kills anybody else, or gets himself in trouble. Hell, I'm already in trouble. I brought you here and you're an escaped convict. I still don't know what all you did back there," Thomas says.

Sheron knocks on the door to announce that she will have dinner ready on the table within the hour. She asks to speak to Thomas privately. David and Thomas look at each other and laugh for a moment before he goes to talk with her.

"Thomas... your *friend* can stay here as long as he pulls his weight. I'm going to try to be *cool* about all of this. Just... can you get him a shower or something? He looks like a *ghost.* I don't know how you boys get so dirty, but please, that smell is awful. I wouldn't want people to think you were hanging around with the lowers!" She whispers the last part, knowing it is offensive.

"Sure, Mom. Would you like us to shower together?" he says quietly, sarcastically.

"What?" she clutches her proverbial pearls.

"Nothing! I said no problem, I'll take care of it."

He informs David of the news, to which he agrees wholeheartedly. She doesn't need to know he has been ghosting for years, or that he had been locked up in a cell for weeks. The idea of a shower and a hot meal seems like a luxury when it isn't tied to a business transaction.

* * *

"Corporal Lance, I need you to go over this with me one more time." She tried to remain impartial but the story was just absurd. The corporal was sweating and she knew he was lying. She tried to take her focus off him and sip her coffee casually. "You said the gorgeous woman knocked you unconscious and was somehow able to break David out of his cell without opening the door. Didn't use the keys. Didn't break it. Didn't walk out with him. And you don't seem to have *any* physical markings to suggest such an altercation," said Detective Clinton.

Her confidence in the entire precinct was dwindling with this reprehensible debriefing. *This was supposed to be a good sector!* At least that's what she'd thought when she'd taken this job. She knew it was only a formality. There would be an endless amount of paperwork over this incident. All will be forgiven and buried deep within the bureaucracy, never to be seen or heard about again. The corporal will resume his post like nothing ever happened, even though he was clearly worthless in that capacity. The degree of incompetence knew no boundaries. Not that the precinct jail was intelligently designed either, but his conduct was still inexcusable.

"Yes ma'am, that's correct. I didn't see her coming. It was just out of nowhere. *Blam!* I don't know what happened. Saw nothing after that until I came to and pulled the alarm," he said.

Clinton leaned in across the desk towards him. "Well, that's interesting because it looks like she's *really* knocking you good in this surveillance footage. While you were *preoccupied,* you can see that a rope descended from the air ducts and David climbed his way out," she said. He shied away from her, defeated. "That's all, Corporal. You can go now."

Detective Clinton was at a total loss. Her principal informant had been stabbed to death, her victim was MIA, her collaborator had broken out of jail. Nothing seemed to be going her way and it definitely made no sense. She felt more lost in this case than ever before. *Carl on Carl crime?*

"How am I going to explain this to Hollander," she said out loud to herself, of course at the precise moment he entered the room.

"Explain what to me, Detective? I've seen the tape." He threw a pile of datapads on her desk. "Already got a workaround on security for that vent system. Before you ask, yes we do keep that hatch locked, and yes they broke the lock off. And yes, due to budget cuts we have no cameras there. No idea who got him out or where he went. Found the clothes abandoned in the alley. He's probably long gone by now. Pressure is mounting from the governor's office. They really want to wrap this up. Don't make me regret my confidence in you. At this point, let's just nail a suspect and call it quits. Bring me somebody. Anybody!" Hollander said, fuming sarcastically and condescendingly towards her

"Sorry, Chief. I won't let you down, sir. I'll do better," she said.

Inside she wanted to yell at him about how none of these events were within her control and about the idiocy of the people around her, or the fact that a guard could be persuaded by a hooker within a matter of minutes. She had instead learned to just say the thing that they wanted to hear. An apology, an affirmation of wrong, and a promise to change, adapt, or grow. It was formulaic, it kept the job moving. The burdens of mid-level management.

Chapter 15

"Good morning employees. By now you should know that I hate you all equally, but unfortunately, I have been forced to choose an *employee of the month.* I realize we're about sixty-three months behind on this practice, but I recently found this plaque in storage and remembered we're supposed to be doing that. Anyways, you'll get your picture taken, and any loser walking by the staff lounge will be able to recognize you for your menial existence," says Xvranbul.

The employees show no enthusiasm for the process whatsoever. They all just hope it isn't them. It was just another shallow gesture, to parade them around for the company newsletter. The kind of thing that says 'we care about our employees', even when you know it's a complete and total lie. No drum roll for the winner.

"And the winner is... Harold!" Xvranbul says.

What? Me? Why thank you! I'm so astonished. Why me? I accept this award with pride! It's just nice to be nominated. Harold rolls his eyes, but internally he's actually smug about it.

"Oh! Believe me I'm as shocked as all of you. I asked the computer who our most mediocre employee is and it immediately came up with Harold. Otherwise, I would never have chosen him!" She turns her attention directly to him.

"Thank you for your dedication to showing up and doing the bare minimum, Harold. Something *all* of our employees should aspire to," she says, bringing the fanfare to an end.

"Also the box-maker union rep will be here today in the foyer, in case you decide you want to pay him to do nothing. Now of course we can't stop you from joining the union, but just know that if you do, you're of course fired! 47,000 microboxes by the end of this week people. Let's move it!" she says. Xvranbul slithers away and they return to their places on the line.

"Wow, Harold! Employee of the month huh? We should celebrate or something," says Baab.

"Oh, I don't know guys. It's an awfully busy week you know. I have a lot of stuff to do"

"Are you still hung up about your cousin Carl? Did you ever find the guy?" asks Baab.

"Yeah no, I haven't. In fact, you might actually be able to help me with that, Baab."

"Sure. Sure. Hey anything you need, Mr. Employee of the Month! What can I do?"

"Well, it's a little on the shady side, but I need a new ID card."

"Why? What did you lose yours or something? Just go down to the Licensing Bureau!"

"No. Not like that. I kind of need *someone else's* ID card, if you know what I mean."

Not that he necessarily *needs* one. He could continue using the one Gharles had given him, but he doesn't want to attract the attention conferred with his double-black platinum access. He can also give that one to Thomas, the next time they go out for another murder spree.

"*Ohhhh!* Say no more, Harold. You need my brother Mu'rrey. He does that shit all the time."

"You always have someone, Baab! Maybe we should go out then. Invite him along!"

"Definitely! Let's go to the Slopicana. It's right by his place. He'll get it done for you. Say, Harold, I been meaning to ask, but Bertrice said she saw you guys the other day and it looked like you have a new pet? Or maybe you spawned a new hatchling or something? I don't know."

"That must be David. He's a friend of Thomas'. He's staying with us for a while. Pet? Seriously, Baab? How can you be so blind with so many eyes?"

"Ah come on Harold! Give me a break. You humans all look the same. My cousin Scurfy is a pet! He loves it. He's kinda slow though. Almost got eaten in the spawn you know."

"Baab! Pay attention. You're going to fry the stitching on that joint at that heat!" Sparks fly haphazardly from his welding gun.

"Sorry! Mr. Employee of the Month. I'd be honored if you'd climb up here and show us how it's done. Go ahead, Harold. Flap your wings!"

* * *

Later that afternoon Harold, Baaab, and Geordon punch out and head for the Slopicana. The place is dark and has big maroon booths, the kind with torn fake leather. The smell of smoking beverages wafts through the air, clinging to the big tapestries and curtains decorating the walls. There is occasionally a floor show on the weekends, but today it's just like any other bar. This one is heavy on the aliens, slurping and guzzling whatever it was they ate.

"Mu'rrey! How you been? I haven't seen you in ages. I assume your brood is prolific?" says Baab. Their wings flutter and their mouth beaks clack.

"Most prolific brother, Baab. Shall I conjure up the usual? Would you like a dipping sponge?"

"Yes, of course, and get two more for my pals here! Not that Harold needs it, but I love watching him fail at things."

The buzzing creature floats away towards the bar, returning with four very dense-looking beverages, smoking, and oversaturated with sucrose. Harold isn't fond of the alien drinks, but he gives it a polite shot.

"So, Harold. Baab tells me that you and I have some business to attend to. Yes?"

"Yeah. I need a new identification card. Something low profile. Sector 1149 clearance."

"*Hmmmm*, I think I can manage it. What species are you again?"

"Human of course! Isn't it obvious? Why is it so hard for everyone to see?"

"Well, I didn't want to be wrong! They don't always come in your size or quite so misshapen."

"Ugh. Well, what's this going to cost me, Mu'rrey?"

"A hundred credits. In advance. Take it or leave it. Risky business I'm in, you know?" "That should be no problem. I'll follow you back to your place later and we'll get it done then."

Geordon chimes in. "Woah! Harold's got that employee of the month money!"

They all laugh and clink their glasses both at his expense and in his honor.

After a pleasant evening of celebration and comradery, Harold and Mu'rrey leave the bar together. Harold, despite having lived here all his life, has never been to this run down alien neighborhood.

It is quite unlike anything Harold has ever seen. It is very small with hanging nests everywhere. It is dark, and littered with strange-looking alien contraptions of every variety. Mu'rrey takes Harold to a small room in the back where his camera and stolen ID machine await him.

He gestures for Harold to have a seat. At least he thinks that's what he is doing.

"Alright, hold still Harold! That's it." A burst of light momentarily blinds Harold. He can feel its radioisotopes penetrating his skin. "Andddd we're all set. Your new name is Alfonso Delacruz!" says Mu'rrey.

"Really? That's the best you could come up with? Can't I change it to something else?"

"I don't make the rules, Harold! Resurrecting a dead guy's identity here. Not many options!"

"Touché. Well, here you are your hundred credits. Pleasure doing business with you. This does work right? I can't handle any trouble."

"Of course it works! Trust me. I do it all the time. It's always easier if no one knew they were dead! Try it somewhere innocuous if you like. It has your photo on record now."

"Thanks. I really appreciate this. And I was never here right? This transaction never occurred?"

"Of course! Strictest confidentiality. Besides, how much longer can I live? By the time they figure it out, I'll be long gone from the swarm!"

Harold departs from the strange abode. He's relieved to smell the somewhat fresher air in the hallway. He heads back home, swiping his new ID card to get on the Transit. *"Welcome Alfonso!" What do you know? It works!*

* * *

When he finally reaches his apartment, he finds it dark. It's unusual to see as Sheron seems quite fond of wasting electricity at all hours of the day and night by keeping the lights on in every room.

He opens the door. *Strange, it's as if no one is here*, another rare occurrence. *Where can they have gone?* He turns on the lights. *Ahhhhh!* A wave of fear falls over him, he panics and withdraws in the terror at what he sees and hears. *Wait what did I hear?*

"Surprise! Oh, Harold, I can't believe it! My Harold, employee of the month."

Sheron has gathered the whole family to sit in the dark in the living area, silently waiting for Harold's return just so they can offer him congratulations. He is smug.

"Wow! You scared me half to death. Well, this is incredible. The whole family here together. And so late on a work night no less. Is that... Is that cake?" Harold says with glee. Not the togetherness aspect, or the lateness, but definitely for the cake.

"Of course! I wanted to make you something real special. Things are really looking up! You think they'll give you a promotion?" Sheron asks.

"Oh dear, you shouldn't have! It looks wonderful... And let's not get ahead of ourselves though!" he says.

No, really, she shouldn't have. Her baking skills are atrocious. He also knows there is no promotion associated with such a petty gesture.

"Congrats Dad!"

"Yeah way to go, Dad! Good job Harold... Okay, can we go to bed now?"

Sheron sends them on to bed. She doesn't understand why her and Martha seem to be the only ones who think that this is a big deal. Of course, she also doesn't know that he is a mass murderer hell-bent on becoming rich at any cost.

Harold decides to relish in a moment of normalcy, though it's not much of a reason to celebrate. Just a stupid old plaque in the break room. It confers no special title, or raise. It is just a veritable 'good job' sticker. It was just a bone to appease the dogs. Harold knows that.

* * *

After a good night's sleep and a hard day's work, Harold sets out again for Sector 1149.

He travels to Carl's building. His entry is unencumbered thanks to his new identity as Alfonso.

This is it. The final showdown. No one to stop him this time. Nothing to stand in his way. Just him and Carl, and the gun.

He follows Carl for a while on his evening routine. Carl can feel himself being watched. Every time he turns to look, there is no one. He stays as much as he can to the well-lit, more popular byways. He swears he hears footsteps. Breathing. Yet nothing.

He turns the keys to his apartment and enters. Instinctively, he knows it's an ambush. He tries to quickly slam the door shut and lock it, but the door is thrust open by the power of the obese assailant. It smashes Carl into the wall. He's disoriented but he is in the battle for his life. He punches, kicks, and claws at him.

They wrestle each other to the ground. Harold hovers over him, forcing a knife ever closer to Carl's heart. The struggle is immense as Carl is easily half his weight. He unexpectedly throws his palm into an uppercut of Harold's nose.

Harold drops the knife, pulling back. Carl runs and dives over the couch. His foot catches it and it flips over. He reaches for one of his guns stored nearby. Setting up over his sofa barricade, he aims towards Harold and looks out into the kitchen. Harold has hidden behind the island also preparing his gun.

"I've got you in my sights, motherfucker! Don't even try it. Why are you here? What do you want?" says Carl. He thinks about it for a moment, maybe he wanted Harold to do it.

Pow! Pow!

The gunshots ring out across the room as Harold fires a blazing round of bullets in Carl's direction, fracturing a lamp, and shattering the exterior window. On second thought maybe he does want to live through this afterall.

"Nothing personal Carl! I just need you to die!"

"That doesn't make any sense! I... I don't even know you! Right?" Carl isn't actually sure. He reflects on the face of his attacker. "Wait... Harold?"

"What? How did you...? No! You must have me confused with someone else. I'm Alfonso!"

"No I'm pretty sure you're Harold. Look around, Harold!" says Carl.

Harold glances around at his surroundings. The apartment seems normal, aside from the flood damage and a huge stockpile of weapons. A pile of sharp knives and skewers resting on the island. Pistols, rifles, explosive grenades, body armor. It is a regular arsenal. *What does this mean? How does he know me? Why the cache?* Then it dawns on him.

"Carl... Are you trying to kill me!?" he says with surprise and concern.

"How am I the one who's trying to kill you! You broke into my apartment, remember?"

"How else would you know who I am? And why the weapons? Did you know I was coming?" That's the only explanation he could come up with for the hoard.

"No Harold! Think about it for a second. *Why* are you trying to kill me?"

"Sorry, Carl. It's just business. I don't know what you did to make someone this mad, but I don't care. I just want to get paid, Carl. So if you could just go ahead and die now that'd be great!" Harold isn't interested in thinking. Thinking might cause hesitation.

"Oh yeah?! Well, I'm trying to kill you for money too! Don't you get it?"

"Wait!? Are you saying that *you* are also trying to kill me for money?"

"Yes, Harold. That's exactly what I'm saying. Can we talk this out? No guns?"

"Nice try, Carl! I think I'll stay over here. For the sake of argument who recruited you?"

"It was this guy from an email. Gharles something. He promised me a fuck ton of money if I killed you. He gave me this picture see?" He holds up the photograph. Harold considers shooting toward it but realizes it's of the exact same size and quality of the one he is carrying of Carl. He begins to realize he has been played.

"What? That's insane. I have the same picture of you! And I also met with Gharles and he promised me a buttload of money!"

"I think we've been set up, Harold!"

Carl slumps down deep into the floor, resting his back on the couch and staring out the broken window.

"For what possible reason? I'm nobody! I mean I was employee of the month, but still nobody! Why would someone want me dead?"

"Why would they want me dead, Harold? He obviously wants us to both kill each other so that he doesn't have to pay either one of us. Some kind of twisted rich man's game."

"That son of a bitch! Probably gets off on this kind of thing. When I get my hands on that low-life scuzzbucket he'll be shitting his teeth out his arse!" says Harold, beyond furious.

"Wait... Harold... Have you... Have you tried to kill me before?"

"Yes! I've tried everything short of burning your building down." Harold begins to wonder why he had not yet taken that approach.

"Ohhh shit... Geeze man. You actually tried to do it?"

"Says the man preparing his army in here! What were you planning to do, a full-frontal assault?" says Harold, pulling one of the assault weapons from the countertop for a closer look.

"I wasn't *actually* going to do it Harold! I just thought about doing it. I'm not like that."

"Sure you're not! So what are we going to do about this?"

"You put your gun down and I'll put mine down?"

"Do you think I'm that stupid, Carl? Okay okay. On the count of three, we're going to both come out at the same time. One... Two.... Three!"

Carl springs up from behind the couch, realizing of course that Harold hasn't moved.

"Damnit Harold! Here just go ahead. Either believe me or stand up and fucking do it. Shoot me," says Carl, throwing his hands out wide.

"Sorry just had to be sure."

Harold stands up. The apartment is a complete disaster zone now. They are both bleeding, bruised, and sweating profusely. An older neighbor peers in through the open door, stunned by the spectacle. Harold moves to close the front door, but it falls off the hinges and crashes to the ground.

"What are you lookin at? Ain't you never seen two people try to kill each other before? Yeah? Mind yah business then!"

The old man walks away terrified and confused.

"Sorry, Mr. Johnstein! We'll try to keep it down! Nice guy. Let it go Harold."

Harold and Carl approach each other, standing face-to-face now. Carl speaks first. "So, we work together on this?"

"Yes. It would seem that is the way. Let's end that bastard and take his money for ourselves."

"Yeah! Okay, so like, what do we do now? Do we hug or something?"

The awkward silence pervades the room. Harold shakes his head in disbelief.

"Carl... not to be bothersome here, but grab your shit and let's go. Now!"

"What's the rush, Harold? We need a plan or something. We can't just walk in there and off a gangster like that right there in the open. Or maybe we can? I don't know, you might!"

"No, Carl. Look out what's left of the damn window and see the Enforcer agent staring right below us with his mouth open. We're already fucked! Let's run for it!"

Carl grabs a few guns and they run from the apartment as fast as they can. They run to the stairwell anticipating the Enforcers will take the elevator. Of course, not being complete idiots, the Enforcers anticipate this. An Enforcer agent is already on his way up, gun drawn.

"Wait! Carl, we just want to talk. Why don't you come down here and we'll work this out okay?" says the Enforcer agent.

"I'm truly sorry, Officer. It's not what it looks like. Look, that was my apartment! I'll pay for the window. Accidental weapons discharge. It's nothing really! We'll surrender peacefully!"

No sooner than the words were out of his mouth before the officer was crushed with a bag of concrete thrown from behind Carl, flying down the stairs. It hits him straight on and smashes him down onto the stairwell. Blood splattering everywhere!

"Harold! Oh my god, Harold, what did you do? Are you crazy? I think you killed him!"

"Yeah! I hope so. Good thing I didn't miss! He probably would have shot you after the first bag. Glad those are laying around up here. Now come on, let's get the fuck outta here."

He tugs at Carl to follow him down the stairs.

Carl is mortified. He can hardly move. Harold somehow manages to drag him out of it and convince him to run down the stairs. Stepping over the dead Enforcer, he tries not to throw up at the sight of it. *How can Harold be so casual about this?*

* * *

They run towards the Transit station. It will be quite some time before the other Enforcers realize their partner is on ice. There isn't enough time. As they reach the Transit station, it's heavily guarded. Enforcer patrols everywhere.

"What's the plan now Harold? We're fucked!" says Carl.

"I don't know Carl! We'll figure something out. I mean on the one hand, they might not even know it was us?"

"Don't be an idiot, Harold. That officer called me by name! They already knew some shit was going to go down. Probably after you went around violently wrecking the town everywhere I go. I have an idea though! Follow me."

Carl takes the lead now. *Where are we going now?* Maybe Carl has a new trick up his sleeve. He leads them across town only to show up at a used spaceship sales lot. *What in blazes are they doing here? Carl can't be serious.*

"Carl, we definitely don't have the cash for this! And you know how aggressive these salesaliens can be." Harold tries to turn around and walk away, but Carl stands his ground.

"Relax, Harold! Look you've already murdered a bunch of people, what's adding grand-theft spaceshuttle to your list?"

"As soon as we steal it, they'll shut it down. We'll never make it anywhere that way."

"We don't have to go far, Harold! Just to the next sector, then pick up the Transit there. Besides, I have a plan," says Carl, with a devious smile on his face.

The stereotypical salesalien emerges from his office. *Here we go! We are already screwed. Carl's plan is already a total failure.*

"You! You again! I thought I made myself perfectly clear the first time. Next credit beatdown won't be so nice," says Ed'die.

"Awww come on, Ed'die. I brought a cosigner this time! See?" says Carl. He motions at Harold. The alien pauses for a moment, thinking about it, but before he comes to a decision, Carl with his hands at his hips casually and with pleasure says, "Light his ass up Harold!"

Harold looks confused and stunned. The alien glances at him, reaching for his own gun.

"Wait what? Why? Carl! Oh shit."

Harold quickly pulls out his pistol, but his hands slip and the gun goes flying. They both dive for it, slamming into each other instead. Ed'die is raising his gun. Everything is in slow motion. Harold's pistol hits the ground and accidentally discharges a round. They all freeze.

Ed'die flops over dead. Carl smiles with delight. Harold is beyond horrified.

"Carl! Next time warn me so I can be ready!" yells Harold.

"What's the problem? I thought you did this all the time?" says Carl.

They take the keys to the ship Carl had hoped to buy and blast off before his credit score gets the better of him. They fire up the engines which flare with that fresh intensity of a new afterburner. The shuttle speeds off into the space traffic with ease. They set it down two sectors over and proceed carefully towards the Transit station before finally boarding the train.

Just before they catch the train, Harold stops.

"This is too hot, Carl. I need to get the pressure off." He pulls out a communicator that he has stolen off the salesalien at the shuttle dealership. He dials the enforcer number for EN1149.

"EN1149 what's your emergency?" says the unsuspecting voice, hoping to help.

"Listen. And listen good. It's a set up! It's all a set up!" says Harold, anonymously.

"What's a setup? Sir? Sir? I don't understand. Can you slow down? Speak calmly."

"I *am* calm! Listen. It was Gharles... Gharles killed the officer. He blew the tram bridge. He's your guy. He took David. He's the one you want!"

"Sir? Are you saying that you know who committed the Tramway murders?"

"Gharles! It was all Gharles!"

He hangs up the communicator before tossing it over the railing into the abyss below.

* * *

"Ma'am there's an audio recording of interest on line seven. Anonymous tip about the Tramway murders. We traced the call to Sector 1147, but it was a stolen communicator. Owner was found dead on his ship lot here in the sector."

"Can we get ID matching on that voice? I've got a dead Enforcer here," said Detective Clinton. She had run down to the dispatch room as soon as she got the call.

"Sorry ma'am, the call was too distorted by the Transit harmonics, impossible to isolate. The call quality is just too poor. We're pulling all area cameras within the dealership and surrounding the Transit station, but so far none were functional."

"Are you kidding me? What kind of a shuttle dealership has non-functional cameras? Why doesn't anything work when I need it to?"

"Well, I can't answer that, but I might posit that perhaps it's because the dealer makes unauthorized trades and has shady business practices."

"Great. More layers to sift through. Thanks for bringing the call to my attention. I'll hear it now."

Detective Clinton tuned in to the call as the dispatcher played it back on the monitor.

"Gharles! It was all Gharles!"

Gharles? Who was Gharles? Carl was now missing. Destroyed apartment, full of weapons. Dead officer. Dead shuttle dealer. Stolen shuttle. Prostitute, prison break David. No camera footage. Blown Tramway car. Burning bar murders. Other Carl was dead. False adoption alibi Harold who showed up on days of murders, but not recently. Then son Thomas on at least one occasion. Wife who doesn't know. *Who the fuck is Gharles? How does all this piece together?* Nothing made sense. No motive. No political claims. No corporate takeovers looming in the sector. Seemingly no connection between victims, except they tended to show up in the vicinity of Carl.

She returned to her own terminal and opened the database. Cross-referencing for Gharles came up with thousands of system-wide profiles. It would take weeks for them to be analyzed and checked. She needed something now. It was time to pay Sheron another visit.

* * *

"David! David! Wake up. Let's go! Come on!"

Thomas shakes him awake. He comes alert, threatened, defensive. *Are we in danger? What is going on?*

"Go where? What's wrong? What's happening?" asks David. Seeing no present danger, he is confused.

"We're going to school today! Come on! Don't be nervous, it's totally fine. You can self-register," says Thomas, anxious to restore some normalcy to his life, and to David's.

The fuck? David hasn't stepped foot in a school since he went ghost. He isn't about to start today. Thomas is so insistent though and he has come to learn that once Thomas has made up his mind about something, he isn't going to let it go. He forces himself to get moving.

"I can't just walk up in there and use my real name. They'll know it's me! It's too risky."

"If I've learned anything from my recent crime sprees, just tell them it's something else! Davin! Your name is Davin now!" says Thomas.

"They'll know though. I don't have an ID card. I'm a ghost, remember? This isn't going to work," says David.

"Trust me. The registrar is a complete moron! Just tell her you don't have one. She'll issue you a new one. Happens all the time with off-worlders. Use our address. Tell her you're my cousin from Atraxia 7."

"Is that even a real planet? Are you sure this is going to work?"

"Who cares! It's not like she would know anyway. Things are way more relaxed here than what you're used to in the business district. Every stamp here is rubber, and if it's not it can be for the right price. If she gives you shit, I'll just pay her off. Everyone has a price here."

Harold might have spent his money from the stolen cards, but Thomas has saved some for times of need. He might have to use it today.

* * *

Sheron drives them to the school in the beat-up old clunker of a shuttle. David is afraid the thing will fall out of the sky any moment. It isn't worth the reduction in walking if they are just going to die in the process. He will definitely be taking the Transit home.

The school building is monolithic. Prison-like even. It is nothing like the ornate schools of the business district. Nonetheless, it seems friendly enough. The disparities within the mid-levels continue to surprise David. He can only imagine the suffering his family must be going through in the lowers if they are even still alive. He knows that he probably made the right choice in ghosting. Thomas escorts him into the central registration office.

"Next! Forms and ID. Oh geez you don't speak this language, do you? Rflurmor k'alarftos mor'quezsh? Plaxos ooflom nzzzb'st? No forms?"

The hideous old alien's voice cracks in a bitter and sarcastic tone. Truly no one has ever seemed more inconvenienced just to do their own job. Her eyes roll. Her fingernails click on her desk. Her plump alien hands flail at the terminal entry keys, almost too large to press them.

"Sorry, I didn't know there were forms. I haven't got an ID card yet," says David.

"Ah hell. What do you mean you don't have an ID? Relocation services is always so behind. Making my job miserable! Name? Address? Planet of origin?"

The line of interrogation continues until she asks for verification. Thomas offers verification by relative.

"Good enough," she says. *This is actually working?* David is surprised.

"How old are you? What was the last grade you were in? Got to get you in the right placement," she says, asking the real tough questions.

David thinks for a long moment. It has been so long since he even thought about it. No one has asked him in years or even cares. The last time he went to school was definitely primary school. How can he have forgotten how old he was? Such a basic simple premise of one's identity. As a ghost, you lose yourself so much to the hustle that you forget who you were.

"Kid? How old are you? Are you sure you speak this language? Thomas, is he slow or what?"

"Thirteen! I think I'm Thirteen? I think I was in Level-4 when I was last in school. Maybe?" says David, with a disappointing lack of confidence behind it.

"What? How do you not even know? I don't even know what to do with that. Those backwater planets! I'm presuming you don't even have prior school records do you? No I figured as much. Okay Davin, welcome to P.S. 8415, the Pride of Mulknosh. We'll just call it Level-9, and go ahead and say agroindustry track. Remedial math for sure," she says.

"Ms. Rathnark, can we get Davin enrolled in Fljrkhorn too? He's an excellent player back home," inquires Thomas.

"*Ugh!* Fine. Probably the only thing he'll pass this year anyway. Okay, there you go, your fitness credit will be Fljrkhorn. Any more changes, cause once I print this to the data tablet, I'm never be changing it again ever?"

"No ma'am, he's good to go!"

She presses the enter key and hands 'Davin' his new ID card and schedule tablet. A place to live, food to eat, a school to go to. He is back on track. Maybe this isn't so bad after all. Even if it is Mulknosh.

They leave the office and venture out into the hallway, bustling with students.

"Thomas, I can't believe that worked! Except I've never played Fljrkhorn. I don't know anything about it," says David, concerned.

"Ah, don't worry about it, you'll learn. I'll train you myself. We need someone with your resilience. But seriously dude, you don't know how old you are? Level-4. That's nuts man."

"When you've been on the run as long as I have, you forget the things that don't matter and just focus on your day-to-day. In the absence of money, the absence of survival, you lose sight of yourself," says David, prophetically, with wisdom beyond his years.

"Geeze. Always so serious! That's rough. That's deep man. Well come on I'll show you to your first class and we'll meet up out front after school. Cool?"

"Yeah, just one last thing. What the hell is agroindustry?"

"Oh! She thinks you're a farmer or some shit, but hey, working for a food plant has its perks!" says Thomas, showing him to a room.

* * *

David's first class is somehow related to written language. He can barely manage to read much of it. He feels like a fish out of water, if he had ever seen fish or water that is. Mastering this class will prove just as elusive. A few of the students introduce themselves, but they are kind of repelled by his standoffish attitude. He has a heavy wave of depression and life experience surrounding him like a storm cloud or a barbed-wire fence.

Who is the saddest looking person in the room? Who was just going through the motions? Who else has known the streets? None quite like him. Though not every alien has the same facial tells as humans. He will have to study them all carefully to determine who he can trust, and who to avoid.

His teacher tries her best to make him feel included but presumes he is just shy. She can tell right away he is going to struggle with the content. The letters jump out at him, and only some of the words have any meaning. He holds the recorder awkwardly like it is almost entirely unfamiliar.

The rest of the day proceeds much the same. He is exhausted from a day of guarding himself against the potential threats of socialization. Thomas doesn't understand why this is such a challenge for him. He will try to do better. He doesn't want to disappoint him. One thing is certain though, he hates Fljrkhorn with a burning passion.

Opting to take the Transit home, they go about discussing the events of their day. At the station they are abruptly stopped in their tracks when they encounter Harold and Carl standing together, demanding to speak with them right away.

"Harold? Carl!? What is going on here? Are you? Are you still? Never mind," says David, alarmed that the two of them would be together.

"Wait, that's Carl? Dad, what the fuck? This is too much. It's like playing with your food or something before you eat it," says Thomas.

"Wait! Harold. You told your *kids* that you were going to murder me? What the fuck?" says Carl.

"Sorry! Actually, they participated. I even paid that one to stalk you for a few weeks, since we're being honest here," says Harold, pointing to David.

"Ugh. So it was like a whole murderous team? How much exactly did you see? Never mind," says Carl.

"Anyways guys, the point is, Gharles set us up! Carl was on a mission to kill me and I was on a mission to kill Carl, but it was the same guy! He offered it to both of us," says Harold.

"Holy shit man. That's fucked up. I mean not that this wasn't already, but wow. So what do you want us to do?" asks David.

"Yeah. Why us? Also, Dad, does this mean we're not going to be rich anymore? Because if so I could just go die right now," says Thomas, fearful his prospects are over.

"Well. We want to involve as few people as possible and since you both already know about this, I was hoping you could help. This is the plan we came up with. We want Thomas to call and set up a meeting with Gharles. He won't suspect us to be there and he certainly won't expect Carl and I to be working together. You lure him out and then Carl and I will kill him. Then we steal his money," says Harold.

"No way! You want me to risk my life and meet with this guy who you know is shady and murderous? How do you know he won't kill me if I decline? Also, what if you fuck it up again? You don't exactly have the best track record. How do we even know he has money?" says Thomas, furiously.

"Thomas, I happen to know on good authority that Gharles is extremely wealthy. Just remember what I said. All who touch his money suffer and perish," says David.

"Wait David knows Gharles too? What, are you trying to kill us too?" says Carl.

"He recruits a lot of street people to carry out his dirty work. The payouts are substantial, but they always end up dead sooner or later. I thought he was just an urban legend, but now that I've heard it from all of you, I think we should take it seriously," says David.

"Fine! I'll set up the meeting. Just don't fuck this up okay? Swear to me you'll get this right!" pleads Thomas.

"Okay! We swear. This is the number. Don't call here though. Wait until we're at home. Gharles has eyes and ears everywhere. Even this is too risky. We have to get Carl back to the house before someone sees us together," says Harold.

Chapter 16

"Who is this? How did you get this number?"

"You're Gharles right? Gharles Darkley?"

"Why yes, I am. Who might you be?"

"This is Thomas. Listen, I know how the game is played. I want to meet with you and discuss financial arrangements. Unlike my father, you can expect me to do the job right. I want in, but I want it all for myself. Okay?"

"Yes, Mr. Thomas. That is certainly good news. I must say that this is unexpected and welcome news. I was beginning to grow impatient with your father. My interest in Carl is waning though. He is, after all, missing and it would seem that his life is already in shambles. I think perhaps I have a new recruit of interest just for you. Shall we meet tomorrow?"

"Whatever. Meet me at 9pm. The Crimson Railroad, Junction 380. Tell the doorman you have a reservation for the High Deck Lounge. I'll be waiting. Come alone Gharles and bring proof of funds. I don't want any trouble. I'm going to great lengths to ensure the privacy of our meeting. Alone Gharles!"

"Of course, Mr. Thomas. A wise precaution. I think you and I are going to do *very* well together. I assure you that you will find our chat to be most satisfying."

The trap is set. David will be monitoring the front entrance. Harold will be waiting just outside the backdoor and Carl will take the side door. They will hide out of sight until Gharles has arrived and gone inside. Then they will kill him on the way out and Thomas will follow behind to make sure the deed is done to completion.

Sheron comes home to find the four of them together, conversing.

Who is this strange man in my home? What is going on here? She has to inquire further. Her face lights up with false pleasantries as she tries to be polite.

"Hello! Harold didn't mention we were having company today. I would have cleaned the house a little better! Has anyone offered you a refreshment? I'm Sheron, Harold's wife. I'm sure he's told you all about me."

"Yes, he certainly has. I'm Carl and I'm here to…" He looks to Harold for assistance. He has actually never heard of Sheron at all.

"And he's David's uncle from off-world, Sheron! He's going to be crashing on the couch for a couple of days. He's trying to get David an off-world permit so he can go live with him!" says Harold. He tenses up, hoping she accepts the explanation.

"I am? I mean yes of course! I can't wait to have my *nephew* here come join our family. *That couch though?*" says Carl.

He stares at the well-used old couch with its faded pattern and scratchy fabric. The springs are so near to coming out from it that you could almost lose an eye if you were to roll over on it the wrong way. He imagines the number of times Harold's disgusting fat ass has sat upon it. Perhaps sleeping in the hallway outside the apartment would be preferable.

"Oh! That's just wonderful news isn't it David?" Sheron says, buying the lie. "Well, you're welcome to stay for a while. Don't mind me, I'll just be in the kitchen making dinner for everyone. This calls for something special, I'll make my famous Slopsagna!"

"Yes. Of course. So wonderful that *Uncle Carl* is here now. Slopsagna, oh boy! That'd be swell," says David.

This is not to anyone's liking, but no one has the gall to tell Sheron what is really going on. Nor will they tell her that her infamous Slopsagna is in fact only notorious for its terrible lack of taste and slippery texture.

"Sher, I'm going to take Carl here out to the bar tomorrow night to meet the guys at work okay?" says Harold. While he has her primed for lies, he hopes to feed her more.

"Yeah. Also, Mom, while we're on the subject, David and I are going to be home really late tomorrow. We've got a school thing to do. Nothing you should worry about though," says Thomas.

By this point, Thomas should know that merely describing something as a 'school thing' is totally insufficient to assuage a mother of her teenager's whereabouts.

"Oh, I get it. Just me and Martha tomorrow. *Again*," says Sheron.

She uses that tone of voice in the hope of illustrating her irritation with the situation, but as usual, her indirect passive-aggressive statements bear no meaning to the men in her life. That or they know exactly what she meant, but take her at her literal word because it suits them.

It is in fact the latter. This bothers them not in the slightest because they intend to execute their mission regardless of her approval. They might have had a thought that if only she knew what they were really doing, she would be understanding, but given their intention is to murder someone and steal his money, that is probably unlikely to occur.

They adjourn to separate areas of the apartment as though nothing is happening. The dinner conversation is excruciatingly awkward, like a telephone game of lies going around in a circle. It is difficult to slurp down the Slopsagna, even for seasoned veterans of her dish.

"Bro! I've been eating trash for years, and this is truly unfit for consumption," whispers David to Thomas.

"Imagine having to maintain this lie for years!" Thomas replies.

Carl feels physically ill after eating it. Then the thought of sleeping on their old worn-out couch continues to disturb him greatly.

* * *

Carl tries as best as he can to ignore how uncomfortable it is to lie upon. *Just look straight up, Carl. Don't turn your head, or your ear might touch this couch.* He confirms his previous suspicions about the smell.

Harold is getting nervous about the operation. In a moment of panic, he awakens in the middle of the night. He slips into the kitchen and picks up a large butcher's knife. He slowly walks over to Carl, thinking he's asleep.

He hovers over Carl with the knife, considering stabbing him to death just to satisfy Gharles and be done with it. Carl opens his eyes to look straight up at Harold. He can see him and make out the reflection on the blade even in the darkness of night.

"Seriously, Harold? Are you really trying to kill me? After all the progress we've made?" says Carl, half asleep.

"Sorry. I panicked! Can't blame a guy for trying, right? You're right though. I was wrong for that," says Harold. He has actually thought about it multiple times since they started working together. It is certainly a good Plan B.

"It's okay." Carl sits up. "If you only knew how many times I almost pushed you in front of the Transit," says Carl. He too has considered murdering Harold, in no small part due to his belief that Harold truly is, at times, a terrible human being.

"Tried? I almost damn near fell in!" says Harold, recounting one such suspicious occasion on the way in which he suspected that Carl had more than accidentally bumped into him.

"Okay, and I already apologized for bumping into you. On another note, don't you think it will be suspicious to Sheron when I don't take David with me? She's going to find out eventually," says Carl.

"I don't know! I just panicked and it made the most sense. Besides, this will all be over tomorrow anyway and then we can get on with our rich lives. She'll forget all about it."

"Right. Just like you were so successful at killing me. Don't fuck this up, Harold," Carl says, trying to return to his abysmal attempt at sleeping.

"*Me?* At least I've actually killed before! How many people have you killed? That's right none! So really it's you I should be worried about. What if you can't pull the trigger?" says Harold, part defensively, part out of legitimate concern.

"This is different. He's a crime lord! Well, I guess so are you, but he's the *reason* you're a crime lord. Besides now I have nothing left to lose."

"What, you got something against criminals now? Mister We Should Steal a Used Space Shuttle!"

"Yeah, but at least I didn't kill the salesalien!"

"That's funny, I seem to remember you saying something like 'light 'em up Harold!'"

"And if you interpreted that to mean kill him, I mean, *pshh*, that's on you!"

None of the four of them sleep well that night. Getting through the day at school and at work will prove to be a chore. David is considering bailing on the entire thing. He has no qualm with Gharles and isn't eager to get any more involved than he already is. Thomas is afraid of what Gharles might do at the meeting or what he might already know.

Harold should have been thinking about Thomas' safety, but he is actually way more concerned about how much money Gharles really has. He might have inferred this from his all-access double-black platinum ID card, had he not already forgotten that it existed.

Carl is having his own doubts about whether he can really kill someone, even if they are evil. Harold is not entirely wrong about what he has said. He is more of a thinker than a doer, especially when it comes to murdering a crime lord.

* * *

Thomas is fortunate enough to have a friend who works at The Crimson Railroad who is able to get him the room for no charge. He doesn't tell him exactly what it's about, but he doesn't need to know. In fact, the less he knows, the better.

The bar has an industrial feel to it. The black and red interiors are illuminated by red lighting. It tries to combine a touch of old grit and modern cosmopolitan imagery. This gives it the illusion of being nice. The bar is on the first floor, along with a wall of booths and a handful of tables. The upstairs lounge is reserved for private functions.

As time grows closer, Thomas becomes more and more apprehensive about the meeting. *Is he still coming? Does he already know about our plan? What will happen?*

As the hour strikes nine, a hovercraft limousine strolls up the back alley, parking there, as though it owns the road. This has to be him. Gharles will be the kind of guy who has a chauffeur open doors for him. Not exactly as alone as Thomas is hoping for. Here he comes into the bar. Walking up the stairs. *Okay Thomas. Poker face, it's game time.*

"Gharles. You're three minutes late. Chauffeur won't be giving us any trouble now will he? I'm already concerned," says Thomas, stern-faced and arms crossed.

"Good evening, Mr. Thomas. Yes, I do apologize. Again you and I are so very much on the same page. My driver is under the strictest orders to remain in the car. We can speak freely here. Just as soon as I inspect the room for a moment." He glances around, checking for cameras and listening devices. Gharles prefers to choose his own meeting places; Thomas has turned the tables on him.

"Is everything to your satisfaction, Gharles?" Thomas asks, trying to rush his process.

"Yes. You have done well, Mr. Thomas. Now let's talk business, shall we? Firstly, you must know by now that I am not a man to be trifled with lightly and that there are of course certain occupational hazards to this kind of work. However, I assure you that the purported disappearances you may have heard about are not as they appear."

He raises a brow at Thomas, probing to see what rumors he might have heard about him, but Thomas gives him no reaction.

"Once people get paid the money that I'm paying them, they don't tend to stay on world. Who would you tell? Wouldn't you vanish as well? Many of these people now work for the Syndicate network. We're an organization you see. We work towards the advancement of a better future for humanity. I hope that one day *you* might become a member. You see, we've been watching you, Thomas. We think that you could be a professional Fljrkhorn player someday, and we would like to help you achieve that goal. Now, there's just of course the matter of actions required. Think of it as an *initiation*. A small sacrifice to our lord, Jefferson. A minor inconvenience at the most."

"Let's start with money for now and then we'll see what else I might be interested in," Thomas replies.

"I've brought you this as a token of my goodwill. Consider it an advance.

As you can see, I have a hundred thousand in unmarked credits. Take them. I am of such great means, I couldn't be bothered to even notice it is gone. A gift. Whether you accept the deal or not. My treat. I think you will though." He opens the briefcase to flash the cash.

"Alright, I'm convinced you are what you claim to be. Let's discuss details then."

"Well you see, Harold has been making such great efforts with Carl, we want to reward him for his hard work. I mean he's not dead yet, that we know of, and we assume Harold is alive right? His communicator appears to be indisposed at the moment. We were considering giving him a *promotion*! Of course, there's that dreadful Ms. Xvranbul who is standing in our way. If you kill her, we'll make sure he gets that promotion."

"Done! How do you want her? Sliced, diced, beheaded?"

"Oh, we'll leave it up to your creative imagination, Mr. Thomas. However, there is another small matter that we'd like you to attend to. There's a boy who has been giving us a difficult time and I'm afraid that he might have been an informant after getting himself caught by the Enforcers. He's of little importance, but we cannot tolerate this kind of dissension in our network, even among subcontractors. Really just riff-raff. His name is David." Gharles flashes the photograph on a data recorder.

Thomas freezes with fear. *How can it be? Is this a trick? Gharles knows? Somehow he knows?* He shakes his head. "No. I can't do that. You must be mistaken. David would never talk to the Enforcers. That's just not who he is. You're wrong."

"I did not realize that the two of you were so intimately acquainted. Perhaps your mother was right about her suspicions." Thomas wonders where Gharles has heard that. "Tell me though, Mr. Thomas, how well do you *really* know David? How do you know that's the *real* David? It's just one little murder, Thomas. Isn't that worth becoming incredibly rich for? He's nobody! He's just a street rodent. No one will miss him and you will be doing him a favor!" says Gharles, his crooked grin widening with anticipation.

"I'm sorry, Gharles. You can keep your money. You'll have to find somebody else to do your dirty work. I won't hurt David. I wish I could help you, but I think we're at an impasse here. I'm out," says Thomas starting to stand from the table, before Gharles reaches across to grab his arm. Thomas sits back down.

"Well, perhaps you are just not ready for the Syndicate yet. That is most unfortunate, Mr. Thomas. I'll prove that I'm a man of my word, Mr. Thomas. I want you to take that cash and I won't take no for an answer on that. If you don't take it, it'll just stay here on the table! Maybe you don't want to do this job today, but sleep on it. Let us know when you change your mind. Especially once you get to know the *real* David. Good evening, Mr. Thomas. Do stay in touch."

Thomas pushes the briefcase towards him. He maintains a stern, aggressive gaze on Gharles. Thomas is in control here, and his no means no.

Gharles is disappointed that Thomas has disagreed with him; perhaps he has mischaracterized him. He sees through this charade though. A man of Thomas's age with that much money will certainly come around. If nothing else, he feels pleased to have elevated a true pure-blood human.

He stands up from the table, not giving Thomas the opportunity to have the last word. As he approaches the staircase down into the bar, he turns once more.

"Oh and one more thing, Mr. Thomas. Do be careful. You may think you can protect David, but if you stand in our way, I cannot be responsible for what ill may come of you. Do send our regards to Mr. Harold. I'll be in touch real soon." He exits the room with a smile on his face, making his way down the stairs in his sharp suit and ornamental cane.

Thomas breathes a sigh of relief. He collapses down onto the table, shaking off his nerves. After a moment, he swipes the cash from the briefcase and puts it into a backpack. He doesn't want to risk the possibility that the briefcase is tracked, but he isn't about to leave that kind of money on the table. He heads downstairs and tips his friend the doorman. He sees that Gharles is heading for the back entrance. His distorted figure can be seen through the stacked block frosted glass windows of the bar. Thomas can see that he is heading to the right, back to his limo as expected. Thomas follows him, exiting through the back door of the bar.

He isn't quick enough. Gharles is helped back into his limo and the door is closed. *Where is Harold?* He was missing his chance. *He had one job and he is fucking it up. Come on, Harold! What happened?* Thomas is furious. He almost thinks about firing on the limo itself but realizes the glass is likely bulletproof and he will be compromised. He turns and walks back through the bar door towards the front instead, steaming with rage, when all of a sudden, the ground shakes.

Kaplow!!

The glasses topple, the drinks in the bar go tumbling to the floor. The back windows shattered . A massive explosion is heard. Thomas' ears are ringing. Everyone is in a total state of shock. He runs back towards the rear door to see Gharles' limo smoldering with flames. Shards of metal and glass everywhere. He turns to run now. He runs for home. He did it! Harold actually pulled it off!

Back at the rendezvous point, David is the first to arrive. Thomas comes second, out of breath, gasping for air. "What the fuck happened? I thought you were dead for sure back there!" says David.

"The meeting went south. He left... the limo. They blew up the limo!" says Thomas.

"Wait, so he actually did it? He actually fucking did it?!"

"Yes. He killed Gharles. I'm sure of it, and I'm glad too."

"Why? What happened?"

"It's nothing... I'll tell you some other time."

"It's not nothing, Thomas! What did he ask you to do?"

"Let's table it for later. Look here comes Carl!"

Carl's clothes are somehow torn and he is bleeding a bit. Black soot from the smoke blankets his face. Covered in sweat, his hair frazzled, he looks like he is in a total daze.

"Ahhhh... arhhh... Gahhh... Harllllllld..." Carl tries to speak, unable to get the words out.

"Carl? Snap out of it! He's not back yet. What happened?" asks David.

As Carl is gathering his wits about him, Harold arrives, sauntering with victorious enthusiasm.

"Did you see it? *Kablamo!* We blew him sky high!"

"Dad! What the fuck happened? I think you broke Carl!" proclaims Thomas.

"Ah, he'll get over it. Man, what a way to go huh? *Boom! Haha!*"

"Dad... How the fuck are we going to get his money now?"

"Oh shit. I don't know. I was so focused on killing him, I forgot why!"

"Harrrrrrllllld!!! You almost killed me you idiot! The.. the flames came *this* close to my face! My whole life flashed before my eyes. And now you're telling me we have no way of getting the money now? Now I really am gonna kill you Harold," yells Carl.

"Relax Carl! You'll survive. But also I have a plan!" says Harold.

"Enough of your plans Harold! Every time you have a plan it gets worse!" says David.

"Perhaps you'd rather go back to your cell then David? Come on, guys. I still have this!" says Harold, pulling the all-access ID card given to him by Gharles from his pocket. It is by luck that he has remembered it.

"Ohhh yeah. I have one of those too! I completely forgot about it. We could trace it back to his accounts that way. Since he's already dead he won't notice the fraud! We just have to get there before the heirs do. Harold, you're not an idiot after all. Well, you are still incredibly stupid, but you know..." says Carl finding his own ID card. They both have at least some connection back to Gharles.

* * *

They journey back home to the apartment, arriving suspiciously at the same time. Sheron sees the gritty conditions of them all, including Carl's tattered clothes, sending her mind into a series of anxieties.

"Hayrolldddd! What happened to him? This poor man. Why do you always go out to the rowdiest bars. I swear! You took the boys with you too? To the bar! Don't tell me it was a school thing, boys."

"Yes, Mom. That's what happened. We took Uncle Carl out for a good time. He tried to ride the mechanical Jhaarthock and got thrown off hard.

Destroyed really. It wasn't his best moment. Dad gave us beers!" says Thomas, using the momentary shock to give him and David time to slip away.

"Harold! I'm ever so pissed! Who does that? Who takes kids to a bar and buys them beer? Is this really the impression you want Carl to have of us? This is not who we are, Carl! We are dignified, honest working, tax-paying Capital City citizens. I apologize for my husband for he is obviously not well and has lost his damn mind!"

"*Ah.* Come on Sheron! Live a little. It's not every day we get offworlders in town!" he says, sending her off in a rage to the bedroom, slamming the door behind her.

He turns on the viewer to try and drown out the sound of her yelling. There is breaking news. The wrong kind of breaking news. "Boys get in here quick!"

"Mulknosh CEO Jez Barbados was rushed to a local hospital this evening to receive emergency intensive care after an assassination attempt was made on his life. Barbados was departing a bar in the mid-levels called The Crimson Railroad. He had just entered his limousine when it unexpectedly exploded from an incendiary device. Barbados narrowly escaped with his life, but sustained severe injuries. His chauffeur Donatello Shaakor was unfortunately incinerated in the blast. No comment yet from the Barbados team on what he was doing in the bar, but they said it was certainly a business transaction and that the public need not concern themselves. Gui'lda W'uthrnm, Capital News. Back to you Caarlito."

Harold and Carl stand, wide-eyed in dismay, mouths hung open. It doesn't seem possible that Barbadosis was Gharles. How could he have survived? Harold saw the entire limo burn up flames. He is sure of it. Carl glares at Harold.

"Gui'lda we're going to roll some footage now of the blast. You can see the edge of his car there around the corner as it explodes! Wow, look at that! Just incredible. That's all we got! What are witnesses on the scene saying? Any suspects so far? Give us the inside scoop!"

They are relieved that none of them are visible in the camera footage. What are the odds that this particular bar has at least one functional camera?

"Well Caarlito, folks here are just as stunned as you are. Mr. Barbados states

that he has no memory of his business meeting there or the events of the past few days. Enforcers do not believe the assailant was inside the bar at the time as the detonator had to be lit manually and was a short fuse device."

Harold is somewhat relieved, as this might take some of the suspicions off Thomas if they are to ever piece more of this together.

"Several witnesses say they saw Barbados heading to a private lounge upstairs. Unsubstantiated rumors believe that they saw what appeared to be two male escorts fleeing the scene shortly after the incident occurred. Barbados' team has staunchly denied this. Unfortunately, guest registration paperwork was burned in the resultant fire which did spread to the bar, but no additional camera footage has been recovered."

"Now Gui'lda, I know it's probably too soon to ask this, but do you believe these attacks could be related to the Anastoncia Tennhausen murder from a few months back? I mean it does seem that there are many similarities – CEOs of massive corporations, explosives used in both cases."

"Yes Caarlito, that is definitely one of the theories Enforcers are investigating. Chief Hollander has reached out to Chief Levitz at Mulknosh EN to offer his support, collaboration, and the manpower to bring an end to this grisly murder spree."

"That's excellent news Gui'lda. We have just received word that President McSlurmins will address Capital City late this evening and is expected to pledge central high command resources to solving these crimes. For commentary on why McSlurmins is wrong, we have with us today a very special guest, presidential hopeful, senator Galxshu! Senator can you hear us?"

"Great to be here Caarlito. Listen, this is exactly what I've been saying. It shouldn't cost this much to live this terrible! McSlurmins' policies are directly responsible for these acts of terror. They say the aliens are to blame, but this is a clear example of human on human crime! The president has done nothing to smooth unrest at VranthCo. and we are no closer to a declaration of victory in the takeover battles. We must dispatch Capital Peacekeepers to these systems of unrest immediately if any changes are going to be made."

"Senator, you've been criticized for many things recently, particularly your stock ownership in both VranthCo. and Mulknosh. How do we know that you're not personally invested in this?"

"That is an absurd, bold-faced lie propagated by the McSlurmins team! I have a very diverse stock profile in many strong companies. McSlurmins has received no such criticism and he was on the board of directors of ArthessIN, and no one has questioned the massive contracting deals he's issued between them and—"

Harold cuts off the viewer.

"Holy shit, I don't believe it! I mean how? Gharles is... Gharles is Barbados? We tried to kill Barbados! But wait, Barbados wanted us to kill each other. I'm so confused. I don't even... He survived? How?! I saw the whole thing go *kaplow!*"

"I can't even believe this! You know that guy was the CEO at my company until I got fired?" says Carl.

"Wait. Barbados was CEO at Mulknosh. You mean he ran your company too?" says Harold.

David and Thomas have caught up by this point and are equally distraught.

"David! Those people who disappeared. You said you knew them. Who did they work for?" asked Thomas.

"*Ugh,* you really don't get it do you? Mulknosh is just the industrial division of a massive subsidiary of an even greater company that all ties back into Barbados. Mulknosh, ArthessIN, VranthCo., HyrOn, Malthex, ZornCo., and at least another thousand companies are all owned by a majority share interest from Galactose Bank. This is in turn owned by a private equity firm called Kronostics. Galxshu, McSlurmins, and Barbados are all big shareholders and sit on the board there too," David says with a rare academic confidence.

"Where did you learn that!? Are you saying they all worked for the same company?" asks Harold.

"Yes... That's exactly what I'm saying. You and Carl both worked for Kronostics. You just didn't know it. And since no one ever sees their CEO, you had no idea it was him the whole time. Everyone that disappeared under Gharles' watch has worked for Kronostics. I learned about all this stuff in History of Inter-Galactic Corporations class yesterday and I kind of put the pieces together in my mind. Truthfully though, several billion people work for them, they just never cared to ask how deep the chain goes."

Sheron returns from the other room frazzled. The conversation stops abruptly.

"See Harold! This is why you don't take the kids to bars. Look what happened. Someone tried to blow up Mr. Barbados right here in this sector! Can you believe it?"

"No Sher! We were just as astonished as you were. How crazy is that?" says Harold, as he attempts to feign ignorance. The tone in his voice lacks sincerity.

"Hey, Sheron. This is probably a bad time to ask, but do you mind if I borrow Harold tomorrow? I've got some errands to run and I could really use some help figuring out the Transit," says Carl, with a calm matter-of-fact attitude about him.

"Oh yeah, sure. Just another day off on my own with a murderer on the loose. That's fine," says Sheron, glancing around to see if any of them pick up on her real meaning.

"Okay great! Thanks for understanding," says Carl.

This leads to a groan from Sheron who presumes Carl must be new to this. *'That's fine'* meant quite the opposite.

Carl has an ingenious idea, but he needs to get back into Sector 1149 to pull it off. Fortunately, they are both now very aware of the ID cards Gharles, or rather Barbados, had given them. The boys will stay behind and keep a low profile for the day in light of the incident. Besides, Thomas still hasn't told Harold about the one-hundred-thousand credits sitting in his backpack. Fortunately for all of them, it is a weekend day, so there are no other inhibitions.

"Thomas. You still never told me what Gharles... er Barbados told you up there," says David.

"And I'm never going to, David. So drop it. It was all lies and manipulations, David. Go to sleep."

Chapter 17

Detective Clinton could tell the case was rapidly escalating now. Dignitaries of the governor's office were pouring in and out of the double doors to the precinct. This usually meant more demands and increased pressures. It would only be a matter of time because the case was escalated further, especially after McSlurmins' declaration.

"Lt. Xanthu, I'm running out of time here and I don't want to lose this case to central command. Please tell me you have something incredible from forensics today?"

"Do I ever! I got you a partial print match on Dead Carl. You know the first Carl who died in front of Missing Carl's apartment? Yeah. Anyways, the partial prints of course align with many, but among the many, there are few. Check it out! Your boy Harold is a high match candidate," says Xanthu.

Clinton's face lit up with excitement. She was so ready to go that she almost ran out of the room but stopped herself.

"Thank you Xanthu. This is amazing. We've already connected Harold to several aspects of this case. I'm actually headed there now. Does the name Gharles mean anything to you?" she asked, still highly perplexed by the connection. Perhaps it was a wrench in the cog thrown by Harold to throw her off track.

"Gharles? Nope. Haven't heard that one before. Why, are they a suspect?"

"I'm not sure. We got an anonymous call that we suspect was from Missing Carl or his captor. It said Gharles was behind it all. Could just be a false lead, but I want to get a search out on it. I could really use your help today though."

"You need me to come, don't you? All the way to Mulknosh!? Come on

Georgette! I'm already working overtime on a weekend here."

He really did not want to be there, and even less wanted to spend all day on the Transit just to end up in some gross dingy industrial sector. She always knew how to get to him, and he had a soft spot for all her requests.

"Don't Georgette me! Look, if I go there now, they're going to drag me into this Barbados crime scene. I want to sweep it, but I suspect this lead on Harold will prove more illuminating in our case. Will you please come with me? I'll let you take the Barbados scene and I can slip off and get the interview I need. Yes?" she said, knowing just how to capture his interest.

"You'll put my name to the Barbados case? Hollander will have your ass for that you know. But you got a deal! I'm in... I don't know how I let you talk me into these things," he said, knowing that she could have talked him into anything just for the off chance of getting to spend more time with her. They would surely want a pure human in the Barbados case, and Hollander would really dislike the optics of the switch.

"Because I pay you!"

She laughed as they both prepared to depart the precinct. She felt like she was closing in on them now, yet she also knew time was limited. The pressure to solve the case had reached critical levels and with witnesses and suspects vanishing off the table, it was becoming less likely she would solve it.

* * *

It was a long ride into Mulknosh as reporters and curious bystanders flooded into the system, all hoping to get photographs with the incinerated limo. Even the Enforcer entry bypass line was long. This was even worse than the tramway incident.

Xanthu kept her well entertained with his jabs. "How do they know it was an explosion and not a trashcan fire? Look at this dump. With mids like this, who needs a lower tier!"

"Simmer down, Lieutenant. someone might hear you!" she said, trying to remain professional.

They arrived at the gate of the entrance set up for law enforcement, which amounted to a set of hastily rigged temporary wire fencing placed in front of a doorway. Two local Enforcers guarded the entrance, manually checking their ID badges. It made the process slow, particularly as each entrant carried on a conversation with the guards *ad nauseum.*

"Oh, you guys must be the pair that Hollander sent over huh?" said the local Enforcer.

"Detective Clinton. EN1149. This is my partner Lt. Xanthu. He'll be leading this investigation and assisting you in this matter. He's more familiar with the forensic evidence as he has been supervising the lab from the beginning. I'll be collecting witness interviews and will rejoin you later today," she said.

Her response caused him to furrow his brow at the sight of the alien sent to run the investigation, and it was obvious he was critical of it. Perhaps she should have kept that to herself if it was going to be a problem.

"Well, it's pretty much a dead end. It happened so fast, no one really remembers anything. We've already got the scene pretty much on lockdown, but come have a look, Xanthu."

The guard provided entry, leaving his post to the other who had to run the line by himself.

With the local force sufficiently off her back, she proceeded out into the Transit plaza, and down the moving walkways toward Harold's apartment. Unbeknownst to her, as she was making her way down, Harold and Carl were already on their way out. They would pass each other on separate lifts without even knowing.

* * *

She knocked on the door.

"Hello? Sheron? Are you home?" She paused for a moment and the door creaked open.

"Oh, it's you again. From the agency. Look, we've already got it figured out. David's going to go live with his uncle," said Sheron, throwing Clinton for a loop.

This was not at all what she expected to hear. She paused a moment to find the best response to maintain her cover.

"Really? His uncle? And where is David now? Can I see him?"

"Oh, you know I'm not sure. They might still be here! Yes, David's uncle Carl! I'm sure you know that already though. Him and Harold already left this morning. Sorry, you came all this way!" she said.

That was everything Clinton needed to hear. Her grasp on the case was tightening again, and that was the piece she needed to link it together.

"Uncle Carl? Oh wow. Sheron, I can't do this anymore" she said, deciding to lay it all out on the table for Sheron. "I'm not with the agency. My name is Detective Clinton, EN1149. What I am about to tell you is not going to be easy. We suspect that Harold may have been involved in some criminal activities in our sector. Can you account for his whereabouts on a few nights for me?"

"What? My Harold? A criminal! No, it can't be true! I won't hear any of these lies. He's been here with me every night," said Sheron, covering for Harold before even considering the proposal. This even surprised her because she knew he had been up to something suspicious. She also knew he was a moron who could easily get involved in crime if it paid.

"Sheron, I know this is difficult. I'm going to show you some pictures okay? This is Harold with a known prostitute. Then there is David, also in the foreground. This prostitute entered my jailhouse and took David out of our custody. David has been connected to a series of murders that have occurred in the vicinity of Carl who has been missing. Is this *Uncle Carl*?"

"Oh my god. I have to sit down," said Sharon, fanning at her flushed face with her hands. "This woman? Who is she? Is this the other woman? I knew it! That dirtball. I knew it all along! What is her name? Oh my god. Harold has a secret double life! Doesn't he?"

Sheron sits on a dining room chair, clutching at her hair in a state of total shock and disappointment. The pictures made it all too real.

"I can't tell you what to believe, but it looks to me like David could be Harold's love child with this woman. Maybe Harold's covering to protect David? I'll ask again. Are you sure he was with you every night?" she said, fueling the fire with an incendiary accusation. She knew that was not the case, but she also knew that would get the most rise out of Sheron.

Sheron agreed to cooperate if the detective supplied her with dates to help her remember. She was furious with Harold and with all the lies she had been told. Her whole world was turning upside down. How had she been so naive? She imagined what might happen if Harold were to be incarcerated. They would have to descend for sure. She wondered how he could have put her in this position.

Clinton reassured her, telling her that she is doing the right thing and that she deserves someone better than Harold. She tried to assuage her economic fears, even though she knew they were well substantiated.

* * *

The boys heard her entrance. David knew her voice immediately. He panics, grabbing a backpack and starting to stuff it with whatever supplies he can get his hands on. He looks around for the escape routes. Vents, windows, doors, weapons – the wheels of strategy turning in his mind.

"Thomas! That's her! That's the bitch that took me in on that raid. She knows! She's onto us," he says.

Thomas had rightfully guessed that the woman is an investigator based on her last visit and the subsequent knowledge he learned about Harold. He knows what is at stake.

"I know her! She's been here before. I knew she wasn't with an agency! Wait… If Mom tells her you're here, then… We have to get you out of here!"

He starts to move as frantically as David, trying to devise their next move.

"How? There's only one way out and she's standing in the way. We got lucky once. We're not going to get that chance again," says David.

"It's dangerous, but I know another way. Follow my lead and do exactly as I do!"

Thomas grabs his backpack containing the money. He tears a piece of a shirt off to cover his face; he gives another to David to do the same. Then he does something totally unexpected in this world and opens the exterior window. Open terraces have external air purifiers and most structures are in some way enclosed to defend against the disgusting pollution of the outside air. This apartment is positioned in the building such that they are on the edge of the sector, and the windows face directly out into the elements. They will have no such defense.

To David's horror, Thomas carefully climbs out the window onto a narrow ledge. The ground is not even visible through the dense clouds of smog. One mistake will send them plunging hundreds of stories to the ground, never to be found.

"Are you coming or what? Come on let's go? Shut the window on your way out, that way they won't suspect anything," says Thomas. The sound of billowing wind fills the room.

"Thomas, I'm afraid of heights!" says David standing at the edge of the window.

"What are you more afraid of? This or dying in prison?" says Thomas, already making his way across the ledge.

"Well, when you put it that way... Just remind me not to look down."

David slowly and painfully manages to get his first leg over the edge of the window. He can tell his feet will barely fit on the ledge. He gets the second leg out, trying not to look down. After a moment he is able to close the window. The wind rips past them in a swirling vortex of heavy pollution, burning at their eyes and exposed skin even through the makeshift masks.

"Thomas! How long? How far are we going? Get me off of this ledge!" David is panicking already within the first few steps, desperately not wanting to let go of the window ledge.

"We just have to slide down this way to the hallway window. Don't worry! I sneak out this way all the time. Just hold on to the pipes to brace yourself. Be careful going around that corner," he says.

David looks up to see a two-inch pipe running the length of the building just above him. He carefully trades the window for the pipe. His hands are shaking. Every muscle in his body tenses with fear.

"Corner? You didn't say anything about corners! I swear if we don't die on this, I'm going to kill you. I can't do it. Please help me!" pleads David.

"David... relax. Don't look down. Just follow the pipe. It's *mostly* secure.

Just take it one step at a time. Nice and easy. There you go. You're getting it now!" says Thomas, trying to coach him through.

The pipe shakes loosely as David grips it. It is clear that the pipe is old and the brackets maintaining it are wearing down and coming loose. He expects it to go at any minute. Thomas has already rounded the corner. It isn't much further but he feels alone now. He hears the crunch of dirt and dust falling from the ledge to the ground distantly below. His foot slides ever so slightly on the dust. He clings to the pipe for dear life. The bracket bends as he applies force to the pipe. This is it. His heart pounding, the bracket holds and the pipe steadies his balance. Finally, he resumes, ever so slowly to the hallway window.

* * *

Back in the apartment, Sheron was briefing the detective on what she remembered. Clinton was encouraging her along, but she was becoming overly emotional and difficult to work with. She decided that now was her chance to check out the remainder of the apartment and see if she could recapture David. She told Sheron that she just wanted to have a chat with him, while she regains her composure.

Truthfully, Sheron had already given her plenty of information to pin the tramway murders on Harold and possibly Carl. This was her chance to recapture David. She kept her hand on her stun blaster. She wanted to be ready this time. He wasn't getting away. She threw open the door to the boy's room. It was empty!

Damn. They must have left before she got there. She decided to search through the room. Nothing out of the ordinary. Typical belongings. Something caught her eye though. A small crumpled strip of paper next to the recycler basket on the ground by the nightstand. *What is it?* She picked it up and opened it. It was a phone number. One word written above it. 'Gharles.' *Ah! There was her big break!* She'd settle the score with David another day, but she had got what she needed.

She informed Sheron that the boys must have stepped out, but that she really has to be going. She told her that she worries that she had overwhelmed her. Her final request is that she keep her visit entirely secret from Harold, Carl, and the boys, to which Sheron agreed.

Sheron knew she couldn't keep a secret of that magnitude and she was so angry at Harold that she just wanted to strangle him. She wondered too what Thomas knew and this gave her elaborate concerns.

Having sufficiently used Sheron for all her worth, Clinton left the apartment to rejoin Xanthu at the crime scene and to investigate her new lead.

* * *

David and Thomas are already well ahead of her, running at full speed across the connecting bridges. David isn't sure where they are going. His knees are still weak from the death-defying ledge experience. This part of town seems more rundown. It reminds David of his street life.

"Thomas... Where are we going?"

"Don't worry. I have a friend. We'll be safe there. Trust me!"

He isn't big on trust, but he follows Thomas into the dilapidated building. The lights flicker on and off and everything is dirty. The lift scares him. He would have preferred they took the stairs, but he doesn't know how far down they are going.

"What is this place?" David asks, his voice filled with concern and doubt.

"Don't worry, we're gonna stay mids. We're just going to go down a while. Thirty-seven floors down actually. It's not dangerous though, *I promise*," he says, like a used shuttle salesalien.

This is not very reassuring. The lift shakes and rattles. It slowly drops through the floors, the lights going in and out. The last thing he wants is to die in a metal box after escaping an Enforcer who wants to put him in a different metal box. He yearns to be free of boxes one day. Ironic in a place known for its box factory.

The hallway is rugged. Piles of trash litter the floor. The carpet is stained and mildewed beyond recognition. They reach an apartment and Thomas knocks. Thomas doesn't even flinch when the door opens but David's eyes grow wide with concern. The giant Y'tarian towers in the doorway, menacing over Thomas, its disgusting centipede-like body coiling around, its fangs dripping, its claw-like hands stretched forward ready to rip him to pieces.

"Hey Geordon! Sorry to just stop by like this, but we're in trouble. We could really use some help and we didn't know where else to go," says Thomas.

"Oh! Salutations Thomas. Welcome. This is most unexpected. Do come in. We're delighted to help in any way we can."

David stands motionless, confused. Thomas doesn't actually expect him to go in there with those beasts?! They are monsters. Eaters of children. Infesters of worlds. The scourge of the galaxy! Thomas is treating them like they are family! It is disgusting.

Thomas can sense David's apprehension. He is disappointed that his friend could be a ghost and yet still harbor such prejudice. He gestures at David to join him inside, reassuring him there won't be any problems.

"I know what you're thinking and stop it. Come in. They're totally harmless. They only eat kids on Mondays!" Thomas says sarcastically, as Geordon just laughs. David reluctantly follows him inside.

"Blindaara, dear! Thomas is here, and he's brought a...? Another human boy with him!"

Blindaara emerges from the back of the apartment. She greets him with enthusiasm and asks about his friend. His awkward and nervous friend who continues to scope out the layout of the apartment for an exit plan. Thomas introduces David and explains their need for assistance, and that things have become very bad for them. She is receptive and apologetic, asking them to elaborate on the problem. For a moment she even raises the concern that it is something her family has done to cause their troubles.

The apartment is actually immaculately clean and inviting. It is filled with strange, ornate and beautiful alien artifacts of an unknown world. David has never seen such treasures. The artistry that went into each handcrafted piece is the kind that only a sentient alien species with hundreds of arms can create. His fear turns to guilt and to sadness. Here he was the criminal, the vagrant, seeking asylum in their home, and yet he had such a vile predisposition to them only moments before.

"It's definitely nothing you did! Geordon, my dad found Carl. Long story short, someone is trying to kill both of them. David here got caught up in it, but we got him out of a bad situation. He's been a ghoster for years. The people who want to kill my dad are after us and we need a place to lie low for a while. This is the last place they would go looking. Will you help us?"

"Of course! Anything for my good pal Harold. Who would want to kill that guy? I can't even imagine. That sounds terrifying. You are welcome to stay with us for as long as you would like. You too, David. A friend of Thomas is a friend of ours!"

They express their overwhelming gratitude. Thomas offers them a generous payment from his backpack for their troubles. They initially refuse, but Thomas is insistent, so Blindaara agrees to apply it to their grocery bills.

"Is that Thomas' voice I hear? It is! Fuulderna, Artynon come, come see Thomas! He has a friend with him!" says Tyxlynor, peering around the hallway corner to see what the commotion is all about.

The whole place is crawling with Y'tarians. A cesspool of alien waste! *Purge these thoughts, David. If they wanted to eat you they already would have. They're even excited to meet you and they're offering to help you. Just be cool. You don't have to touch one.*

"Tyxlynor, this is David. We're going to be staying with you guys for a while if that's cool?" he says, not wanting to tread on the space of his good friend.

"Oh yeah! I remember you were telling us about Davin at school. The off-world recruit. What position do you think he'll be good for?" he says, accepting them without question.

Thomas has nearly forgotten they are maintaining the lie of *Davin*. "We'll just have to wait and see, Davin hasn't played in a while, and you know they play the game a little bit different on the off-world. Between you and me I hear they only have a single-tier surface in the boon planets!" he says.

Thomas's disgusting friend slithers up to David, offering a traditional greeting in Y'tarian. A slithery embrace of the midsection, like a body hug. He tries not to cringe. *Oh no it's touching me. It's touching me. Gross get it off.* He cringes, trying not to react strongly.

"You guys want to see the new console game I got? We can all play. *Dartroxs VII*. It's the coolest one yet!" says Tyxlynor.

This is interesting. Y'tarian adolescents played digital console games? David hasn't seen one in years. Entertainment has become such a luxury, he has forgotten to be a kid. He makes the mistake of asking a foolish question about what the game is about. He has certainly never heard of it. Apparently, this is quite surprising to the two of them.

Thomas and Tyxlynor look at each other menacingly. "Oh, you'll love it. It's a first-person shooter game, but all the CPs are humans. You're a Y'tarian and your goal is to devour the flesh off of as many human infants as possible to win!" says Tyxlynor.

David looks horrified. They laugh hysterically at his expense.

"The expression on your face! Can you believe this guy? No, but really. You create your own avatar and you choose a class. Depending on what class you choose, you get certain perks. Then we have to go on these missions and rescue the princess from Dartroxs. He's the main boss of the game. It's awesome. You'll love it," says Tyxlynor.

* * *

Detective Clinton appeared on the scene at The Crimson Railroad, at least what was left of it. Shards of broken glass littered the ground and its wells were black from incineration. The crowds of spectators were gathered shoulder to shoulder trying to get a glimpse of the burnt-up limo.

"Xanthu! I got something good. How are things going here? Any leads?" she said.

"The device isn't a match to the Tramway. Doesn't mean it's not our guy, but it's a totally different model. It does however match the style of Latanian grenade we found in missing Carl's apartment. It's a fairly common black-market purchase, there's tons of them out here, but I think that's quite a coincidence wouldn't you say?"

"Oh, I wholeheartedly agree. Harold's wife cracked. Turns out Carl has been living over there pretending to be David's uncle. Oh yes, that's right.

David has been living there as well. I'm going to take an extraction team back there and bring them all in. The struggle is they're on the move again right now. Harold and Carl have been working together, and Thomas has been helping all of them stay out of trouble. To make matters more interesting I got *Gharles'* communicator number. I tried calling it and got nothing, but I'm running a number trace right now."

"Unbelievable. You got all that from the wife? You are good, Clinton. Question is, should we tell the locals or leave them hanging? I don't want to start a turf war."

"Agreed. Let's keep it low. Hollander is going to want to know about this and I'll have to get approval for an extrajurisdictional arrest team."

Chapter 18

Carl's brilliant idea has taken them right back into Sector 1149. Harold thinks this is reckless and dangerous. Carl already knows that. He tells Harold that they are going to find a place to lie low for a couple of days in order for his undisclosed plan to work. Harold is livid.

"Days? Carl, I can't be here for days. I'll lose my job! Then I'll really be fucked," he says, as they disembark the Transit.

As they are heading up the stairs to the exit lobby, Harold tries to reason with him. He pleads with Carl, who seems unstoppable. He heads straight for the resident entrance with his special Gharles pass, hoping that it will still work.

Carl reminds Harold of everything Thomas had just told them on the communicator. They already knew who they are. The detective is onto them, and Sheron has told them everything she knows.

"You'll never be going back to work again anyway. I promise you, Harold, by the end of the week, you'll have your money. I just need to do something first," says Carl.

"I'm so fucked, Carl! This whole thing has ruined me. I should just throw myself over the ledge" says Harold melodramatically.

The guard waves them on as their passes light up the gate green and grant them passage.

"Trust me, I know how you feel. Unfortunately, you'll have to wait. We're meeting a business associate of mine. Ma'arl Abeurstei. Promise me you'll just stand there and not talk?" he begs Harold not to be his usual mouthy self.

Harold mocks him for several minutes of their walk about all the stupid things that he could say during this meeting, just to piss off Carl. He wants more explanation from Carl, but Carl suspects the more Harold knows, the more opportunities he will have to somehow ruin it, so he keeps him in the dark. As they approach their destination he gives him a small taste of his plan.

"We're getting tickets to a business conference, Harold"

"What? Why? What possible reason could we have for that?"

"*The* business conference Harold. The one so big, Barbados himself will be there speaking."

"Carl! You're a genius! Wait... Who's paying for these tickets? Carl? Carl?"

They go to a classy stately office building. It is nice enough to have an escalator. They ride it about three floors up and stroll into an office of an alien who sells financial instruments of some kind. This is an alien to Harold's own liking. Though he wears some semblance of a suit, he seems like a fun guy, and his portly figure indicates that this alien has a mutual appreciation of food.

"Hey, Ma'arl man! What's happening! Long time no see pal!" says Carl, switching into his awful work meeting voice, making finger guns at the alien.

"Ah! Carl, is that you? Oh man, it's been ages. What can I do you for? Stocks? Bonds? Tickets?" The alien holds up one of each in his many tentacles.

"Actually, I have a favor to ask of you. Remember that time I... Yeah, of course, you do. Look I know this is a challenge, but I have to get into AscentCon."

Ma'arl laughs. His tentacles giggle with delight. He has not forgotten the situation Carl had fixed for him years earlier. He informs Carl that the tickets have been sold out for months. It is a complete impossibility. He also has the nerve to tell Carl that he knows he can't afford them anyway.

"Ma'arl, I know you've got something up your sleeve. You've always got something!" says Carl.

Both literally and figuratively speaking, Ma'arl is known to keep all matter of objects in his sleeves, making it easier to make a sale, light a potential client's cigarette, or hand them a pen to sign with. He is the jovial business alien with the tickets to anything, and everyone knows it.

"Okay okay. Well, I can't get you tickets of course, but there might be something else I can do. How do you feel about food service?" He gives Carl that look, knowing his reaction.

There are so many feelings Carl has about food service, and he knows it. All of them highly negative of course. It is perhaps the last thing he wants to go back to. He begs him for any other alternative. Whatever he has planned, Carl is going to hate it.

"I'll talk to my buddy Dino over at the Hotel Chauffann. He runs that high-dollar restaurant Chateau d'la Merde. They always bring in extra wait staff for these high-profile events. He owes me a favor, so I'm sure he'll take you on. Got to put up a convincing act though. How you get out of there and where you need to go is up to you. Security is probably going to be on overdrive this year after, you know, that thing with Barbados!"

Carl agrees reluctantly. He asks Ma'arl to contact him as soon as possible to ensure that the deal is set. He doesn't have much time and there is a great deal of pressure to get in there. If he needs another option, he will need it sooner rather than later.

"I'll call you by tomorrow. I'll have everything handled. Don't worry, but listen. Carl, you're out of favors. We're even now? Yes?" says Ma'arl, hoping to be exonerated from Carl.

"Definitely. Our agreement is fulfilled."

They leave the office with a certain sense of victory. They have found a way in, they just aren't sure how to pull it off. It isn't as easy as they had hoped for but these days nothing is. Carl sees the potential in having an employee pass. It allows them opportunities to shuffle through doors and exits that other patrons won't even take notice of.

"Harold, I don't know about this. Maybe we should tell them you're a cook or something?"

"What do you mean! This was your idea, pal. I don't know the first thing about cooking no fancy upper-level food. What are you saying anyways?"

"Well, you don't exactly look like the kind of person who would be serving in a place like *this*. I mean or anywhere. I mean where people might see you."

"Oh, that's rich coming from you! You look fit to deliver salads. Is that order too heavy for you? Besides, who trusts a skinny cook anyhow!"

"See, there it is! That temperament of yours. Perfect chef material. Somewhere far, far in the back. In the freezer even!"

"I'll be sure to stash your body there after I murder you and serve you to our guests!"

"Great, Harold. Thank you for that lovely imagery. So now there's the next part of this plan that I don't really know. You know of a place where we can lie low for a few days?"

"Well, I might have an idea but you're not going to like it."

* * *

Harold leads Carl to a seedy-looking neighborhood that Carl had lived somewhat near, but certainly had never been to, at least not that he would tell anyone. Drunk patrons are exiting the casinos and there is a tremendous amount of foot traffic. The neon lights around them are blinding. Carl is beginning to have his suspicions that Harold intends to murder him after all, or maybe just steal his organs, or maybe pimp him out. It isn't abundantly clear.

"Harold! Where are we? Are you trying to kill me again? I thought we got over this."

"Just be cool Carl. As soon as they find out you don't have money, they'll stop bothering you real quick. Stay close, we're almost there. Under the bridge."

Why is Harold stopping? Who can he possibly know over here? Is that a hooker? Come on Harold, this can't be your plan. Focus on the mission, Harold. This is insane. The hooker speaks!

"Harold, I swear on my life that better not be your ugly face again. What the hell is wrong with you, coming back here? I don't want to be seen with you. But most important, is that Carl? I'm not getting involved in this. You planning to kill his ass right here or what?" says Duchess.

"Duchess! It's great to see you again too. Listen, first of all, the whole thing was a setup. Gharles wasn't Gharles, and Carl was trying to kill me too, so it's okay. Anyways, we're working together now, but we need a place to hide out for a couple days."

"No! Hell no. Would you get somewhere with your broke ass Harold? I'm trying to work here and you're scaring away all the potential clients," she says, looking at him with the utmost irritation. On a night as busy as this she can make a substantial haul, but not if Harold is just standing there annoying her.

"Look, I know you're pissed at me, but I got David out. He's been living with us, you know, in a *real* house. He has food. He's even back in school. I'm trying to make things right here. You gotta believe me. Just three days or so tops!" He pleads with her, without considering the bizarre request. It's not as though she owns the streets necessarily. There are plenty of back alleys to sleep in.

"That's great for you, Harold. Why don't you and old Carl here go stay in David's place since he's on *vacation*. Nobody's moved in yet. Might give you some perspective. Now let me do my work! And I mean it Harold, I hope I never see you again. Not you though, Carl. I don't have a reason to hate you yet, so if you want to pay to play, the option is open," she says. As much as she hates Harold, she thinks Carl wasn't so bad-looking. He might have money even.

"Yeah, no thanks. I'm also completely broke now, so sorry," says Carl, heeding Harold's advice to ensure all around know he is strapped for cash.

"Oh, okay then. You can get the hell out too! Bye!" she says, thinking he is rude.

They leave Duchess to her work and proceed towards the opposite side of the bridge. Carl is shocked when he sees Harold walking up the embankment toward a dilapidated storm runoff gate.

Carl is dying to know why she was so mad at Harold, but he also wants to know where they are going. The gate is punctured enough for them to crawl through, but Carl is not a willing participant. It seems incredibly unsafe. It is dark. It smells like sewage and mold. There is garbage everywhere. He is not even sure it is legal to be there.

Harold asks him to just accept it and move on. He has got them a place as far as he is concerned, and Carl can just deal with that or get them another one. It is only three days after all until the conference. A mere three days, how hard can it be to stay there?

Carl looks around. The storm drain is certainly ancient. The planet has long since given up on liquid precipitation with all the water being captured into the central water networks. The only reason they tend to keep the drains is to recapture any that falls from the upper tiers above. They are often overlooked and run bone dry.

"Harold! Come on seriously, what's your plan? Is this some kind of twisted joke or what?"

"No, Carl. This is it. Welcome to David's house of late. What do you think Carl?" asks Harold, before going off into some kind of tirade on the tyranny of poverty.

He wonders if it is better to sacrifice everything to stay in the mids, living in this storm drain and hustling the streets just to survive, or to be demoted to the top of the lowers. The king of the lesser castle would choose to be a peasant in the emperor's palace. It makes a man wonder if greed is worth it.

"Woah! You mean he lived here? Harold, if I didn't know you better I would think you were getting feelings or empathy or something. It's like a street version where the ghost of Christmas future shows Scrooge where Tiny Tim will die if he doesn't change, except with hookers instead of ghosts, and instead of being rich, Scrooge murders people and steals their money."

"Keep talking Carl! You can find your own storm drain to sleep in!"

There is a broken raised inlet in the concrete just surely wide enough and long enough for a body to lie out on. Upon it is the remnants of a worn hastily thrown-together mattress. The rest of the trash begins to take on the semblance of a makeshift living establishment. A board haphazardly covers the massive drain pipe leading down into the abyss from which there is surely no return. A pile of clothes serves as a closet. A stack of trash forms the basis of a bench to sit on and another a makeshift table. An area of it has a pile of what amounts to a collection of used discarded food packages, no doubt the pantry.

"You know, if it rains, we're fucked! I call dibs on that mattress, Harold! I got us into the conference after all."

"Relax, Carl, it hasn't rained in two-thousand years! If it does, I would much prefer to perish quickly than suffer the toxic radiation poisoning slowly burning my flesh! I suppose I deserve it. I'll take the bench."

Getting through the night is rough. Sounds echo throughout the chamber. The lack of temperature controls makes the place alternate between being too hot and too cold. The digs are most uncomfortable and there is a constant threat of insects and rodents needing to be fought off.

* * *

The next morning the communicator rings, disrupting their late morning slumber.

"Harold! Who is it? Get it quick! It might be Ma'arl!" Of course, it wasn't.

"Hi Harold! It's your boss, Mrs. Xvranbul. I'm looking at my desk clock and I see that it's been five seconds since the start of your shift. It is with great pleasure that I inform you that you're fired! *Haha.* It's unfortunate I can't see your reaction in person," she hisses into the communicator.

"Wait! I can explain! Listen, you got to listen to me. It's not my fault! I'm being held against my will by a psychopath!"

"Well, I'm sorry Harold. Next time try not to get yourself kidnapped. Besides, you should be used to it, that pretty much describes your job already! You're welcome to apply for our affiliates in the lower sector. I'm sure they'd love to have you! If you're still alive of course! Bye now!" she says, hanging up on him abruptly.

Was Harold crying? It's more like a defeated sobbing. It's amazing that after twenty-three years with Mulknosh, making boxes day after day, he can be dismissed on a whim for being only seconds late. No wonder so many people in Capital City turn to crime.

"A psychopath? Trapped by yourself maybe. You're the one who murdered all those people and that's the best you could come up with? I thought you were an expert liar, Harold?"

"I just... I need a moment... I'm trying really hard not to stuff your corpse down in that drain pipe after I rip your face off and feed it to you!" says Harold.

"Would you rather have been arrested on the job? You're liberated from it now! Forget about it. It's over. They can't hurt you anymore," says Carl, like he has just become the king of trash mountain.

The three days pass glacially. Carl and Harold are at each other's throats. Things are so insufferable that Carl considers risking going back to the apartment. Worst case scenario they arrest him and at least he will get his own place and three meals a day that he doesn't have to work for anymore. Most importantly, he will be away from Harold! Either way, it is a dim-lit concrete box. At least that one has some semblance of plumbing. How David has managed to survive here for years is a mystery to him.

At last, the communicator rings, days late at that. It is Ma'arl.

"Alright guys, you're in. You're going to go to Side Entrance B. Tell the gate guard that you guys is there to see Dino. He'll get you set up. Good luck! Let me know if there's anything else I can ever sell you!"

Harold and Carl have never exited an area as quickly as they do their sewage bunker. It is showtime. All the pent-up frustration over the past three days is lost. They are looking and probably smelling worse for wear.

* * *

Carl leads them to a massive towering building in a central area of the terraces. Its very presence announced itself as a conference center, with its chic massive glass windows, open concept floor plans, and multiple entrance doors all the way around.

They approached the guard at Entrance B who is made apprehensive by their appearance.

"Excuse me, gentlemen this is a secure area. This is a private event. I'm going to have to ask you to leave."

"Wait! We're here to see Dino. We're his new servers," says Carl.

"Ah geez. Ma'arl sent *you* guys over? *Whooo* Dino is gonna get a kick outta this!" he phones into his radio. "Hey uh Dino, your new guys are here from Ma'arl's place, lookin' like they just ascended from below."

Dino's harsh voice fires back across the radio. "*Ah* fuck, are you serious? Dammit Ma'arl! Send 'em up to Al's, and take the back way. I don't want the building guests to see that."

"Sir! I promise you we don't normally look this way! Well okay, maybe he does, but I assur—" says Carl, before being cut-off.

"Look, Mister, I Don't Give a Fuck. We're gonna take the stairs up to Al's place. He'll get you cleaned up and fitted for a suit. Well, you anyway. I don't know about the fat one, might just cover his ass with a tablecloth. He a chef or some shit? Whatever. Anyways, if you see any conference-goers, don't talk to them. *Be seen, not heard!*" says the guard.

Harold struggles with the stairs. Though his job had been physically active, somehow the action of climbing the stairs is exhausting. They must have gone up sixteen floors. The stairwell is repetitive and unassuming. Everything is left to its concrete and steel elements. By the time they reach their destination floor, Harold is sweating profusely and breathing heavily. His calves burn and his feet ache.

"Alright gentlemen, here we are at Al's place," says the guard, gesturing them on.

This floor is a commercial center designated for employees. Among them is Al's, a store specializing in employee formal wear. Al, as it turns out, is unexpectedly alien. Having six arms with small dexterous hands makes him an exceptional tailor. Upon seeing the sight of them his antennae curl back in disgust.

"Difficult. You fix self. Then come. Employee showers. There," he says, pointing with

three arms at a time, as though one is insufficient to get his point across. Didn't have to tell Carl twice, he is ready to be clean again.

Al fits Harold, finding an oversized suit in the back. It hangs off him, surprisingly baggy. The alien takes it in as he is wearing it. It is certainly the nicest suit he's ever worn in his life, *and all to do what, serve food with? Geeze.*

He has certainly never had one tailored like this, or come to think of it, at all.

Carl is more comfortable in this setting of course but he cannot help but take amusement in Harold's awkwardness. "Wow Harold, you sure clean up nice!" Carl says. Seems that he spoke too soon as he tries and fails to tie a bowtie. Al comes and offers his assistance.

* * *

Fortunately, they are able to take the freight lift the rest of the way up fifty-six floors to the very precipice of the division mark between the upper and mid-tier society. The restaurant features a three-hundred-and-sixty-five degree view of the whole mid-level in Sector 1149, or at least as much as the narrow space between towering buildings allow them. It at least presents the illusion of depth, which on this world is as close as you get.

This is the closest Harold has ever come to his dreams. The upper-level security gate rests just opposite the restaurant with golden elevators that can carry them up to the tiers of wealth and prestige bestowed to the highest of society. You might think that seeing a steel and concrete horizon above you would be a deterrence to the view of restaurant-goers, however, its proximity to the upper-flats makes it all the more alluring, even if you are just staring up at its under surface. In many sectors, the upper-tier decks are so extensive that they essentially represent the middle-class sky and stars, comforted only by the notion that somewhere on the surface level, the lowers are looking up at the mid-tiers thinking the same thing. *It must be dark down there.*

It is through this golden elevator between worlds that they expect to find Barbados coming down for the conference. It is here where they will use the ID cards he had given them to gain access. Harold and Carl's first trip into the rich man's world, outside the recent luxuries Harold had enjoyed on the nautilus cruiser.

As they stare wide-eyed around the hustling, bustling restaurant preparing for its evening of fine dining, they catch the attention of Dino the owner, manager, and head chef. Wait staff are frantically moving in chairs and tables, putting on the white table clothes for the dinner hour. Lighting the fake candles. Putting out the sauces and spices. The display trays of desserts, some of them still living to show their freshness. Fake flowers even, they really did go all out.

"Gentlemen, welcome to Chateau d'la Merde. We do things a certain way around here as we try to provide *an upper-class experience on a middle-class budget!* That's our motto anyway. Normally, I would have weeks to coach my staff in the art of service, but today I am of course short-handed as reservations are completely booked," says Dino, somehow gruff, but pretentious at the same time.

"Is this really how the upper-class eat? What does Chateau d'la Merde mean anyway?" says Harold, desperately searching for the right pronunciation.

"*Ah* yes, you must be Harold! The fat uncultured one. How should I know what it means? We receive few complaints in any event. It just has a nice ring to it don't you think?"

"Sure, whatever you say, boss man! So what is it you want us to be doing?"

"Hmmm... Can you roll silverware? Do *you people* use silverware? I haven't the slightest idea. I'll have someone show you how to do that. A non-speaking role. Then perhaps we can graduate you to delivering plates."

"Yeah. Sure. Whatever. Just let me know."

Dino turns to Carl much more satisfied. He is, after all, licensed to serve! That makes him significantly more marketable. If only he had a Master's degree in serving he might have made something out of it.

"Carl, you might not actually be terrible at this. You've been a server before? At one of those low-brow plebeian establishments? I think you can manage. Just make sure to use your largest vocabulary. The less comprehensible the better. Remember it's not about being correct, it's about the illusion you know what you're talking about. For example, our slopster tartar is handcrafted from the finest crustaceans of the moons of Klarnash III. It features a bourgeois butter garlic bourbon sauce, lightly pan-seared in lemon pledge and fresh verbs."

"What does that even mean? Half of those things aren't even food ingredients?" says Carl.

"Exactly! But when you string a bunch of shit together that sounds rich, people eat it up. I boil the slopster in a pot and throw some butter simulant cubes on it and serve it on a fancy plate. We can charge an extra fifty credits for it just by making it sound expensive. That's our goal here!"

"So, you mean I don't have to know anything I'm talking about? I just recommend some made-up shit to upsell people on basic cuisine?" says Carl. He is actually genuinely pleased by this idea. Not that he has done anything differently before, but this time it is sanctioned!

"That's right, Carl! You've got it down my friend. Think you can handle it?"

"I mean, I'll give it my best shot, but if you want someone with quality lying skills, Harold is your guy. No offense."

"None taken! I'd sell my grandmother for a floor above. Promise I won't disappoint," says Harold.

"We're going for a certain *look* here at the restaurant and I'm not sure Harold is who our clientele want to see... or be seen with."

"We understand completely. Right, Harold? Thank you for giving us the opportunity."

"Great. Okay, well time for you to get busy then. Talk to the assistant manager Jeanene, she'll tell you what to do and all the remaining shit that I don't have time for."

Harold is of course terrible at rolling silverware, but he likens it to his former box-making job. Methodical. He will figure it out eventually, much to the frustration of a very stressed-out Jeanene. Carl on the other hand seems to relish the server life. Carefully setting the linens, silverware, and various dainty decor on the tables, preparing for the arrival of the guests. He is practically dancing, it is so natural.

The sound of the great hall echoes through the building and can even be partially heard inside the empty restaurant. This is the main stage of the conference. Speech after speech to thunderous applause.

'How to dismantle a robot union.' Naturally.

'Psychological techniques for making overworked employees think they're happy about it.' A corporate essential.'Expanding profits with off-world slavery.' Money is everything after all.

Then, lastly, an army of security guards descend in the lift, passing right in front of Harold as he rolls the silverware haphazardly. Barbados has made his arrival. It is more security than they ever expected. It will be more difficult to kill him than they had previously imagined. They will have to be cautious and wait until the precise moment to make their move.

Barbados never really speaks on any matter of substance. Only about how others can achieve greatness like he has achieved greatness. Nothing he says has any meaning, but people eat it up anyway. He always just speaks in thought-provoking metaphors.

"Believe in yourself! Be like the grain of sand in the pond. If you think positive, you will be positively rich. In my new book Surviving Assassination, *you can get real insight into how almost dying can increase your profits. Get your copy today at the official Barbados Exchange."*

It has only been a matter of days since his limo accident and he had already written a book. That is truly unbelievable, except that his writing has such little substance it may as well have been auto-generated robotically. Maybe it was. Harold is furious.

"Surviving an assassination attempt is a lot like business. You just have to get in there and get your hands dirty and do whatever it takes to meet your challenge and you never stop challenging yourself. Every day, I wake up and I say, 'Jez, you're absolute fucking human garbage. You can do better, no you will do better' and then I do one-thousand-four-hundred pushups just to prove I can. And so can you. Buying this book is better than one-thousand-four-hundred pushups. I guarantee it."

The crowd roars with thunderous applause. It seems to continue forever. The brown-nosing is so stellar that the crowds have to be told when to stop applauding, and a countdown for seating is imposed as no one wants to be the first to stop or the first to be seated. Even after he has already long left the stage. It will be quite sometime after the speech before he makes his way back up. In the meantime, the restaurant is becoming bustling with customers eager to enjoy their early reservations.

"Waiter… What do you recommend?"

Can't you read, you illiterate swine? Thinks Carl.

"Well ma'am, as I see you're enjoying the Pilquist Don Linguini wine this evening, might I recommend pairing it with the lemon braised salamander? It's stuffed with the finest grains, seared in a platinum skilled, and served over a bed of lies. It really brings out the nuttiness."

"Oh! Well, that sounds wonderful! I'll have that then. Can we substitute the lemon for gjriovios sauce? I'm allergic to hypochlorofalconiquin. Also I want it braised lightly, but also burnt, and hold the onions."

"Of course, madame!"

He writes none of it down because he is just going to bring her whatever the fuck he wants to anyway. *Next table!*

"Sir! These moths are not crispy enough. My splurlglast is having a hard time consuming them. Can you bring out the blow torch again?"

"I'm sorry… *Just say when!*" He thinks for a moment of angling the blow torch just the slightest bit further to incinerate the strange alien customer instead. *Next table!*

"We've been waiting for thirty-seven nanoids! I demand to speak to the manager!"

"*Awww.* I'm sorry that our service has disappointed you. Can I interest you in some complementary slacon wrapped slopapeños?"

He returns to the host stand where Jeanene is reviewing the reservation lists.

"Hey, Jeanene. We got a couple of Ka'arons at table seven. They're asking for a manager. Enjoy!"

It is at this moment that Harold grabs him by the arm.

"This is it, Carl! Look, it's Barbados he's coming down the hallway. How are we going to play this out? He can't see us, he'll know it's us!"

Carl leads the way with a new plan. They slip away from the restaurant as best as they can. It is so busy that it will be quite some time before anyone notices they left. They proceed ahead of Barbados to the upper-level security gate. People are still surrounding him, trying to get autographs or shake his hand. Most of them just want to pitch their business proposals. Harold and

Carl swipe their special platinum access IDs 'Gharles' had given them. They work, they are in! Carl leads them straight to the elevator.

"Carl? How do you know which lift they're using? Are you crazy? He'll see us. This better be a good plan." There are two possible lifts leading to the upper- tiers on this level.

"Shut up, Harold. Just bend down!"

He produces a piece of paper from the host stand. This restaurant is so fancy it has a very expensive paper guestlist instead of digital. He produces a pen as well and in his best effort scribbles out 'Out of Order' using Harold's back as a writing desk. He slaps the sign on the right elevator with some sort of sticky adhesive-like dessert item from the restaurant.

"Carl, you're a genius, but now what? We're running out of time!"

They enter the left elevator. Harold has no idea what they are doing.

"Okay. Harold. Lift me up on your shoulders, I'm going to take off the top access panel."

"Are you crazy? I'll never make it up there."

"Just do it, Harold!"

He kneels down and Carl climbs on him. Slowly and awkwardly they rise from the floor. Carl fights with the panel for a moment before it finally comes loose. Barbados and his company are coming closer and closer to the lift.

With the panel off, they now start the process of trying to get up there. They try to get Carl up first, but he has no upper body strength whatsoever. He tries to lift up Harold, but he's so heavy he just crushes Carl underneath. He tries using the hand railing as a step, to no avail.

Eventually, Harold manages to just throw Carl up into the ceiling and he finally makes his way up onto the top of the elevator. He reaches his arm down as though he's going to pull Harold up. He struggles for a while. His muscles stretched to the max. Face red. Sweating. *It's no use!* Harold isn't budging. Carl lets go and disappears from view.

"Damnit, Carl! You set me up, didn't you? I hope this elevator crushes you on the way up. You're still trying to kill me aren't you?"

No sooner than he complains, does he get nearly knocked out by a steel dropdown ladder. He falls to the floor disoriented.

"Harold! Climb up!" says Carl, hoping he hurries.

"There was a ladder there this entire time! Why didn't you do that from the beginning?"

"How was I supposed to know? I don't exactly go breaking into maintenance hatches every day. Not all of us are as criminal as you are, Harold."

"What is that supposed to mean? I ought to—"

"Harold! Shut up and help me get this ladder back up and close this damn hatch."

No sooner do they get the hatch resealed than the lift doors open. They are just in time to avoid Barbados and his security detail.

"Great speech today, sir."

"Very inspirational."

"What floor sir?"

"Top floor today, gentlemen. I have business to attend to. As always just wait with the other security in the executive lounge."

This is excellent news. Barbados is going to be alone! They are finally going to get him. At least that's what they think. The elevator stops short. This isn't the top floor. There is another above. They can both see it.

The security detail exits the elevator at the 'top floor' and the doors close. Barbados remains on board. He pulls a key out from his vestments and inserts it into a hidden terminal on the lift. It continues to rise. Higher. Higher. Too high! Carl and Harold are about to be crushed by the ceiling. Higher and higher!

The space is getting narrower and narrower. They cringe and brace themselves for imminent death. The lift comes to a halt with just enough space to spare them. Barbados gets off the lift and goes on his way into the secret penthouse suite. Harold and Carl try to follow. Unfortunately, as they are about to return to the inside of the lift, it starts to descend.

"Harold, what do we do? Try to stop it or something!"

"No time to think, Carl, just grab onto something!."

Harold reaches out to grab the access ladder. Carl in his infinite wisdom grabs the cable and starts rising back towards the pulley at the ceiling. Quickly realizing his error, he jumps to catch the edge of the door ledge to the penthouse floor. He dangles precariously as the lift gets lower and lower, increasing the distance of his potential fall.

"Help! Harold quick! Do something. I can't hold on much longer!"

Harold carefully pulls himself up the ladder to the door. He tries as best he can to step around Carl's hands. They're slipping. Slipping. He's about to fall to his death!

Harold uses all his might to thrust the doors open manually. They struggle to open. He forces himself in between the doors, and reaches for Carl's arm, just as it slips from the ledge. He pulls him with all his strength and thrusts him through the door and then himself before it closes behind them. They lie there for a second, gasping with adrenaline and exhaustion. Then they immediately realize the danger. Fortunately, no one is around to see them enter the floor.

One direction of the hallway is well decorated with luxurious amenities and it is obvious that it leads to the main entrance. The other direction leads to an unassuming service door. Opting to avoid attention, they choose the service route. It leads them to a dark black spiral staircase which leads up to the roof infrastructure. Most buildings in Capital are glass-domed, but this particular rooftop is completely covered. Not a window in sight and it was very dimly lit. They find a series of catwalks suspended over the lights that look down on the great room. No one will see them up there in the dark.

The great room is set up like a theater in a way, where there are stands to hold people looking down upon a flat circular stage, all painted in shiny black lacquer. The patrons of the hall are making their way into the venue in an orderly fashion. All of them are dressed the same in deep red robes with hoods and a variety of masks shielding their identity.

Some of them carry torches lit by actual flame, which they position in various locations around the circle giving it light. The rest carry tall staffs which they bang on the ground in one syncopated daunting rhythm. *Thud. Thud. Thud.* The pace resembles the human heartbeat. Carl decides to start filming with his communicator from their secret hiding place.

With all the guests in position, a booming voice is heard. The voice of Barbados! He arrives in a black robe, hood, and distinctive golden mask with two great horns protruding from it. He is wielding a golden dagger of the most ornate design. It is encrusted in jewels and detail work, its sharp edges gleaming across the room. His robe contains a symbol, a blue circle emblazoned with a red emblem across the front. *What is happening here?* The hammering of the staffs stops.

"Welcome distinguished and honorable guests of the Order. It is with great pleasure that I call this meeting of the Syndicate to order on this thirteenth day of April, in the year of our creator 4079."

It seemed that Barbados is the ring leader at some sort of cult-like circus.

"Nothing is unchangeable but the inherent and unalienable rights of man. If you want something you've never had, you must be willing to do something you've never done. Do you then prefer dangerous freedom over peaceful slavery?"

He pauses for dramatic effect, a non-rhetorical question, the audience responds in unison "*No!*"

"Be bold in the pursuit of knowledge, never fearing to follow truth and reason to whatever results they lead, and conquer every authority which stands in our way. Do you want to know who you are? Don't ask. Act! Action will delineate and define you."

The crowd cheers at this point in the speech ritualistically.

"There is nothing more unequal than the equal treatment of unequal people. My brothers and sisters, the blood we spill here today is the blood that keeps us free. They would have us be brought down before them. They would see our freedom taken and redistributed to the masses so that none shall live well."

They boo and hiss at this interpretation. All of them are in concordance with his statements.

"We will not descend. We are entitled by our divine right to the appropriation of property in absolute dominion. Let none challenge the dominion of the Syndicate. To our Lord Jefferson, may he reign supreme. We make this sacrifice unto you."

A fearful alien woman is brought into the arena, held against her will by two guards of the Syndicate. Their faces are covered by black cloth masks, such that their identity remains anonymous. The woman pleads for her life and her release. Barbados places his hand above her head and pricks himself with the blade. The blood rains down from his hand onto her face as she screams in terror, Carl capturing the whole ritual on film.

Barbados raises the dagger high above his head and plunges it deep into her throat. Repeatedly he stabs her. Over and over again. The guards release her to drop to the floor, they bring forth golden chalices to fill with her blood. The robed audience each takes their turn to drink from them. Carl and Harold are horrified. Carl suppressing the urge to vomit, nearly passes out from the heinous act.

"My friends, it is time for our toast! Raise your chalices and join me! On this day, the birth of our lord Jefferson, we celebrate the elevation of the human race and our work there untoward. May the free exercise of industry exist for all eternity!" His voice raises into thunderous verbal agreement.

They throw back their blood goblets and guzzle down their contents to the last drop. The body is dragged away. The audience claps and they begin to remove their hoods and masks to mingle and socialize as though nothing out of the ordinary has happened.

To Carl and Harold's astonishment, among the audience is none other than President McSlurmins himself! Yet directly across from him is none other than his chief opponent Senator Rosnarth Galxshu. They both approach Barbados with joyous expressions.

"Barbados! A fine and murderous celebration today! It was the best yet. Truly none better. The greatest. I must congratulate you on some of your late selections. We have found them to be quite entertaining. Harold has turned out to be quite the prolific imbecile! The films you have sent have indeed been most splendid. To see Ms. Tennhausen wasted in such fashion was quite entertaining!"

"Thank you, Mr. President. I hope that you are honored and pleased with our service. A blessed Jefferson's Day to you, my liege. I told you that while laying waste to an entire lower class subsector was enjoyable, that pitting the worst and weakest humans against each other would provide a more entertaining display of murder and violence, while also enhancing our human purity and supremacy."

Galxshu speaks next. "Premiere Barbados, your presumptions have again proved to be correct. This is indeed far more interesting and productive than we had expected. I do look forward to the next installment of films. Do you suppose they have killed each other by now? The last I heard, Carl was missing and Harold was nowhere to be found. I was hoping for an exciting finale to that series."

"You must forgive me, Senator, but I have lost track of them at the moment. There are of course plenty of other participants for your amusement, but that particular pair may be unavailable at the moment. I promise that as soon as we reestablish connection, we will send out a mass update. In the meantime perhaps your office can send over your next list of prospective recruits for promotion and elimination?"

"That would be perfect indeed. Now it is your turn to forgive me, but I must ask, do you have any reasonable suspicions on who might have made the dastardly attempt on your life Barbados? Undoubtedly the work of those unspeakable Y'tarian barbarians!"

"Unfortunately, I have not yet ascertained the identity of the assassins, but rest assured I plan to bring those responsible directly to the Grand Syndicate Arena to be personally sacrificed upon our great altar, in a showing guaranteed to obtain the most favorable ratings."

"Well, blessings of Jefferson to you and your family, Barbados. The President and I have many matters to discuss if you will join me in your chambers, sir?"

"Of course, Senator! May you conduct business freely. *Remember a penny saved is a wasted investment opportunity!*"

Carl and Harold look at each other in shock and horror. Carl ends the recording. The Syndicate as it turns out is a cult of elite humanoid supremacists. The Order represents the elite of the elite in fact. Murdering the lower classes and non-humanoid aliens for their own amusement! Harold and Carl are but characters in their overtly fascist viewer show.

"Harold! I'm sending this video to you right now. We need to have more copies. This has to get out. The whole galaxy needs to know about this! Are you as blindsided as I am?"

"This is the proof we need, Carl! We can get the Enforcers off our backs now. Let's send it to that detective!"

"That's one idea anyway. What about the money though? I didn't come this far to walk away with nothing. Bribery? Extortion? What should we do?" says Carl. This takes Harold by surprise, he is astonished to hear Carl finally be the voice of finance.

"You know as well as I do they will just kill us for knowing this information. We're better off just using these access passes to steal from the rich. We could just start killing them the same as I did the others?" says Harold, figuring that he may as well continue.

"Damnit, Harold! That just makes us no better off than they are. We have to get close to Barbados. We need to infiltrate a Syndicate meeting somehow. We can use the robes to hide ourselves."

"Fine. Have it your way. Just wait until they pass you a blood chalice! Sounds like a death wish to me. As soon as we kill Barbados, what's to stop them from coming for us?"

"I don't know, Harold. Why don't we start with how the hell are we going to get out of here first?" says Carl. They have almost forgotten that they are trapped there and could be discovered at any moment.

"Well Carl, I have your answer, but you're not going to like it. That panel over there is roof access. I say up and out. Every building has to have outside maintenance access tunnels."

"Harold, we have no protective equipment. You want us to go out into the hazardous pollution in the hopes of maybe finding an unlocked maintenance access tunnel, and then climb all the way down it to the base floor in order to reconnect to the mids? That's like seventy floors, Harold."

"Told you, you wouldn't like it. What's your other plan? Wait for the lift with the senator?"

"I see your point, Harold. Well, fuck it. Let's get out of here."

They proceed to the ladder for the roof access hatch. They are careful to open and shut the chamber. The exit hatch is double sealed like a submarine to ensure there's no pollution blowback into the building. Knowing that they don't want to breathe the toxic outside air, they resolve to tie their cummerbunds on their faces as masks. They look completely ridiculous.

Harold throws open the hatch. A vortex of brown air surrounds them, vacuuming out the clean air around them. It burns all around. They proceed to the roof of the building, looking around them frantically for a maintenance hatch. The wind is ferocious. The toxic poison singes their eyes and burns their skin.

Neither of them can hear anything except the deafening roar of space traffic all around them. Inside the buildings, these sounds are buffered out by their filters, walls, and windows, but out here there is nothing but the elements. Nothing in sight, they fear the worst, until Carl spots a raised doorway in the distance.

As they trudge along, trying not to be blown right off the roof, holding their breaths as long as they can, there is a certain surreal value to it. They have both been privileged to go into space, but this is still their first true dose of reality, standing in the clouds of the planet. The real planet. No filters, no screens, no false air. This is what had actually been done to a planet once teeming with life, now a desolate wilderness of smog.

Carl tugs hard at the maintenance door. It's rusted shut and locked. No matter how hard they pull, they can't get it to budge. This is it. They are going to die here. This is the end. Harold gives up and sends the video to the detective's number. After everything, this is his legacy. Someone has to know what happened. He has time to send just one last message before death overtakes them.

It is in this moment that Carl remembers that they both came in carrying guns. He yells out to Harold to stand back. Harold tries to stop him, but it's too late. He fires off the gun towards the door lock. In doing so, he ignites a toxic gas cloud around them in a blaze of glory. The door dislodges itself open, remarkably still hinged. They run inside and pull the door to as best as they can, still shaken from the blast.

"Son of a bitch, Carl, you nearly incinerated the whole planet!"

"Maybe that wouldn't be such a bad thing. Look what we've made of this world. Maybe the whole thing should burn down. Lucky for us there's never enough oxygen outside to stay burning, otherwise, we'd all have burnt up millennia ago!"

They cough and sputter. Their lungs are bleeding, their eyes red and bloodshot. Minor chemical burns cover their skin. They will heal, but it will take some time. They have managed to ruin their nice suits. Al will be pissed! If they ever plan to return there anyway.

The way down is a narrow claustrophobia-inducing spiral staircase. The air is stale. It is lit only by rudimentary emergency lighting, dust and spider webs everywhere. The descent is disorienting and endless. Harold feels himself becoming nauseous. They have to keep stopping just to keep themselves from falling over.

They have no idea how many floors they have to descend before reaching an access door. The typical design makes these access points as much unseen as they are difficult to find. Only a handful of maintenance staff know them and the entrances are rarely on a prestigious floor. Some of them are forgotten entirely, lost to the passage of time. It must be something close to thirty-three floors down before they reach a doorway, if you can call it a doorway. It is a hatch leading to a horizontal crawl space. As if this is not bad enough already, they have to squeeze their way through on their hands and knees.

At the end of the tunnel is a small room. *At last!* This must be the exit. A small half doorway leads to an even more claustrophobic hand-cranked lift, just barely wide enough for Harold and Carl to fit in and not even tall enough for them to stand upright.

"You've got to be kidding me. Harold, I don't think both of us can do this at once. I mean I'm concerned about the weight," says Carl.

"It will have to work. No way I'm cranking this thing back up again just to crank it back down!"

"Harold, should we be concerned that it's up here? That means the last person who came up here, never came down."

"They probably ended themselves after going up that spiral staircase! I know I would."

They cram themselves into the elevator. It slowly creeps downward at the slowest of slow speeds. Would this tiny lift really have been the downfall of the power grid if it were automatic? The air is thin. It is unusually hot inside. The stench is terrible. Carl's arms are wearing out fast; he isn't sure how much longer he can last.

"Harold, I can't. I can't do it anymore. You gotta take over. Here!"

"Just how do you propose we achieve that, Carl? I can barely move as it is!"

"I'm going to just squeeze under you and you're going to go over. Like this." He starts to push his way past Harold. They start to scuffle and argue. A clank is heard in the lift chain. All of a sudden, they are in a free fall. *Down, down, down!*

The lift falls at an incredible speed. All they can do is scream. Carl is at this point suffocating on Harold's chunky stomach, unable to shift position. *Thud!* The lift jerks to a halt. No way out in sight. There is no escape now. No exit in sight. They're trapped inside a tiny steel death box. Paralyzed with fear, they frantically pull at the crank handle.

"Give it to me! Let me do it! I'm not going to die in here with you!" says Harold, reaching for the crank. During their scuffle Harold pulls at the crank and it snaps off in his hand.

Carl starts panicking even more, yelling that they are going to die, placing the blame squarely on Harold as though it mattered somehow who it was that killed them. Carl starts to pound on the walls of the tiny steel coffin. It shakes a bit but doesn't budge. Harold starts to push on the roof.

"Help me out here, Carl. Let's see if we can bust the lid off this thing!" yells Harold.

Before Carl can even respond, the force of Harold pushing on the ceiling causes a different unintended consequence. The bottom of the lift had been weakened by the heavy weight of both men at once, and due to its antiquity, came dislodged from the lift entirely. The floor falls right out from under them.

They scream and throw up their arms trying desperately to stop the fall. *Thud!* They hit the ground hard, but fortunately, it doesn't have much further left to go. The entrance door is just a few feet above them now. They pry open the gate of the exit door. It hasn't been moved in ages. It's rusty and difficult to maneuver. They manage to dislodge it and find themselves in a janitorial closet.

"Carl... I swear on my life if what's beyond that door isn't a normal hallway, I'm going to rip one of these cables off the wall and electrocute myself to death with it," says Harold.

They thrust open the door, expecting it to be difficult to open. To their surprise, it flies open with ease. This shocks a bystander passing by who sees both men looking their worst, coming out of the maintenance closet. The hallway is splendid with textured wallpapers and marble floors. Exquisite furnishings and artistry from all across the galaxy. Most importantly, light and fresh air. They both heave a sigh of relief and joy.

"Oh goodness me! How horrid and unsightly! Gareth! Gareth! Come right away. Should we call security? Two beasts from the lowers have found their way in from the outside!" says the bystander, an old and proper woman of sophistication.

"Ma'am, I assure you we're platinum ID holders. Just doing some maintenance to keep your building running safe and clean. We ran into some trouble with an electric fire. Pretty dangerous. You should leave the area just to be sure," says Carl.

"I've never seen you before! You're not the usual maintenance personnel. I'm calling the enforcers! Gareth! Where are you? Fetch my communicator right away." The bystander calls for an unseen companion.

"Fuck this. We don't have time for this, Carl," says Harold as he pulls out his gun pointing it straight at her. She throws her hands in the air, panicking.

"What are you doing? She's harmless!" says Carl.

"Into the closet bitch! Give us all your money and jewelry and nobody gets hurt," says Harold.

"Harold, come on man, what the fuck! This isn't who we are. Come on!"

"You want to join her, Carl? I didn't think so. Now hand it over!"

She dumps her purse on the ground and throws her rings and necklaces on the ground. Harold shoves her into the maintenance closet, breaks a leg off a nearby table, and uses it to brace the door shut. As he's collecting his prize, he sees Gareth, a ten-foot-tall, extremely athletic alien approaching them. He looks somewhat like a centaur, if centaurs spent all day focusing on their gains and getting ripped.

"I'm sorry, sir, there's been a misunderstanding you see— *oof,*" says Harold, in a desperate attempt to save his own ass.

The alien grabs Harold by the throat, holding him up in the air choking him near to death. He grabs the gun from Harold and crushes it in his strong hands.

"That's an interesting concept, outsider. It seems pretty clear to me what's going on here. Now I could wait for the Enforcers to come and arrest you, but all I see is trash, and I hate littering!" says Gareth, his deep voice shaking even the walls.

"Oh, we're tremendously sorry sir. Please forgive him, he's totally mental. We'll just be on our way now and won't give you any more trouble— *bleh,*" says Carl. The alien grasps Carl with his other giant hand and starts carrying both of them effortlessly down the hallway, both of them desperately pleading through the chokehold.

The alien takes them to the trash shoot at the end of the hallway, it's quite fanciful and hidden from view to some degree. The rich don't want to be seen throwing away their garbage. He tosses a pleading Carl down head first, like a garbage sack. Then he gives Harold a blow to the chest with his other fist, knocking the wind out of him before tossing him down the trash slide.

The metallic shoot gives them roadburn as they descend. It smells and is covered in the fluid remains of centuries of garbage. They land in a massive pile of trash sacks. The smell is unbearable. The energy radiating off the compactor makes it unbearably hot. There's a small alien shoveling the trash bags into it. He glares at them, irritated, before returning to work as normal. As though this had happened before.

"Nice going, Harold. Truly great. You couldn't just fucking walk away, could you? No! Had to start some shit. Who knows where we are now!" says Carl.

Harold comes to, gasping for air. It takes him a bit longer to bring himself to move from the pile of garbage. "Joke's on him. I still have that broad's ring! Bet I can get two to three kay for this!"

"Harold, you're fucking disgusting. Immoral piece of shit. Come on let's get out of here," says Carl.

They open the door to the trash room to find themselves back in the mids at a hallway extending just past the restaurant. A maintenance alien is desperately trying to explain to a very annoyed woman in a suit that the lift was in fact not out of order and that someone was pulling a prank.

Trying to slip by the restaurant unnoticed would be impossible, the entire patronage staring and whispering as they approach. Then here comes Dino! Burning rage in his eyes. "What the fuck happened to you two? Where have you been?! You guys are fired as fuck," says Dino.

Carl responds, "Yeah, well we'll go ahead and see ourselves out. Oh and Dino. I put Chateau d'la Merde into the translator. It's French. Means *shit castle.* Just like your cooking!"

Dino furiously returns to trying to reassure the customers in the most pretentious way possible that he has removed the distracting riff-raff from the building.

"Nice one, Carl. It's nice to see you standing up for yourself every once in a while," says Harold.

Chapter 19

"Detective! We got that phone number trace you asked for on that Gharles account. You're not going to believe this," said Xanthu, hurrying across the room with the datapad in hand. Detective Clinton looked up from her massive piles of paperwork to hear the exciting news.

"The account is owned by none other than Jez Barbados himself!" he said.

She paused for a moment, her face furled in confusion. "You mean like his business accounts right?" This plot was getting denser by the moment and this would be a big change up in the case and could spell real trouble.

"No... Barbados' *personal* accounts. No business connections. Get this though, when you cross-reference it to outgoing and incoming calls, you find thousands of match-ups to unsolved homicides and missing persons cases."

Clinton was shocked by what she heard. That was the last thing she wanted. While this was great news for the progress of the case, it was actually going to most likely end her assignment. This was precisely the kind of politics that Hollander had mentioned would take the case off her hands. Someone as powerful as Barbados brought a tremendous amount of heat with them. She had to consider whether her principles justified the hardship that would be placed on her by coming forward with an accusation. On the one hand, the governor wanted *someone* to burn for it, and Harold was an obvious shoe-in candidate. It was becoming more apparent to her that there was some merit to this 'Gharles did it' argument. Except, if Gharles was Barbados, they were screwed anyway. She asked who else he had told.

"Not another soul! You think I would leak information that heavy? I don't think so. As far as I'm concerned this information is already forgotten."

"Good. Let's keep it that way. I got to take this straight to Hollander."

It was then when she received a notification on her communicator. Harold was sending her something directly? He must have got the number from Sheron. What could this possibly be? Maybe she could trace his whereabouts. It had been days since he had been reported missing. She opened the attachment. It was a video.

The contents of the video had unbelievable implications. Barbados, the President, the Senator and other high-society individuals were murdering people for their amusement and participating in a ritualistic cult together. It seemed impossible, but also terrifying.

She ran up to Hollander's office and burst through the door without even knocking. He was in the middle of a meeting, but amidst her look of urgency, he sent them on their way.

"This had better be something real big, Detective. *Huge.* Case blown wide open. What is it?"

"Sir, I know this is going to sound insane, but I've traced the architect of these heinous crimes. Jez Barbados is masquerading as a man named Gharles Darkley. He uses his money to convince unsuspecting citizens to murder each other. It gets worse though. He's part of a larger crime network called the Syndicate. I have evidence that Barbados himself has committed murder as part of a ritual sacrifice. This is a powerful organization, that includes President McSlurmins and Senator Galxshu. They are conspirators to murder."

To her astonishment, Hollander didn't seem at all that shocked or even taken aback by what she had said. Perhaps he thought she had lost her mind. It might also be that after forty-two years on the force, the idea that prominent businessmen and politicians would murder people was unsurprising. He just stared at her quietly for a moment before speaking to her calmly. "Who else knows about this?"

"No one sir. I thought you should be the first to know. You did after all say that if—"

"Yes, I remember what I said. And no one else has seen this video?"

"Well no. No one from the precinct. I believe, sir, that the two suspects, Harold and Carl, were witnesses to this atrocity and have been working on behalf of Barbados, but I have reason to believe they want out."

"That's good work, Detective. Your assignment is now concluded. Thank you for your service in this case. I'll be sure to tell the governor you were instrumental in the investigation. Why not take yourself a well-deserved vacation and let's keep this between us okay?"

"Sir? You're ending the case now? How? How can you just ignore this?"

"Listen... Clinton... This is *way* above either of our pay grades. I'm going to refer this matter up to the central command and let them investigate this matter. If it's all the same to you, could you give me that communicator? It would really speed up the process you know. That way they have the evidence in hand. I just couldn't live with myself if something were to happen to you and that tape disappeared."

She trusted him. She handed over her communicator. Something gnawed at her. She couldn't let this one go. She left his office feeling a deep sense of regret and helplessness.

She went straight to Xanthu.

"Well, how did it go? Are we going to swoop in and make some big arrests or what?"

"Xanthu, I've been removed from the case. He's sealing it up and sending it up to central. He says it's too big for us to wear. You know as well as I do that central is never going to handle this problem. They're too slow and corrupt. I gotta do something!"

"Maybe he's right? I mean if this is as big as you think it is, what can we even do about it? They would come for you and me and everybody. Of course, I know you and I know what you're thinking. Why don't you take that *vacation*? I think it would do you some good."

"You know what, you're right. I *should* take that vacation. You're a real friend, Xanthu. I mean that. I really do. You're a good Enforcer too."

"Yeah, I guess now would be a bad time to ask you out?" he said, half-joking.

She blushed. He could sense she was falling for him. "Hold that thought!

Plenty of time to discuss that after the *vacation*."

Meanwhile, in Hollander's office, a conversation of a very different and sinister nature was occurring.

"Yes. Mr. Barbados... I have the footage sir... Yeah, I trust her enough... She is a liability though. She knows too much... You, the President, the Syndicate... Yes as a matter of fact... The video came from your old friends Harold and Carl... It would seem that they're collaborating and conspiring against you.... Well, that's up to you sir. Handle her as you see fit... Of course my loyalty is always to you sir... It is done... Blessings of Jefferson."

* * *

Sheron is a nervous wreck. She hasn't slept in days, since the day she had spoken to the detective. Her husband is missing and might be a murderer. Thomas and David never came home either. They are, as it turns out, still going to school. She ought to have checked there first, but it has been such an emotional rollercoaster of a week, she thought that would be the last place two missing teenagers would go. She decides to confront Thomas there.

After a few days have gone by, Thomas is finally feeling more comfortable. No one has come for him or David. Maybe they have escaped unscathed, or at least have hidden well enough. It never occurs to him that the school is keeping daily track of his attendance and of course the whole community knows he is a Fljrkhorn player, and certainly the Enforcers will too.

As he heads to the Transit, a voice pierces his soul.

"Thomas! Thomas! Where have you been!? It's been days and I don't hear from you or your father or anyone! I've been worried sick, you could have been dead somewhere! What the hell is going on? Answer me!" says Sheron.

"Look, Mom I'm sorry," he says, pushing at her emotions with his palms, so as to hold her back. "It's just that it's complicated. We just needed to get out for a while. David is fine too, thank you for asking," he says, glancing all around, hoping no one is paying attention to the scene she is causing.

"Thomas, I don't mean to pry into your life. It's just I'm your mother and I have every right to be worried about you at all times always. Now, I know this is going to sound crazy, but I know that you David have been sleeping together or dating or whatever, but David is your half-brother! And I just cannot allow you to continue down this path. It's just not right Thomas!" Her eyes are bulging from her head with insanity.

Of all the many things he expected her to say or be upset about, this is possibly the last and most incorrect he could have ever imagined. Now he really hopes no one else heard her.

"WHAT!? Are you crazy? First of all, we're *not* like *that* together, like at all. Second of all, he's not Harold's son! Trust me, I've already been through this episode of panic. And that hooker isn't his mother either and no Dad hasn't fucked her yet. At least I think, but that's beside the point. Where the hell did you get this lunacy?" he says, hoping the last comment doesn't get him slapped again.

"Oh... Oh dear... Thomas, I apologize. It just seemed like...? Oh never mind. So, you knew this entire time all of these things? How much of this is true? I had to hear everything from the detective," she says, completely awash.

He comes up with a quick and easy lie to throw her off track. It is better if she doesn't know the whole truth, but one more lie couldn't make matters any worse.

"Mom, that's not a detective! She's not an agency worker. She's just a crazy person who is desperately in love with Dad! Don't talk to her and don't believe anything she says. We're hiding from her actually because she wants to kill us all so she can have Dad for herself."

"What? How could she lie to me like that!? Why didn't anyone tell me this? I let that woman into our house! She could have killed me, or Martha even. This is what I mean about communication! You never listen and you never keep me informed. Now I want answers, Thomas. Real answers," she says, figuring the lies are already deep enough and she might have leverage to hear more.

"Mom, sometimes you know as much as you need to know. Trust us to tell you what you *need* to know. Listen, I gotta go okay? I promise things will change for the better soon okay? Trust me." He gives her a reassuring side hug.

That's not very reassuring, she thinks. Thomas walks away from her toward the Transit, waving goodbye to her. She has the urge to run up and slap him but knows it would do no good. She is slightly relieved that Thomas is not in fact in an incestuous relationship with David, but now incredibly angry that she has let this woman into her home who told her all these lies and is trying to steal her husband away. For all she knows, Harold is with her right now! *Why didn't they tell her?*

* * *

Sheron goes to pick up Martha from school but is shocked to have a *mom moment* of terror when she is told that Martha has already been picked up from school. She tries to calm her nerves, thinking it must surely have been Harold. She rushes home as quickly as she can in the beat-up old clunker of a hovercar. She bursts through the front door. *"Martha?! Martha?"* Martha does not answer. Instead, she finds a soaking wet Carl naked in her living room. She has to admit that for a moment she's slightly interested in the scene but then returns to her panic. *"CARL!?* What the fuck is going on?"

"*Woahhhhh!* Hold up! It's not what it looks like. Or maybe it is. Look I just took a shower, and my stuff is in here, so I'm just... I'm just getting some clothes," he says, turning to leave the room.

Harold bursts into the room at the same time. "Oh shit. Sheron. I can explain. I... Carl, fuck man put some pants on or something. Animal."

Sheron's tone shifts to a rage previously unknown to humanity. "Harold! Where have you been! Who is she? Who is Carl, really? This crazy bitch was trying to kill us and you didn't tell me, and where is Martha?"

"Calm down, Sheron! I promise I will explain it all in good time. But how the hell should I know where Martha is. You didn't pick her up?"

"No! I didn't pick her up, she wasn't there. They said someone came and picked her up! But it wasn't you!? Oh Harold... Oh Harold...."

"Fuck. Sheron, I'm sure there's a logical explanation for this."

"There is actually."

All three gazes shift to the doorway. Detective Clinton stands before them.

"It was you! You did this! You crazy psycho bitch, I'll kill you!"

Sheron lunges at her, but Harold holds her back.

"Sheron, it's not what you think. Whatever it is you think." He turns his attention to Clinton. "I presume you got our video?"

"I did and now I'm here. Not in an official capacity, but on my own accord."

"So, then you must know that Carl and I are totally innocent."

Carl pipes up, "Well not totally."

"Shut up Carl!"

"I know you two are *involved*, but you're not the main problem. Not that it matters anymore, we have bigger problems. The case is out of my hands. Pushed up to central."

"Oh, wonderful! It'll never go anywhere there," says Carl, familiar with the government.

"Yes, I know. That's why I'm here. I can't let it go after seeing what you've seen. I have to do something about it. Sheron, I want to apologize to you. I manipulated you for my job. It's what I do as an investigator. When you didn't show up to the school as expected, I feared the worst. I picked up Martha. Here she is," she says.

Everyone breathes a sigh of relief, but it is short-lived. "Sheron, where are Thomas and David? I need to speak to them right away," says Harold, panicked.

"I don't know. Thomas won't tell me. He thinks the detective is a jealous girlfriend or something and he and David are hiding out from her. Harold, what's going on? Are you involved in something crazy? Is it the drugs? What is this?" asks Sheron.

"Sheron, I'm not sure how to say this, but a very powerful man is trying to make me and Carl kill each other. He's hurt a lot of people and I'm afraid he will hurt you as well. I need you to take Martha and go to your sister's place for a while. Don't say a word to anyone, don't even leave her house. Just stay there."

"Oh, I will Harold. I'll definitely be leaving alright. That's the stupidest thing I've ever heard. My mother was right, you know. You're nothing but trouble, Harold. I never should have married you. I always knew you would ruin me someday," she says. She bursts into tears and storms out of the room.

Harold has no words for her. He decides for once to say nothing at all and just let her be.

"Detective. There is something you can do for us, actually. My apartment back in 1149. I've got a serious weapons cache there. I can't go back, as you know, but you can. They won't suspect you. Bring us what you can. We're going after that son of a bitch," says Carl.

"Smart thinking, Carl. I'll see what I can do. Anything else the two of you want to tell me before I head over there? No? Okay then. Also, geeze Carl, put some pants on!" she says.

Just as quickly as she had entered, she is on her way out.

Harold calls Thomas repeatedly, but there is no answer. Typical. When he really needs him, he is silent.

Where have they been staying for the past week?

"Okay, Carl. We need a plan of action. How are we going to do this? And if you say we're going back up that spiral staircase one more time I swear..." says Harold.

"I'd like to avoid stairs if I can, or lifts for that matter. Barbados is unlikely to make any public appearances for a while, and if he does it will be in the upper tiers. I think our best chance will be to try and infiltrate the top-tier society. I say we sneak into the next Syndicate meeting, put on some robes and a creepy mask. Then, when he least expects it, we sack him," says Carl.

"Now you're just delusional, Carl! What are the odds we would go unnoticed? You heard McSlurmins. He knows who we are! They watch us on the viewer. We can't just go to the upper-tiers. They have cameras and watchers everywhere," he says.

"That's interesting because you didn't seem to mind when you were robbing that old lady of her jewelry. You think they got that on video? Or what about when the giant manhorse beat the shit out of us and threw us out like garbage?" says Carl.

"That was different! She walked into it. She would have stirred up security and then we would have been really fucked. It would have been more suspicious if I didn't rob her," he says.

Sheron storms from the back room, bags and Martha in tow. Harold thinks about all the times recently he had almost died and how his daughter knows so little of him, and he of her. Sheron says nothing at all; she has already said enough. Harold tries to say something, but he can't find the words. He just lets her go and turns his attention back to the matter at hand.

* * *

Harold has another one of his brilliantly stupid ideas. He calls the guys from work for an emergency meeting at the bar, to which they responded affirmatively. He brings Carl along with him. Carl feels that too much time has already been wasted, and that this is but one more thing that Harold is doing to stall the inevitable.

"Harold! We thought you were dead. Xvranbul took such great pleasure in announcing you were abducted. What are you going to do now man?" says Baab.

"Not dead yet Baab. Guys, this here is Carl. Yes, *the* Carl."

"Woah! *The* Carl! We finally get to meet him! Who is he again?" asks Baab, twitching his wings, forgetting what Harold was even searching for.

"We got mutually screwed over by the same guy," says Harold.

"You know, I haven't said anything Harold, but that son of yours and his friend David have been staying at our place. Said somebody was out to kill you guys or something. I assume that's why we're here," says Geordon.

"Geordon! We work together every fucking day and you never once mentioned it!" says Baab, surprised that he would sit on a secret that big. "Work is so boring already, that might have passed the time better."

"It wasn't your business. Besides, I was sworn to secrecy," says Geordon.

"Wait!? So the boys have been living with you? At your place? That's amazing. And strange. Why you though?" says Harold, as surprised as he feels somewhat betrayed.

"I suppose we're the last people they would expect," he says, shrugging his claws.

247

"Thank you. That's truly astonishing. But yes, someone is trying to kill me. Well *us*. What I'm about to tell you is going to sound insane, but Jez Barbados is part of some kind of evil cult of rich powerful people who kill for amusement. He tried to get us to kill each other, but we found out about it and now we are working together. Our plan is to turn it back around by killing him and stealing his money."

A chorus of laughter erupts.

"You humans are all alike. That don't surprise me one bit!" Baab is laughing so hard he is buzzing.

"Honestly, Harold, you guys didn't know about the Syndicate? Y'tarians have been campaigning against it for centuries. Why do you think the humanoids hate us so much?" says Geordon, as though this is highly common knowledge.

"Wait!? You guys knew about the Syndicate this whole time? And never said anything?" says Harold, feeling somewhat betrayed.

"Well yeah, Harold. I mean you didn't actually answer the viewer ad, did you? Oh man, that would be rich. Yeah, Jez Barbados is a total piece of shit. But what can you do, we're just one species among millions, and considerably less fortunate economically at that," says Geordon.

"Wait, Geordon, you know how people feel about Y'tarians?" says Harold also surprised, as though the victims of xenophobia were oblivious to it.

"Yeah, Harold. You don't experience two thousand years of systematic oppression and xenophobia without coming to some understanding about how people feel. They hate us because the Syndicate tells them they hate us, because we stand opposed to them. It's okay though. We would rather suffer in our truth than accept the human lie. The truth is, we have nothing against the normal human. We don't even really eat you guys. Well *most of us* anyway," says Geordon, clicking his claws around his beer.

"Anything else anyone wants to tell me while we're at it? This is incredibly illuminating. Why the fuck did I never know about this?" asks Harold.

"Because you didn't have to, Harold. You just went with the flow. Your boy, Thomas, is a great kid that way. He asks the questions. He challenges the norms. You should be proud of him. He gives you a hard time to help you grow. That's why he gets to stay at my house. And as our religion requires us to feed and house the poor, we're even taking in that racist homeless kid you conjured up," says Geordon.

"Geeze, Geordon. I had no idea you felt this way. I feel like a huge asshole now," says Harold, in a rare moment of apology.

Carl saw this as his moment to shine. "Now? Now you feel like an asshole! Fuck off, Harold."

Baab decides to lighten the mood. "You know, Harold, Gharles' ad only comes on during porn hours! Please don't tell me you thought Gruntilda was going to meet with you?"

"Baab! Be still. Look, we need a plan. We're going to end this and end it all," says Harold.

Rancorous laughter ensues

"Yeah, Harold. You and Carl are going to single-handedly bring down the entire galactic order that's existed since the dawn of space-faring society? What a human-savior complex! I give it three days before you're praising Jefferson with the rest of them," says Baab.

"Harold, they don't know what to do any more than we do. Come on. We're wasting our time here. Didn't I tell you this was a waste?" says Carl.

"Wait! We're not without suggestions. When you noticed the Syndicate, did it not change your outlook? Your perspective has been altered and now you cannot unsee what you have seen. If you want to defeat the Syndicate, you have to make them seen. Right now the public only sees money, they don't see the big picture." says Geordon.

Geordon's profound wisdom is powerful. Harold and Carl finally realize what they must do. If only there was a way to infiltrate the central media network building, they could just broadcast it to the whole world. This is next to impossible. They are heavily guarded and tightly regulated for many reasons, mostly political.

It is at that moment that Blindaara phones Geordon on his communicator. It isn't like her to call during his nights out as she respects and trusts his autonomy. He takes the call. She is concerned. Thomas and David did not come home and it is getting late. She asks if they have gone back to Harold's.

Maybe they are just being teenagers? Maybe they have gone back? He doesn't know. He tells her not to worry.

"Hey, Harold. Wife says the boys didn't come home this evening. They might have gone back to your place. You might ought to check there. Just to be safe you know," says Geordon.

"Thanks, Geordon. We'll do that. Well, gentlemen, pleasure as always. Send my regards to that fat bitch, Xvranbul! I'm sure she'll be thrilled to know I'm alive," says Harold.

"Will do Harold!"

* * *

They return to find the apartment still empty. If they aren't here, and they weren't at Geordon's, and it was too late for a school function, where did they go? He doesn't know where they might be. Not that he would ever know. He never keeps tabs on where they are. He himself is always gone.

Where could they have gone?

Chapter 20

A chilling call to his communicator. It is Barbados calling. *Should I answer? What will he want? Does he know? What if I just didn't answer it?* He has this new communicator and number specifically to keep him out of it, but here he is somehow showing up again.

"Mr. Harold... Mr. Carl... Let's get to the point, gentlemen. It seems that you have stumbled upon our little secret. I would have paid one of you handsomely for the life of the other, but you just couldn't ever pull the trigger. I was surprised to see you were working together. Targets have never made a mutual discovery before. I'm not sure how you even managed to get in here or leave without being seen. I assume that you can do it again? Well, we couldn't have all that baggage and collateral damage laying around, could we? We had to take out a bit of an insurance policy, you see Mr. Harold. We have your son Thomas, and we have taken David as well. If you should wish to see them alive, you and Carl will come unarmed and alone to this address at 9:00 pm sharp tomorrow evening."

"What! Listen, you sick son of a bitch, you lay one hand on him, and I swear I'll dismantle you into so many pieces they won't even find your DNA. I'll kill you for this Barbados! I'll kill you!" says Harold.

"Save that energy for the arena, Mr. Harold. Paying customers will take great joy in your vengeful pleas. I'm giving you the opportunity to spare their lives, Mr. Harold. You just have to come willingly."

"You better believe we'll be there! And it will be your last night on this planet!"

He slams down the communicator to an astonished Carl.

"What the fuck was that!? What did he want?" says Carl.

"They have Thomas and David... Barbados says he'll kill them if we don't come to this address at 9:00 pm tomorrow."

"Harold, you and I both know what happens if we go there right? I mean, you saw?"

"It's either me or Thomas and David. What choice do I have?"

"I don't know, Harold. I've never known you to be selfless or virtuous."

"This is different. This is serious, Carl. You'll come right?"

"Yes, Harold. I'll go. I don't know why. But I'll go. Thomas and David deserve a chance, even if you don't. "

* * *

Detective Clinton approached Carl's apartment. The usual Enforcer guard was keeping watch in case Carl returned. He pointed his gun at her momentarily when she entered before realizing it was her.

"Detective! This is unexpected. Nothing to report today. You got a break in the case?"

"Actually, I've come to retrieve some evidence that I think might have been left here. No stone left unturned you know! Have to be thorough."

She knew that they were notoriously unthorough. She found no less than fifteen concealed guns and three belts of explosive grenades. She pretended to bag it as evidence. The guard applauded her for her efforts. She strolled out of the apartment effortlessly. As she made her way down the hall she could sense she was being watched. She turned back but saw nothing.

As she passed by a stairwell door, she had the inclination to peek inside to see what she could find. That is when she felt the silencer of the pistol pressing into her spine, at level with her heart.

"So, you *were* following me. Before you kill me, can I at least know *why*? Think of it as a last rite," she said.

"Nothing personal, Detective. *Just business.* The Syndicate feels that you've become a liability. Then we both know your silence can't be bought. Not when the price is this high. For what it's worth, you occupied this office with resounding strength and honor. You were a good Enforcer. Too good. Please understand, I never would have assigned you to this case if I had known where it would lead us. Forgive me," he says.

Pow! The gun discharged. The body slumped down to the floor, sprawled out in shock, bleeding from the mouth, chest, and back, the smoke still clearing the barrel. Yet it was the detective who remained alive. She turned to face her accuser and her saving grace.

"Xanthu? You saved me? How did you know?" she said in shock. Chief Hollander lay dead at the top of the stairwell. The gun was still in his hand.

"Because Clinton... I love you. I've always been in love with you. From the first time I saw you work a case. You must have felt it. What you call rivalry, I call flirting. It doesn't matter if Hollander was right or wrong. All I know is that I'm by your side."

"If you truly love me, you'll stay as far away from this one as possible. It's dangerous. Too dangerous. If Hollander was one of them, that means the evidence has likely been destroyed. We have to warn Harold and Carl! Barbados will know they're coming. That also means the evidence never got pushed up to central. Xanthu, I need you to do something. Go back to the precinct, go to Hollander's office and see if you can find my old communicator there. We have to try."

"Anything for you. I'll take all the evidence I find, and bring it to a trustworthy person at the bureau."

"Careful Xanthu, I thought I trusted Hollander. Now see what that got me."

* * *

Gentech Sector 455. There is industrial class, there is business class, but technical class sectors are another matter entirely. It had been built on the outskirts of Capital City. Settlements on the periphery tend to have the newest most advanced buildings. Aside from the city core, this is definitely a place you wanted to be. Tucked into the side of a mountain, this sector boasts some incredulous amenities for the planet.

The buildings start in the flats where it picks up the Transit. As you go higher up the mountain, the buildings become increasingly taller. As they begin on higher ground, this sector has buildings where even the lowest tier intersects with the upper regions of the Capital flats.

As a result, they have created a class above even the highest of the high. Supreme tiers as they are known, where the giants of the galactic tech industry can lord over even the wealthiest Capital citizens. It is into such a building Harold and Carl are directed to go by Barbados.

Massive server facilities underground host vast portions of galactic terminal data. There is a running joke on the planet that the mountain is just a decorative rock, placed upon a server farm. Indeed the rock is a prominent feature of this community, as a place where the rich can be 'connected to the land.' The irony of those who are most responsible for disconnecting people from reality are the most covetous of nature's possessions. Their sleek black glass buildings feature towering indoor gardens and water features. It should come as no surprise that the Syndicate has a building at the base of the mount.

"Well, Carl, I guess this is the place. At least we'll die in a place of great wealth. I had always hoped it might end this way, I just presumed I would also be wealthy in the process."

"You can thank me in the next life, Harold. This is going to be a rough ride."

The security guards make no question of their arrival. Dark visors shield their eyes. They are emotionless. It is as if they know who they are and why they are here.

As black as the outside is, the inside is almost pure white. The silence is deafening in the building compared to the intense noise they have become accustomed to. No one can hear you scream here. They are approached by a woman in a red robe. Her shoes echo as they cross the polished marble floors.

"Welcome, noble gladiators Harold and Carl. It is my pleasure to welcome you on behalf of the Capital City Order of Jefferson, leaders of the Syndicate. I am Umpaala, chief matron of Victory Tower. In a moment you will be escorted to your accommodations, where you will be attended by twelve virgin servants. I have taken the liberty of selecting a compliment that I believe you will enjoy, though if you find that they are unsatisfactory we have a wide selection of genders and species that it would be our pleasure to exchange with you. Gentlemen, each of you has an opportunity to taste their winnings should you be made a Knight of Jefferson. May the excess and splendor be your motivation!"

"No thanks, lady. Where's Barbados? Let's just get this over with, okay? We're not here for your games, are we Carl?"

"Well, I don't know Harold, did she say twelve virgins? I mean maybe we should at least hear her out. I mean if that's what Barbados wants, I wouldn't want to refuse him."

"Oh my. I'm sorry that we have disappointed you, Mr. Harold. The Executive Committee of the Order will send a luxurious transport for you in the morning, departing from our superior hovercar terminal. You will each be conveyed separately to an undisclosed arena location.

They feel that this is necessary to minimize *disruptions*."

"They think we have some kind of daring escape plan, Harold. They don't want us to be able to pull anything over on them by knowing the location in advance."

"Fascinating. Well, I guess they'll be really disappointed they wasted the funds."

Two guards approach them. They are dressed in the same ceremonial attire that they had witnessed at the sacrifice only a few days ago. Not a great sign, but remember, *it could always be worse!* They come to escort each of the distinguished guests of honor to their rooms. Each is loaded in a separate lift. Carl is just relieved that it isn't broken or manual. If there is a special place in hell reserved for Carl, it is certainly in a crank elevator.

The suite is unlike anything Harold has ever seen. The massive floor-to-ceiling windows reveal the entire city before it. The building even rivals the central government plexus in height. The furnishings are unparalleled. Real wood, golden fabrics, living plants, and wasteful water features. Then most importantly, twelve unbelievably attractive servants.

The massive dining table is set full of fresh food. *Real food!* A banquet fit for a king. The bed is a massive towering structure with a canopy. In this brief moment, Harold forgets everything else in the world. Carl, Barbados, Thomas – it all fades away into the indulgence of selfish pleasures.

He gorges on his dinner with reckless abandon. His servants tend to his every need. They offer him eccentric baths with essential oils. They offer him *favors* which he gladly accepts. This will prove to be perhaps the greatest night of his life.

Carl, meanwhile, is having a similar but more awkward experience. The setting is everything he has ever dreamed of. The company of the servants is, on the other hand, more of a terrifying experience really. He finds himself shy and unnerved by their advances. They try to normalize the experience, making him feel more comfortable, but it doesn't work. He is still apprehensive about it. Perhaps if he just selects one from the group, he might have a more intimate experience. It is difficult to choose. He spends most of his evening engaging them in existential conversation.

* * *

They both sleep well. Better perhaps than they ever had. They wake up in the morning refreshed. Their servants hurry to dress them in their battle armor, an unusual and foreboding choice. The impending situation is unclear. *What are we doing? Why this?* They both assume whatever it is will most likely be terrible.

A gong is heard in the hallway, summoning them to their private hovercars. They are attended by their servants who shuffle them out onto the platform. Neither of them can see each other as they are on opposite sides of the building. The hovercars are truly the height of luxury. Nicer even then Barbados' limousine. They are flown to a completely different part of the city.

"You will be victorious Harold! Make us proud Harold! Harness your strength Harold.""

Think of me while you're in the arena!"

"No. think of me Harold!"

"You're so intelligent Carl! Use your emotional sensitivity! You can still win! We're all rooting for you Carl. Be the champion you were born to be!"

The servants stroke their egos the entire way. They are caught up in yet another unknown game. It is only fitting that Barbados chose this means of destruction. Whatever it was would certainly be violent. There is no escaping the Syndicate. Their only choice is to participate or die, whatever the outcome may be.

This sector is completely unfamiliar to either of them. In their defense, Capital City consumes nearly half the planet in its jurisdiction, and there is really no true separation between it and the next city. At this point, it doesn't matter where they were. It is time to find out the rules of the game.

They are each escorted to separate rooms where they are told to wait until the door opens. Each is handed a knife, crafted from ivory. It is the kind of weapon that is only effective in close combat. Harold figures he will probably be fighting a vicious beast of some kind, perhaps a sewer dweller. Carl thinks it might be to use it on himself. He does not know.

At last, the doors open into the arena and they are pushed out into it with the doors closing behind them. Arena is a strong statement. It is really more of an intimate theater. Much like the last one, except a high wall keeps the patrons from the immediate threat of the participants. There are also two poles raised high upon the wall. Thomas and David are tied captive upon the poles overlooking the arena. The audience is waiting in their robes and masks. Among them, front and center, is Barbados, their maître d' for the afternoon affair.

Barbados' voice booms over a loudspeaker. "Distinguished guests. I welcome you. Today is a special occasion. I present to you your favorite gladiators of late, Harold and Carl. I know that many of you have already placed your bets, but you now have them presented before you in the flesh, if you wish to do so now. Today's grand prize is the price of freedom. The victor will receive a supreme-tier lifestyle, which he may maintain by continuing his loyalty to the Syndicate. The victor shall also receive a bonus prize of his choice of these two slaves to serve him in his new life. Thomas or David.

The other shall be given away to the highest winning bidder from today's games."

"Enough Barbados! Tell us why we are here. We came at your request. We're playing your game. Release the kids," says Harold, shouting back up into the stands at him.

"Ah, the spirited Mr. Harold! The odds are certainly tipped for you today! I will turn my attention to the combatants. Gladiators, today you fight to the death. As you failed to kill your opponent by act of surprise, each of you shall have the pleasure of direct confrontation in the arena today."

"Oh yeah? What happens if we refuse to play your game? I've never killed anyone and I'm not going to start today, Barbados. Don't you have any sense of decency?" asks Carl, surprised by his own sudden act of bravery.

"An excellent question, Mr. Carl. In short answer, no. My decency is only predicated on the will of my position. Should you refuse to participate, I shall have no choice but to execute the slaves and come up with an equally heinous death for you both. The good citizens have come to witness the bloodshed of the week, and they shall be made whole on their tickets. Prove yourself a worthy human."

Thomas and David try to speak, but they are restrained from speech by muzzles. It is clear that they are not interested in another of Barbados' games either. Harold and Carl turn their attention toward each other.

"Carl, I'm sorry. This is for my family. I know if the tables were turned, you would do the same," says Harold, preparing his knife stance.

"Yeah, well if I'm going to be *Uncle Carl*, I'll have to live through this. I guess I fight for David."

"There really is no victor here. Ultimately it was always just business," says Harold.

"Gladiators. Prepare yourself for battle! Long live the Syndicate, by the will of Jefferson! May his liberty shine upon you and bring you property and profit. On the count of three gentlemen. Three... Two... One..."

Bshhhhh.

The gong of battle has been rung. Carl and Harold must now fight to the death.

Each takes a defensive stance. They circle each other for a while, neither one making the first move. Neither of them can. The audience chants with murderous rage and boos. *"Fight! Fight! Kill! Get him Harold! Come on Carl let him have it!"* Harold takes the first swing. An obvious miss. He has killed almost a hundred people in pursuit of killing Carl, and in his moment of opportunity, he finds himself to have gone soft.

McSlurmins is at Barbados' side. "Gharles. This cat and mouse game tires me. Is there nothing we can do to raise the stakes? Minutes have gone by and no blood spilled! Not even a scratch. I expected a better performance. Perhaps they are both unworthy?"

"Of course, Mr. President. All in good time. This is mere foreplay. The show will begin in earnest momentarily." He yells out to the guards, "Bring forth the sticks of motivation!" Two of the guards emerge, wielding burning hot iron rods. They position themselves each with a prisoner. To the horror of Harold and Carl they jab the sticks at Thomas and David. The audience cheers at their muffled screams. Carl lunges towards Harold, cutting his upper arm. The cut is weak as the knife is dull. Harold catches him in the shoulder with his blade.

The knife combat continues. Each cutting at the other, neither getting a direct stab. The armor makes it nearly impossible. The blades chip and weaken with each passing blow.

Harold lunges towards Carl's neck with a direct stab attempt. The knife instead splits in half and cracks on his chest piece. He kicks Harold, sending him falling to the ground.

Carl dives on top of him, trying to drive the knife directly into his skull. Harold struggles only for a moment to repel his knife-wielding arm before overpowering him. The knife goes flying across the arena. They begin to engage in hand-to-hand combat, each trying to retrieve the knife.

"Carl, I've said a million times. Why won't you just die already?"

"Because, Harold, I have nothing left to lose!"

Each is now bloody, cut, and bruised. Carl is of course no match for Harold's physical strength. Harold wins the day, retrieving the knife. Carl is now defenseless. His armor is coming unraveled, torn from combat. It is over.

Carl will die today. This is the end. The finale the audience has been waiting for. The odds are certainly two-to-one on Harold as it were already.

"I'm sorry, Carl. For what's it worth I considered you to be a friend."

"It's nothing personal, right Harold? *Just business.* Go ahead then and make the transaction."

Harold pauses for a moment. He looks up at the cheering audience. He looks into Thomas' eyes; his look of fear and disappointment. He thinks back to the words of his friend Geordon. He thinks back to all the murders he has committed in the name of the Syndicate. Harold is not the one who deserves to live through this. His final gift to Thomas will be his self-sacrifice; a symbolic reformation of who he is. Someone that Thomas can be proud to speak about, even as a slave. Afterall, it is better to suffer in our truth, than accept the human lie. He presents the knife to Carl by the handle.

Carl takes the knife from him, astonished. Harold backs away, throwing out his arms open to the sacrifice. He will not die today without his honor. Barbados will have his bloodbath, but it will not be on the terms he wanted. Harold will have the last laugh.

The audience is stunned. The chatter intensifies, as does the cheering and booing. Barbados himself seems shocked. He thinks about doing something about it, but decides to let it play out. Senator Galxshu, on his other side, reassures him. "Let us see where this leads. An underdog win could prove very popular. I think the viewers will appreciate the sentiments."

"Harold. You're a braver man than I am. I take no satisfaction in what I have to do. I'll try everything in my power to achieve their freedom. You have my promise on that," says Carl.

Chapter 21

Carl approaches Harold with the knife. He draws it back. Ready to strike. Right as he is about to make the kill an explosion goes off in the audience. More explosions! Thick smoke bombs fill the room. Dozens of audience members lay dead and dying. A portion of the wall collapses. David's pole snaps and falls toward the arena stage. It lodges itself against the back wall, bracing his fall. The confusion abounds, as the most distinguished guests struggle to escape. In this brief moment, Carl springs to action. He scales the wall, knife in his mouth, held by his teeth. He climbs along the pole to cut David free. They both end up falling to the ground, slowing them down as they struggle to recover.

Meanwhile, Harold drags himself up the broken wall. He has nothing to get Thomas down with, but he knows his time is limited. A member of the audience tosses him a gun. It slips through his hands but he catches it. The guard is coming at him with the burning stick of motivation. Harold fires off the gun at just the right moment, laying him to waste.

He takes the stick and uses it to burn away the rope holding Thomas, who drops down into the arena. Carl and David help him up and they all four proceed to the exit. Before they do, Harold glances back to see who their unknown rescuer is.

He ever so briefly makes out the face of Detective Clinton. She has saved them all, and in the process probably doomed herself. Barbados, Galxshu, and McSlurmins all have made their escape, and armies of heavily- armed security guards begin pouring into the arena, firing in their direction. He can't tell if the detective made it out or not.

They're running as fast as they can through hallways, through doors, frantically trying to find an escape route. The guards are in hot pursuit, firing bullets all around them. They turn a corner, losing them momentarily. Then the unthinkable happens. They're trapped on a terrace, with no way out and no way down.

"We're fucked, Harold! But it was worth it. Bastards."

"I haven't lost a fight yet, Carl! Look there, the fire chut!"

"Are you insane?! Who knows where that thing goes. It's a one-way ticket to free fall to our deaths"

Carl was right. All buildings in the Capital were close together and connected. Firefighting was of great global concern. Every building was fitted with fire chutess on certain levels. These were designed to be slid down. That way those above could escape to safety at lower levels on an adjacent building that may not be on fire. As there was rarely if ever any inspection process, the majority of these had fallen into disrepair if they even existed at all. This tended to lead unexpected entrants to fall to their deaths at the disconnected or broken end of a fire chute.

"Would you rather stand here and wait for the firing squad?" says Harold.

"I see your point."

David and Thomas are already sliding down. Carl follows. Harold waits briefly, hesitating, but he can hear the guards rapidly approaching. "Here goes nothing!"

The guards emerge onto the terrace and see it empty, Barbados closely in tow behind them. "Where could they have gone? This is outrageous!"

"Sir, perhaps they were picked up by shuttle?"

"That seems impossible!? We certainly would have seen it on our scanner."

Galxshu speaks up. "I told you we should have installed the tracking chips!"

The President offers his suggestion. "Perhaps it was the Y'tarians conspiring against us once again. Who else would know where to find us?"

* * *

The fire escape chute is dark, though somewhat translucent to the outside light. That just made it seem more shoddy and terrifying. Sliding faster. Faster. It seems to proceed with no end. Nothing to stop them. Nothing to hold onto. Nothing to slow them down. Just gravity pulling them, accelerating ever faster.

"Harold! If I live through this, I swear I really will kill you this time," says Carl.

Whoosh! Carl flies out of the tunnel, landing on a pile of garbage. Clouds of dust fly up all around him. He is alive. He celebrates being alive. Not but seconds later, Harold comes bursting through the tunnel, landing square on top of him, burying him deep down into the garbage pile, nearly knocking him unconscious.

David and Thomas are already back on their feet and help them up.

"Fortunately all this garbage was here to brace our fall! Did the people who designed this ever test the damn thing out?" says Harold. "Fortunately, people have been dumping their shit down here for years."

"They once had a padding system in place, but it was long ago stolen. At least that's what the old ones say."

An alien stands opposite to them. Its vibrant, terrifying yellow eyes are nonchalant as though they are not the first to have come down this way. The alien leans against a wall, smoking.

"Pardon the intrusion. We were just in a bit of a situation," says Thomas.

"It is no intrusion. Tis a public space. It belongs to all the people. Let me presume there was no fire? So lest you be criminal or refugee. Tis no difference to us here. You in the lowers now," says the alien.

"Where do we go now?" asks Thomas

"Wherever you wish to go." The alien throws up its arms, gesturing to the entirety of their surroundings. Its skin keeps changing color as it continues smoking.

"Well who's in charge around here?" asks Harold.

The alien chuckles. "Der are but three goddesses here. Sufferin' and Releasin'."

"And who is the third?" David inquires.

"Tis what you make of it!" The alien chuckles again. It is of no service to weary travelers.

"Well, what is it you do around here?" Carl asks of the alien.

"I do as I do! I watch the chute. I catch the prey fall its victim. Eat and sell to smoke. "

"You're not going to eat us, right?" Carl is concerned now.

The alien chuckles again. "No, I had my fill today. Human meat, worth a pound of nothing here. I think of you as large and gamey. Not to my taste anyway."

The alien creature slithers up the side of the walls and suspends itself above the tunnel on the ceiling. The gang decides to leave the area before it changes its mind.

They find themselves in an absolutely trashed corridor. Mold grows from the walls. Lights flicker. Doors to rooms that have collapsed or are filled with trash. Water spills across the floors, dripping from pipes. It reminds Carl of his apartment after the flood. The initial shock of the adrenaline wears off and they are finally able to discuss what has happened to them.

"Thomas! What happened? I feared the worst when you and David turned up missing, and then when they said they had you, I couldn't let that happen," says Harold.

"They snatched us up in plain sight at the Transit station. No warning. Just a bag over the head and dragged away before we could even react. You got us in a real fucked up mess, Dad," says Thomas.

"Not to disrupt this family reunion, but having had some experience in street living, if we don't get busy, the busy get gotten. We have no IDs, no communicators, a shitty bone knife, and one gun. At least they can't track us down here, but welcome to our new life," says David, reminding them all of the impending tasks ahead.

They round the corner to find the corridor is completely collapsed. They try another hallway. This leads them to an overgrown stairwell. They take the stairs down several floors and it opens out into a large open room, which a commercial center might have previously occupied. It stands mostly abandoned. Barely lit. Moss grows from the railings and hangs from the ceiling. A few of the shops appear to be open, but they're fortified with makeshift barricades and the counters are only narrow enough to inquire of the shopkeepers. The scene is entirely post-apocalyptic.

Carl approaches one of the shops. "Excuse me! You there, sir. Sorry to bother you like this, but can you tell me what sector we're in?" asks Carl.

"Who cares? You ain't nowhere now. And nowhere don't matter where is or isn't. Buy, sell, trade, or move on." The first shopkeeper is no help, but at least he speaks human.

A panhandling alien approaches them in the courtyard, begging them for support in an unknown language. They can offer it no assistance.

The air is stale, musty, and polluted. There are few if any purifiers or functioning oxygen transformers. About the only relief they have is that the toxic gases tended to rise, but the smells are almost unbearable. It appears that they are significantly underdressed for the occasion. They follow the sounds of music, in hopes of finding a more lively area.

Where the exit to the outside of the building should be, there is just a massive pile of dirt, rock, and debris. In order to reach the actual ground level, they have to climb at least three stories worth of this garbage mountain to reach a blown-out hole where the new ground level is located. The buildings have not as much sunk deeper, as the ground has come up to meet them. They follow through a tunnel of makeshift tarps, bits of cloth stretched across discarded metal poles. Eventually, they reach an alleyway market.

The patrons and stallholders of the market are primarily aliens, non-humanoid aliens in fact. This presents a wide variety of language barriers, to which Thomas, in his limited language capacity, can sometimes translate for them. It is mostly unhelpful. Requests for assistance are laughed at. Locations unknown, unconsidered. Finally, they ask for a government office, to which they are readily pointed towards.

As they venture through the market, a sudden spree of loud shouting occurs just in front of them with people pointing and looking up towards the mid-level tiers, towering in the pollution clouds above them. A loud crash is heard, and the tarp-way collapses only two segments ahead of them. Market-goers swoop in on the opportunity. The corpse had obviously just been discarded by funeral. It's completely crushed on arrival, blood splattering everywhere. The aliens of the market rush in to take whatever items the corpse has to offer before finally one comes forward and drags the remnants of the body off to an undisclosed location. Just as quickly, a new tarp is erected back in its place. It seemed that the constant falling of trash is quite the occupational hazard in these parts, as much as it is an opportunity.

Incidentally, the body is being dragged off in the direction of the government office. A red-stained ground lies in its path. By this point, all four of them have torn pieces of their clothes to cover their nose, as the smell of decay is horrific. They approach a bridge covering a river. An ancient decayed riverwalk and waterway of what might have once been a riverside boardwalk of grandeur. The remnants of a bridge have been assembled entirely out of loosely fashioned garbage but it seems to support a high volume of foot traffic.

The river is horrific. A fog of radiation rolls off it. Green and glowing in parts, brown in parts, red with blood in parts. The bodies that go unconsumed, are dumped here. This forms a toxic sludge river of blood, decomposition, and industrial waste. The river runs off into massive ancient drain pipes leading to the city sewers, undoubtedly sustaining the horrifying beasts that lurk below. One might expect it to be swarming with insects, but even insects daren't consume it. It burns just to stand near it.

The government building is heavily fortified. Massive barbed wire fences. Heavily armed militarized enforcers guarding it. They point their guns towards them as they approach.

"ID? ID? Show me your hands!" they shout at them commandingly, forcefully.

"I'm afraid our IDs have been stolen sir! We've come to seek a reissue," says Carl.

The Enforcer rolls his eyes. "No ID, use the back security entrance!" As though they should already know that. As though it is common knowledge.

At the rear security gate, a massive line awaits them. It takes hours to get up to the gate. They can see the inside. It is an archaic monolithic institution that appears in pristine condition, like it has hardly aged a day since it was built. As they are next in line, the doors slam shut, killing their hopes and dreams.

"What's going on, why are you shutting the doors?" Carl asks frantically.

"Oh. We closed. Bye!" The alien government employee gives no consideration to their presence.

"But we waited in this line for hours. Can't you make just one exception?" asks David.

"*Hummm.* Let me see. NOPE! Still closed. Come back in the morning. We open at 9:30 am, or some shit. Whenever I open the door really."

Harold screams and pounds at the door. "Wait! You have to help me! We're not even supposed to be down here."

To his surprise, she walks back over to the door and opens it ever so slightly.

"*Oh!* Well, why didn't you say so before? I would've let you in!" she says cheerfully.

Harold gleefully steps forward to try and enter. "You would?"

"Nope!" she zaps him with a taser and he falls to the ground convulsing. He's fried for a moment but comes to.

"Nice going, Dad! You really showed her didn't you?" says Thomas, helping him back up.

"I told all of you this was a waste of time, but you didn't listen. If you expect to survive out here, we're going to need to get good at something fast. And the clientele down here won't be as nice or profitable as they are in the mids. We're the poorest of the poor now. Harold is extra fucked, he can't even sell himself out," David exclaims.

"Wait. But you think I could sell myself out?" Carl asks, somewhat intrigued but also frightened.

"You got a pretty face, Carl. Soft hands. You would do well on the corner," David says.

"Is there anything else I might be talented at? Anything at all?" asks Carl.

"Probably not honestly. What did you do before crunch numbers? You see any numbers down here?" David is just making fun of him now.

"Woah, that was a lot of juice guys. Check this out!" Harold reaches out and zaps Carl with his residual electricity.

"Ow! Cut it out!"

This is when Harold has another one of his brilliant ideas.

"Guys, we need to find a Y'tarian building. Remember what Geordon said? They have to take us in. It's like a religious thing."

"Dad, are you seriously suggesting we take advantage of an alien religious obligation?" says Thomas.

"Would you rather sell yourself on the corner with Carl?" Harold laughs, still loopy from the taser.

"I'm not selling myself! Next person to suggest it is going in the radioactive blood river!" says Carl.

Thomas sees the point. The real question is how will they locate a Y'tarian settlement? Fortunately, they don't have to think long, because they encounter a group of parishioners spreading the gospel of Y'tra. Amidst an open square between four buildings, the small group of Y'tarian evangelicals are yammering on to passersby who largely ignore them. Some stop to listen, but most cannot be bothered.

"Be oppressed no further under the humanoid footprint! Y'tra is your key to salvation! Come and experience the benevolence of his endless legs. You there! Humans! Don't be strangers among us. The Syndicate oppresses all! Won't you come and worship with us?"

Seeing this as their cue to entry, they migrate over to the pilgrims and inquire for further information about the deity, hoping that it might spark some assistance in their direction.

"Ah, weary travelers! It is rare that humans cross our paths with intention. I can see that Y'tra has brought you here for a reason. To hear of his tales. Y'tra the powerful! Y'tra the brave! Y'tra liberator of worlds! May he wrap you in his segments and brush you with his antennas of compassion! Do you see? Do you see the evils of the Syndicate? Y'tra will purge them of this galaxy!"

"Oh yes. We're quite familiar with the evils of the Syndicate. And where is Y'tra now exactly?" Thomas speaks, being the only cultured one of the group.

"Ah! Perhaps you are worthy of his glory. Y'tra exists within us all. His spirit inhabits you and guides you wherever you go. This is why the human only walks on two legs! Human has abandoned Y'tra and lost his favor. In his sympathy, he gives just enough to walk upon, in the hopes that one day you will change and embrace him back into your heart!"

"I am so persuaded... Y'tra is the way. Glory be to Y'tra. He's filling my heart right now... I must grow more legs," says Thomas. He can hardly continue the charade without rolling his eyes.

"Ah yes! Lost souls brought back into the light. See that Y'tra is good? Y'tra is holy among the holiest in all things. Visit us at our temple! Then we may pray together in solidarity for his mercy and good fortune."

"Yes... We absolutely must do that... Where is this church exactly? Uh huh. How many blocks is that from here? Excellent. Uh, praise Y'tra!"

Maybe Harold was right after all, this is a good idea. Or at least it is *an idea*. They aren't about to get stuck sleeping out here. Their exposure to the pollution is already intolerable to their skin. They will need to obtain additional clothing and protection to stay out in it much longer. At least it is a clear enough day that the fog is rising toward the mids. Besides, this also looks like a great place to get murdered and they do not wish to be stuck outdoors with no defenses.

"Thomas, are you certain this is the way? This looks even worse than where we were before if that is even possible." Harold is concerned, he glances around at the abandoned rubble, at the foundations of the hulking towers. "Yes. He said three blocks and to the left. At least we're upwind of the blood river now!"

It makes sense that even in the lowers, the Y'tarians would still be in the worst segments of society. How will they even know when they have reached the temple? *Oh, that's how*... Two massive centipede-alien-looking statues stand outside of its doorway. The neighborhood around it is atrocious, in dilapidated condition, but somehow the temple is quite nice and clean. Well for the lowers anyway. It is a welcome sight. The place is crawling with Y'tarians everywhere, as one might expect, and they attract a serious amount of attention, being that humans rarely if ever come there. The high priestess of the temple is the first to come and greet them. She wears a tall white hat upon her head and some semblance of ceremonial garb. At least as much as can accommodate her strange body style.

"Blessings of Y'tra be upon you. You have entered a sacred Y'tarian temple. I am High Priestess T'paala, the matriarch of this community. I welcome you to stay and worship with us. Though, forgive my trespasses, but may I ask *why* you have come? The humanoids rarely interact with us if they do not have to, and I cannot recall an occasion where one has come here. I just want to know your intentions, so that I might put our congregation at ease."

"We are friends of Y'tra. We have been exiled by the Syndicate, and we know the evils of their ways. We are without identification, adequate clothing, or shelter. They have left us with nothing. We were hoping that in your compassion you might take us in, as the enemy of your enemy is your friend." Thomas speaks from the heart.

"Ah, Your eyes have been opened! You fight for noble causes. Our mission of outreach is working! You are welcome in our halls," says T'paala.

"Thank you for your generosity. And blessings to Y'tra be upon you," he says.

They are put up in a hostel designated for traveling missionaries of Y'tra. It isn't much, but it is out of the elements. They are given something resembling food, a bed, and blankets to fashion into clothing. The Y'tarians obviously didn't have much in the way of human wear.

"I'm afraid all we had today was rslothgar stew. Do humans eat that? I hope it is to your satisfaction."

They all nod in agreement. While it tastes like old dirty shoes, it is highly fulfilling given the events of their endless day.

They sleep for many hours. For several days all they do is seek to recuperate from their nightmare adventure. More strange meals. Most importantly, they gain valuable daily insights on the writings of Y'tra. It isn't exactly living, but it is a life. David adjusts quite easily, as might be expected. Carl, on the other hand, spends much of his time nauseated.

"Carl, you alright in there? We can hear you vomiting," says Harold.

"How could you possibly be okay? I think the frzendan worms went bad or something."

"How could you even tell? I don't know my frzendans from my rslothgar, but it all tastes like shit to me. Better then Sheron's Slopsagna!" Harold tries to be a useful friend. He is trying to think more of others after his recent brush with self-sacrifice.

* * *

Each day they attempt to return to the government plaza to get new identity cards, but each time they are denied.

"Insufficient Funds."

"Proof of Address."

"Forms 4789.2736 A-S."

Every time there are more and more obstacles.

"I didn't spend years in the streets to end up down here, sluffing it with a commune of alien zealots. Meanwhile, Barbados is out there killing people, living his best life."

David is frustrated. He feels that it is time for them to move on. Gaining access to any higher levels is difficult without any ID. There is of course a huge black-market for false IDs in the lowers, but the demand is so high, the supply is always low and expensive..

"I agree. We have to do something. We have lives to live dammit!" Carl snaps in agreement.

"And these people don't? Look around you, Carl. How do we live our lives when their lives are like this because of how we live?" asks Thomas, pulling out the deep moral wisdom.

"It's easier than you think, son. You just live your best life, and ignore every possible social problem that doesn't impact you," says Harold, with ignorant confidence.

"Remember how you said, if only you could get a copy of that tape broadcasted at the central media complex it would end the Syndicate? Let's fucking do it," says Thomas, sounding frustrated and deranged.

"That's hilarious, son. If only that were possible! Can you imagine?" Harold laughs to himself. He makes hand gestures and impersonations of

271

their march into the central media building.

"No. I'm serious. What if we just fucking do it?" Thomas says, more urgently this time.

"Even if we raised an army to fight our way through, the recording is on our comms, which are back at Barbados' pleasure mountain. Probably long destroyed by now. We just have to admit defeat and move on," says Harold, sounding resigned to defeat.

"Actually, Harold, there is another possibility. That detective has a copy. Maybe we can get it from her. Assuming she survived and escaped. It's a slim chance, but I got nothing else." Carl was starting to consider it.

"Assuming she's alive, she can't come down here and give it to us. It would register on the security grid right away. You know Barbados has people everywhere. *Even here*," says David leaning in so as to whisper it.

"So then who do we know that can without suspicion?" Thomas pondered.

"Ah fuck, we should call Geordon!" says Harold. He is the perfect candidate. While everyone hates the Y'tarians no one would think anything about seeing one visiting the lowers. They just need a communicator to contact him on.

Thomas ventures off to ask the high priestess if she has a communicator they can borrow.

"Oh dear. I'm afraid due to financial limitations, our communicators only *receive* calls. We couldn't afford both," says T'paala.

Thomas explains who they are looking to contact, as though she will know some random alien of the same species in a completely different sector.

"*Ah!* Of course. Geordon. His sister Plxolara lives here in the building. Perhaps she can be of service in helping you contact him." *What are the odds?* This truly is the strangest of alien species. *Blessings of Y'tra indeed...*

"Wonderful! Any idea where I can find her?"

"Yes, she lives on the forty-seventh-floor apartment 29C."

Of course she does! Why would she be easily accessible?

Thomas returns to the group.

"Okay, so the communicator is a no go. But, crazy fucking coincidence, Geordon's sister lives here in the building."

"Oh wow, that's unbelievable! Where is she exactly?" says Harold.

"Well, we kind of have to go to the forty-seventh floor," he says. Carl looks incredibly unenthused.

Chapter 22

"No! Absolutely not. I'm not doing it."

Carl stares at the lift. It looks like a death trap. One of the doors is missing, and the lights flicker off and on. On top of it all, it is yet another damn manual crank elevator. Fortunately for Carl, the handle is stuck anyways.

"What's your aversion to lifts?" Thomas says, perplexed by Carl's strange phobia. Harold simply responds not to ask, so he figures it had something to do with Harold and then it makes all the sense in the world

The hike up forty-seven floors takes something close to two hours to complete. Except for Harold, who has given up somewhere in the thirties and may or may not make it up to them later. Hopefully, she's home and this whole trip wasn't for nothing. If it is they are going to just camp out at her door until she is there.

Knock knock.

The door opens partially, her antennae feeling the air. Upon seeing the humans, she screams and shuts the door.

"Wait! We know your brother! Please. We're not here to cause problems."

She opens the door again. "Which brother?"

"Geordon. He works with my dad, they're friends. Listen. It's very important that we talk to him. We were wondering if you have a way to reach him?"

Thomas is trying to persuade her, but she seems quite suspect.

She invites them in as long as they "don't mind her cats." At first they say it was fine, until they enter the tiny apartment littered with almost twenty cats, some of them maybe even dead. *Do they eat cats? Maybe? Who knows?*

"Here, this is the number. What? *Oh,* you want to use my communicator. Well... You don't exactly get service here. If you go back down to the ground floor and walk about a block towards that building, you'll get some bars. But you can borrow it, just return it when you're done, okay?"

Incredible. This means they will be going back down all forty-seven flights of stairs, and then all the way back up again.

Carl doesn't skip a beat. "Yeah, I know how this goes. Let's go ahead and get it over with. Better tell Harold to just stay down there."

David chimes in, "What if we just *don't* give her communicator back?" He is sneezing and dying from the cat fur invading his sinuses.

They take the communicator back down the forty-seven flights of stairs. They're completely worn out now. They find Harold, still in the thirties. They explain the news to him. He curses and begins his descent. They of course arrive at the ground floor long before he makes it to the twenties.

After walking a few blocks, they finally see that the communicator has service. They're going to place the call now, but then come to the horrible realization that it is locked! Not one of them had thought to get the password from her before they left.

"Are you fucking kidding me!? Why didn't anyone think to open it before we left?" Carl is pissed.

"David try 'CATS' or 'CAT.'"

This is a great idea from Thomas, too bad it doesn't work at all. There is no other way about it. They will be making another two trips up and down the stairs. This time they just send Thomas, as this was his idea in the first place.

He encounters Harold on the tenth floor or so and explains the situation. It had been almost three hours now since they decided to pursue this plan. All of it has been spent just walking up and down stairs. No Fljrkhorn workout could have prepared him for this!

At last, he reaches her door once more. "There you are! I was beginning to think you weren't coming."

Thomas is out of breath, dying really. "I... the... password... communica-tor..."

"*Oh Y'tra!* I'm so scatterbrained sometimes. I just forget the simplest things. The password is Kats. With a K!" she says, cheerfully.

Thomas wants to stuff a cat down her throat and murder her. "Also for your information, it takes a human an hour to get up here," he says.

"Really? Well, if you would just grow more segments, you would have more legs. Why it doesn't tire me at all! The blessings of Y'tra are with me."

Thomas can't get out of there fast enough. Kats with a K! *What a stupid bitch.* He has no plan to return her communicator now. David is right. *Fuck it.*

By the time he reaches the bottom of the stairs again, he just wants to collapse. Somehow he still manages to get there about the same time as Harold!

"The fucking... password... is 'KATS'! With a fucking K," he says.

Carl and David could honestly die after hearing that.

They finally succeed in unlocking the communicator at the point of service. The call is made to Geordon, who fortunately answers.

" Plxolara? For the love of Y'tra! I'm not going to help you find one of your damn cats again. You probably accidentally ate it in your sleep again!"

"No! Geordon, wait, it's me, Thomas."

There is some static at the end of the line.

"Thomas? How in the hell? What's going on? We haven't seen or heard from any of you in a week. Sheron is worried sick, and you show up at my sister's?"

"We're on the run from the Syndicate. No time to explain. We have evidence on video that Barbados is a murderous cult leader. We just can't access it, and we can't get to it either. We need you to do it and bring it back here."

"*Ah geez.* Thomas, you know I hold Y'tra in high regard and everything, but the temple is a little extreme. I mean, *I believe,* but I'm not really in your face about it you know?"

"Geordon! Listen, it's the only way. Just come down from the mids. We'll meet you at the security gate. You're the only one we know that we can trust to do this. You don't have to see or talk to anyone. Except you do have to make a slight detour to pick it up in Sector 1149."

"Woah that is quite a detour. Who or what am I looking for there?"

"I know this is going to sound bad, but I need you to go into the Enforcer precinct there and ask for Detective Clinton. Give no reason why. Trust no one but her directly. Tell her we must have the Syndicate footage. She'll know what it means. Just get it from her and go. Don't say nothing to nobody else."

"*Oh wow.* Thomas, that's quite a journey. I'll do it this time. But I don't know how much further I go into this. You guys are in way too deep, and I don't want to be involved in something this dangerous. I've worked too hard for what I have to be brought down by this. Sector 1149 won't be friendly. Walking into an Enforcer station, that's bad news."

"I understand. Thank you. How soon do you think you can do it? Tonight? Okay fine. We'll meet you there at the security gate at 11 pm."

The deal is made. Now all they have to do is climb seventy-five steps to reach the security gate!

* * *

All hell had broken loose at the precinct. Hollander had vanished without a trace, Clinton had gone rogue and was missing in action. Seventeen high-profile murders at some performance venue in the city were rocking the corporate world, unleashing violent turmoil throughout the Capital.

President McSlurmins was stretching Central Forces thin, launching search party after search party. Galxshu was criticizing him on the viewer as commanding the single greatest policing expense in the history of Capital. Units of the Capital military were being deployed all over the city, quashing a multitude of uprisings. The President had to call a moratorium on corporate acquisition battles until they could properly sort out the findings in the case. The trouble was that evidence was scarce, and only the President's own hand-picked elite team were allowed access to it. All because the President himself had been there and knew exactly what had happened.

Xanthu was appointed to the position of Chief. It was a dream for him, but he knew that the causality was by default, and not on merit. He wondered if he would ever see her again. He had to launch a nonsensical investigation into the disappearance of Hollander, but they would never find his body. Xanthu took it upon himself personally to search the Chief's office, just as Clinton had requested.

"Sorry to bother you, sir. I know you're still getting settled in, but duty calls. There's a... There's a Y'tarian downstairs. I tried to get rid of him, but he's insistent on speaking to Detective Clinton. I asked if he could just share the information with me, but he said it was for her ears only."

"Well send him up then! I'll talk to him. Maybe he's got some news on a case she was working on."

"Oh sir... Are you sure you want the *thing* in your office?"

"I let *you* in here, didn't I! Now are you going to send him up or what?"

She left in a fit, but she sent the man up as he requested. Not the greatest looking fellow, and he certainly took up some space in the office.

"I'm sorry. You are not Detective Clinton are you? I am not at liberty to disclose this information to anyone else. My apologies for your wasted time," said Geordon.

"Why not? I'm the Chief! She works for me after all. What can't I know and why?"

"Again, I will only confide in her on this matter. Do you know when she will return?"

"Would you believe me if I told you she was missing in action? Rumor is she went rogue, started working for the criminals. But I don't believe that. You're here because of the Syndicate. Aren't you? And I'm guessing you ain't a member, which makes you a friend. Well I'm not part of that club neither, so you can say what you got to say."

"You are very perceptive Chief Xanthu. Yet trust is so hard to come by these days."

"Alright, I'll take a risk then. You don't actually have anything to say. You're looking for the communicator aren't you? The one that has the footage? She sent you didn't she?"

"Yes. Yes that is correct. It was she who sent me. Do you possess this item?"

"I do. I thought it was lost myself. I came back here to Hollander's office to search for it. The Syndicate almost certainly asked him to get rid of it. Found it in the desk trash can. Now Hollander isn't an idiot. I think he wanted to do right by her in the end. There was a note attached to it. 'Forgive me. It was just business. I had no choice.' Can you believe that? Whether that's redemption or not, you'll have to decide. I was going to follow the chain of command. I was going to turn this evidence over to central, but when I saw the footage, I knew then that no case would ever be made. Turns out, giving it to you is probably the best thing I can do with it. Passcode 784291."

He handed the communicator over to Geordon, who thanked him graciously before exiting. His decision made him nervous, but he figured with all the crazy things happening in the world, this was the sign he needed. His secretary popped in on him to make sure he wasn't consumed during the meeting. "I'm fine Debra! Leave the man alone. They're just trying to make their way in the world the same as we are."

"Well was the information worth it, sir?" She was nosey with her inquiry.

"It was nothing to be concerned about. Just returning some belongings. That's all."

* * *

Thomas and David go alone to the drop point. Harold and Carl are too exhausted to make the seventy-five-floor journey to the security gate. The temptation to gate hop is high. They can easily cross over when Geordon opens the doors. They would be apprehended by Barbados for sure though. They stay clear of the cameras, whether they are working or not.

Geordon almost wonders if they are there at all. He strolls out into the hallway, looking guilty. At least he has made it.

"Geordon! Over here... look natural" Or at least as natural as he can look.

"It is good to see you both. Here is the communicator. The passcode is 784291. If I may ask what you intend to do with it? The video I mean. I see why Syndicate wishes to kill you all, given its contents."

"Our plan is to broadcast this video across the entire Capital Network. Let them *see* what their eyes have failed to show them."

"You do realize that the Syndicate's grip over the media is equally as powerful, and they are armed to the teeth? They will never air that broadcast. McSlurmins will see to that."

"I know that... That's why we're not giving them a choice. We're taking the Central Media Building by force. Just have to put together enough of a militia to pull it off."

"Thomas... As wonderful as that sounds, I just don't think it could ever be done. If you slowly change the hearts and minds of the people you might erode their power over time, but a call to action will surely be crushed."

"That's what they want you to think. Don't you see it? They keep the mids hanging by a string as a buffer. They convince you that even minor changes will disrupt the whole system. That we would somehow be torn down if we didn't keep propping up the rich. They want you to believe that you are closer to them than you are to those beneath you. Look around at this place. How does a building stand without a solid foundation? The price of inaction is worse than the pain of change today," says Thomas, imploring him to see his point of view.

"I see your point. It is not without truth. For me though the price of failure is a grave burden. I risk all the progress I have made to fit in with the middle world. I cannot support a course of action leading to violent confrontation. Even if it results in a favorable outcome. The alternative, if you fail, becomes very detrimental to my species. You have seen the exterminations. Those above us here today will view them as you once did. They will not see *us*. They see criminals to be repressed and feared. Any uprising will be blamed on us it always is."

"Then we leave nothing to lose. We put everything we have into it. They have bigger guns, but there are far more of us than there are of them."

"I wish you luck, my friend. I will not press you further on the matter. You seem tired. I do think you should get some rest before deciding on a course of action."

"Oh! It's nothing to do with that. We had to take stairs. Thousands of them. All-day long."

"Why did you not simply take the lift?"

"Well, there are only two. One of them is completely missing, and the other is stuck on the first floor."

"Well yes, of course! Everyone knows that. Just take the freight elevator next time!"

David sprang to life with rage. "The what?!"

"Yes. The freight elevator is right around the corner. Fully electric, in working order. Paid for by the Guardians of Y'tra, a society for the betterment of Y'trian neighborhoods. It is best for commerce to keep that lift open, and it is more suited to our large bodies. I bid you farewell!"

Thomas and David are furious at each other, blaming the other for missing the additional elevator in the building. They reflect back upon it and determine that perhaps they ought to plan and investigate more carefully before just leaping headfirst into a project.

Carl is astonished to see them come around a different corner. "What happened? There's no fucking way y'all made it all the way up there and back already."

"Turns out... There was a functional electric freight elevator in the back this whole time. Sorry guys!" says Thomas. They are all royally pissed. The entire day's energy could have been salvaged. "Well, not that anywhere cares, but he came through for us. We got it!"

"That's great! Now we just have to figure out how we're going to get it into the Central Media Complex. I presume we're not just going to walk in and hand it over?" Carl says.

"This is going to be complicated. I want to talk with the Y'tarians. Other disenfranchised aliens. See if we can launch a coordinated assault," says Thomas, the mastermind.

"Thomas. That's a terrible plan. These people are way too beat down for that. They're not going to care enough to do anything. Why would they even follow us? Besides, you would lose badly," says Carl.

Because Carl's plan was so enlightening. Oh, wait he has none!

"The goal is not to win the battle. The battle is a diversion. We take advantage of the distraction and the confusion as our ticket in. Then all we have to do is get to the broadcasting room. Then it's only a handful of guards to take out instead of an army," says Thomas.

"You know something, that might actually work. Sorry I doubted you. Harold what do you think?" asks Carl.

"Come on, Carl, it's easy to get people to care! We literally tried to murder each other for cash. All I have to do is convince them they all have a chance at being on television for money. Instantaneous riot! You don't even have to have a coordinated army then.

"Well fuck, Harold. That's actually not your worst plan. As much of a joke as that is, it might actually work."

Carl is genuinely surprised, but he figures like most of Harold's plans it could go wrong quickly.

"Okay, so Harold instigates a riot, drawing out security forces and overpowering them. This gives Thomas' army a chance to come in and catch them in a vulnerable state. What's your plan David?"

"Ghosts stick together. There's a network. We have a code. If a customer roughs us up, underpays, or skips out on a bill, we all go after them. Harold, you've been there. Duchess had my back. If I tell them we have a chance to avenge the fallen of Gharles, and about what he tried to do to me, they will come. We're already invisible. We live in the shadows. They won't see us coming. Basically, we have your back."

"Well, these are all actually really great plans you guys have made!" Carl is satisfied.

"Well Carl, what's your plan? What are you going to do?" Harold inquires.

"Oh you wanted me to participate in this? I thought we had it covered!" They stare at him blankly. "For real though, I'm going to send an email."

"An email? That's it? That's your contribution!? Of all the stupid ideas, Carl..." Harold laughs at him, they all do, finding him completely incredulous.

"Hey, I'm serious! You can't take the whole building from below. You're going to need mid-level support. Nothing stirs up businessmen like a good chain letter. 'All employees must report to the Central Media Building, on such and such date and time, or else they'll be fined ten thousand credits. And if you don't forward this email to ten other people you'll be fired! Something along those lines."

"And you're certain that this will work?" David is studying the plan meticulously.

"Oh, absolutely. People will do anything to avoid being fined, paying taxes, or getting fired. Hell, I was fired how long ago? They still haven't removed me from the server. I'll broadcast it on the whole network. Plus, I've got a few tricks up my sleeve. There's a group that I'm a part of that might be interested in a little mayhem."

"Wow. That's disappointing really. I figured they would be smarter or something in the business sector?" Thomas raises his continued concern.

"Oh no! *No no noooo.* Not even the slightest. In fact, the more money you make the less work you do, and the dumber you are! They tell us to dumb down our email language to a Level-5 just to make sure the managers can understand it."

"I knew it! I knew it all along! Just like that bitch Xvranbul!" Harold feels vindicated. He knew he was smarter than her.

"Speaking of, Harold, know any way of getting your box worker friends to contribute?

"Definitely not. We're the most complacent group on the planet. We're willing to do that all day! Why would we care who controlled the Syndicate anyways? As long as we're making boxes and getting paid, everyone is happy."

"Psh! As if. Harold, you murdered people for the cash! Actually that gives me an idea... You should call up Baab, and tell him that Barbados is shutting down the box factory for good. That will keep him off our ass, and create external diversions." Carl thinks it is a great idea.

Then comes the question of timing. When was the timing right? How will they specifically go about their plan? There is no better time than the present. There are already multitudes of uprisings in progress over the deaths of the seventeen executives at the Syndicate meeting. The heirs threaten each other with war, massive buying, selling, trading, the whole system is in turmoil as shareholders raise their armies against each other in sectors all throughout the city. The military and Enforcers will be too dispersed to launch an effective counteroffensive in time. The government is much more tolerant of these riots, viewing them from a perspective of neutrality, at least in theory. As for the question of *how* they are less certain.

* * *

Thomas decides to share their grand scheme with the high priestess, to at least test its viability. She is surprisingly quite supportive.

"Many generations, we have waited for such an opportunity. Trying to study the humanoids, learn from them, find common ground. Always those among us who pursue avenues of peace, avenues of understanding, tolerance. The track of slow progress. Because they believe in Y'tra the benevolent, the gracious, the forgiving. But they miss out on a critical element of our lord. Y'tra the just. For there can be no others before justice. Justice is the hallmark of a civilized society. Let me show you something Thomas," she gestures for him to follow to the main sanctuary.

He follows her to the sacred temple altar. A massive statue of Y'tra coiled around a tall obelisk, his antennae pointing upward toward the heavens. She reaches toward the statue, turning one of its stone legs like a lever. It reveals a hidden doorway, leading downward into darkness. They descend down the old rusty metal staircase. What Thomas finds is unbelievable.

The stairs lead down into a massive underground complex. The place is teeming with Y'tarians, monitoring hundreds of complex terminal read-outs. Massive stockpiles of weapons, military equipment, and data centers. The Y'tarians have been preparing for war for quite some time in this strange underground bunker.

"T'paala? What is this place? It's unbelievable." Thomas is astonished.

"This is but one of many of our command centers. In the times before the corporate uprising, this was once a military facility on the planet, left long abandoned. We have retrofitted it to our purpose. We have been monitoring the Syndicate for quite some time. Our survival depends in part on the humanoid fear of the planetary sewer system. That is why they do not venture down here. That is why they keep us around, to maintain it. While it is true there are monsters that lurk beneath, we are quite well defended here. We have discovered many such bunkers."

"These must be thousands of years old! Was anything left behind? Who built these?"

"That is among the many things that we do not understand. We believe that among our discoveries so far that they are derived of two factions. One of which we are familiar with, the Warriors of Y'tra, correlate to our own ancient history, like this one, placed beneath the old temple. The building was added above much later. The other is a mystery. The data was too heavily damaged, the writing eroded, the artifacts unexplainable, unusable. All that we could decipher was a piece of humanoid writing set afront a blue circular symbol that says 'NASA'."

"NASA? I wonder what it means?" Thomas's mind is blown.

"We believe that it suggests the conflict between the humanoids and the Y'tarians has been going on for millennia. In any event, we track members of the Syndicate here. Their whereabouts, their business dealings. We in turn present them with nothing. They see only our destitution. We tithe heavily to the cause of Y'tra the Just. It is our belief that they know very little about our present weapons capabilities. What's more, is that we have extensive maps of the subterranean complex. A place we know well, that those with their heads up in the clouds know nothing. That is because they only have the late-term city blueprint schematics. We however have been able to put together a more complete picture of the ancient tunnel structures. In part, due to the data we find in bunkers like these."

"So, what you're saying is you might have a way into the Central Media Complex that even the Syndicate doesn't know about?"

"That is exactly what I am saying. Thomas, the evidence that Harold and Carl have obtained is the most damning surveillance ever captured of the Syndicate. We have never successfully infiltrated a ceremony of the Order of Jefferson. This could change everything and help sway the public opinion towards our favor. I will speak with the other temple matriarchs and ask them to pledge their support. Once the rioters have drawn out the security forces, we will attack them from beneath the surface, from within the building."

"Once we're in, what's the best way to proceed to the broadcast room?" he asks.

"As you may be aware the CMB is a Colossus Type II Reinforced Pyramidal Structure. While its mains are heavily guarded, there are of course several maintenance access hatches that we can slip through, sight unseen. It is revered though for its massive clock tower, the mechanics of which are actually located behind the control room and the main broadcast stage. Our objective will be to deliver your party to the clock basin, where you may scale the steps. We will storm the control room first, and then the main stage. We mustn't delay in airing the broadcast. We will only get at most twenty minutes before the grid link is severed."

"So it is done then. We need to act swiftly on this, T'paala. There hasn't been this much instability in the corporate sectors for centuries. What day are viewers most likely to be tuned in?"

"Our data suggests that Thursday, prime-time evening news at seven pm has the highest ratings. Workers are tired from their week, but not yet on their weekend. What do they all do? Sit in front of the viewer."

"It's settled then. T'paala we're go for this on Thursday okay? That's less than a week from now. Can we pull it off?"

"It is as you say. No better time than the present. I will rally our warriors at once."

Thomas returns to the group who is growing impatient, wondering where he has run off to. After explaining the entirety of the plan, the group decides it is best to go their separate ways. They will each orchestrate their part of the plan on their own, only reconvening on the day of the uprising. Given that Thomas is the most likely to reach the control room, they determine that he should be the one who carries the communicator footage. He does after all have a real army behind him.

Chapter 23

Harold stands in the busy back alley market passing out digital flyers to bystanders.

"That's right folks step right on up here! The first ten people to enter the Central Media Building at 6:00 pm on Thursday will get the chance to be on Capital City television! Huge cash prize! That's right FREE MONEY!"

The flyers go quickly. He passes out boxes and boxes worth of them. People are spreading them rapidly amongst their social circles. The response is working perfectly.

Carl's chain letter email is also off to a great start, spreading like a virus on the company servers. His inbox is being spammed with it thousands of times a day, therefore he knows people are just hitting 'Reply All' to forward it. This is going to work. He and David just have to find a way back into Sector 1149 for their final act.

Using a map obtained from T'paala they are able to enter through an unused sewer access tunnel. Unfortunately, it triggers David and Carl's mutual fear of heights.

"After you!"

"No, I insist you go first!"

Eventually, Carl gets the short straw. The tunnel is pitch black except for the headlights T'paala had supplied them. The smell of rust hangs in the air.

They have to wear gloves to climb the ladder as it has been calcified over from years of dripping water. The rusted rungs are flush with stalactites. Carl has to be cautious not to disturb them, lest they might fall and pierce David's eye.

"Don't look down, Carl. Don't look down."

It turns out that Carl and David share a mutual fear of heights and yet are somehow made to climb the seventy-eight-story maintenance ladder.

As they approach the halfway point, Carl reaches for the next rung and starts to pull himself up when it completely snaps off. His hand flies back. He drops the rung, which narrowly misses David below. He nearly loses his grip but is able to regain his footing. In the process, he looks down, to reveal the black hole from which they came. He clings to the ladder in panic.

"Carl! Carl! We've got a job to do. I know it's hard, but you have to keep going!" says David, terrified that Carl could at any moment fall on him, sending them both spiraling to their deaths. There isn't enough room in the tunnel for Carl to fall around him. He would be directly in the path.

Carl is not about to let this kid upstage him in the courage game. He propels himself up onto the next rung. It is a true struggle to get over the gap, but he eventually succeeds. David crosses it with ease of course, by virtue of his youth. The burdens of being middle-aged. Carl's joints hurt. They pop and crack. He can't do half the things he used to be able to do. Not that he was ever very good at doing them to begin with.

At last, they emerge at the top, pushing up on the hatch. It doesn't budge. Centuries of neglect have corroded it into the concrete. So close, yet impossible. Carl curses at it, pounding it with his fists. He is about to concede defeat when he hears a voice on the other side.

"Is someone down there? Are you trapped?" asks the concerned voice.

"Yes! Please help us! We're *maintenance workers*. We're trapped down here!"

"You hold on now! I've got you. Don't you worry!"

Chiseling sounds can now be heard overhead. The crusted layer between the hatch and the concrete begins to separate. At last, it breaks free, and the blinding lights of the business district penetrate their eyes. They climb up from the tunnel, revealing their savior. A very confused-looking alien stands staring at them. They are in the middle of his space shuttle repair shop.

"You sure you guys are maintenance workers?" he asks, puzzled by their appearance.

"What are you trying to say? Not *all* maintenance workers dress the same," says Carl.

"What about you? Ain't you a little young to be working this gig?"

"For your information, sir, my species is always this longevous! How offensive," says David.

"How'd you get down there anyway?" he asks.

"I don't suppose *you* want to tell us where you get your parts from?" asks Carl.

It is a well-known stereotype that space shuttle repair aliens always have stolen or used foreign parts that they pass off as new.

The alien understands the implications and backs down. "Fine, I won't ask then."

"Thank you again for getting us out of there! You might want to seal that back up though. It's a long way down. Trust me," Carl says.

They exit the shop and get their bearings about them.

"Well, David... This is it. It's been a pleasure working with you."

They shake hands and head in opposite directions.

* * *

Back at the command center, Thomas arrives at the meeting. The table has clearly been designed for Y'tarians. He has to stand on his chair just to be seen over the table. T'paala has assembled five Chief Matrons of War from a variety of temples loyal to the cause. They stare at him with irritation and frustration.

"So, this is the humanoid for which you speak? Y'tra has certainly created him to be hideous and weak. I bring you fifty of my strongest women, and you expect them to fight for a man? A man-child no less! This evidence with which you speak must be the greatest which has ever been seen on this planet if you expect my temple to participate," says Hlxtochuuba.

"Yes, Sister Hlxtochuuba speaks truth! It is not our custom to fight alongside men. They are after all weak and emotionally stunted. They cannot even birth an egg sack. They should be at home tending to their larvae. Y'tra gave more legs to females for a reason!" says another.

"Sisters, please... I have heard your concerns, but Thomas has seen the light of Y'tra and basked in his glory. Sure, he is helpless, weak, and has few legs, but we are not going into battle with his sword drawn. We are his protectors. He is just the deliverer. He speaks to the humanoids. He is a face of reason that they will listen to. He has seen. Now so shall they see. Now behold the evidence!" says T'paala.

She slams her claws down on the table to solidify her authority and turns their attention to the viewer screen.

Thomas isn't sure if that was a compliment or not but T'paala sure can work a crowd. The hoard of Y'tarian warrioresses is truly a terrifying spectacle that no human guard would want to reckon with. She plays the video of the Order.

The evidence is compelling enough, as the fearsome ladies burst into their war chant. The deal is made. Each gives their consent and support to the cause. They are brought chalices of beer so that they might drink heartily from the warrioress's brew. Thomas takes the opportunity to assert himself more at the table. He raises his chalice in a toast. "To Y'tra the Just!" The excitement intensifies as they pound the table with conviction, shaking the ground below. It is now time to prepare their armor and sharpen their blades. Not that they needed weapons.

The stage is set. The 6:00 hour approaches.

* * *

"Good evening! Gui'lda W'uthrnm here with Capital News. The most-watched news station in Capital City! With the highest ratings. The biggest ratings. None truly more great than mine," she says, while plastering on her fake reporter smile.

"Join us tonight as we report on the issues that you really care about. The investigation into the murders of the Capital Seventeen continuing onward this evening. Special forces units seen rolling into the central square in Sector 167,

narrowly averting a crisis as tensions boiled between groups loyal to Gontnor and C'higuo over who would become the new majority shareholder of Nabilasto Foods. Then a special interview tonight with gazillionaire Jez Barbados to comment on his recent assassination attempt, his ideas on how to reduce city-wide crime, and dispelling rumors about a factory closing in the Mulknosh sector. Join us tonight for Prime-Time News at 7 with Gui'lda W'uthrnm. I'm Gui'lda W'uthrnm, Capital News. Remember! It could always be worse.

None of the four groups would see the commercial, as they are getting into position. The moment to strike is upon them. Nothing will stop them now.

As Harold predicted, a massive mob of citizens from the lower levels are pouring in from all sides towards the Central Media Building. Screaming, shouting, pushing each other out of the way. The windows are being broken in neighboring buildings. Security starts pouring out of the building as the mob rushes in. They fire into the crowd with tear gas and a rain of bullets. The mob stirs like an angry hornets nest. Security officials are struggling to maintain their position, many are getting dismembered by the riotous crowd. All of them fighting for their chance to get on the viewer.

At the mid-level entrances, something else is happening. A crowd of businessmen is forming outside the gates demanding entry.

"Let us in! We're not getting fined! I only know eight people. Can I still be fired? No more government fines! Why are we here?"

The security guards are in a panic. Alarm bells begin to ring out. "Code Red! All personnel proceed with Plan 7." Unfortunately plan 7 is unavailable. Local law enforcement is scrambling to contain their own sectors as it is. There are few agents to spare. Ghosts are wreaking mayhem throughout the city, on top of the already sensitive corporate hostilities. Enforcers are being called to all manner of locations. Arsons, lootings, bombings, Transit blockades. It is total chaos.

Large machine guns emerge from the mid-tier windows to the sides of the gate, spraying the crowd of suits with a sea of bullets. Many bodies tumble over the edge of the terrace, crashing down on the mob below. They are winning the containment war. So far the mob is being kept at bay and out of the building.

Nonetheless the suits remain undeterred. "Shoot us all you want! We're still not paying that fine. I'm getting in there!"

A strange disturbance of honking horns sounds in the distance. The guards have geared up in robotic suits designed to amplify their strength. This particular portion of the terrace has multiple overlays. While the businessmen are at the lower entrance level, there is a recessed upper deck area that remains virtually empty. It is from here that the sounds grew louder.

Vrmmmmmmm honkkkkk!

The sound of a revving engine. The whir of the wheels. The sound of a smashed barrier. A moment of suspended disbelief. A silence as time stands still. The massive city bus comes careening over the edge of the top deck at full speed towards the building, amplified by the force of gravity.

"Today the bus runs on time!" Carl shouts his victory cry from the driver's seat of the now airborne bus hurtling toward the side of the building.

The bus crashes straight into the glass facade of the building, tearing a massive hole in the side of it. The bus, managing to stay upright, comes to a screeching halt among a sea of destroyed cubicles. The crowds at middle and below are cheering him on. To their dismay, a whole fleet of buses follows behind him. Carl has merely led the charge.

He has been on the low attending a group session for citizens who are irate about the notoriously awful ground transportation in their sector. It was an easy sell. They have hijacked the city buses at gunpoint. *Boom! Crash!* Bus after bus. Perhaps even ten or more crashing into the side of the building. Portions of it are now erupting in flames. One bus lands square upon the gate, crushing the guards and destroying the machine gun turrets. The crowd of suits storm the facility, pushing through the carnage.

David emerges from one of the buses with Duchess and her army of heavily-armed prostitutes. They begin smashing everything they can with bats, clubs, and crowbars. They fan out in every direction and every floor, heading towards the lowers. They dismantle security systems, destroy cameras. Sneak up on unsuspecting guards from behind.

Three military battalions are airlifted from the Central Government Office to the upper decks. They anticipate a swift end to the ragtag rebellion of poorly-armed citizens, but they have no idea what awaits them inside. They enter the complex and begin their descent, attempting to contain the chaos before it reaches the control room.

An explosion comes up through the first floor from beneath the ground, throwing guards in its wake. From out of the ground emerges a battalion of Y'tarian warrioresses. Their shiny metallic armor gleaming as they charge into battle. The guards are no match. The women tear them limb from limb. Some of them are even consumed whole. The warrioresses can easily wrap their bodies around unsuspecting guards, crushing them and dismembering them. Their swords stab through the hearts of their enemies, like human kabobs. The mob charges in around them, flooding the building.

Meanwhile, more Y'tarians are emerging from the maintenance hatches. The military commanders are caught completely off guard. Explosions, gunshots, yelling, smoke filling the corridors. Thomas and his team have successfully reached the base of the clock tower. A towering staircase looms before them. More armored military units are being recalled from throughout the city now and the Y'tarians become more indisposed as the battle thickens.

Thomas, Harold, Carl, David, T'paala, Duchess and her gang all arrive at approximately the same time. The prostitutes are the first to seize the control room. Barbados is nowhere to be found by this point. Gui'lda W'uthrnm is cowering behind a decorative plant.

"Duchess, hurry and roll the tape!" shouts Thomas.

"There isn't much time left Thomas, they're starting to cut the power relays now! Ready or not, you're on in three... two... one..."

The silence could have filled the room suspended in time. Audiences all throughout the city pause in their tracks to see the broadcast. The whole town was engulfed in chaos, but everything is brought to a momentary halt. Rioters have breached the central media complex for the first time in Capital City history. Whether it is out of solidarity, shock, or curiosity Thomas has the attention of the entire world.

"My fellow Capital City citizens. I stand before you today, a son of

Mulknosh. A humble and proud middle-class district. A strong student, an intrepid Fljrkhorn player, and generally a morally upstanding human citizen. By now you have heard so many lies it must be hard to believe what is true, but feast your eyes upon this moment, the power of collective action. The true power lies within the hands of the people.

"The rich would have you believe that this is their dominion, that they are kings to grant you mobility or destruction. You might point to the sanctity of our democratic election process as a sign of our freedom. You have been deceived in plain sight. We have grown complacent to their treachery and accepted their ways and their lies as truths. President McSlurmins, Senator Galxshu, Jez Barbados, the Capital 17, are all part of a secret cult organization known as the Syndicate. Though it appears that these parties are at odds with each other, they are in fact very much so operating from the same plan. They consolidate our corporations, erode our power, oppress us in the name of security, all while our city crumbles in ruins at our feet, on a planet they helped destroy.

"But tonight you will see the most egregious act of their sinister ideologies. The murder of those they perceive as inferior for their entertainment. I too bore witness to these atrocities, held captive in their arena. Justice must be served. Justice will be served. We must unite as one people, as one voice. The Y'tarians, the lowers, the working-class, the businessmen. The vilification must end here. It must end now. On the ashes of this society, we shall build a new, more prosperous future with equity and opportunity for all. This is Thomas signing off. Watch the video and see the evidence with your own eyes."

The footage rolls. Instantaneously viewed by over five-hundred-and-twenty-six billion citizens of Capital City, and it quickly spread throughout the galactic core and even beyond. The most viewed news story of all time.

* * *

Harold is beaming with pride. He would have enjoyed hearing all of Thomas's speech, but his moment is brought down by a familiar voice that shouts out to him in all its anger.

Barbados stands at the center of the massive clock mechanism. "I'll get you for this, Harold! I'll kill you! Do you hear me! If it's the last thing I do. Everyone you love will die before you!" he says, abandoning his calm formal demeanor for something more primal.

The others turn to offer their support. They will kill him together, they say. "No! This fight is mine and mine alone. I got us into this mess, and now I will end it," says Harold. This is Harold's fight to win. He pulls out his knife for one final kill. Barbados is deranged, maddened by the destruction of his empire. The gears swirl around them. He pulls his knife. An equal match. Like the arena. Only these blades will kill much easier than the bone knives. "Your reign of tyranny is over, Barbados. You cannot win now."

"You're nothing but a murderer, Harold. A fat pompous criminal. You will die poor and alone."

"And I shall take you down with me. You fucked with the wrong family, Barbados."

They lunge at each other. Knife to knife, it clinks. Their teeth grit. The punches unfurling. Locked in combat now. Losing their balance, they fall from the platform, landing on one of the giant spinning gears. The disorienting battle rages on, both still holding their knives.

"This changes nothing, Harold. You'll see. Nothing! Thomas will join us. In the image of his father, he will become the Syndicate's next great leader! You'll see!"

"You're delusional, Barbados."

Harold goes for a low stab, it pierces deep into Barbados abdomen. He drops his knife as Harold churns the knife upward. He grabs at his wound. Blood is dripping everywhere. The gears are still spinning. He loses his balance and falls to a vertical gear below. His spine fractures, bleeding out. He looks at Harold with his piercing evil eyes.

"You will always be... middle-trash!"

The vertical gear meets another, crushing Barbados in between. His now lifeless body stays wedged in the gears, bringing the clock to an abrupt halt. The horizontal gear stops dead, sending Harold flying off balance. He is hanging precariously off the edge. His friends rush towards him.

Slipping, slipping.

"Harold!!! I'm coming Harold! Hang on!"

Carl has never ran so fast in his life. He jumps down onto the gear, sliding towards Harold, grasping his hand just as he can hold on no longer. To his dismay, he is able to pull Harold back up onto the gear in his moment of adrenaline.

"Harold... I take back every shitty thing I ever said about you. Well most of them."

"I'm sorry I tried to kill you, Carl. It turns out you're pretty alright," says Harold, giving Carl a friendly hug for the first time in his life.

* * *

The power to the building was severed, but they were free to leave. As the military chiefs defected within their ranks, Enforcers stormed the central administration towers. McSlurmins, Galxshu and dozens of other high-profile Syndicate leaders were arrested one-by-one.

"That was not me! I never said that. Fake news I tell you! The media is rigged. I told you it would get worse! See it got worse! I'm not your enemy. The aliens are your enemy! Exterminate them before they bring about our extinction! I've never heard of the Syndicate! I'm the president! I'm the presidentttt!"

McSlurmins' arrest would be broadcast across the galaxy as well. It was his last great presidential address.

Galxshu took an ever so slightly more dignified approach to his departure. "I have submitted myself to the authorities until I can be exempted from this heinous accusation. Clearly, this is a ploy by my opponent to slander my good name. I maintain my candidacy. My fellow citizens, ask yourself. Is this what you wanted? A lawless disorderly society? It shouldn't cost you this much to live this terrible. You have to vote for one of us! And it might as well be me."

Stories of the atrocities of the Syndicate began flooding out across the

Capital. The Order of Jefferson disbanded or went into hiding. Syndicate cells severed their connections and denounced their involvement. McSlurmins and Galxshu were quickly convicted of high mega treason and sentenced to life in a maximum-security prison sector. A third-party candidate would end up becoming victorious in the election, promising to bring about great reforms and changes. A promise they would later renege on.

Harold and Carl were rewarded handsomely for their actions. They both received the wealth and supreme lifestyle they always wanted. Their mega penthouses were right across from each other, as they decided to become neighbors.

Thomas would go on to lead the Fljrkhorn team to a Capital City championship. He would be recruited by the highest and most prestigious university in all of the planet on a full-ride scholarship for Fljrkhorn

Harold made good on his promise to himself by adopting David into their family. David continued his education, forging his own path that definitely did not involve Fljrkhorn.

Sheron finally had a husband she could be proud of, well as much as anyone could be, who was available and gave her the support she had desperately wanted. Harold would finally get to know Martha and she would know him.

Geordon was promoted to a management position at the box factory. A step forward for the Y'tarian people. He and Harold would later mourn the loss of their friend Baab at the ripe old age of eleven.

The Y'tarian journey for acceptance was far from over, but they had the Syndicate on the run. They turned their attention away from waging war and focused on the changes to be made ahead for a more integrated future.

Duchess ended up becoming the newest spokeswoman of Capital News. Ghosts were no longer in the shadows. Many of them would come to work for Duchess as reporters. They had after all been everywhere in their districts and knew every street. They knew where the real news was.

Xanthu continued to man the lonely chief desk, hoping that one day, Detective Clinton would return, always wondering if she was alive and where she had gone. Her sacrifice and bravery changed the face of the planet and the political dynamics of the galaxy, proving once and for all that one person, steadfast in their virtues, can change the world. Few knew her, and her accomplishments went unspoken, but those who did know... well, they always kept her in their gratitude.

There were many who denied the allegations, refusing to believe even what they saw. The prospects of liberty was still a far cry away for many. Many of the rich had abandoned the planet in hordes, retreating to the outer worlds. Mass rioting brought about the destruction of gates between worlds. Buildings came crashing down in some cases. It was a spectacle both beautiful and unspeakably disconcerting all at the same time. The exercise of freedom is never for the weary. It is constantly fought for and never won. It is better to live poor in truth than to live rich in lies.

* * *

"Harold... We did it... We've finally arrived!" says Carl, kicking back in a plush chair at Harold's luxurious penthouse suite.

"I don't know, Carl... I'm holding out for an off-world palace!" says Harold, guzzling his favorite beer.

"Give me a break! You know you'd miss this place. It's imperfect, it's noisy, it's busy, but it's home and you love it."

Oh yes, Harold and Carl had arrived. But like most arrivals, departure was inevitable. Live in the moment today gentlemen, because this is but the eye of the storm...

* * *

But wait? What happened to Carl?

Carl rings the doorbell at Melissa's apartment. He has gone to the elaborate effort of tracking her down. He had called up her communicator and finally worked up the conviction to ask her out on a date.

"Wait who are you again?" she asks.

"It's Carl, you know from the office. You saw me every day for years," he says.

"Gosh, well I guess I just don't remember. Maybe if I saw you in person I would recognize you," she says.

"That's actually what I'm calling about," says Carl, annoyed.

"Your lack of memory? I'm not sure I can help you with that," she says cheerfully.

"No, I mean you and me seeing each other in person," he says.

"Like at the office?" she asks.

"No, like you and me, dinner or something," he says. He worries that she doesn't understand and that he's blowing his chances.

"Well, I don't really know you. At least I think I don't know you?" she says.

"I understand if you're not interested. I'll just cancel this upper tier reservation then," says Carl.

"Wait! You didn't say you were ascended," she says.

"Of course. I'm surprised you don't recognize me. I was one of the leaders of the riot that took down the Syndicate," he says, beaming with pride.

"Woah! No way. You're Harold?" she says astonished.

"What? No! Absolutely not," he says.

"I guess I don't remember seeing you there and you're too old to be David or Thomas," she says.

"Nevermind that. Are you interested then?" he asks.

"Sure thing Connor, it's a date," she says.

"Carl! It's Carl. C–A–R–L," he says.

"Right. That's what I said," she says.

* * *

Later that evening at a stately upper-tier eatery, Carl anxiously awaits his date with Melissa.

He shows up with real flowers in hand, an exceedingly rare commodity on this planet. Now that he is rich he can afford live plants, the height of luxury. There is surely no greater sign of his affection.

He is nervous at first. Will she actually like him for who he is, or is she just saying yes for his money or his newfound celebrity status? The waiting is truly unbelievable. It seems to be taking her forever to arrive.

Looking at the hands ticking slowly on his solid gold watch, he begins to grow annoyed. For all he knows she forgot who he was and went off with someone else thinking it was the man she set out to meet. He sees a rush of enforcer units converging at an event just around the corner from the restaurant. In his curiosity and irritation, he decides to investigate.

A tragic accident had occurred only moments earlier. It seems that a piano was being lifted into an upper-tier unit when the cables holding it snapped. The carnage of a full-size grand piano litters the sidewalk, the bulk of its sleek black exterior stands in sharp juxtaposition to the bleeding corpse of its unfortunate victim. Pools of blood ooze out from under it. The scene is particularly traumatizing as it appears to have decapitated the unfortunate soul.

He sees an enforcer carrying the remnants of a human head by its long hair. Carl reacts with disgust and horror. It is clearly Melissa. The enforcer takes notice and approaches Carl with the head in hand.

"Pardon me sir, but you don't happen to know who this is do you?" he asks.

Carl thinks long and hard for a moment. He could tell the enforcer exactly who she was, but in that moment a sinister joy takes hold.

"Nope. Never seen her in my life. She looks familiar though. Try searching the database for Morgan," says Carl.

"Sorry to waste your time sir, but one more question. This isn't your piano is it?" he asks.

"No, but whoever it is, needs to get a great tuner," says Carl.

"Oh yeah? Why is that?" asks the enforcer.

"It's a little flat," says Carl.

* * *

Join us next time as your not-so-heroes return in Untitled Space-Murder Comedy

II. McSlurmins and Galxshu are exonerated of their crimes and seek vengeance upon the famous four. They reconstitute the Syndicate and chase them down into the furthest depths of the city. All the way down in the sewer levels they rescue a beautiful woman who leads them on a four-way love triangle. The gang discovers the secret origins of the Y'tarian mystery bunkers. Harold and Carl must escape the planet. Thomas takes on a troubling new leadership role. Detective Clinton's fate is revealed. You'll never believe what happens to David! New discoveries are made and the real truth of the Order is exposed!